TECH DUINN

Book One of the ETHERFLOWS Series
Written by RYAN DEBRUYN

MOUNTAINDALE
PRESS

TABLE OF CONTENTS

ACKNOWLEDGMENTS

For the readers. With whom none of us writers could do what we love.

PROLOGUE

Danu stood on the observation deck of her battleship and surveyed the cataclysmic scene through the port window. She checked her updated calculations on her tablet screen and smiled. Everything was within acceptable limits—as she expected.

A massive blue streak of lightning took her attention away from her numbers. The huge bolt struck close to her ship and she hastily adjusted a few calculations. Her crew behind her slid the ship backwards in response. She smiled at the raging storm that spread out before her. The vibrant colors stood out starkly in the darkness of space. Clouds of crystalline ice exploded from forks of blue lightning, creating a mist. A growing dark black rock swirled in that mist and lightning collided with it, causing the rock to liquify to magma. The crystals of ice crashed with these fragments of liquid red, turning to steam and reinforcing the mist. This process would repeat itself until her new planet formed.

A sob forced her to look away from her beautiful creation. Beside her stood her second son, Ogma. As usual, he was unkempt. His ruddy brown mane of hair intermingled into his long fiery red beard. She sniffed haughtily at his appearance. Was he trying to look homeless?

Heat suffused her face and she spat, "Stop blubbering. This is a moment of triumph. Your brother is ascending!"

She shook her head and returned to her notes. The sad sack beside her wouldn't ruin this moment for her. Then she sighed and tried to cheer him up. He was her son after all. "All *our* work is paying off. The Tuatha De Danaan Guild will become the most powerful force in all the Etherverse. One day we will even supplant the Gaian Military and the other superpowers."

Her son sniffed once, and she shrugged. At least she'd tried. Returning her attention to the swirling vortex of cosmic energy brought a broad smile to her face. "Today your brother, my first son, Dagda, becomes our first Planetary God!"

In my pocket, she added internally.

The crew behind clicked away at their stations, continuing to take their readings and adding the numbers to her calculations. She sensed her steward, Oberan, approaching and waited. He bowed low. "Mother, the Lady Brigid is watching the display as well." He indicated a ship visible off their starboard, then continued, "She has requested to communicate with you about the Guild debt."

Danu took a deep breath before finally responding with a sneer, "Patch her through, Oberan."

The image of the muscular, fiery redhead flickered onto the viewing window. Brigid was the adventuring warrior type and Danu's least favorite officer in the Tuatha. She admitted that her hatred stemmed from Brigid always challenging her on every decision. The woman even lobbied for her removal from *her* leadership position.

"*Mother,*" Brigid used the honorific with the barest dip of her head. Every action of the woman conveyed her lack of respect for Danu. Danu ground her molars, letting Brigid continue. "You have spent every Crystal the guild possesses to set up this display in space. While I can see its offensive capabilities if used near a planet—I don't see any other way it will crush our enemies."

Danu forced a smile—the meathead was always so direct. Brigid didn't understand the subtle plans Danu had in motion; the angry-looking woman preferred swinging her forge hammer or standing toe to toe with her enemies on a battlefield. Sighing theatrically, Danu responded, "While the Guild has invested heavily in this endeavor, I assure you that my years of lobbying on Gaia weren't for nothing. I have studied this problem from every angle. And might I remind you the rest of the council agreed?"

Brigid shook her head and retorted, "*Mother,* you cannot take full credit for the changes to the stagnating Atlantean System. The Atlantean Council all had agendas, and you piggybacked off of them. Each Guild that formed from this new opportunity is moving, and we are watching a storm in space!"

Danu breathed in through her nose. Shaking her head, she snapped back, "Ah, Lady Brigid. The new formation of Guilds is only the first step of a much greater plan. You are right that other groups are forming and using Guilds to build a power base or conquer small Territories. We, on the other hand, have thought bigger—an entire planet—and, in time, a collection of planets! It might be hard for a dungeon diver like yourself to understand."

Brigid's face grew fiery. Danu understood the state of her family—the Guild. She knew they were nearly bankrupt. It had taken everything they had to purchase all of the Planetary Essence that this power play had required. Danu held up a hand to forestall a response. "Lady Brigid, today is only the beginning. The Atlantean System has also added class templates. The Council is working tirelessly to create optimal paths for our recruits to take. In time, we will try to conquer the Ancestral Quest and lock those classes to our Guild. Atlantis was not built in a day, *child*."

The muscular redhead's face grew darker still and her nose crinkled as she bowed jerkily, "As you say, *Mother*. If this fails, be prepared to face the Guild Council, and the united officers."

Brigid winked off the screen after her empty threat. Danu had nothing to fear from the Guild Council. First, this was going to work, and secondly, no one would dare cross her when her son may one day ascend further. A God of their very own.

Danu breathed in a deep lungful of air. These were her Guild's first steps on its rise to power. Yes, they would need to rebuild, but with an entire planet under their control, that would be exponentially faster.

Ogma had stopped crying, at least. She wrinkled her nose. That was right, he had a thing for Brigid. No matter. She had a marriage alliance with Cathodiem in the works.

"What shall we name your brother's planet, Ogma?" she asked.

Ogma looked at her, his eyes sparkling with unshed tears. "Tech Duinn," he whispered.

She tilted her head and muttered the translation, "The house of the dead?"

That fit her plans rather well. If only her teachers at the Atlantean Academy could see her now!

CHAPTER ONE

Azrael's ribs reverberated a thud through his body and his eyes flew open as pain from the booted kick reached his brain. The low hanging sun informed him of the early hour. He jumped to his feet and tried to catch his breath. He scanned the clearing; there was another threat out there. A slash across his arm told him he had run out of time.

His hand shot up to cover the shallow wound, and he stated, "Come on. Don't you think this is too much? A simple 'it's morning, wake up' would be sufficient!"

Verimy shook his head sadly. "We trained you for years at the Sovereign Hall! You are better than this, Azrael!"

His wife, Dara, cleaned her bloody dagger while hiding a smile. "We are holding back, Azrael, but you really have to get better at staying mindful of your surroundings. Even as you sleep."

He winced as he prodded his ribs and sucked in a breath when he found the tender area. "Yeah, but now I have to walk around with my chest hurting for the next hour as the bones heal! Holding back or not, you both know I don't have a class yet!"

Verimy shrugged. "A class doesn't give you awareness. Still, the system heals and you must learn. Just because the Sovereign Halls were destroyed doesn't mean your training should stop—the ends justify the means."

Azrael spat—he had always hated that saying. The stupid thing had been carved into the training arena on Lars, the planet he had grown up on. Yeah, he knew that he was lucky to have been allowed to grow up in the Territory his entire life, and that he had received constant training for four years. Still, sometimes he wondered what his childhood would have been like if he hadn't started training at the age of three.

Yet his 'luck' led to his capture and subsequent enslavement by the Tuatha. So that credo was absurdly ironic. His captors definitely followed the same justifications.

He twirled his ring. The dappled sun from the trees overhead glinted off the moon crossing a sword. The iron ring was his one remaining keepsake from the Sovereign Halls—a signet ring of the Sovereign King himself. A father he had never met.

"Do you two still hope that the Sovereign King is coming to rescue us too?" He sneered.

Dara's mouth fell open and she quickly covered it with her hand.

He knew he had gone too far. "I'm sorry, Dara, Verimy," He nodded his head at the man to include him. "I am just tired of all this hiding. I'm sick of waiting for my eighth birthday. We don't even know exactly when it is!"

It didn't help that he wasn't even sure if the Sovereign King was his father. What did he know? Well, his mother dropped him just inside the gate of the Sovereign Halls around a week after his birth. His early trainers had turned their noses up at him. Until he became the best in every class...

Why were the training grounds of the Sovereign Elite taking orphans in? Well, that would be his bastard father's famous libido.

Based on the sheer number of Sovereign Sons Azrael trained with, Erebus Sovereign had an insatiable appetite for the pleasures of the flesh. Erebus must have indulged himself at every opportunity to sire more than thirty 'students' a semester.

Azrael's first nursemaid had supposedly given up three of her children to the Sovereign Halls. Azrael wasn't stupid, and he assumed that not every student was a true son of the Sovereign. Erebus had to be taking in children that weren't his.

Not that Erebus was actually the one who supported them. No, he created a training ground in one of his Territories called the Sovereign Halls—Sovereign like his last name, get it?

Azrael shook his head, clearing his mixed feelings for his father and the Empire he represented.

He hadn't always felt this conflicted. Since the very first day of his classes, Azrael had pushed with everything he could to make his father proud. To join the elite soldiers the Sovereign Halls created for Erebus.

Why, then, had his father allowed one of his planets to be ransacked? Especially one as important as Lars.

He studied the prison planet of Tech Duinn. The ashy leaves and slightly mushy ground were under the unflappable control of the powerful Tuatha De Danaan guild.

Verimy cuffed him. "Stop standing around. You have morning duties and training to do. Erebus doesn't help those that don't help themselves!"

He turned his back on Dara and Verimy and rolled his eyes—another stupid saying of the Halls. He jogged to the double buckets and staff that always started his day. He weaved through the trees, practicing his foot techniques. The trick was to maintain balance and ensure minimal shifting from the buckets. The route to the streambed was about speed and control.

He rinsed off the light sweat he built up during the sprint in the shallow water. The way back was always more difficult. He tried to mimic Dara's feminine voice, "This type of training is good for you. Once you get your class, your skills will grow faster. It's all part of the plan."

He kept his time to a minimum at the stream. Took a swig of water from the bucket and refilled it. Then jogged back the way he came. Today he chose to twirl the buckets above his head as he ran. The circular pattern was hard to maintain. But if he did it correctly, the added gravity would hold the water firmly inside the containers.

"Do you remember the exact day he was left by the gate?" Dara's voice filtered through the trees to him. A slight falter in his controlled spin of the buckets caused water to slosh to the ground. He adjusted his wrist and recovered before any more liquid escaped.

"No… I only remember… when the… ordered… to keep him," Verimy's response was fractured as Azrael's spinning increased the whir of the bucket.

"Well, he is going to be eight any day now—"

Whatever else Dara was going to say cut off as he stepped on a branch. *Imbecile*, he scolded himself. He was too focused on listening and hadn't minded his surroundings like he was supposed to.

No one knew his exact age when he arrived at the gate, so while he was definitely seven, the precise time of his birthday was still unknown. But did they know more than they had shared?

Verimy called, "I thought you were top of your class in forestry. I taught you myself. What was that horrendous—" Verimy rounded the corner and froze. He stood there blinking at

Azrael and his spinning buckets of water. His eyebrows rose and he coughed. "Combining training methods, are you? I think that means you can answer additional questions during sword katas!"

He travelled the rest of the way to the fire pit and went through the methodical process of slowing down the spin. Dara watched him the whole time. She offered, "If you don't keep your wrists level it's going to spill." He bit his tongue in concentration and managed to place the buckets down with only the tiniest amount of water escaping.

He had enough time to take a deep breath before his training sword hit him in the stomach. "While Dara checks the traps and gets some food prepared, let's go through your forms."

Verimy wasn't the Swordmaster trainer that Azrael had learned from. But he knew enough to correct improper footwork and sloppy wrist movement.

"Where are we?" Verimy asked as he walked in front of Azrael, unstrung bow ready as a 'correction' stick.

"Trainer. We are on the outer edge of the Muradin Territory. It is a Territory under the control of Lord Ogma."

"Why don't we stay within the Territory borders?"

"Trainer. The Territory's forest is regulated by 'The King's Forest' decree. No hunting within its zone will provide Etherience or loot. The town itself is taxed. Each 'building' must pay a tithe to occupy the land. So, we camp outside and make quick trips into the city to sell our goods."

His trainer paused and squinted at Azrael as he slowly moved through his first form in the kata, Glas Wen. This form maintained a low posture and upward strikes. He, in turn, studied his trainer and examined his feelings towards the man and, by extension, Dara.

In a way, they were like surrogate parents. Without them, he may have died during the assault on the Sovereign Halls, or again on the spaceship journey here, and again several times over from local predators, both humanoid and monster. Perhaps they genuinely did care—a slap and stinging in his shoulder told him Verimy noticed his distraction.

Do you really think they aren't going to get something out of all this?

"What is the function of the Sovereign Sons?"

"Trainer. To protect the citizens of the Empire. To defend those who need it, and destroy those who deserve it. To use the ancestral Sovereign class to maintain peace, order, and justice." Azrael recited the words from memory, and repetition.

Sovereign class from his last name—just like the training school, *real original.*

"What is our current plan to get off this rock?"

Azrael clenched his jaw. "To wait for my father to send his army to rescue his citizens from the arenas and wildernesses of this world." He received a hard cuff from the supple wood of Verimy's bow. The cuff meant he had performed something improperly, but he knew he hadn't. So, this cuff was for his answer.

"Trainer," Verimy corrected. "What is the second option?"

Or he cuffed me because I didn't say trainer—come on, we are out in the middle of nowhere.

"*Trainer.* To gain strength and farm enough Crystals to buy our way off the world." Just because Azrael thought the formal address was unnecessary didn't mean he was stupid enough to push the issue.

"Better. What is the third option?"

"Trainer?" Azrael didn't know they had a third option.

"Improvise!" Verimy stated as he hit him again.

The questioning continued to topics covered in the classes in the Sovereign Halls.

Dara put a stop to his exercise. "That's enough, breakfast is finished! Come get it while it's hot."

"Final question," Verimy clipped out. Azrael knew what was coming before Verimy said it. Every session in the Halls ended this way. "What does any opponent of a Sovereign Son lose once the fight begins?"

"My opponent loses its identity, it loses all future, and finally it loses its very life!" Azrael returned the rote answer. It seemed like a slogan but in fact was far deeper than words. It was an early lesson taught to every Sovereign Son, usually with a pet. After killing something that Azrael had grown attached to, the slogan finally took on a greater meaning.

They lose their identity—opponents are no longer male or female—they become an object with a name. Losing its future may seem self-explanatory, but to Azrael was a reminder that the opponent forfeited that future by choosing to fight him. Finally, its life—the outcome of the fights were a forgone conclusion and Azrael should fight with that confidence in mind. Never giving up.

He wiped up his sweat with a rag Verimy threw at him after his answer. They strode to the firepit and both took a helping of the large rabbit haunch. Azrael looked to Dara, waiting to take a bite as it was her turn to ask questions. He noticed her quiver beside her with only two arrows. Both his trainers had superb skills with a bow, but when ammo ran dry it necessitated a trip into town.

Their second plan required a large sum of Crystals, so the trainers sold all of their hides and spare looted items at the same time. He knew some Crystalized Ether dropped from the wildlife out here but, conversely, being on a prison planet seemed to increase the price of all the wares they needed.

Dara asked, "What are the superpowers of the Etherverse?"

"Trainer. Martians, Gaians, Sovereign Empire, and the Coalition of Dragons."

She nodded, and he took a mouthful of his soup.

Dara fired the next question, "The greatest tool in those Dynasties' rule?"

Azrael groaned; this was a long-answered question. "Trainer. Well, for the Gaians they possess Leviathan class starships, several colonized worlds and boast the most powerful recruitment school ever founded. The Martians have several colonized worlds as well, but their strength is mostly based on the template classes they started hundreds of thousands of years ago and were recently adopted by other planetary systems. The Sovereign Empire is the bastion of freedom for individual strength and has access to the strongest ancestral class ever known."

He took a deep breath, as he had never understood the strength of the Coalition of Dragons. "According to Professor Trall, the Coalition of Dragons derives its strength from its communication network and structure."

Dara nodded, but chose to add to his knowledge as he ate. "The Coalition of Dragons operates in small cells that infiltrate groups and worlds. For protection, each cell is effectively blind to all other cells around it and utilizes communication methods that no one has been able to intercept or decode."

Azrael shrugged, and she shook her head exasperatedly, before musing, "We should probably add the Tuatha De Danaan Guild to that list of superpowers. To attack the Empire, they must be very confident about their strength."

Verimy was blowing on his rabbit haunch to cool it, but answered, "Or they have a death wish. I do agree with you though, Dara, the fact that we had never heard of this planet or the Tuatha before their attack seems to point to a great deal of strength."

Dara smiled and shrugged. "We have been here a full month already and still haven't seen another person from the Sovereign Halls. I am surprised our ship of a thousand inhabitants of Lars only had us three from there. Still, we know there were more than a hundred ships loaded with prisoners. Do you think they have more planets like this one?"

Azrael shrugged; the Sovereign Halls taught you to be cold and detached from others. While he was interested in the premise brought forward, he had already written off the rest of the students and teachers as dead. At least until proven otherwise. "This planet has limited travel, so they could be two towns over, and we would be hard-pressed to find them. This has also given us a certain level of anonymity within Mur. It might have been an issue if anyone discovered I was a trained son of the Sovereign. Luckily, the prison transport ships were all just automated and you two kept combat classers away from me. Regardless, we still haven't made any real plans to get ourselves off of Tech Duinn."

His lack of emotion and criticism caused Dara to look at him sharply. She had a slight sheen in her eyes. Azrael tilted his head. Had she not learned to distance herself from her emotions?

Verimy nodded sagely, though, and stated, "Those words are true, Azrael, but we need to have all of the pieces together before we can make a full plan. We have two options, but both require you to reach your eighth birthday. A single step taken in the right direction is worth hundreds of others in the wrong one."

Dara continued to look at him, and he felt his skin crawl. She noticed his shudder and she explained, "Sorry, Azrael. I am just studying your face. While the increased growth rate helps all of you Sovereign Sons become stronger, it makes it easy to forget how young you actually are. You may look eighteen, but haven't even made it past your eighth birthday."

This was the woman's favorite excuse for when she was looking at him. He had heard her say the same thing on numerous other occasions.

Perhaps it was strange to others, but all of Azrael's classmates were similar. He had never known anything different.

Azrael shuddered, considering not being himself. While he knew his body had been changed and altered, those changes were part of him. Perhaps his quick learning and superior strength were a product of where he had grown up. Maybe it was entirely dependent on it, or perhaps it was a partial factor, but second-guessing wouldn't change his circumstances.

His trainers relented and gave him the signal to eat his fill. Azrael began to wolf down his portion of the rabbit haunch. He swallowed his last bite and stood, walking over to the tent. Dara and Verimy cleaned up the cookware.

He cleared the tent of ragged pillows and patchwork blankets. Next, he folded down the pavilion into a four-sided square metal box that hovered about a foot above the ground. He efficiently strapped tightly-packed bundles to it and then moved to collect the recently cleaned plates and utensils.

Verimy unlatched a small circular disc from the tent and clipped it onto his belt. "We have everything? We might not come back this way after we enter the town. I am still hoping that an Adventurer's Tavern or even a Guild might have popped up since our last visit."

Dara shook her head. "You know that isn't going to happen, but the sentiment still holds." She looked around. "This area is starting to get crowded, and it might be best to find another, less populated, hunting camp."

Azrael looked around, his brow furrowed; he hadn't seen signs of other groups. Then again, he was often kept well back from those groups if his trainers discovered them. But what was Dara referring to?

"Yes, perhaps it might be time to head to a new Territory. The journey might be a good opportunity for Az to learn more about traveling. Soon this area will become overhunted anyway," Verimy added.

His trainers' unwillingness to look at Azrael during their reasoning made him sure he had missed something.

Azrael coughed politely. "You do remember that I took a class on travel with Jerimiah, right?"

Dara blushed, and Verimy laughed nervously. "Right, completely forgot about that. Let's get to town. Perhaps instead of learning about travel, we will find a dungeon that we can explore once you're eight!"

The condescending tone of his voice told Azrael that he wouldn't receive a real answer to the unspoken question. The fact that Verimy and Dara seemed to treat him like a child, even though he was one, was frustrating.

Dara broke into a loping run and Verimy followed her. Azrael had no choice but to follow. The hover tent floated behind Verimy at a meter's distance. Azrael knew that the two hunters weren't running at their top speed and neither was he. The stupid junker of a hover tent could never keep up with even him at his top speed.

Or at least that's what Verimy and Dara told him.

CHAPTER TWO

Azrael ran after his two trainers through the dense forests. The hover tent floated just in front of him and he bumped into it as Verimy came to a halt. He pushed around the heavily-laden contraption as it puttered ominously. It was probably long past the time to replace the gravity engine. But on Tech Duinn, things like this were repaired to function again. New technology was reserved for the wealthy, and Azrael would likely never see something new near the Muradin Territory. He was fairly certain of that.

Verimy had stopped at a wide thoroughfare that led to Mur.

Azrael called, "Are we meeting Mark on this path like usual?"

The back of Verimy's head bobbed and Azrael rolled his eyes. His trainer often got quiet as they neared Mur. Azrael thought the man believed that speaking less was a sure-fire strategy to revealing little. That was true, but he thought it just made Verimy come across as suspicious.

Verimy and Dara began making hand gestures to each other. Azrael sighed, knowing they were communicating in their unique way. He could understand parts of their gestures but not enough to put together the topic. From his limited knowledge, Dara was asking about the time.

Azrael looked up at the sun. He knew that Dara could tell time based on its position, but assumed she also had a clock that came with her interface. They continued to argue and he felt himself grow angrier. The only reason they would be talking with their hand signals was because they were discussing something they didn't think he should hear. Or something that was about him.

He tried to ignore them and considered the man they were planning on meeting. Mark was an oily Karacy travelling merchant. Verimy had some way of keeping in contact with the dwarf that Azrael had yet to discover.

Whenever Dara, Verimy, and he went to town, the travelling salesman was always in Mur. How this coincidence existed Azrael had never figured—

Verimy turned, his face serious and Azrael instantly paid attention. "Azrael, we need to tell you something before we head into town. With all the unrest right now, if something were to happen to us, you may never hear this tale." He looked to Dara.

Dara smiled, then began, "This is the story of how you came to join us in the Sovereign Hall."

Azrael's fists clenched hard and his cheeks flushed with heat.

She saw his scowl and her smile dimmed slightly. "Just like today, you were red in the face. You were swaddled liberally in a black blanket and thrown through the Sovereign Hall castle gates. The trip must have been a bit uncomfortable because after you bounced to a stop, you began to cry and shout. That, of course, was how the guards were alerted to your presence."

Azrael felt himself bristle. Why would they not have shared this with him sooner? Why wouldn't the school?

"As everyone knows, only sons of the Sovereign King himself train in the sacred halls of the academy. At first, people pondered why someone would throw a baby through the gates, and why the note they found bundled up with him claimed he was a bastard son of the King," Dara continued.

Azrael interrupted, "My last name is Sovereign. How can they have doubted my heritage?" Azrael tilted his head as his jaw muscles bulged out on his cheek. He had hoped he was the son of the King this whole time, with little to no proof. His last name was one of his two biggest arguments with himself—the other being that he had trained in the Sovereign Halls. Now, he wasn't sure if he was ready to hear his trainer's response to his question.

Verimy placed a hand on Azrael's shoulder. "Calm down, Azrael. Yes, there is a way, but don't worry. You are a Sovereign Son. The system affixes the last name of the father to the son. However, the system also allows name changes by the mother at birth. Many parents have brought children to the Halls, claiming they were the son of the King. Just listen to the tale and you will have your proof."

Dara continued, "After the council discussed this issue, the headmaster of the institution decreed you would be given to the nearby monastery to raise, like the other children who weren't confirmed sons of the Sovereign. However, on the day we swaddled you back up to hand over, a note from the King himself arrived and ordered that you remain."

Azrael's brow furrowed and he bit the tip of his tongue. He wanted to interject, to ask more questions. But he worried it might interrupt the story.

The King himself interceded on my behalf?

The snide jokes from other Sovereign Sons. The name calling. The teachers' reverence—all of it made a lot more sense now. He just wished he had known sooner. In time, he had risen above the other students, but knowing this would have helped him understand the strangeness of it all.

Maybe this is why I had no true friends? I could only ever be revered or hated.

Was this why Verimy and Dara had saved him, over all the other students? Because he was the only student who the King had confirmed...

Verimy looked down the road. "You were the strongest son the teachers had seen in a long while, Azrael. I am shocked that even you had doubts who your father was. Your superiority could only have come from your bloodline."

Azrael didn't speak. He thought back on all the 'compliments' he had received from these two. He couldn't help but see this untold story as the reason for why they had chosen to save him. They were too smart to not see the increased chances of rescue from having a strong chess piece in their possession.

Dara patted Verimy's hand consolingly. "It wasn't all that easy. I remember having to console our young man here, a few nights. The other sons were cruel. He was the only one who wasn't brought to the complex by one of the King's guards."

You caught me crying when I was three years old, Dara! I am not that child anymore!

"You two should have shared this with me then. Or at any point in my years at the Halls. Why is it only now that I'm hearing this story?" Azrael heard the heat in his voice and turned away from his trainers to not glare at them.

Dara's eyes held tears and Verimy reached out to hold her hand just as Azrael averted his gaze. "We weren't permitted to tell you anything, Azrael. Who do you think the guards were that found you as a baby?" asked Verimy.

Azrael turned back, confused. His hands began to sweat. No, it couldn't be.

"Yes, we were guards at the time, stationed at the gate. That's the only reason we know the story. We only found out about the letter from the King much later, as a teacher gossiped about it near us," Verimy continued.

He closed his eyes and fought to control his breathing. Breath was the first step to control of the body. After his breathing came his racing heart. Finally, he opened his eyes and nodded. His trainers met his eyes and looked away, faces flushed.

He repeated his lessons the other Sovereign Sons had taught him. *Don't ever expect help from others. Friends will only stab you in the back.*

"Speak of the man, and he isn't far behind." Verimy's mumbled comment broke the awkward silence. Mark's beat up transport truck floated into view, coming down the packed dirt pathway towards them.

The sun that filtered through the canopy shone off a rusted roof. The front cab had only two chairs in its boxy design. The cab connected to a large shipping container through a small doorway that Mark left open when he drove. Azrael always sat in the back with Dara, and Verimy always sat up front.

Azrael glanced at the hover tent. How did Mark even afford the truck? This tent had cost them an entire week's worth of farming. The truck would have likely taken a lifetime and Azrael didn't get the impression that the salesman was well off.

The gravity engines on the truck coughed to a stop as the anchors churned the ground behind it, stirring up black pine needles, leaves and dirt. The passenger door creaked open and the group climbed in.

"Hello again, Azrael, you've sure grown," Mark smarmed.

No, I haven't. You have barely known me for a month.

Azrael pressed his tongue into the back of his teeth and put on a false smile. Once he was through the doorway to the large openness of the container, he rolled his eyes and sat down to think on what his trainers had just told him.

"Verimy," Mark called as Dara walked through the doorway to join Azrael. "I have had to increase my price for this service, I'm afraid."

Dara blinked. She opened her mouth and closed it a few times. Azrael was the reason why Verimy paid the man to take them into town. He couldn't see what Verimy liked in the greasy trader.

He missed Verimy's response, but Mark's was loud and clear. "Your little child mercenary back there is worth quite a bit to the right people. His last name is Sovereign for Athena's sake. The first person who Analyzes him will scamper off to rat him out."

The truck lurched into a side rotation. And came to another stop facing back towards Mur. "Listen, they have hiked taxes in Mur again. There is even a rumor that King Oberan will soon control Muradin. Deal? Or get out and walk."

Verimy's head peeked through the door. He said, "Dara, drop two bags worth of goods with his inventory." His head disappeared and the front seats springs groaned. The truck lurched forward this time and began to hum as the gravity pulsar engines sped up and stabilized.

The rest of the trip to the city entrance was quiet. Then the anchor brakes got dropped into the dirt and jerked them all to a grinding halt. Verimy asked, "Why is the line going out longer than the one headed in?"

Azrael felt his eyes widen and stuck his head into the front. There was a long, snaking line of dirty, bedraggled sapients waiting on the guards to allow them exit. Azrael studied the mismatched colored paneling that created a rusting wall rimming Mur. The large metal plates were leaned haphazardly against standing trees and overlapped to create a defense a strong wind could collapse.

The interior of the city was even more dangerously built. Bent rods were driven into the earth and plates were screwed, nailed, tarred, or sapped into place. The effect was an almost never-ending sprawl of 'buildings' leaning against one another. Azrael scowled; if there was a single fire, or a bad storm, this whole shanty town would be decimated. However, bad weather never happened in a Territory.

Azrael studied the sticky sap that was leaking out of the nearest tree. He was actually surprised that the Tuatha allowed the collection of the sap, when cutting down trees was a crime that landed you in the arenas. Otherwise known as a death sentence.

Mark inched the transport forward. "Told you, tax hike and rumors of new ownership. Everyone leaving has to prove they have paid the new tithe. Most people are choosing to move on rather than risk a trip to the Pit. Other than those idiots." Mark indicated a line of people waiting at a bar door.

Verimy pushed Azrael's head back through the door. "No one survives the arenas." Verimy kissed two of his fingers and then touched his heart. "It appears you were telling the truth earlier. You still have merchant rights?"

"That's what you're paying me for," Mark quipped.

Verimy joined Azrael and Dara in the back.

Azrael coughed. "Does that change the plan?"

Verimy shook his head. "Dara, you're still going to be Mark's shop assistant when he sets down for the day. Azrael, you're staying in the office."

Azrael's shoulders slumped and he closed his eyes. The office was a small compartment within the floating transport truck. It was right behind the passenger seat and had one lockable door and a small window that allowed Mark and Dara to pass him Crystals, gems, marks and chips as they were collected. Azrael opened his eyes. "Wait. What about you, Verimy?"

"Mark is going to put out the yellow flag and I will be in the cab trying to buy information."

Yellow flag? Right. For adventurers, that often meant they were looking for maps, quests or locations.

That was new. But the look on Verimy's face told him that he wouldn't be getting an explanation. What sort of information would be worth some of their saved Crystals? Verimy didn't show a hint of emotion but something about his behavior was odd.

Mark maneuvered the massive vehicle into position and slowly lowered it to the ground with a thud. All four walls shook around them. Azrael raised a single eyebrow and Dara punched him in the arm with a chuckle. The rusted-out shipping container didn't collapse. *This time.*

Once on the ground, Dara and Mark got to work efficiently rearranging metal shop panels that folded off the side of the truck. Within half an hour, everyone was in their assigned positions.

For the next few hours, Azrael meditated within the miniscule space of the office. It had a single chair, a table, and a small safe stowed under it. Azrael evened his breathing to long silent intakes and controlled exhales. His goal was to hear Verimy when the man found an information broker. He was sitting just a few feet away, so it should be pretty simple.

"Heya, Gurdy. We have the usual pelts, extra meat, and assortments of other drops to trade," Dara's best cheery voice filtered through the passenger side walls.

Gurdy was a gnome vendor. Her high-pitched squealing penetrated the metal as if it was paper. "What are you hoping to get in return?"

"The usual—"

"You're hoping to purchase some maps, I hear." A low baritone coming from the front of the truck overrode Dara. Azrael inhaled sharply. Verimy was buying the information at the same time as Dara negotiated with Gurdy. Azrael couldn't have expected this and leaned nearer to the front of the vehicle. He wanted to hear Verimy and the unknown information broker, not Dara and Gurdy.

"I can't do the usual pricing after the tithe has been levied, Dara. I can get you four hundred arrows as usual, but the salts, peppers, and oils will cost you extra." It was impossible to hear Verimy's responses over the shrieks of the gnome.

"—I do have a few maps with what you're looking for. Lord Ogma used to buy up all these types of maps himself—"

"Four pelts. I can't trade the extras for less than four."

"With a possible change of ownership, you might not see Lord Ogma for a long time." Verimy's soft voice carried back to Azrael from the driver seat.

What would Lord Ogma be looking for? Azrael tried to listen further, but both devolved into price negotiations after that.

"If you are back this way and have any locations to share, let me know. Not many people venture out that far," the salesman with Verimy finished.

"Mark, have you paid your taxes yet?" an arrogant sounding voice called from the front of the shop, just as a money pouch dropped in through the office slot. Gurdy's shrieking must have garnered the wrong sort of attention.

That voice sounds more authoritative. I'm guessing a patrol, or military?

Azrael began sorting it out, placing the Crystals, gems, marks, and diamonds into slots that led into the safe by his feet. Mark responded as the currency slid down the slots with a rattle. "I certainly have, Captain Colten. All according to my Merchant Writ."

"The one signed by Lord Ogma? I don't know if you heard, but Mur will be changing ownership, Mark," Colten retorted and a few grunts told Azrael he had company. "What about your pretty little shopkeeper? She could settle any tax issues and line her pockets besides—"

A slap like gunfire sounded and Azrael tried to peek through the opening but couldn't see anything.

Someone coughed, but the silence that followed was deafening. Azrael strained to hear what came next. What had just happened?

"Sweetheart? Everything okay?" Verimy's voice called from up front, seeming to come from the passenger side of the front seats.

"Everything's just fine. Colten here just needed a reminder to keep his hands to himself."

"Tax papers, all three of you. Now!" Colten's voice cracked like a whip.

Shuffling of papers sounded through the wall. Then Colten said, "This is one paper."

"Look right here, Captain Coltan. It is for me and two assistants."

"Alright, it does say three people. Who's in the office if you three are out here, then?"

"My son," Mark responded quickly. "He is under the age of eight and exempt from taxation."

Colton went over every inch of the stall after that. Loudly banging through each item and storage compartment. Finally, with an audible sigh the Captain said, "Good day, Mark. That document is only good until tomorrow. Be out of my town or I will run you out. Merchant Writ or not."

Verimy whispered, "Is there a law against taxing children under the age of eight?"

Mark snorted. "No, but that idiot doesn't know that." A short pause before he spoke again, "Dara, you are lucky that the Captain still fears Lord Ogma. I think we have overstayed our welcome, though. Let's close up and get inside for the night. We will leave at first light."

CHAPTER THREE

Azrael sawed his jaw, trying to bite a piece out of a trail ration Mark had handed him. Was the taste always this bad? The hover transport wasn't leaving until morning, and the group had sat inside since the Captain had confronted them.

Mark ran a hand through his hair, pushing it out of his face. Azrael tilted his head. The oily look was gone. In place of a rodent sat a businessman. Mark leaned forward. "I heard an interesting rumor about why the tax hike happened."

Azrael squinted at the change in Mark's speech pattern and glanced at Dara and Verimy. They continued to fight with their own trail rations. Verimy managed a bite and held it up. "What is this made of, Mark, rocks?"

Mark's eyes crinkled and he ran a hand through his long beard. "The Karacy were born of rocks. I would never dream of being cannibalistic." His face sobered, and he continued, "Recently there has been a downturn in citizens willing to sign up for the arenas. Usually, this wouldn't be a problem, but I have seen fewer ships of prisoners arriving in the capitals and outlying Territories.

"So, if the rumor I heard is true, King Oberan needs more slaves in the Pit. According to everything I was told, King Oberan is farming the people on this planet for Essence."

Verimy laughed. "Mark, come on, you know better than that. Planetary Gods hoard Essence and they definitely don't take sides in conflicts. No one even knows how to produce Essence, just that it is the second tier energy formed of Ether."

Dara smiled and nodded along with her significant other. "Not to mention all they would achieve by feeding the planet more Essence would be to strengthen the planet. That might be beneficial if the Tuatha wanted this planet as a training ground. However, killing people inside of a dungeon increases the dungeon's Essence, not the planet's specifically. It would be a very inefficient method to collect Essence, no?"

Mark shrugged and smiled sheepishly. "You are probably right. I heard it recently and now realize it is probably just someone's bad dream. They could be planning to use the dungeons as training grounds, though."

Verimy stroked his chin but gave no verbal response. Azrael followed the conversation but hadn't taken his eyes off Mark. While Mark had seemed to laugh off the dismissal, Azrael could tell the Dwarf was still worried.

Mark's eyes met Azrael's, and the dwarf tried to smile, but it didn't reach his silver irises. Azrael shivered and looked away as the conversation turned to other things.

"Azrael, it's time for bed," Verimy ordered.

More like time for the adults to speak.

Azrael lay down and feigned sleep, modulating his breathing to sound convincing. After a time, the others began speaking again. As he had expected.

"If we can find an area deep into the wilderness, we can probably avoid patrols and eat off the land. Dara and I can start to make arrows instead of buying them, but our damage will probably suffer because of it. Mark, what class are you?"

Mark snorted, "Trader, so don't go expecting much help from me."

"Well, we have a map to a nearby dungeon. Once Azrael turns eight, we should be able to farm it for a time."

Paper rustled and noises of approval were made from the others as they likely studied the map. Azrael strained his ears, but the others chose to call it a night.

Azrael fell asleep shortly after.

He woke up to banging on the door to the hover transport and loud catcalls. "We're hungry and have no place to sleep, but you get to sleep in opulence, huh!"

"You think you're above us?"

"We know you're in there, Mark! Give us some food!"

Azrael looked around worriedly and noticed that everyone was awake. Verimy shook his head and mimicked falling back to sleep before he closed his eyes and attempted the task himself. Azrael tried to sleep again, but every bang on the shipping container shook the rickety sheet metal walls.

He swore they were trying to tear it apart for scraps at times. Mark sat up, wide-eyed and shaking. Dara peeked from the front. "There is an entire mob out there, Ver."

"We are much safer locked in here, then. Go back to sleep, Dara. In the morning, the guards will disperse everyone. Probably," Verimy responded without opening his eyes.

***

Azrael woke again as low morning sunlight penetrated the high windows of the transport. A noise woke him up; a loud sound that was akin to dropping a ball down a long tube. Azrael recognized the familiar noise; it was the gravity pulsar booting up.

Mark sat in the driver seat, and Verimy sat beside him as they made their way towards the northern gate. It was the exact opposite direction they had entered from. Azrael tried to look around surreptitiously for the map his trainer had purchased. There wasn't an obvious slip of paper out on a counter and he yawned theatrically to hide his perusal.

At the gate, Mark supplied their papers to the guards on duty, and Azrael hid in the office to avoid scrutiny. Mark was pretty sure they wouldn't care about a minor, but they figured it was best to just answer the questions asked and move on. Since the gate guards didn't ask them if anyone else was with them, they didn't even have to lie.

Once they were moving, Verimy poked his head into the trailer from the front seat. "Do you think this is a day off, Azrael? Get to work on your kata forms."

Dara watched over him this time. She didn't ask him any questions as he flowed from stance to stance, instead only using her bow to correct his postures when she deemed it necessary. It gave Azrael some time to think. Where would they keep the map now that they had studied it?

Azrael finished his katas and ate another atrocious travel bar as an early lunch. According to the conversations he overheard as he tried to stay invisible, this side of the Territory was much larger than the other. It made sense, in a way, because his trainers had never taken this route out of Mur to hunt.

They travelled for a few hours, and were just nearing the border of the Territory according to Mark, when something went wrong. The gravity pulsar engines made a sound like they were throwing up a hairball, and then the transport flopped like a beached whale onto the ground. The momentum of the travel jerked to a quick stop and Azrael flew forward. He tried to see what happened to Dara but was a bit preoccupied with attempting to not hit the wall headfirst.

He turned enough to collide with the container wall back first, and his ribs made a noise like dead branches breaking in a storm. He fell to the floor, breathing becoming hard. He fought his own body for each inhale as a sharp pain stabbed into him.

Dara shouted, "Azrael is hurt. Mark, what was that?"

Mark growled, "We ran out of power, but that doesn't make sense. The batteries should have been converting all night."

Azrael wheezed in a lungful of air as the driver side door slammed. Verimy came to kneel beside him. Azrael's vision began to darken as his brain started to feel the starvation of oxygen. "He needs a healing potion, Dara. Take out the one we have."

A taste like the ripest berry juice dripped into his mouth. He accidentally breathed some into the wrong pipe, causing him to cough. The pain of the cough sent him into unconsciousness for a moment. However, he woke as his brain signaled that he was drowning. Drowning on that same berry juice.

He fought the urge to spit it out and was able to swallow mouthful after mouthful.

He finally cleared his airway and managed a breath. Then the pain quadrupled, and he felt bones start shifting again in his back and ribs. He passed out.

***

Azrael woke up again to Mark's voice and the sound of two metal objects hitting the floor. "One of the citizens from last night plugged some old appliances into the outside sockets."

Verimy grunted. "Two heaters? At least that explains why we couldn't hear them. How long until the battery recharges?"

Mark shook his head. "Unfortunately, once it is fully depleted, it needs six hours to recharge. You can't use it during that time." Azrael managed to move his head. Mark was rubbing a large dent in the wall. Likely where Azrael had collided and nearly killed himself.

Mark let his hand fall to his side and his head fell. "Can you help me move it to the side of the road? If a patrol comes this way, I don't want trouble for blocking the path."

Azrael felt the truck slide across the ground and managed to sit up. Once the motion stopped, he stood and went outside. Verimy saw him and said, "Go gather fallen branches and kindling. Only things on the ground, mind you; there is a law against cutting down anything inside the Territory borders."

Azrael groaned but did as he was asked. When he returned to dump his wood, he found his trusty quarterstaff and the buckets waiting for him to fill up. He closed his eyes. "I did just almost die, you know?"

Dara ruefully shook her head. "You probably wouldn't have died. I don't think the ribs pierced your lungs. Anyway, water is about a mile or more in that direction. You know the routine."

He sighed—that was right, no one cared. He lifted the staff and buckets and jogged off half-heartedly. Better to finish quickly since he knew he would have to practice sword forms when he got back. Then after that he might have time for a rest.

He was spared from the sword forms, to make another trip for water. Another body meant they needed more. Well, at least the routine wasn't the same as it had been for weeks.

He stacked kindling and coaxed the fire to life once he had brought enough water.

The entire time, the others chatted, and he continued to try to be invisible.

"You know of a cabin that we might be able to use?" Verimy asked skeptically. "Out in the middle of nowhere?"

Dara squinted her eyes and took a deep breath, but Mark nodded.

"Actually, I have stayed there on a few occasions. The person who owns it moves around a lot, so he often isn't even home. However, I know he is there presently. I think you should meet him."

There was a sort of reverence mixed with worry about the way Mark spoke that made Azrael want to hear what came next. Either this man was powerful, or Mark was about to reveal something dangerous. "If you two are interested in opposing

King Oberan or finding a way off this rock, he is probably the best source for options."

Azrael felt his eyebrows raise as he worked his stick back and forth over the split kindling. If what Mark had just stated was right, it was both—this man was both secretive and powerful.

A puff of smoke rose from the split kindling and he missed the response as he added air, literally breathing the fire to life. Dara set up a stew pot and began throwing trail rations, water, and some herbs into it. The combination didn't look appealing, but maybe the water would make the trail rations softer. A good stew would take a few hours to cook and would likely be ready right before the batteries of the transport would be recharged.

Dara shooed him. "Go get to your sword forms again."

He had gotten too close to the fire and failed to remain invisible. He scowled at his failure. But walked over and picked up his training sword from the back of the truck.

For the next few hours, he flowed from form to form and tried to listen, but the adults were too far away. Verimy didn't even come to correct forms or ask questions—changing routines indeed.

What has them so worried?

He was in the middle of Dancing Dragonfly when the final rays of sunshine fled the sky, making room for the darkness that swallowed everything but the fire.

Dara called, "Dinner is ready. Come get a bowl, Azrael."

Azrael put his practice sword back into the truck, then walked over to the firelight. As if in perfect sync, six other people carrying weapons did the same.

Azrael scanned them all quickly and saw three cocked crossbows, two spears, and one sword.

They weren't here to talk.

CHAPTER FOUR

"No one move, no one does anything heroic, and no one gets hurt!" the mugger holding the sword exclaimed. Azrael assessed the man, taking in his weak grip on his rusty sword, his ragged clothing, and his gaunt frame. This man wasn't a threat, and probably wasn't even the leader of these hooligans.

Why was this weakling doing the talking? Trying to conceal the true threat maybe?

Azrael continued his study of the enemies. Two of the crossbowmen were barely able to lift the weapons to shoulder height, and instead were bracing the butts against their stomachs. The limbs of the contraptions were dry-looking and had webwork cracks marring them. The strings were even fraying! If these two nincompoops fired, they were likely to wound themselves with recoil and break their weapons at the same time.

Not just them, either. Azrael shifted his gaze to the spearmen and noticed that they both were a bit beefier. At least they had a semblance of proper form with their legs spread just past shoulder width and the spearheads aimed at targets. His eyes narrowed. The slightly healthier appearance was because they wore rusty chainmail under their shirts. They were just as gaunt as the others.

What in the world would possess these men to attack healthy, able-bodied travelers? Azrael felt a smile tug at the corners of his mouth. Dara and Verimy would make quick work of these wannabe thugs.

But the two both had hands raised into the air. Were they waiting to surprise the would-be crooks?

Azrael double-checked his assessment and even scrutinized the trees—triple-checking. Verimy opened his mouth and slowly intoned, "We don't want any trouble. Perhaps we can offer you some food and a place by our fire for the night—"

The 'swordsman' cut Verimy off, "You will stay there as my colleagues go through your truck. Don't move!"

Mark spoke up, his voice wavering, "You need my biometric to open the back—eek!" The merchant actually squeaked when a crossbow twitched in his direction. Why in Sovereign's name weren't Verimy and Dara attacking?

One of the crossbowmen kept his stirrup pointed at Mark while the other continued to aim at Azrael. The swordsman motioned sloppily with his rusted piece of metal for Mark to stand and open the truck. He sneered as he directed his next words to Azrael. "Kid, come join the others at the fire!"

Slowly, Azrael made his way over to the firepit. He still couldn't figure out why his trainers had done nothing to stop this.

He lowered himself into a crouch, his muscles tight with the strain of inaction. These men were such weaklings, he felt like he could kill them all himself! Yet, he knew he was at a severe disadvantage without levels and access to skills, but—

Then it hit him. It felt like a kick between the legs. His stomach clenched and his fingernails dug into his palm.

Dara and Verimy were protecting him!

Azrael's eyes widened, and he looked to Dara, who was observing him from the corner of her eye. He felt his blood cool. His two high-level trainers were currently sitting still and allowing muggers to take their gear because Azrael was too much of a burden.

It turned into a rather polite mugging, as each time one of the ragged morons approached Verimy or Dara to loot their gear, they grew too scared and retreated. Azrael would have laughed if he wasn't so upset. The muggers packed up what they could carry, which was a pitifully small amount, from the truck. Verimy chimed in as they prepared to leave, "Were you the group that was tracking us at our last campsite?"

The leader sneered. "We were just waiting for you to let your guard down!"

Verimy laughed in response, and it seemed to unnerve the man, who hastened to pick up his load of mismatched spoils. The group of muggers ran off, towards town, and Verimy stood slowly. "Was there anything valuable that they took?"

Mark shrugged. "Nothing that I can't recover. Mostly food, and leathers I was planning on trading in the next town."

Dara stood up during Mark's response and placed a hand on Verimy's arm. "Let's just eat and get back in the truck. One of us will keep watch for more muggers. No need to go after them; I'm sure they're starving and desperate."

Mark's eyes widened comically at the exchange, and Azrael felt his ire flare again. They should have just handled the imbeciles when they attacked. Verimy's head fell and he muttered, "Dropping *your* guard because you were in the Territory! Not smart, Verimy!"

The group ate. His trainers weren't in the mood to talk. Azrael wasn't either. Whenever he thought of the muggers, he wanted to punch both of the high-levelled trainers.

Was that compassion Dara just showed?

Mark, on the other hand, ate with so much speed Azrael wondered if he would choke. His eyes moved in every direction but toward his food. A lot of the merchant's meal ended up on his tunic.

"We should be able to leave soon. We could travel through the night and get into the deep wilderness before we would need to stop and recharge. Do you think that would be safer?" Mark's voice wavered. Azrael could tell the merchant hadn't seen much combat before.

Verimy stroked his chin and looked at Dara. Together they nodded, and just like that, it was decided—probably for Azrael's safety!

He clenched his teeth so he wouldn't scream at them, or at the universe. He didn't need protecting. He had been trained his whole life for this. Would he ever be able to make his own decisions?

After the food was finished and the stew pot was cleaned, the group got into the truck.

Mark fired up the gravity engines as soon as they got inside, and within a few minutes they began bouncing down the path. Still no one talked, and Azrael seethed.

He gave up on calming down and moved to the back of the truck, hoping he might fall asleep. The only problem was that his mind wanted to rage. He let the anger and frustrations of the night wash over him.

He didn't need anyone else. He hadn't needed to be coddled by his two trainers—he could and would have taken care of himself. Who cares if he didn't have a Class—

Tech Duinn welcomes you and congratulates you for making it *past* your VIIIth orbit of Farghul!

You have now been granted access to your personal interface to help you navigate. Become strong and help Tech Duinn survive!

- **To check your personal interface, please use thought, and intention commands.**

Azrael felt his breathing slip out of his control—he let it and his heart have their way. This was far too exciting. Hands shaking with adrenaline, he navigated to his character sheet and then to his class selection page.

Azrael Sovereign Level 1
    Class: Awaiting Selection
Class Skills: Awaiting Class
    Health Points = 110/110 Points
    Ether Pool = 130/130 Points
You have 5 stat points and 1 skill point to distribute.
    Stamina – 11
    Strength – 13
    Agility – 11
    Dexterity – 12
    Intelligence – 13
    Wisdom – 9
    Charisma – 13
    Luck – 12
    Would you like to assign statistic points now?
        <Yes> | No

A hurried review of his available classes using his search parameters yielded *unexpected* results.

Where was the Sovereign Class?

CHAPTER FIVE

The truck hovered along, and Azrael looked through the list of classes one at a time. He found the alphabetical listing function and scanned the area where Sovereign should have been. Nothing.

His body felt like it had been on a roller coaster. His chest ached and his eyes burned, but he fought to stay awake. Maybe it was one of these other search functions?

***

He woke up as the truck bed bounced and tried to open his eyes. They felt glued shut and he rubbed them, forcing the crust to fall away. That finally allowed him to open them. He had spent all last night searching through classes to no avail and had slept in.

The truck bounced and shook as the gravity engines tried to compensate for uneven ground. Azrael looked out the front and saw that they had definitely gone off road. They likely would have to stop soon to allow the battery some recharge time as well. He wondered how far off the grid they were.

He looked at his two trainers, and took a deep breath. They were his next reluctant option for finding his Ancestral Class. It was possible they knew something, after all.

***

"The King himself recognized him as a Sovereign. Why would he not have access to his Ancestral Class?" Verimy asked no one in particular.

Azrael regretted the decision to talk to them. They now spoke to each other as if he wasn't present.

Dara shook her head. "This is our first time talking with one of the kids after they turn the appropriate age. Perhaps there was something at the Halls we missed. Remember, they were always taken away by the principal for a week. Maybe an item granted access."

I am right here, you know!

Verimy snapped his fingers. "That's right. Then they also received special training for a year afterward, before moving to the King's special forces!"

Mark's face firmed when he saw Azrael's clenched jaw and red face. Mark tapped Verimy on the shoulder, and Azrael turned to go. He needed some fresh air. He grabbed his training sword and swiped a piece of paper that was open on the tabletop. Perhaps it was the map…

"Let him go work through his forms. This is probably harder on him than anyone else," Dara's soft voice called.

More sympathy? I don't need your sympathy. I don't need an Ancestral Class. I don't need to be a Sovereign Son!

"I thought they were emotionless monsters," Mark began, before he coughed to a stop. "I mean, that's what people say about the Sovereign Sons," Mark stuttered.

*I will become a monster. I **will** become emotionless.*

Azrael jumped down the few feet to the forest floor, stomping into his landing, and surveyed his surroundings. They were deep in the wilderness. He punched the door button without looking back.

Mark must have shut down the engines sometime earlier this morning. He stormed into the forest and sat down on a black boulder covered in brown moss.

He unfolded the parchment he had swiped. It was just a hand drawn version of an original map. Jackpot. Azrael tried to interpret the hastily drawn lines. Mur was depicted as a house with the name scrawled in chicken scratch above it. The star must be where they were now, a few leagues outside the Territorial boundary. What was the treasure chest, and the X?

The treasure chest was nearly on top of the star. The words above it said Training Site. The X had the word Cabin. He oriented himself and turned in the direction of the nearby Training Site. What could his trainers have in mind?

He folded the map and began his warm up exercises for sword forms.

Congratulations! You have learned a new skill.

Swordsmanship

- **Swordsmanship skill will help you better wield any weapon classified as a sword.**
  - **Each level, you will gain some small tidbit of knowledge about wielding your blade.**
  - **Each level reduces the chance of being disarmed by 0.5%.**

Current Rank: Weak level 1.

He finished his first kata, and the twenty skill level increases convinced him to continue into the next. He knew his trainers and they wouldn't bring him to some random place in the forest and mark it on a map. Or buy a map for that matter.

What would Verimy buy a map to, on Tech Duinn? What did you buy a map for in general?

Treasure, which was indicated by the treasure chest. But that was a kid's fantasy. Or a really stupid writer's delusional attempt to create an end goal out of nothing. Couldn't be that.

The goal of his trainers was to get off this planet. Did the mark on the map depict a pickup point? But then why would some random person in the market have it? Why would Lord Ogma be interested in it?

A dungeon. They had spoken of a dungeon. It was the only logical training device that fit. His trainers had bought a map to a dungeon out in the middle of nowhere. Dungeons could give treasure.

He advanced into the Moderate swordsman ranks, and a grim smile crossed his face.

Stats page open, he watched the skill tick up steadily as he entered the third kata.

He seized onto the salve that this show of strength provided. His starting stats were further proof of his gains from his time at the Sovereign Hall. On average, his race of human would average 8 in all categories. Through the classes and training, he was above that in all of them. He entered his fourth kata and ranked up Swordsmanship again to the Strong rank.

His growth after that, while fast, slowed down enough that he knew he wouldn't reach the Greater rank in Swordsmanship unless he trained all day.

He finished his ten katas and sat down, mind feeling clearer than it had the previous night. He had options now, and one of those options was to get away from his trainers. Dara and Verimy had hidden things from him his entire life. Did he really want to stay with them?

He twirled his ring. He wanted revenge for the Tuathan attacks on his home. Dara and Verimy followed the laws of that place. Could he fault them for their loyalty when he longed to return to the same?

The iron signet ring caught the light. The half-moon or ax head, and the crossing sword or fragment of a star's light. So many theories existed about what the sigil represented.

Azrael didn't care. To him, the sigil had always represented the fight each Sovereign Son battled through. The metal backdrop was the shield the Sovereign Empire created with their strength. All the people of the Empire were behind that shield. His mother was somewhere behind that shield.

He reached out to turn the ring again—seriously considering throwing it away.

Ring of Holding
Soulbound
Size: Small
Weight Reduction: 90%
Inventory
- **Note**
- **500 Crystals**
- **Sovereign Sword**
- **Scroll of Strong Obfuscate**

Azrael's breath caught. The strange weight of the ring suddenly made a lot of sense. It wasn't some foreign metal mixed with iron. How could his trainers not know about this? For it to be Soulbound meant that this ring was exceptionally rare.

A Soulbound item couldn't be removed from a small radius from around a person unless they wanted it to be. Most Soulbound items would be overlooked by others as well. The system somehow created an unknown effect that forced people to skip over the item in question. Soulbound items had other effects—

He shook his head; no point dwelling on the ring when it had things inside. He pulled out the sword first.

Sovereign Sword
- **This sword is a near-perfect replica of the Sword of the Sovereign King.**
    Ether Pool: Large
    Current Ether Pool: 130/130

Enchantments: Stats X (+3), Ether Edge V

Stats X
- **Increases all stats by 3, except for Luck.**

Ether Edge V
- **Increases the penetration of this sword versus Ether Armor, and inherent Ether. This enchantment also prevents the need to clean this sword, as an Ether film protects it.**

From his classes at the Sovereign Halls, Azrael would classify this sword as extremely rare. It could even pass for an Heirloom or Soul Blade with the large Ether pool and enchantments. He placed it back into the ring. Why would every trainee get this ring if they had a Soul Blade waiting for them?

He pulled out the bag of Crystals. He didn't bother counting them, just hefted it in a palm, peeked inside the bag, and placed it back in the ring. He had no use for currency at the moment, not buried in the wilderness. Would he have had a use for Crystals at the Sovereign Halls?

Will five-hundred Crystals buy me transport off this planet? Where would I even go to find a ship leaving?

He resolved to possibly ask Verimy and Dara about that—if he returned to them.

He pulled the skill scroll out next, marveling at the Strong classification, but not knowing precisely what Obfuscate was.

Scroll of Strong Obfuscate

- **Obfuscate allows a user to change the name or description of an item or their character sheet at will. This new name or description will appear genuine unless the individual's Perception skill is high enough to detect it.**
  Learn Obfuscate?
  <Yes> | No

This was a strange skill scroll to impart to trainees. Azrael wasn't naïve and knew that this ring was of standard issue. What exactly was the purpose of these four items? The note might give him some clue and so, holding his breath, he pulled it out and began to read.

Hello Trainee,

Please provide the bag of Crystals to the headmaster. This is his payment for another trainee making it to his eighth year.

This note may be a copy of the original, but it does not change the severity of the information within. Do not share what you read below with anyone. It is knowledge shared only with the sons and daughters of the King.

Welcome to the Sovereign Elite,

First and foremost, congratulations on completing your training, and I look forward to your rise through the ranks of my other alleged children. You may have already noticed that there isn't a Sovereign Class available for you to choose. That's because my class of Sovereign isn't truly a class.

That's right, I will not share with you what my actual class is, but I can tell you that if you are reading this, I have yet to complete 'The Quest' to lock my class to familial relations. Why then do all of your 'brothers' and 'sisters' have a class of Sovereign when you see them? That's because of the skill imparted to you. Your instructions are as follows:

Choose a Combat Class.

Obfuscate the name of the class to Sovereign.

Obfuscate the name of the sword to appear as a Soul Blade.

By completing these steps, you too will be a member of the 'Ancestral' Class.

Your father,

Erebus Sovereign

The Sovereign King

Added:

If this addition is still penned, it means that the war between Guilds and the Sovereign Empire still wages. Unfortunately, the Guilds have discovered our secret and thus do not fear the power of the Sovereign class anymore. They are fighting to begin controlling planets, and through those planets, they hope to gain power. Unfortunately, with most new worlds under oppressive planetary occupation, their best option is to secure weakly defended, already existing planets. Their unfortunately timed discovery of our secret has placed the once supreme Sovereign Empire directly in their crosshairs, as I cannot be everywhere at once.

> *Erebus Sovereign*
> *The Sovereign King*

Azrael crumpled the note and threw it. That explained quite a bit. Pieces of the puzzle fell into place. He hadn't missed the 'alleged children' line either. *His father* didn't care if Azrael really was his son. He only wanted more *children* to carry on his ruse.

After a moment, he went and collected the note and placed it back in the ring. He still didn't have an explanation for the letter telling the Headmaster to keep him.

One thing in the letter had his heart pumping magma through his veins, though. The King had known about the war and still left the Sovereign Halls so under defended?

CHAPTER SIX

He practiced some unarmed combat forms to vent his final, clinging frustrations. Part of him wanted to run away. To abandon his trainers and Mark. But Azrael knew better.

As for the information of the fake Ancestral Class, Azrael could use it to continue the lie, but he would gain nothing from it. His trainers may believe the discovery of his *Ancestral* Class when he returned, but what would that achieve?

> **Congratulations! You have learned a new skill.**
> **Martial Arts**
> - **Martial arts are a highly practiced form of defending and attacking without a weapon. Practitioners of Martial Arts are said to be able to create attacks and defenses that rival all other combat forms.**
>> **Each level of Martial Arts increases the inherent Ether in your fists, feet, elbows, knees, head, and shoulder by 0.1%.**
>
> **Current Rank: Weak level 1.**

If anything, his deception would put himself and his group in more danger on Tech Duinn. His trainers likely believed that his Ancestral Class would grant them amnesty or alert someone to rescue them. Azrael now knew the truth, and none of those things were going to happen. He punched out viciously, pretending the air in front of him was his 'father's' face.

The year's worth of training after a Son reached his eighth birthday also made a sick sort of sense. They likely increased the level of obfuscation in some way, while also placing the individual son or daughter under a compulsion to never reveal the information. The plan was destined to fail, of course, as a high level individual would, and did, see through Obfuscate—but Azrael also began to understand why Sovereign Elites were never stationed near the edges of the Empire...

From his training at the Hall, he knew of the history of the system. In the early days, individuals absorbed Ether and learned to control and manipulate it to create skills. Often fighters would take centuries to craft a single skill, and then they would level it. skills varied greatly, and practitioners rarely taught their life's work to anyone but descendants.

In a way, this was very effective as family lines formed kingdoms and passed on skills to the main branches and sub-branches of their lineage. However, it was also vastly inefficient, as skills often duplicated in multiple nations, under different names. Trainers would offer to teach a skill, only to discover that the trainee already knew the technique under a different name. In time, the Atlantean Council passed the Globalization of Skills law, and all the same or similar skills became grouped under one name.

Then more changes were necessary because vast disparities began to form between Lords and peasants, between crafters and the less fortunate. Slavery began to grow rampant. Until slaves stole techniques, and a rebellion occurred. Once the slaves rose to significant stature, they petitioned the council, and classes were created, for equality of opportunity.

People were happy for nearly five hundred years, as class options slowly built, until individuals had access to many options. Although classes were now beginning to cause a universal issue, as any individual could choose the custom class. Once named, this class became an option for others to accept. However, that new 'class' may have the same skills as another. Since skills formed groups and paths known as skill trees, this created multiple named classes that were mostly the same.

The solution put forward was Ancestral Classes, a middle ground to remove skills from the global list. Of course, this was a bill pushed through by the Lords. Their influence needed a way to gain back what they lost.

The Sovereign King, his *father*, was so powerful and famous because he was the first to complete 'The Quest' to obtain an Ancestral Class. Or so everyone believed...

Azrael spit onto the black ground, feeling disabused. The history he had learned was the propaganda of his *father*. However, there was a tidbit in the story for those who paid close attention. Currently, there still existed a custom class option, and through it, you could create a class that became powerful. Of course, you were just as likely to develop something badly broken.

Azrael navigated through the thousands of classes available on Tech Duinn. The planet's system was probably a carbon copy of all other Planetary Systems—derived from Gaia, the eldest planet. He confirmed that thought when he found the Custom option. He finished his tenth martial kata and placed his hands on his knees, sweat dripping down his face, breathing heavy.

Was this what he wanted?

He chose the option, and a prompt appeared.

What is the name of your Class?
<Revenant>

He mentally typed in Revenant, a character in one of his only books growing up. In the story, the wronged man came back from the dead and claimed revenge on the people who had hurt him. It felt fitting—trapped on this prison planet, abandoned by his father and the Sovereign Empire. Abused by the Tuatha De Danaan.

Once the name registered, he waded through a list of thousands of first-tier skill options. Unsurprisingly, he didn't find a soul sword option like the Sovereign tree was fabled to contain. What a joke! His 'father' might just be carrying around an obfuscated enchanted sword for all he knew.

How did he choose from hundreds of viable skills?

Azrael felt himself reeling at the sheer quantity of them. He had expected a large number, but this was terrifying.

It was easy to filter out the crafting skills. He wasn't particularly drawn to Non-Power Classes. They often grew to be extremely valuable and influential, but very few of the NPC's would ever be on the front line—and to achieve his goal, he needed to not only be on the front lines but to survive it. The skills shrunk to half.

Did he want casting skills, and ranged abilities? Yes, but those would be secondary. If he couldn't survive a close-range fight, he would likely never achieve revenge. Still, perhaps skills existed with dual purposes. Instead of removing range, mage, or melee, he checked the <and> modifier and included abilities that contained all of them.

The list shrank to a hundred, which was much more manageable. Could he narrow it further? Possibly.

He read through the skills. One hundred was not a bad number. It gave him options. At a mental command, Azrael favorited skills that appealed to his combat sense.

In the end, he had four skills on the list.

Phantasmal Blade
- **This skill coats your sword in personal Ether, which can project an invisible attack at enemies. The density of the fired sword-like Blade increases in strength as more points are placed in the skill.**
  Skill gained at 1/5, "<u>Phantasmal Blade.</u>"
  Ether cost is 25 Ether per stack.

--

Blink
- **This skill uses personal Ether to teleport through space. It can be used offensively and defensively for a range of five feet. More skill points increase the distance one can travel with this spell.**
  Skill gained at 1/5, "<u>Blink.</u>"
  Ether cost is 50 Ether per use.

--

Impact Absorb
- **This skill can absorb the impact of a single object and store it. The user can then release that same impact on a future contact of their own. More points in this skill reduces the Ether cost.**
  Skill gained at 1/5, "<u>Absorb.</u>"
  Ether cost is 10% of force absorbed.

--

Charge
- **This skill uses personal Ether to increase speed and momentum. Users can Charge to a place or**

target an opponent. More skill points increase the distance the skill travels.
   Skill gained at 1/5, "<u>Charge</u>."
   Ether cost is 25 Ether per use.

Azrael had one point and getting to tier two of skills only became available after maxing the first tier. That was a significant consideration, as most skills increased in potency as tiers increased. Still, sometimes the second tier of a skill was just plain useless. He groaned. Custom class might have been a mistake.

He removed Blink. While it was probably the most potent skill available, it had too high of a chance of linking to strictly mage skills at higher levels. Charge had a similar problem, with the opposite specialty. It may lead to only close-range combat.

That left him Impact Absorb and Phantasmal Blade. Impact Absorb was theoretically infinitely powerful. However, two rather significant problems existed. First, if the strike overwhelmed his Ether pool, he assumed the remaining power of the attack would still connect. The second consideration, of course, was Ether sickness. Bottoming out your Ether pool left the user feeling weak. Bottoming out your Ether pool in one shot left most people catatonic—at least according to his teachers.

So he chose Phantasmal Blade. Not because it was the most potent option; no, rather it was the most reliable choice when he considered its flexibility. Just because it was a ranged strike didn't mean it couldn't function in close quarters. It had a set Ether cost, and as he grew his Ether pool, it would gain additional functionality. Finally, because of its ambiguity, he assumed he would have more versatile options at the next tier.

Once he placed the point and confirmed it, his mind expanded and warbled. Then suddenly, he knew how to use his first Revenant ability. He charged his blade with the skill and slashed his sword through in the air. Instantly he noticed that the skill had coated his brand-new sword in an invisible layer of energy. He didn't have to release the Phantasmal Blade as a ranged attack, which made this skill even more versatile.

It looks like I got a good one!

To test how the blade would function in melee, he moved to a tree and slashed it. Then he removed the skill by reabsorbing his Ether from it and cut another tree with just the sword. His first casual strike nearly doubled the penetration depth of his second!

He smiled, despite simultaneously noticing the ability had a small downside. Azrael discovered that Ether was lost for each swing that connected. Still extremely functional, but not all powerful as he had secretly hoped.

Next, he charged and released the skill at a tree from ten feet away.

The skill began splintering the wood and creating a strange, almost tube-like cutting pattern. The ability made it more than halfway through the tree before it ran out of juice. He moved to examine the damage and discovered what the skill points meant. Right now, his released Blade was wide and almost circular, and it appeared to use a continually rotating front end to cut. If Azrael placed five points, he surmised that would sharpen and increase its penetration.

Still smiling, he chose to find some wildlife to test his new skill on. Perhaps he should go back and bring a trainer with him? He shook his head, expelling the notion. They were probably just going to scold him for choosing a class before *they* decided one for him.

He jogged off, deeper into the woods, towards the treasure chest on the map. He jogged over the ground, reveling at the feeling of finally being able to do something he determined. He could level, and like a liquid under pressure finally given its escape, he was ready to burst.

The ground disappeared under his next step.

I should have been paying more attention.

Azrael shot his arms and his legs out, attempting to catch an edge of—the crumbling ground? Someone had placed a pitfall out here. Thinking fast, he dug the tip of his sword into the packed soil beside him.

His descent slowed but didn't stop. He touched down at the bottom of the pit and didn't break anything. He sighed with relief, feeling tension drain from his body. Maybe he could just climb back—

Welcome to "Apep's Pitfall"!

>**You have entered in a group of one, suggested group size 2+.**

Good luck.

Level: Unknown

Age: 155 Days

Best time: N/A

Clears: 0

Ether Concentration: Low

Looks like he had found the treasure…

CHAPTER SEVEN

Azrael was in an antechamber made of dark black stone. In front of him, a reflective archway made from onyx formed a doorway into deeper darkness. He had wanted to find the dungeon. But he had been hoping to discover its location and have time to prepare. Not fall into it…

He pulled the hand drawn map back out. Maybe it had a bit more information.

Nope, just the treasure chest.

Entering the next room may begin a puzzle, a delve, a reverse climb, an arena, a mob encounter, a timed challenge, or so many other options. Azrael glanced back up the shaft he had fallen through. Sadly, there was no climbing out; it was just too high, and the soil was too soft. He took a deep breath and checked the walls nearest him. They didn't have any distinguishing features that might give him more information.

He only had the information the system provided. One hundred and fifty-five days old. Low Ether concentration and no clears. He could work with that.

He did some quick mental math based on his Dungeon Diving class. With low Ether concentration and its age, the monsters inside would range from level seven to ten of the Apprentice rank.

That was only if no sapient lifeforms had perished down here. Zero clears didn't mean zero attempts.

Better put in five wild card levels. Even if no sapient lifeforms had died down here, it was common for dungeons to trap wildlife and gain levels that way. So, with a great deal of guesswork, this dungeon could classify as a level twelve to fifteen Apprentice rank, with a boss difficulty as great as Journeyman level five.

Theoretically he could clear a dungeon with those mobs. His chances were probably ninety percent if he had time to prepare and recharge his health and Ether. If the dungeon came at him non-stop, those chances were probably closer to fifty-fifty.

Of course, if multiple people had attempted its depths, the mobs inside could all be Journeyman rank. In that case, his chances plummeted and it was better to sit in the antechamber waiting for his trainers to come find him.

Another consideration—not all dungeons locked people in. The odds worked out to a coin flip on that front. Azrael could roll the dice. This antechamber would remain a safe zone and he could retreat here. Then, of course, this could be a delving dungeon or a reverse climb. In that case, he wouldn't have to enter the boss chamber or leave the first floor. He could just farm the first level until Dara and Verimy arrived.

Don't ever expect help from others...

He repeated the hard-learned mantra in his head. That was right. He wouldn't count on them to arrive. He wouldn't count on any help from anyone. He redid his earlier assessment and left Verimy and Dara out of it.

The best chance for survival with his trainers out of the picture was to continue to fight on the first level, gaining enough strength to advance to the second. So for his best-case scenario, this would be a delving or climber dungeon. He would also need to find food and water to make that strategy work, of course.

Azrael's heart increased its tempo as he squared his shoulders and walked through the archway into the next room. Lights blinked on in all directions. He shaded his eyes from the sudden change in lumens. A boom sounded behind him before his eyes could adjust. That roll of the dice had come up poorly. He was locked in.

He blinked the spots from his eyes and felt his heart stutter. His stomach clenched and seemed to fall towards his colon. He was greeted by a gargantuan, seat-less Coliseum. An Arena Dungeon?

He was standing on a balcony, and stairs descended to the sands on the ground floor.

Azrael's teeth ground together, and he spat. This was possibly the worst type of dungeon for his current predicament. He checked the archway behind him. He needed to be sure it was sealed.

It was.

Too late now. Time to reassess.

Arena Dungeons slowly ramped up challenges. So, his early calculations weren't accurate. Statistically, the first challenge would be below the dungeon's power base, and the last would be above. That meant he could fight through waves of spawns and gain levels for the final challenge. That was the good news.

The bad news was that there was no way to avoid the final showdown in an Arena Dungeon. No way to gain levels until he was ready. There was a finite number of Etherience available before the challenges escalated.

A countdown of sixty seconds began in his interface. Next consideration. Would he be better off on the stairs or down in the sands? The stairs were a natural chokepoint for any creature that couldn't fly. He stayed on the stairs and readied his sword.

Grinding assaulted his ears. And it was coming from below him. The stairs began to tilt, and his jaw clenched. The dungeon was going to make his decision for him. A heartbeat later, the inertia in his feet was broken and he slid off his balcony onto the slide the stairs had become.

He crashed onto the sand and spat out the granules that got into his mouth. Azrael heaved himself to his feet and ran towards the nearest wall—the next best option. The timer counted down from fifteen seconds and he went through his breathing exercises to center himself.

At zero, a section of the far wall slid away with a grinding noise, and an insect chittered out. Its six legs moved mechanically as its antennae adjusted like individual satellite rods. One of those antennae twitched in his direction and he took in a breath. The other jolted to join the first and the six legs began to propel it over the sand in a clicking run.

He scrutinized it, attempting to prompt an Analyze skill.

Ant
Apprentice-Drone
Level 2

This would be the first time using his Sovereign Sword, which was quite overpowered for a low-level dungeon, though he couldn't be sure how well it would function, especially against an insect. He needed to find a weakness, to increase his odds in this fight and subsequent ones, as dungeons normally followed a theme. So, if one ant was present, he was likely to find more.

Insect chitin was naturally high in inherent Ether. Azrael remembered a lesson about the Antinium, a sapient species of insectoids. Their joints were the weakest point in their chitinous plate armor. Azrael assessed the enemy. Its joints were low to the ground.

He got into a stance that excelled in waist high and lower strikes. Threshing Wheat. He leaped left and simultaneously torqued his body. He left his sword extended and braced against his right hip. He felt the blade catch and drag before his wrists clicked as the pressure released. He landed, brought his feet together, and pushed off again. His body spun and he was facing his enemy, again, just as it arched around on five limbs. Its sixth limb twitched on the sand nearby.

It screeched and clicked its mandibles in his direction. Its antennae and head followed him, even as its feet made a small circle.

He resumed Threshing Wheat. Using that form, his blade had severed a leg from the creature and proven its strength. The limb now ended in a short stump that spat ichor onto the sand. He could continue to whittle the ant down, but he figured it was time to test his Phantasmal Blade. He needed to know how it would fare against a living sentient creature.

He loaded the skill on the edge of his sword and performed the exact same attack pattern, but this time in the other direction.

On his landing, he turned around to assess the damage. This time the blade had severed a limb right in the middle of the chitin, instead of at the joint. The ant wavered on its turn, before it crumpled to the ground. He nodded and absorbed the Ether back into himself, choosing to assess the actual cost of that strike. Fifteen Ether returned to his pool, and he nodded again—a fee of ten from his one hundred and sixty.

He recharged his Blade and released the ranged version of the skill at his downed opponent. The creature was just getting its four legs under it when his skill circulated through, bisecting it. A single charge of his skill could counter the chitin's inherent Ether. Test two complete.

Azrael walked over to the ichor-stained sands and looted what remained.

He used Analyze on the strange shard he had just picked up.

Half of Sphere of Sweet Perfume
- **The crystal shard is half of an item. To learn more, assemble all parts.**

He placed the small shard into his ring and studied the sands. No other monsters had rushed out of the opening during his encounter. A grinding began, followed by an ominous boom as the stone closed again. The timer in his interface reset to sixty seconds.

Standing over the ant corpse, he checked how much Etherience the kill had earned him.

A measly sixty-two points. That wasn't much, but more than enough to advance to level two. Azrael instantly dumped his skill point into Phantasmal Blade. He would experiment with it again in the upcoming fight.

He was going to need to place all of his free stat points as well. No opportunity to hoard them at this time.

Azrael Sovereign Level 2
Class: Revenant
Class Skills: Phantasmal Blade (II)
   Health Points = 140/160 Points
   Ether Pool = 134/160 Points
You have 0 stat points and 0 skill points to distribute.
   Stamina – 16 (+2) (Stats X +3)
   Strength – 16 (Stats X +3)
   Agility – 16 (Stats X +3)
   Dexterity – 17 (Stats X +3)
   Intelligence – 16 (Stats X +3)
   Wisdom – 16 (+4) (Stats X +3)
   Charisma – 16 (Stats X +3)
   Luck – 12
Skills:
Analyze – Weak 12
Combatant – Weak 5
Martial Arts – Moderate 29

Swordsmanship – Strong 8

He placed his free stat points to remain in balance. This meant most of his points went into Wisdom. Wisdom increased Ether pool regeneration, which he would need as fights ramped up. It also increased the speed at which his neurons could fire, making decisions faster. He may choose to specialize later, but right now Azrael had no idea where this particular skill tree would lead him.

How many waves would he have to fight through in this dungeon? That unknown alone solidified his need for the regeneration.

He dropped into a ready stance and waited as the countdown continued. The door ground back open to reveal a slightly larger Ant.

Ant
Apprentice-Fighter
Level 3

Azrael checked his Ether pool. One hundred and fifty-three points. He didn't bother testing the close-range improvements of his Blade. He just fired the ranged version at his charging opponent and watched it run right into an invisible circular saw. The corner of his mouth twitched up. He rather liked his first skill choice.

He made a mental note to recheck his skill's capabilities once it was level five. That kill had leveled him again and he didn't want to waste time assessing the skill when his levels were flying up.

He looted the second bisected ant corpse.

Half of Sphere of Silence
- **The crystal shard is half of an item. To learn more, assemble all parts.**

Azrael continued his slaughter of the first six waves. Each wave was an enlarged ant of some variety. The sixth wave had been a Soldier Ant and had been the first creature to survive his Phantasmal Blade. However, surviving and continuing to fight were two vastly different things. He had simply walked up and pierced the creature's eye. Ending that stage.

The encounters netted Azrael four-hundred and fourteen Etherience, which catapulted him to level five. As soon as he placed his final point in Phantasmal Blade, the Fog of Discovery, as his teachers had called it, flowed back to reveal two new options on the second tier.

He had no time to read the new skills. They were currently unavailable anyway. He glanced at the timer and his Ether pool. Unfortunately, the speed of combat was beginning to place him in a bind. His Ether was recovering from ninety-two points. If he continued like this, he would run dry near the eleventh fight. The timer was at twenty-two seconds. Hoping to conserve some Ether, he had made the decision to place his points in strength as he leveled up.

The three extra points in strength would increase his melee penetration and damage, which should allow him to hold onto more of his precious resource.

As the timer neared zero, Azrael charged his fully-upgraded skill and placed it on his sword. It was time for a change of tactics.

The next creature that exited the monsterside chamber wasn't an Ant, however.

Beetle
Apprentice-Shell
Level 7
Mini-boss

Oh great! He really needed a mini-boss when he was hovering just above fifty percent Ether. He shook his head and let the slow-moving creature meander its way around the sand. It took a strange path. Not coming directly for him. Azrael's eyes narrowed, wondering why it wasn't attacking—at forty feet, it shot towards him like a bullet, sand spraying out behind it.

Azrael hadn't relaxed his stance and managed to jump sideways and tuck into a roll. Despite this, the domed back of the beetle connected with his right ankle and jolted his entire body, but his quick thinking and action mitigated a large portion of the possible damage.

He shot to his feet and winced at the pain his ankle pumped to his brain. He entered into his deep-mind space that his Swordmaster had taught him. It helped him ignore the screaming agony his ankle wanted him to focus on.

The beetle's speed had been too much to handle. He couldn't allow the creature to use that charge skill again, and so he closed with the mini-boss.

He managed two strikes, one to its back, and one to a leg, as it turned to face him. Its mandibles came forward, attempting to surround and crush him in their sharpened vice. Azrael swayed and performed Descending Curtains, sweeping his sword from high to low on a trajectory away from the beetle's body.

The blow caught the joint of its right front leg, and the combination of his skill and his strength tore the limb off. The boss screeched in his face and swung its head, choosing to batter Azrael. It connected with his chest, but instead of resisting the blow, Azrael continued to sway, absorbing some force and pushing off with his toes and calves to add more. He screamed as his ankle protested this motion. His assisted leap turned into a somersaulting roll that carried him ten feet from the boss.

He immediately realized his mistake. Sand shot into the air behind the back legs of the creature, as it propelled itself using Charge—again! Azrael came out of his roll and jumped straight up. His ankle bloomed in agony again and he clenched his teeth. He'd barely cleared the five-foot-high back of the monstrous insect.

He dragged his skill-surrounded blade over the face and back of the beetle.

His skill managed to sheer off a mandible before the momentum bounced the blade up. It was everything Azrael could do to hold onto the weapon and land without impaling himself as he was forced to avoid putting weight on his bad ankle.

The creature, now short a mandible and a leg, took some time to turn. Azrael limped into range and resumed his close combat.

The beetle still hadn't fully turned, and Azrael severed another leg from its right side. The bug reacted by flexing all of its left legs and body checking Azrael into the nearby wall. It attempted to activate the Charge again, but instead of rocketing forward, the skill misfired. The face of the boss crunched into the sand as its back legs pushed with skill-assisted maximum effort. Its mandible caught, and instead of a charge, the bug somersaulted onto its back, where it lay waving its remaining legs in the air helplessly.

Azrael tilted his head. The beetle just waved its three remaining limbs uselessly. It couldn't get back up. He walked over and prepared his blade to kill it. Then thought better of it, and waited for nearly fifteen minutes.

His health ticked to full first and Azrael tested his ankle. No pain. He checked on the boss continually, and while it had begun re-growing mandibles and limbs, it stayed trapped on its back.

Once his Ether was also back to full, he dispatched the mini-boss.

The timer that joined his interface gave him three-hundred seconds, and he shrugged. His precautions became somewhat unnecessary, but now he knew for the future.

He gained eight-hundred Etherience for the level seven beast and was propelled into level six and partway towards level seven. He knew from school that the first fifteen or so levels in the Apprentice ranks were the fastest anyone reached. That was why he had made the assumption of being capable of beating a low-level dungeon.

The five-minute timer meant he could check his new tier two skills.

Tier 2 Skills
En Sphere
- **This skill creates a sphere of converted Ether around the user. Within this sphere, the user can feel all movements as it disturbs the En. At one skill point, the En Sphere reaches one foot from the heart of the user. Increase points to increase the radius of skill.**

Passive Skill gained at 1/5, "<u>En.</u>"
0/5

--

Mend
- Mend increases the natural healing of a body. At higher levels, it will even rearrange structures within the organism to ensure healing occurs most effectively. At one skill point, healing speed is increased by 100%.

Skill gained at 1/5, "<u>Mend.</u>"
0/5
Ether cost is 40 Ether per stack.

Azrael then looted the boss's body and surveyed the items he had managed to compile in the first seven fights. Each of the first six waves had dropped a half sphere which he combined, while the Beetle boss had dropped a shield.

Sphere of Silence
- This sphere, when broken, will cast Silence in a twenty-foot area. Can only be used in Apep's Dungeon.

--

Sphere of Sweet Perfume
- This sphere, when broken, will spew forth a sweet-smelling perfume, created from the local flora above. Can only be used in Apep's Dungeon.

--

Sphere of Command Interrupt
- This sphere, when broken, will interrupt communications between creatures. Can only be used in Apep's Dungeon.

--

Beetle Shell Shield
- This shield is created from the hard exoskeleton of a Beetle. It has naturally high inherent Ether and has an Enchantment to increase strength.

  Ether Pool: Small

Current Ether Pool: 5/40
Enchantments: Deflect I (10%)
Deflect I

- **Increases the chance this shield will turn or rebound an attack away from the user by 10%. This shield is extremely effective against stingers.**

The shield was a disappointment. Using it would force him to wield his sword in a single hand and make his sword strikes far less powerful. Still, it did give him a huge amount of information. The fact that it was unlocked right after looting gave him hope. Some dungeons locked the enchantments, and others didn't. If he could defeat the final boss, he might receive loot that was immediately valuable.

The spheres seemed to be strategic items. He would look for opportunities to use them.

Lastly, he chose to place his skill point in En. While Mend would be useful to have, it was reactionary. Only of value after damage had been taken. En was preventative, and Azrael hoped that it would stop the injuries Mend would be useful for from occurring.

CHAPTER EIGHT

He had finished dispatching the eleventh challenge and the sixty second countdown timer for the twelfth challenge ticked down to zero. The monster entrance door slid open but nothing emerged. Azrael's arms were burning, his heart was pounding, and he kept having to blink the sting of sweat from his eyes. The dungeon wanted to throw something new at him, again?

At least he had gained another level and a skill point. Still, the combat was getting more difficult.

The last four rounds had been humanoid ants. They stood on two legs and used their other four limbs to strike at Azrael with ferocious intensity. There was no longer an easy win. He scanned the air above him and saw nothing. Where was his opponent? Were they too small to see?

His En flared, warning him of something being within the three-foot perimeter around his heart. He reacted immediately and stepped left, allowing the En to act as his eyes. Just because he couldn't see the opponent didn't mean the opponent wasn't there. Using a downward slash, he connected with something his En highlighted as the probable neck of the creature. He felt no resistance, like he was swinging at air.

Had he missed?

A bodiless head materialized and flopped to the ground, rolling away as it became visible mid-collapse. His En flared again from two directions and Azrael leaped into the air. Turning and swinging below him in a flurry of movements directed at the area where his En indicated the opponents were.

Two more ant corpses hit the sand, ichor spreading out from head wounds. He examined their exoskeletons and saw why there was no resistance to his attacks. Their chitin was dull black and absorbed what little light the arena provided. It was also as thin and light as cotton. That was all the time he had because his En flared again.

Twisting in mid-air, Azrael moved flawlessly and deflected two strikes from two more Ant Assassins. The dagger-like fists of the creatures almost broke through his blade's barrier. He hadn't noticed during his rushed examination, but those things must have been as hard as Eternium. Landing, he assumed a ready posture, then flowed through stances. Using his En sense, the final two Assassins posed no threat. In a few short minutes, he had managed to dispatch them both. And he hadn't even needed to use Ether attacks—just physical endurance, which admittedly was starting to waver.

He moved throughout the bodies and collected an additional sphere as the counter reset to sixty seconds with the telltale boom.

He now had two of the silence and perfume spheres, but only one and a half of the command interrupt. Based on his previous experience, he was assuming that the next wave would finish the sixth sphere, and then he would face another mini-boss.

This wave was unlucky number thirteen, and he labored to catch his breath. At least he was power leveling. How long would it be before Dara and Verimy started searching for him? How long would it take before they discovered the dungeon above? Finally, could they even break in here?

Don't count on anyone.

The Assassins had been level fourteen, and his earlier calculations suggested the final boss would be in the Journeyman rank. This wouldn't end at a fourteenth challenge. Maybe twenty-one or twenty-eight. All he could do was keep pushing forward. After the fourteenth stage he might get another five-minute break. The fact that he hadn't found a use for the orbs yet added to his feeling of unease.

Even with his Ether rationing, he was at ninety points and considered dumping free stat points into Intelligence or Wisdom. His health was hovering near one hundred despite not having any serious injuries.

The arena door swung open to admit his next opponent. This time the creature was an amalgamation of an Ant and a Beetle, and he groaned. This dungeon was running out of ideas it seemed. Unfortunately, this idea could be the death of him. Especially when he combined it with the level increase.

Beetle Ant
Apprentice-Warrior
Level 15

The beast had the back shell of a beetle with six legs, and the two first segments of an ant. The ant portion of the mutation stuck straight up like a humanoid, and its four limbs ended in sharp chitin blades, like the Assassins.

Azrael, seeing the Warrior class, chose to wait until it came to him. Warriors were notorious for having limited or no ranged attacks.

The Beetle Ant didn't possess the Charge skill of the beetle mini-boss—luckily. Azrael had been ready to dodge in any direction to avoid ending up skewered on the end of those chitin blades if it charged. The enemy was forced to close slowly and when it had, all four of its arms shot straight up above its head. The arms began to glow, and Azrael dove under the beetle's backside to avoid the telegraphed hammer blow.

A muted boom sounded, and he was peppered with sand. His legs screamed as he slid, and his sweaty arms were now caked in sand. Instead of rolling, he shot his sword up at the tender underbelly of the insect. His skill-assisted blade pierced through the underside, then stuck hard.

He got to his knees and lunged, levering his sword with every ounce of strength he could summon. The wound opened wider, and ichor poured out on top of him. The sand that coated him turned a sickly green.

He gagged from the smell of burnt rubber the blood exuded, but continued to step forward. The back end began to collapse under the severity of the damage he was inflicting, and he abandoned his blade to roll out from his cover. The ant half of the body continued to thrash around, attempting to turn and attack Azrael, but without its beetle legs, it was rather useless.

The sword-like appendages were slicing through the sand as it tried to drag itself around unsuccessfully.

Azrael calmly walked over and extricated his sword. The dungeon needed to learn that beetles had a mobility issue. Once he had caught his breath and his two bars were full, Azrael executed the Beetle Ant.

He looted the beetle and completed his second Sphere of Command Interrupt. If he was right, he would have three of each completed sphere at level twenty-one, which was looking like the final boss according to calculations. At least, as he began using the new data from each wave.

He felt his body tingle. He had a shot at this. If all this dungeon was going to throw at him were beetles and ants, and various combinations, he could win. Possibly.

The timer ended with Azrael feeling a rush of adrenaline and hope. He could beat this mini-boss.

The doors opened with a sliding hiss of stone on stone. Something black and yellow began squeezing out of the room. It was too big to exit all at once. Instead, the creature dragged its head out, followed by its middle, and lastly its abdomen. Its translucent wings began to blur, and the air hummed.

Do not let an opponent fight from strength.

Azrael licked his lips, then spat insect ichor onto the sand and charged. Allowing that insect into the air would be a very bad choice.

Wasp
Apprentice-Stinger
Level 18
Mini-Boss

Mid run, Azrael loaded a Phantasmal Blade into his Sovereign Sword. The insect flexed its legs as the wings' humming became steady. Azrael released his slash. The wasp jumped up, and the invisible skill connected. A line of ichor bloomed along the shiny black abdomen of the wasp.

Azrael sighed in relief, seeing his skill connect. It should be torn apart by his Phantasmal Blade. Or not...

The wasp barrel rolled and landed back on the ground. Azrael's skill no longer pushed it back through the air. The skill's momentum had created more of a separation gap and the wings began to pump again.

He sprinted toward the insect, again trying to close the distance. What other options did he have?

He was fifteen feet from it, and still out of range of a melee slash. He charged his blade with the skill in preparation and closed.

The wasp jumped back into the air.

His eyes widened—he had been limiting himself to a single charge of Phantasmal Blade. He forced Ether into his blade, and it worked. He had a double charge of his skill. He hesitated for an infinitesimal moment, not knowing what to expect, before releasing the new double-stacked skill in a horizontal trajectory.

Had Azrael missed? Nothing happened for a strained heartbeat. Then he saw the six legs and the wings separate simultaneously. The wasp fell back to the ground, screeching. What had just happened?

Something hit the back wall behind the wasp. Azrael felt his mouth twitch and he leaned over to see around the fallen insect. Two grooves slowly ground into the wall, accompanied by a deafening cacophony. They were spaced six feet apart and acted exactly the same as a single Phantasmal Blade. He was liking his first skill more and more.

Azrael glanced at his Ether, which was at eighty-seven, and charged his melee strike with a single stack. Without wings or legs, the wasp wasn't moving to attack but still managed to spin in quick circles. He would kill it soon. But first he would let his resources recharge a bit.

As soon as his bar was nearly full, he executed the struggling bug.

Stinger Sword
- **This stinger is forged from a mutated wasp's stinger. It has unusually high inherent Ether, which is strengthened even further by an Enchantment.**
    Ether Pool: Small
    Current Ether Pool: 1/45

Enchantment: Poison I
Poison I
- **Adds a wasp's poison damage to any physical wound made by the weapon. This adds severe damage and a chance for anaphylaxis.**

His sword was much more reliable than this new weapon, but he had to admit that, for a low-level adventurer, it was quite something. If this was the quality of the gear it dropped, he had a real chance to defeat it. A real chance to use this as a stage for leveling.

His skill tree was turning out to be very beneficial. Both En Sphere and Phantasmal Blade were strong.

The Etherience Azrael gained for the wasp only amounted to a thousand, unfortunately, and that wasn't enough to push through level eight.

The five-minute timer counted down, and Azrael scanned the coliseum. As he moved around to fight, each kill had sunken into the sand. Absorbed back into the dungeon once he was farther away from the corpse. His adventuring teacher in the Sovereign Halls claimed that the dungeon cores gained back some of their spent Essence, if not all of it, in this way.

His heart sped up, sending heat into all of his extremities. Only seven challenges left. A first clear dropped the rarest gear the dungeon could create. Of course, the sword and shield he had acquired weren't fantastic, but that didn't mean the final boss wouldn't be better.

***

Azrael fought through six more waves. The fifteenth and sixteenth were flying ants and had been hardest to deal with because they were agile and ferocious. Waves seventeen and eighteen, however, were beetles that he assumed were meant to fly but couldn't. Instead, the dungeon had messed up the wing to body ratio. They could jump and sail for a period before landing.

At first, the beetles froze him in place when they took to the skies. A mobile tank would be devastating. However, they could only coast in straight lines and always travelled a set distance. He had managed to incapacitate both specimens and regenerate full resources before starting the next stage. Beetles in this dungeon were turning out to be his savior.

The final two waves were insects that were hard to look at. He gazed pityingly down at the twentieth wave's single creature and grimaced. It had the abdomen of a wasp, with two 'stingers' that moved like a beetle's mandibles. Its thorax was the hard carapace of a beetle, and its head contained the maneuverability of an ant, with long thin antennae.

Instead of making the creature more powerful, the amalgamation had seemed to want to attack and defend in three different ways. The beetle portion wished to stand in and tank blows, the wasp section wanted to be airborne to avoid them, and lastly, the ant head seemed overwhelmed by the conflicting signals.

This failure of amalgamation told him that he was likely one of the first adventurers in this dungeon. At least the first to make it this far. If the dungeon got it working together in unison, it would be more powerful than either of the two mini-bosses. That didn't bode well for his plan to farm this dungeon. Young dungeons grew in strength very fast when adventurers arrived and began giving them demonstrations of weaknesses to fix.

He ended the ghastly insect's suffering and prepared for the final stage. He looked in his ring at the three stacks of different kinds of spheres.

The last six stages of the arena had managed to fill his Etherience bar for level eight, and Azrael placed his skill point into En, which increased the radius of the sphere to six feet. He held onto his free statistic points, hoping for a glimpse of his third-tier Skills before deciding. He just hoped that the four unplaced points wouldn't be the death of him.

When the timer reached zero, Azrael looked to the spawning chamber door. It didn't open, but he could swear he heard the stone grating sound he had expected to accompany it. He listened intently and instead his ears picked up the slow hiss of—falling sand?

He scanned the arena and found small circles of what could only be described as churning, vortex-like patterns in the white grains.

Each pattern was spaced evenly around the combat floor and near the wall. Azrael moved slowly away from the twisters closest to him—eventually finding himself in the center of the coliseum. He scolded himself and began a slow shuffle back towards a wall. Suddenly the subtle sound of falling grains was eclipsed by a hum that mutated into a buzzing roar.

As Azrael watched, fat black and yellow bodies began shooting from the holes. The creatures were five feet long and matched that in girth. It was a hive of wasps. Wait—they were furry. He gasped. Bees!

The hive continued to pour out of the holes in all directions.

He managed to Analyze one that hovered near the ceiling.

Worker Bee
Apprentice-Buzzsaw
Level 15

He continued scanning through the ever-multiplying creatures and found that there were two different types.

Drone Bee
Apprentice-Warrior
Level 21

The creatures didn't attack him. And that was the only reason he was still alive.

If they all descended on him, he was beyond screwed.

He looked back up the slide he had entered from. Was it better to try to break back into the antechamber?

The humming was oppressive. He could feel it through his bones. A cacophony of demise.

He noticed a change in the light of the room when a golden glow began to coalesce behind him, stretching a shadow self out in front of him.

His head snapped around and he found a bee slowly gathering Ether. A spell! He kicked forward off the sand and faced front. He sprinted through the sand in random patterns as the light grew in intensity.

Just when his shadow stuttered, Azrael pivoted hard and reversed direction. His shadow grew and then reversed, telling him the spell had gone above him. Just before the shadow elongated to his actual height, he dove forward and rolled. Something flashed behind him before wind and sand blasted his shabby tunic and pants.

He turned and found a massive crater. He looked back up and desperately tried to find that bee again. He hadn't had time to Analyze it the last time.

Three sharp hums sounded through the buzzing din. The drones landed all over the arena and attempted to bulldoze him out of existence. They weren't agile or dexterous, though, especially on the ground.

He ducked and dodged, making each movement purposeful and concise, as he had been taught. He counterattacked when he could and even managed to cripple two drones. But truthfully, the drones' bulk saved him, as they often ran into an ally, preventing multiple bees from attacking in unison.

A quick assessment told him that the Worker Bees had stayed out of this conflict.

Two sharp buzzes cut the din again. The drones took back to the air, and suddenly bees were attacking him from above.

The bees were trying to pick him up. They surrounded him, creating a circular stack of bodies hovering just above his head. Again, their bulk made it so only three to four were attempting to grab him at one time. He entered into Cooling Fan and circled his sword above his head in continual slashes. This was somewhat effective, but then the Worker Bees started landing to try another avenue of assault.

Azrael couldn't stop Cooling Fan for the risk of the attacks above. Instead, he used En and footwork to avoid grasping forelegs from the ground. His body began to sweat desperately from the exertion. One loud buzz signaled the bees to take back off into the air.

Azrael stopped his technique and examined the room, expecting a new method of attack. Golden light caught his eye, and he nodded. Three spheres, three attack patterns—he pulled out a Sphere of Silence, turned, and threw it at the magic-wielding bee. As the orb flew, he Analyzed the creature.

Queen Bee
Apprentice-Mage Queen
Level 25
Boss

As soon as the orb connected, the spell cut off, and the Queen buzzed violently. Azrael watched closely, and that likely saved his life. The Queen dove so fast that it blurred. He felt it enter his En sphere and swayed as soon as he could. Its stinger missed him, but its abdomen hit his arm and torso, spinning him like a top. He hurtled away from the impact and rolled to absorb momentum. Gaining his feet, he looked at his health bar. The attack had removed thirty points, and his right shoulder was currently throbbing. He moved the limb and breathed a sigh of relief, not finding it broken.

He attempted to locate the Queen in the swarm but failed. Three loud buzzes rang out.

This time he pulled out the Sphere of Command Interrupt and lobbed it into the air. One of the attacking drones collided with it, and a pulse of blue shot out like an electromagnetic pulse. All of the drones fell from the air, and Azrael dodged massive bee hail.

An angry buzz was his only warning, and he dove behind one of the incapacitated drones. The Queen collided with its subordinate, and the momentum shot the drone's body into Azrael, who reeled backward into another incapacitated drone. The fur and bulk of both organisms softened the blow, so he only took five points of damage. The Queen struggled to free its stinger, and Azrael attacked all out. His melee version of Phantasmal Blade connected three times, leaving shallow crisscrossing cuts on the thorax of the Queen before it detached its stinger and flew away. As he watched it retreat, another stinger grew to replace the old one.

All around him, the drones began to buzz and slowly rise back into the air.

Two agitated buzzes emanated from his retreating foe, and Azrael responded by pulling the Sphere of Sweet Perfume from his ring. He lobbed it across the arena and watched as a gold fog sprang forth from where it impacted. The Worker Bees swarmed the mist, and Azrael was beginning to congratulate himself when the angry buzz reminded him of what came next. He realized he shouldn't have thrown the sphere so far, as it left him without cover or a way to trap the boss.

Instead of swaying, he fell to his stomach, face down on the floor, as wind and a screech tore by overhead. He shot back up and waited as the fog seemed to drain into a nearby open hole in the sand floor.

The workers rejoined the rest of the bees in the air. Azrael continued his search, attempting to find the spell that came next. Based on his minimal damage inflicted during the Drone phase of the fight, he needed to figure out a way to make the last two sets of spheres count. How could he ground the boss in the Silence phase?

He accepted that he would need to attempt a counterstrike and rely on the other two phases for more significant progress.

A glow of golden light alerted him, and he pulled the sphere and threw. Then he entered into Highway Robbery, sword held above his head. The angry buzz gave him some warning, and he began a split-step. This technique was usually completely unsuited for traditional duels, but it was the only way he could think of to react fast enough.

He had timed the maneuver well, and when his En flared its warning, his feet touched the sand, allowing him to kick left, and swing down. He scored a triple-charged Phantasmal Blade melee strike against the fast blur that shot past. Unfortunately, the creature didn't fall from the air as he had hoped.

He reabsorbed the Ether and instantly groaned—of the seventy-five points he had placed in the blow, he only received ten back. That meant the attack had cost him sixty-five points and hadn't managed to down the boss. He hoped it had done some significant damage, at least.

Three buzzes rang again, and his colon clenched. He was dripping sweat and wasn't doing a ton of damage to the boss. At least, not yet.

The command interrupt sphere pulsed blue, and he managed to trap the Queen on the next dive bomb. He single-charged his blade this time, needing to conserve Ether or risk running out, which would spell death as surely as any of the stingers would. Its trapped body allowed him to glimpse the damage from his triple-stacked strike.

A deep cut scored the abdomen of the boss and leaked ichor onto the sands. Azrael chose that spot as his target and managed to deepen it infinitesimally in two quick strikes. The Queen escaped into the air again and Azrael grimaced.

Next time, I'll try a thrust.

Two sharp buzzes and his jaw clenched tight. Come on—he could do this!

The perfume sphere exploded a few feet away this time, and while this left a few Worker Bees close enough to jostle him, they ignored him otherwise. Angry buzz—and dive behind the swarm. He popped up to find the Queen stuck to a Worker it had struck from the air. He attempted a thrust and had some success widening the wound.

As it abandoned its stinger and fled, Azrael found two snags. His sword was somewhat stuck, and he was forced to pour Ether into the blade, creating a second stack of Phantasmal Blade, to free it. This left him with twenty-nine Ether remaining, and that was the second hitch. The phases were advancing rapidly, and he was now low on Ether. He spat to the side and soon heard the single buzz, which signaled the drain of the fog and the soon to be charging spell.

His Ether ticked up one point, but a charged attack in this phase would likely hit a new area. Without the compromised inherent Ether, he would probably just waste the blow. He debated about not tossing the Sphere of Silence, but admitted that he had been lucky to avoid damage the first time the spell exploded. He couldn't hope for the same kind of fortune twice.

He threw the last silence sphere and struck without his skill coating his blade. It felt like he was trying to cut through a tree with a mace, but at least he connected!

Small victories may win the day.

Azrael caught it on each of the next phases but didn't have enough Ether on the Worker Bee phase to recharge his skill.

His head throbbed as he surveyed the air for the telltale signs of the Queen's charging spell. Sweat fell into his eyes, and he bit his lip, trying to jolt himself into full awareness. He was out of spheres and couldn't see a way to beat the boss—he felt his knee hit the sand unbidden. No! He tried to stand and managed to make it to wobbly feet before falling the entire way back to the ground.

The moaning he was unconsciously making caused his mind to quiver as he wondered if he had missed a signal.

How could he dodge the devastating spell from his prone position on the ground? He took a deep breath and got to all fours. He needed to calm down—panic wouldn't help him. He concentrated on his hearing, keeping his eyes closed as he gained control of his breathing.

The first thing he noticed was the absence of buzzing. He was either dead, or the bees weren't flying anymore. He cracked an eyelid and found the bees in a circle around him, the Queen tilting its head back and forth right in front of him.

He swallowed, attempting to wet his tongue. He strived to stand and made it back to his wobbly feet. Smiling sardonically, he forced out, "If I am to be the first and only challenger of this arena, I wish to die fighting."

The Queen didn't attack, and Azrael slowly regained his senses as his Ether ticked up, point by point. Why wasn't he dead?

"Why are you the only challenger I have had?" a windy whisper asked from all around him.

Azrael fell back to his butt in front of the Queen. In his addled state, he'd forgotten that dungeons could speak. They rarely chose to do so, but this did change things. Maybe he could still make it out of here alive!

He swallowed and knelt again before attempting a response. "Well, someone did find you and mapped the location. But likely, since you had no level assigned, they didn't attempt your depths. I bought the only copy of the map. So, unfortunately, your location dies with me."

"Could you tell others?" the dungeon asked.

"Not if I'm dead!"

CHAPTER NINE

"So, if I don't kill you, you promise to ensure more people will challenge my depths?" the dungeon asked Azrael.

He nodded his head and a pragmatic pause later the dungeon, Apep, continued, "I will admit I learned quite a bit from your single attempt. With more participants, I am sure I could grow and evolve!"

Azrael swallowed his nerves. He was still surrounded by bees and sat on the sand to regenerate resources faster. This could still turn bad and he needed to be ready. Unfortunately, the time had also regenerated the Boss and he didn't have a single sphere remaining.

This has to work!

He spoke to the Queen Bee, preferring to have an object to address. "I mean, you may have to adjust that final encounter, though. People won't want to challenge this place if you kill everyone."

The Queen Bee's mandibles clacked together. Was it laughing? Azrael shivered.

"I gave you everything you needed. You failed to use all your tools. How is that my fault?" Apep retorted haughtily.

What was it talking about? He had used all the spheres. What other *tools* did it bestow?

He slapped his forehead. "The shield and sword?"

"That's correct. The Queen has a severe allergy to Wasp venom, and the shield deflects one hundred percent of her charges into the sand, which stuns her for five seconds. I will admit that you surprised me by forcing her to attack the Drones and Workers. I hadn't considered that option."

Azrael shuddered, his face burned, and his fists clenched. He was better than this! He should have figured out the drops were needed, especially after the spheres had proven so effective. If he had died here, he could only have blamed his stupidity.

He hadn't placed his free stat points either. He'd gotten cocky. Even some extra points in intelligence would have given him a final round of combat.

If I survive this. I won't make that mistake again.

"I will let you go if you return the sword and shield. You don't deserve any loot if you failed to complete my challenges. In exchange, I will expect someone to challenge my depths within seven days. Agreed?"

Binding Agreement
System Binding
Ultimatum of the Apep Dungeon
- **Apep has offered for you to leave its depth to spread its location and existence to the world. Apep wants back all items but otherwise has made the requirements pitifully small at one new person in the next seven days. We guess that one challenger in 155 days of isolation has made it drop its standards. Lucky you!**

Rewards:
Variable Etherience
Your Life

Consequences:
Removal of all Etherience gained in Apep's depths
Do you agree with the terms?
<Yes> | No

Saying no would mean he would have to fight the Queen again. And likely die.

So, Azrael chose yes. He quickly placed the items onto the floor before standing. He dusted off his butt and smiled hesitantly at the Queen. It tilted its head then buzzed four times.

The familiar buzz that had signaled the change of phases caused him to flinch. All the bees filed back into the still-open holes around the arena. The Queen stayed, regarding him for a long period. Azrael tilted his head and the Queen juked forward a step.

He jumped backward and landed back on his butt in the sand. The Queen Bee swaggered away from him.

Azrael's face turned crimson. "When I come back, I am going to stab you with the Stinger Sword—tough girl!"

The abdomen of the Queen Bee waved back and forth, while its two back legs grabbed its butt!

His cheeks got hotter and he forced himself to take a deep calming breath.

No one is here to see this. You can deny it ever happened.

The holes in the sand began to grind and slide closed after the Queen disappeared. Stairs formed, in what he believed was the opposite direction of the entrance he had *discovered*.

He pointed, as a door at the top opened, and asked, "These lead to the surface?"

No response came. Azrael walked up the stairs which continued to climb straight through the doorway. He came out on the leeward side of a large boulder. He recalled the large black boulder. He had been training in this clearing and could even see the marks left by his testing of Phantasmal Blades. He glanced at the sun to determine how long he had been underground—maybe two hours. He should have checked his interface clock before he started...

He hoped his trainers hadn't gotten too worried. He began walking back to the truck. Together they could run the dungeon. That would clear the depths and Apep's quest, simultaneously. He couldn't wait to stick that Queen with the Wasp sword.

He was already trying to calculate how much Etherience, and what level he might achieve, when he arrived in the clearing. The truck was on its side, and all of Mark's belongings were strewn haphazardly around it. Azrael saw the bucket staff, the buckets, broken crates, and so much more. He jumped back into the trees and circled the clearing, using his forestry training to stay hidden.

The clearing was empty and after an hour of searching he hadn't discovered any lingering guards or monitoring devices. He stayed cautious and moved towards the truck. He found signs of a struggle, broken arrows, and even a few patches of blood on fallen leaves. His trainers had put up a fight this time, it seemed.

Once inside the truck, he discovered that it had been thoroughly tossed. Even the safe was cracked open and emptied. He exited and took a look at the tracks and signs of fighting more closely. It would appear the attackers came in some sort of hover vehicle themselves. They had exited and spread out, standing in one place. That was a tactic only used by law enforcement or the military.

How had they found them way out here?

The fighting must have started sometime after an ultimatum was offered. A few of the footprints had handprints and blood in front of them. An arrow to a limb or non-lethal area, dropping the lawmen to the ground. From there, it became chaotic. A true battle. No way of telling the order of events; just that the lawmen or military had won.

A small piece of clothing was snagged on the metal of the truck and Azrael inspected it. King Oberan's colors. Was this attack under order of the King?

Azrael felt his stomach lurch. Had King Oberan been looking for him?

He considered trying to track the hover vehicle and liberate his trainers but knew he had no real idea of where the vehicle had gone. Some broken branches indicated they had headed back to the road, but once on the road they could have turned either way, with no sign. His stomach grew more knotted, and his chest hurt. He felt heat suffuse his eyes. He was alone.

For the first time in his life, he was without a trainer near at hand. He had trained for this exact situation. Why was his body reacting this way? He had always thought this would be exhilarating. Not sad. He wasn't a kid anymore! They were just his trainers and his other teachers would scold him if they saw his emotional reaction. He took some deep breaths and managed to regain control.

He walked through the scene with fresh eyes and noticed a few leaves in a strange pattern on the ground. They stood out starkly as they were clearly picked off the nearby bush. Each leaf was then torn in half and placed on the ground to form an arrow. At the tip of the arrow, the word "Ogma" was spelled. Someone had knelt in the grass here and Azrael assumed it was Mark. His trainers had fought, but Mark had left a message. Why should Azrael go to Lord Ogma?

Another inspection confirmed the Ether Converter and Battery Banks were torn out of the truck. That made the truck just a pile of scrap metal. There was no point staying around here, either. He collected what pieces of gear or equipment might come in handy. His practice sword, a water bucket, a bow, the two bundles of arrows, sleeping bag, mobile tent, and a few sets of spare clothing. Azrael changed out of his current rags and into a plain black set. He even scored a pair of boots that were pretty close to fitting him. Nothing enchanted, but all of it was serviceable.

That patrol was likely to come back through this area and he needed to be away from here before they did. He jogged off into the woods and set up his camp for the night. He dug a deep pit, got a fire going and fetched water from a nearby stream. It was easy to find some animal tracks and follow them to the water source. He shot two rabbits and began cooking them as the sun began to set.

He took a sip of the water first and was going to wait an hour. This way he could see if he reacted poorly to the stream water, but then smacked his forehead. He had an interface now! Checking his debuff list, and then adding it to his interface, was the work of a few mental clicks. The water didn't need to be boiled and was potable.

With some sand from near the shore, he cleaned off the dried insect ichor and patches of sticky sand that still clung to him from Apep's arena.

The next decision—should he go find Lord Ogma? The arrow on the ground and the map lined up with the crudely drawn cabin. But with just a rough bearing, he could miss the location by miles depending on how far away it was. His trainers, or their captors, likely had the real map they had followed to the dungeon.

He figured it was a good option but then considered the problems with that plan. Mark's reaction to his last name was the biggest issue. But there was also a relatively easy solution at hand. Using Obfuscate, he removed his last name and even changed his sword's name. If he ran into anyone strong, it might not pass inspection but it also might. Most people didn't dig deeper into their Analyze skill unless they had reason to be suspicious.

If he ran into someone who had a high enough Perception skill, they still had to find a reason to use it...

He ate his rabbit and climbed a tree to sleep, because he didn't feel comfortable sleeping on the ground without a lookout.

He lay awake for hours, each noise the forest made somehow louder than it had ever been before.

***

Azrael woke up the next morning just as the sun rose over the horizon. He coaxed the banked coals back to life and pulled the second rabbit carcass from his ring. He set it on a spit to cook before beginning his sword katas.

After each one, he turned the spit and continued until he had finished all ten. He fetched water again, filling up the two buckets like his training dictated. He would use the second to clean off his sweat.

Then he ate his breakfast and even gathered some nearby greens to satisfy his internal Dara. "You need to eat your vegetables!" he muttered to himself in mimicry. He needed to stay healthy, to survive, and that was why he continued to follow her advice. There wasn't any other reason. He shoved down all thoughts he had to the contrary.

He packed everything back up onto the portable tent and turned on its auto follow feature. Now was the moment. Should he go find Lord Ogma? It was likely the only chance he had to save Mark, Dara, and Verimy. Would Lord Ogma even care, or was Azrael walking into the hands of a potential enemy? He chose to find the cabin first and then make a decision on approaching it.

He killed any wildlife he came across, skinned the corpses and parceled some of the meat for later meals. On the fourth kill, a shell-backed rodent half the size of Azrael, he realized he was avoiding continuing onwards. Did he fear Lord Ogma? Yes, he definitely feared meeting a powerful person he had never met before. On a whim, the man could kill him. But for some reason Verimy, Dara, and Mark were going to see this possible enemy.

His musings were interrupted.

"Don't let it get away! We have been tracking it for months, and we won't get another chance at it." Shouting echoed through the long grass and trees in front of him.

Tracking what?

He sprinted to the edge of the forest and clambered up a tree. Through the long grass he made out five people running after something large and white. Sun glinted off the pure white fur, highlighting the bloody places arrows protruded. A rainbow patina struck Azrael in the eyes, and he jerked back. The rainbow had reflected off of a pearl protrusion from the horse's forehead.

A unicorn?

The five men ran after the mythical, nearly unheard-of creature. The unicorn was stuck out in a kill zone. Two more arrows sunk home into its hind legs. It wouldn't make it to the tree line.

The men reminded him of the bandits that had robbed the transport truck. He dropped the tent's tracking beacon to the ground and charged into the clearing.

He activated his En and infused his sword with a single Phantasmal Blade.

He Analyzed the Unicorn as he ran by.

Dagda's Unicorn
Apprentice-Catalyst
Level 39

Once past the unicorn, the closest pursuer noticed the strange pattern he was causing in the long grass. "What the? Something is counterattacking!"

Azrael was now committed, and he quickly analyzed the humanoid who had yelled.

Ulec Westin
Apprentice-Tracker
Level 19

Ulec was a beastkin and had the head of a wolf. So, Azrael made a logical deduction that it was from the wolf tribe. The wolfman was likely the reason they had been able to track a unicorn down. Azrael lunged forward, trying to pierce the heart of the tracker and end this fight quickly. Ulec reacted and batted his sword blade aside with its claws. The coating of Phantasmal Blade sheared off quite a bit of those claws, though. And Ulec pulled its hand back with a growl.

"Why do you attack us, cub?" Ulec asked as it assumed a battle stance.

Azrael could hear the four others converging on his position and knew that talking was just a distraction method. He entered Bull Rush and attacked Ulec with everything he had. The fact that Ulec had no weapon gave Azrael the advantage, and he planned to capitalize on it. The wolfman dodged the blade to the left, not wanting to risk parrying again after the last deflection cost its claws. He expected the move and paused his downward chop and slashed at his opponent. He released the double stacked Phantasmal Blade and heard a whine before he was liberally coated in blood.

He couldn't stand still and instead charged one of the approaching hunters. His quick disposal of Ulec and his blatant aggression gave him his only advantage. He wouldn't let it slip away. When he popped through the grass in front of the snake woman, its mouth fell open. It attempted to recover and spit something at him but he drove the tip of his coated sword into its fanged mouth.

Two projectiles zipped into the back of his six-foot En field and he turned sideways, barely avoiding one and feeling the sting in his arm from the other. He clenched his teeth to stop his scream and checked the wound. Glancing. That was better than he could have hoped.

He turned and released Phantasmal Blade horizontally in the direction the arrows had come from. The grass flew, cut midway up the stalk by the invisible blade. Azrael heard two shouts that morphed into terrible death cries. He ducked into the nearby grass and listened. At least one more lived. Assuming that his blade had finished off the two archers, that was.

He heard footsteps running away and he took a deep breath, still waiting to see if anything else moved. Nothing. He checked his health. That arrow had taken off more than he thought. He lost another point as he watched. They had envenomed arrows!

He checked his debuff bar.

Boomslang Venom
1 Health point per second. Last until cured or removed
from the system.

He instantly moved his wound to his mouth. It was a bit of a feat of flexibility, but he managed to wrap his lips around the cut. He sucked and spat blood for the next thirty seconds. He managed to remove enough of the venom from his system that its damage was only 0.1 health points per second. At that rate, his regeneration could counter it. He still needed to find a cure, but he would live.

He could hear the noise of the final attacker fleeing, and waited until silence reigned again.

He looted his four dead attackers and found that they had very little of value. Four Crystals total, two bows and forty arrows. But no cure!

Their clothing was standard cotton, and he managed to find a few spare changes in the hunters' bags. He took the clean sets—he never knew when he might need additional changes of clothes.

There was a trail of blood leading into the forest, and Azrael followed it. Perhaps he could still save the unicorn. He didn't hold to hope, especially after he discovered the envenomed arrows. But he had to try.

The beautiful creature was lying on its side, heaving as it attempted to pull in air. Azrael sighed and moved closer. It tried to stand and run but it didn't have much strength left. He removed the four arrows and threw them aside. He couldn't tell how many hit points were remaining with his low skill level in Analyze.

Chest tight, Azrael began sucking blood from the wound and spitting it aside. He spent thirty seconds on each wound like he had his own. The unicorn watched him work, its eyes unblinking, and its sides heaving with each strained breath. As soon as he finished with the last wound, the sides of the creature stopped rising.

Azrael felt a cool line trace down his cheek. He breathed in sharply and shook his head, forcing down his feelings on the matter. He wasn't supposed to be emotional. Why had he even tried to save this thing in the first place?

He checked his debuff and found a surprise.

Unicorn Savior

You attempted to save a Unicorn from Dagda's menagerie. You are marked.

Another shock waited for him. The poison was back up to 0.2 health per second. That was slightly higher than his health regeneration. Had it automatically increased because he hadn't cured it yet? Or was it higher because he had tried to purge the venom from the Unicorn?

A moment later it ticked up to 0.3 per second and his jaw hurt from clenching his teeth. He had perhaps thirty minutes at this rate. He needed to get to that cabin and fast.

He was about to take off when he remembered to loot the fallen Unicorn.

Bottle of Tech Duinn Essence
- **Rare Crafting Component**
    Increase Analyze Skill to learn more.

He held the ornate bottle in his hand and ran through the woods. He left his portable tent behind and told himself he would come back for it. If he survived. His indecision from earlier was gone. Lord Ogma was his only hope to survive.

Ten minutes in, and the poison was ticking at 0.5 health per second. He had seventy points remaining and he could feel himself growing weak. He wasn't even sure where this cabin was. After all of his training—was he going to stumble through the woods on this toilet of a planet and die?

He felt his erratic heartbeat thudding in his chest. His sickly sweat coating his body in a cool film. Driblets of sweat mixed with the red blood from his opponent and ran down his skin. This wasn't good.

He had eleven free stat points. It would increase his health regeneration if he dumped them into Stamina. He checked his character sheet on the run and placed those stat points.

Azrael Sovereign Level 12
    Class: Revenant
Class Skills: Phantasmal Blade (V), En (IV)

Health Points = 69/270 Points
Ether Pool = 160/160 Points
You have 0 stat points and 2 skill points to distribute.
   Stamina – 27 (+11) (Stats X +3)
   Strength – 19 (Stats X +3)
   Agility – 26 (Stats X +3)
   Dexterity – 27 (Stats X +3)
   Intelligence – 16 (Stats X +3)
   Wisdom – 16 (Stats X +3)
   Charisma – 16 (Stats X +3)
   Luck – 12
Skills:
Analyze – Weak 24 (Rank up?!)
Combatant – Moderate 12
Endurance – Weak 17
Martial Arts – Moderate 42
Obfuscate – Strong 1
Sneak – Weak 16
Swordsmanship – Strong 21
Tracking – Weak 12

He also filled out his En skill and saw the fog of discovery roll back. Maybe he would have a cleanse or heal spell available in the next tier. Doubtful, but still possible.

Tier 3 Skills
Stored Action
   - **Stored Action allows the user to store an attack and trigger it at will. The attack stored can be any skill you possess or any attack you can muster. Each invested skill point reduces the Ether cost of the skill.**
      Skill gained at 1/5, "Storage."
      0/5
      Ether cost is 100.

--
Desperado
   - **Desperado allows the user to freeze a single opponent for 0.1 seconds. The freeze can be**

shortened based off the level disparity between the user and the target. Each subsequent skill point invested increases the freeze time.
Skill gained at 1/5, "<u>Desperado</u>."
0/5
Ether cost is 50.

He breathed out and kept running. He looked at Mend. It would be a temporary measure at best. The skill had no properties that would cure venoms or poisons…

The extra stamina had bought him a bit more time, but he was out of other options. Could the bottle of Essence in his sweaty palm heal him?

Ten additional minutes into his run the poison was up to 0.9 health per second and he had fifteen health points left. He had failed to calculate the increasing poison damage into his thirty-minute estimate. He had less than a minute to live.

He looked at the bottle of Essence, unstoppered it, and chugged it back.

His throat felt like he had just poured molten metal down his esophagus. The liquid reached his stomach and ignited whatever food he had in there into a raging bonfire. He screamed at the top of his lungs as the liquid fire consumed him.

The pain wouldn't allow him to take a breath. His lungs froze and his heart tried to break through his sternum. The lack of air and pain combined to stop his heart. His whole body tensed in the throes of death. His eyes rolled up and he fell to the ground.

What had possessed him to save that Unicorn?

CHAPTER TEN

Azrael groaned and shot a hand to the back of his head. What happened? How had he ended up on this wooden floor with the smell of burning birch permeating the air? He cracked an eyelid and shut it tight again as the light hurt his sensitive pupils. The spikes of pain the bright whiteness shoved into his brain made him wonder if he had died all over again.

Dead people don't feel pain. Probably...

Okay, well, he likely wasn't dead, but he would have to lay here for a bit and recover some more. At least he was conscious. Instead of an attack on him, he heard the door close, and a man's gruff voice say, "I followed his trail, and found Mark's truck ransacked. There were tracks from soldiers who appear to have been Oberan's. I found this piece of livery on the truck."

The gruff voice sounded worried but was responded to by a soft womanly one, "My dear, do not worry, Oberan cannot touch you."

"It isn't me I am worried about, Jophi—"

"He wouldn't dare touch me. I am your betrothed, and the Tuatha's one bargaining chip with Cathodiem. My father will scorch this entire planet if Oberan dares."

"My mother cares very little for the affairs of Cathodiem. She will stand behind Oberan if it's just you. Your father placed you here to garner information on the Tuatha, and she knows that this *marriage* is a sham. If your father attacks, she will use that knowledge to erode his support."

There was a lull in the conversation before Jophi continued, "Ogma, if what you told me about your brother is true, how can anyone stop her?"

"Let's figure out what to do with the boy first, and then we can run before Oberan finds you. I don't think Mark knew much, but I need to hide you somewhere safe."

He heard the blanket over the door get pulled back, and two people entered the room. Ogma must have Analyzed him because he said, "I can tell you aren't unconscious any longer, Azrael. What were you running from?"

Azrael cracked an eyelid again and studied the figure of the gargantuan man before him. Ogma was tall, in the category of small giant actually, and his face sported a beard so bushy and dark that Azrael had to consider if he was part bear. His mane of hair was full of twigs and moss, while a large wooden handle for some form of weapon poked over his shoulder. Azrael guessed it was a mace or a club based on the sheer strength the man exuded.

He Analyzed him.

Ogma Tract
Master-Firbolg
Level 115
Moderate Analyze failed to reveal additional information.

He squinted at the box and swallowed hard. No wonder Ogma didn't have to fear Oberan. Ogma was the highest-leveled individual Azrael had ever met.

His high level was the second oddity today, though.

On average, Apprentice levels ranked up at twenty-five. But the Unicorn had been fourteen levels above that average. At the time of his Analyze, Azrael was willing to believe that was just an outlier.

Similarly, Journeyman ranked up at fifty and Master ranked up at seventy-five. Those were all averages, of course, but for Ogma to be forty levels above the average and not ranked up? He should be in stasis. Waiting to rank up and storing Etherience. But he wasn't. Was Ogma's class that rare?

Azrael cleared his throat. "I came because I was traveling with Mark. He was going to bring me and my two companions here."

"Why were you unconscious then?" Lord Ogma prompted further.

Should Azrael tell him?

Lord Ogma, I almost died saving a Unicorn in the woods and drank a bottle of Dagda's Essence hoping to live. Now? Here I am. Alive.

He coughed to hide his thoughts. Yeah, it sounded absolutely ridiculous.

"I got in a fight with some hunters on my way here. They injured me pretty badly," Azrael said.

"Yes, I found the four bodies of the beastkin you murde—"

Someone hit Lord Ogma's arm, and Azrael remembered Jophi was in the room. "That is enough, Ogma. You're scaring him. He is only an Apprentice."

He tensed up, expecting the Firbolg to backhand her through a wall. Instead, he cut off mid-sentence and looked to her softly. She was diminutive next to the monstrous man. Azrael tried to gauge her actual size compared to himself from his place on the ground. She likely was around the same height as him. Wiry, and dark haired.

She was not dressed fancily or extravagantly. Azrael would call her pretty, but also didn't have a lot of experience with women. Still, Azrael hadn't expected someone as strong as Lord Ogma to stop mid-sentence on her account.

Azrael Analyzed her. Trying to understand why someone as strong as the giant would listen to her.

Jophiel Turendal
Journeyman-Sorceress
Level 3
Moderate Analyze failed to reveal additional information.

She was weak. Well, that was unfair. She was weak compared to Lord Ogma.

She looked to Azrael. "We probably can't help your friends. I hope that isn't your request."

His stomach clenched. And his heart felt heavy. He coughed. "No, I wasn't going to ask that." Or was he?

The silence in the room grew unbearable. Azrael volunteered his story, with a few parts edited out. They didn't need to know about his Sovereign blood, or about whatever happened with the Unicorn. He hoped Ogma wouldn't dig into his Analyze and find out more despite the omissions.

"I believed your absurd tale right up until the dungeon let you escape! I will ask it myself," Lord Ogma said. He pulled a purple smoky sphere from his pocket.

Azrael tilted his head. That looked a lot like the depictions of a dungeon core. It pulsed with soft light and a voice spoke into the room. "Azrael, did you send this barbarian to challenge my depths?"

"Apep!" Azrael exclaimed. He looked from the massive fist wrapped around the glowing stone to Ogma. "Why do you have Apep's core?"

His notification for a completed quest popped up, but he mentally closed it, waiting on an answer.

Ogma looked between him and the stone. "Wait, you actually let this boy go?"

"I did let the boy go. He told me I would gain popularity. But now I have lost my body," Apep complained.

Jophi looked between Azrael on the floor and Ogma, who towered over her. "What is going on? Why did you capture another dungeon core?"

"Jophi, I am trying to gather more strength for my Cardinal Dungeons. If I feed them more, then we can reach the Tectonic Dungeons."

Jophi hugged her shoulders and shuddered. "The Prime Dungeon under your Territory is terrifying. It is so powerful already, and is even deeper than the Cathodiem's Prime Dungeon. The Silver Spires have been around a lot longer than Tech Duinn. Something just feels off about that. You know the old saying of 'don't rush anything'…"

"Wait. You're planning on feeding me to another dungeon? Come on, that seems unfair. I didn't kill the boy…" Apep complained.

Lord Ogma sneered at the stone. "Quiet, or I will crush you in my hand!" He put the stone on a nearby table and began massaging Jophi's shoulders. The disparity in size made him look like a father comforting a child. Her shaking stopped and she tilted her head back to smile up at Ogma. Her love for the giant man was obvious to Azrael but he seemed to treat her like a little sister.

He coughed. "Lord Ogma, you traced my trail all the way to Mark's truck. You know Oberan took him, and my friends. But didn't ask about Mur and Oberan's plan to capture it."

"What?" Ogma shouted. His tone caused Jophi to flinch out from under his hands and step away. "Oberan wouldn't dare to take from me. My mother's favor only stretches so far."

Azrael looked to Jophi. She was looking at Ogma, her eyes wild.

"Lord Ogma, I can only tell you what I heard."

"Tell me all that you heard, then."

Azrael told him about the tax increases, the unrest and the rumors of invasion in Mur. Jophi's blood fled her face and when Azrael finished, she was white as a sheet.

"Ogma, honey, I think it's time we left this cabin."

Ogma growled, looked to Jophi, and softened. "Start packing. I need to check out a few things. We will leave in an hour."

Ogma left the room, and the door of the cabin slammed a moment later. Jophi met Azrael's eyes. "Want to give me a hand?" she asked.

CHAPTER ELEVEN

Azrael took a moment in the room by himself. All of his gear was in there, including the portable tent. He hadn't expected that. Lord Ogma had truly found everything. He grimaced.

"Don't leave me with that monster," Apep's voice whispered into the room.

He had forgotten all about Apep and found the dungeon core on the same table where Ogma had placed him. He didn't like the idea of Apep dying, especially after the dungeon had let him live.

"I can hide you in dimensional storage. But I'm not sure if that will kill you," Azrael whispered back.

He stood staring at the pulsing purple crystal. Waiting. "Better if I die trying to escape," Apep finally said.

Azrael picked up the dungeon core, crossed his fingers, and placed it into his ring.

He then instantly pulled it back out. "Are you still alive?"

"Yes. I felt like I was in there for a few minutes. Why didn't you pull me out right away?" Apep scolded.

"I did…"

"Time dilation. Right, well, please don't leave me in there too long!" Apep said.

Azrael nodded and placed the dungeon core back into the ring.

Next he checked his statistics. He still needed to assign those two skill points into his third-tier skills.

Azrael Level 12
    Class: Revenant
Class Skills: Soul Strike (V), Soul Cloak (V)
    Health Points = 270/270 Points
    Ether Pool = 160/160 Points
You have 0 stat points and 2 skill points to distribute.
    Stamina – 27 (Stats X +3)
    Strength – 19 (Stats X +3)
    Agility – 26 (Stats X +3)

Dexterity – 27 (Stats X +3)
Intelligence – 16 (Stats X +3)
Wisdom – 16 (Stats X +3)
Charisma – 16 (Stats X +3)
Luck – 12

Skills:
Analyze – Moderate 5
Combatant – Moderate 12
Endurance – Weak 17
Martial Arts – Moderate 42
Obfuscate – Strong 1
Sneak – Weak 16
Swordsmanship – Strong 21
Tracking – Weak 12

His heart caught. He hadn't chosen Soul Strike or Soul Cloak. What was going on? He hastened to open his skills, his heart in his throat.

Skills
Tier 1 Skills
Soul Strike

- **Soul Strike coats your sword in personal Ether and Soul, which can project an invisible attack at enemies. The density of the sword-like blade increases as you level and increase your Intelligence.**

Skill gained, "Soul Strike V."
Cost is 10% of Revenant Ether pool per stack of this skill.
5/5

--

Blood Mend

- **Blood Mend increases the natural healing of a body by controlling your very blood flow. At one Skill point, it will close wounds and regenerate blood, increasing healing speed by 200%.**

Skill gained at 1/5, "Blood Mend."
0/5

Cost is 10% of Revenant Ether pool per stack of this skill.

--

Tier 2 Skills
Soul Cloak

- Soul Cloak creates a 10-foot sphere of converted Ether and Soul around the user. Within this sphere, the user can 'feel' disturbances. The Soul in this cloak will try to adjust incoming attacks, helping the user avoid them.
  Skill gained, "<u>Soul Cloak V.</u>"
  5/5

Ether cost is 10 Ether initiation and 2 Ether per minute upkeep.

--

Blood Poison

- Blood Poison stacks a debuff on your opponent with each cut made. At one Skill point, the Blood Poison Debuff reduces all stats by 1% per wound, up to a maximum of 15%. Debuff lasts five minutes.
  Passive Skill gained at 1/5, "<u>Blood Poison.</u>"
  0/5
  No Ether cost.

--

Tier 3 Skills
Soul Storage

- Soul Storage allows the user to store an attack and trigger it at will. Users can save any attack or Skill they can perform. Additionally, with permission, the user can store other individuals' attacks. The attack stored is performed exactly as stored when released.
  Skill gained, "<u>Soul Storage.</u>"
  0/5
  Cost is Ether invested in the stored attack.

--

Blood Boon

- **Blood Boon stacks a buff onto the user whenever blood hits their skin. One Skill point increases statistics by 0.5% per stack up, to a maximum of five points. Buff lasts five minutes.**
  Passive Skill gained at 1/5, "Blood Boon."
  0/5
  No Ether cost.

What had happened to his original skill tree?

Azrael read and reread each skill. The skills he had chosen were the same as before but also different. He felt stuck between euphoria and frustration. It felt almost like his entire class had changed, but without his consent.

However, based on his lessons, soul and blood were options for class specializations which suggested that his class had upgraded. The blood options were entirely new to his class as well. Maybe if they had been there before, he would have chosen differently.

He considered the skills tree carefully, noticing that Mend had morphed to Blood Mend and moved to the first tier. From everything he could tell, the skill was more powerful and available at a lower tier rank. This discovery convinced his body to settle on the feeling of excitement at the changes.

Caught up in that excitement, he scanned both of his tier three skills.

Was Blood Boon worth it for the passive buff? An increase of five stat points was nothing at high levels but would be very powerful right now. It also had the potential to increase in potency as he added more skill points, but the additional points could also just increase the buff duration.

He turned his attention to the other available skill, Soul Storage. It was an obvious offensive powerhouse. He could theoretically have a trump card stored for each battle. It felt like it was the stronger of the two, with far less guesswork. He placed his two points into Soul Storage and looked over his skill tree again.

I am not sure how I feel about the change to percentage costs on skill use. But that does usually mean that the skills automatically increase in power as the user's Ether pool increases.

He joined Jophiel and together they began packing up the cabin onto a portable tent of Ogma and Jophi's. Admittedly, Jophi's looked much larger and newer than Verimy and Dara's. He sighed and continued to load bundles she handed to him. Had he just traded his two trainers for two others?

According to Mark, these two might have a way offworld, which would be invaluable. Since these two knew nothing about him, he could theoretically hang around and catch a ride. If anything went terribly wrong, he could likely escape as well. Lord Ogma might make escape difficult, but Azrael was well-trained and could be patient, if it came to that.

They waited in the main room in uncomfortable silence. The packing had gone quickly. Lord Ogma and Jophi were quite prepared to leave at a moment's notice, it seemed.

Azrael didn't understand any of the political complexities here, and he didn't like that. He cleared his throat. "Care to explain some of what is going on?"

Jophi shook her head and gave him a strange look. "I assume you are quite young to only be at level twelve. It is very strange to see people below level fifteen of the Apprentice rank and still alive. Especially on Tech Duinn."

Azrael's blood froze in his veins. She was seeing discrepancies based on his sheet. If she was already poking holes in his backstory based on his low level and older appearance, Ogma might dig deeper. If Ogma did dig, he likely would discover Azrael's heritage...

He forced a neutral expression onto his face and breathed out, "I thought you were the one who wanted to help me?"

No point worrying about the blood on your shirt when you had a knife to your aorta.

Jophi frowned. "I don't want to see another person chewed up and spit out by the Tuatha. This entire planet is wrong. To force free citizens into slavery. To call them prisoners and subject them to the dangers of this planet with practically no protection."

He narrowed his eyes. Altruistic much? Out loud, he said, "Well, I will take all the help I can get—I think?"

She laughed. The sound relaxed his nerves. She likely wouldn't laugh so freely if she suspected his heritage.

The door flew open and Lord Ogma rushed inside. He was sweating and pale.

He caught his breath and gasped, "Oberan's army has this place surrounded."

Azrael looked at the Master ranked Firbolg. Why was he worried in the slightest about a few grunts?

"Can't we just sneak through the line?" Jophi asked.

Lord Ogma shook his head. "He sent an entire Legion. We would have to fight our way through."

Yeah, that's exactly what we should do. I could likely do it myself. A Master rank should be able to sneeze his way through.

Jophi's shoulders crumpled like wet paper. "Diplomacy, then?"

Lord Ogma stood up straight and took a deep breath. Once collected, he nodded.

"Wait. What?" Azrael asked. "Why not just bowl through the encirclement?"

"They are members of the Tuatha De Danaan. Any fighting would void my diplomatic immunity. Oberan could come after me himself after that," Lord Ogma stated.

"Lord Ogma, based on your earlier conversation, Jophi has no immunity. And I definitely don't. So, if you don't mind, I am going to leave," Azrael spat.

"Azrael, don't be stupid. Ogma rushed back to ensure he was here for the army's arrival. We are safe as long as we stay inside. An officer in Oberan's army wouldn't dare trespass in the home of a son of Danu," Jophi countered.

"*Lord* Ogma, come out and talk. I don't want to have to dig you out of there, but I will," a deep baritone interrupted, through the log walls.

Jophi began shaking as she fell to the floor, hugging her knees. From her reaction, Azrael knew that wasn't just any officer.

"Oberan… came himself," Lord Ogma stated as his head fell.

CHAPTER TWELVE

Azrael looked around the cabin. Was there a back door out of here? He took a step and a hand on his shoulder stopped him.

The hand belonged to Ogma. The giant man stood straight and took a deep breath. "I am coming out, Oberan." He made some hand motions at Jophi that might have meant lay down and die. Or stay where they were. Azrael assumed the latter, but honestly...

Ogma stepped through the door and called, "What brings my mother's servant to my cabin?"

"Still haven't accepted your fate, I see. Wait a moment. Would you look at that! It looks like you figured out a way around Stasis, but staying in the Master ranks can no longer save you, kiddo."

"Ah yes. Well, I see you were all too happy to take up the kingly seat. Go kiss Danu's boots and leave me be, *King* Oberan."

"I'm afraid I can't do that, kiddo. Danu was absolutely heartbroken when she heard that you were harboring an enemy of the Guild."

Azrael's eyes narrowed. He looked to Jophiel, head tilted, and she was looking right back at him, mouth hanging open. There was a moment of confusion for Azrael, before he felt his mouth drop open and his heart kick into overdrive. Oberan knew!

"I am not sure what you told Danu. But I can assure you that there is no enemy of the Tuatha here. Only my wife and a young man."

"*Lord* Ogma, you are under arrest for conspiracy against the Tuatha De Danaan. If you come quietly, your mother will hear your story—"

"What? You dare. Search the cabin if you must. I am not harboring an enemy."

"You just admitted to harboring a young man a moment ago, *Lord* Ogma. I have reason to believe that the young man is a Sovereign Son."

Jophi was glaring at Azrael. He could feel his skin heating up as adrenaline increased the tempo of his heart. He needed to get out of here.

Azrael took off towards the opposite side of the house. The most logical place for a back door. There wasn't a door, but a massive window dominated a wall. He sent a Soul Strike through the glass and followed after the crash and tinkling shards.

He rolled to his feet and engaged his Soul Cloak. He needed to get out of this clearing right—

The Soul Cloak cried a warning, but the speed of the strike overwhelmed any reaction Azrael might have been able to make. A thump sounded through his bones as fire and pressure built at the back of his head. He saw the corners of his vision begin to blacken as a debuff floated onto his interface.

Unconscious
- **Your brain has bumped into the inside of your skull. Your skull refused to let your brain out of your head and resorted to imposing a time-out.**
Time remaining: 5 hours, 59 minutes.

***

Something jolted Azrael, and the split-second feeling of weightlessness roused him fully awake. He blinked his eyes, trying to remember where he had fallen asleep the night before. He could hear the sound of a gravity engine. Right, sleeping on Mark's transport truck. Dreaming of his eighth birthday— definitely a strange dream to imagine Oberan, Ogma and Jophi.

"The *Sovereign Son* is awake." Ogma's scathing voice cut through his fantasy.

Azrael sat up. Wind whipped through his shabby clothing, cooling the sweat on his skin. His eyes could see the bluish light of stars. Nighttime. He was sitting in some sort of prison transport. Thick metal bars ran from the floor to the ceiling, leaving the sides of the truck exposed to the elements. He slid over the shiny floor to steady himself on the bars and felt his heart stop as something jolted through his hands.

He sat back up, breathing hard. His arms felt like someone had burned them from the inside. He looked at his fingers and saw two black marks. Lightning. He moved away from the bars and closed his eyes, trying to slow down his breathing and regain control of his emotions.

"Tell me. How much did *King* Oberan pay you to come to my cabin?" Ogma prompted again. This idiot got all three of them captured, and now blamed Azrael? He was done calling this man Lord. High and mighty Ogma probably hadn't even put up a fight.

Azrael opened his eyes. Ogma sat cross legged in the middle of the metal floor. Jophi leaned into his side. Figured that they would just surrender. What did they have to fear? A high-ranking member of Cathodiem and the leader of the Tuatha's son.

Azrael raised his chin. "I have never met Oberan before in my life. If you two have a stat point of intelligence between you, you should be able to figure out what happened."

Both Jophi and Ogma's faces went bright red and the Firbolg's knuckles cracked. Azrael shook his head. He didn't care about these two idiots. They had gotten him captured because of their naivety. Clearly, Oberan had taken the opportunity presented to him after he captured Mark, Verimy, and Dara. Azrael doubted that the slimy merchant held out long before he told Oberan's men about Azrael's heritage.

He examined the cage around them. Enchanted. Ogma could probably still break out if he wanted to. "Why don't you just break out of here?"

"Those bars are enchanted Iridium. It would take everything I had to break out. Then what? Become an enemy to the entire Tuatha. Right now, Oberan still must try Jophiel. And he can't even think about touching me. If we break out, then we would be giving him the excuse he needs," Ogma said.

Azrael shook his head again. Even he could see that something had changed. "Come on. You think that Oberan, in a day, mobilized the entire army to surround your cabin, after he found out I was a Sovereign Son? You can't be that naïve. Your capture was coming with or without the excuse I provided."

Jophi gripped Ogma's wrist, her knuckles going white. "If Oberan didn't plant the boy or pay him, Azrael is right. You can't mobilize all of this in a day. To travel to your cabin from Samheim takes a full day or more. Oberan was already nearby!"

Azrael pointed his open palm at Jophi. "I'm assuming that's why his army captured Mark's transport. They must have seen the transport cross the perimeter they had set. Oberan didn't want anyone coming to give you an excuse to flee."

Ogma's face had changed colors drastically through the revelations. It flushed red when Azrael insulted them. Then paled considerably when Jophi agreed. Now it was a sickly shade of green. "We were getting too close to the Tectonic Dungeons," Ogma whispered.

Jophi tried to comfort the bear of a man. But Azrael was fed up. "Explain. What have you been doing that would stir up the Tuatha, enough that even your own mother would turn against you?"

"We don't owe any answer to you, kingly dog," Jophi spat.

Azrael had been told that Sovereign Sons weren't well received by others, but this was the first time experiencing it himself. And from Jophi…

His heart clenched tightly, and he breathed in to regain control over the organ. Ogma held up a hand and shook his head. He sighed, "This is not his fault, Jophiel. Please begin to explain. I will fill in what I can."

Jophi glared at her *husband*. But relented after he patted her hand and motioned to Azrael. "Fine. Ogma is one of three sons of Danu, the de facto leader of the Tuatha De Danaan Guild."

Yeah, I kind of caught on to that…

"As Ogma tells it, his brother became the first sacrificial pawn of his mother. She used a vat, of untold proportions, filled with mixed Planetary Essence, and transformed her first son into this very planet."

Azrael rolled his eyes. He hadn't asked for a fantasy story. "People don't create Planetary Gods, Jophi. Planetary Gods create sapient life forms. This is well documented."

Jophi sniffed disdainfully. "Azrael, that is what is fed to the common people, yes. Listen and think! What happens after someone reaches the Legendary rank? What comes next?"

Azrael's brain stuttered and he blinked. "They kill all their enemies, become rich, own entire planets, and one day die?"

Jophi smiled at his blunt words, then, chuckling softly, said, "That is an… interesting way of looking at it. Yet, Cathodiem's leadership shared the truth with me. After Legendary ranks exists Planetary God, and a further theorized God rank after that."

Azrael blinked, stunned by the information just shared. While it made a logical sort of sense, he was skeptical. "Why would you tell me, a *kingly dog,* something so secret?"

Jophi squeezed Ogma's forearm with one hand and hugged her knees with the other. "It's essential to understanding what Ogma and I have been doing. About understanding Tech Duinn and why shiploads of people arrive here. May I continue *now?"*

Azrael nodded, realizing he wasn't in a position to give her permission and that her asking for it was sarcastic. She continued, "Dagda was the eldest twin-brother of Ogma. They always had a strange connection. When Danu placed Dagda into the vat of Essence, Ogma felt incredible pain emanate from his brother. Since that day, Ogma has been feeling that same pain coming from something deep within Tech Duinn. Dagda was only in the Epic ranks when he ascended. And everyone knows nothing good comes of fast-tracking ranks."

Azrael nodded to her, showing his understanding. All students took a course on this in the Sovereign Halls. There were a ton of items and methods to advance ranks. Pills created by necromancy, technologies designed to convert your body, alchemical solutions that transformed your very blood, enchanted gems that enhanced your mind, and the list just kept going. Each item the teacher showed them and lectured about came with the same warning: Do not accept any unearned rank increases.

He turned the Sovereign signet ring on his finger distractedly. Ogma glanced at his hands and squinted for a brief moment before moving on. Azrael felt his heart stutter when Ogma looked at his hands. Luckily, Ogma hadn't commented on the ring and must have thought Azrael was just playing with his hands.

Jophi followed Ogma's eyes to his hands and frowned at him before continuing the story. "Since that day, Ogma has refused to increase his rank from Master to Epic. After all this time, he found a way to bypass Stasis, but he worries that entering the Epic rank will trigger his mother to place him in the same type of experiment."

Ogma picked up the hanging thread of conversation. "For Oberan to have already been given permission to track me down, I'm afraid she has enough Essence to perform the experiment a second time.

"I should have tried to escape, but I fear I have stayed in seclusion too long—Oberan is Epic ranked now and likely can beat me like I used to beat my red-headed step-brother, Lugh!"

"Jophi mentioned the shiploads of prisoners delivered to the planet. What possible reason could Danu have for that?" Azrael asked.

"The Essence Danu used the first time was purchased from all over the Etherverse. In shops, quests; any way the Tuatha could find it. Still, once Tech Duinn was habitable, she discovered that she could farm it here. The infrastructure to handle life, Ether, and Essence is in its juvenile stages on a new planet. Danu is overloading the ecostructure by dumping massive amounts of slaves here. At first, Danu just wanted living races as filters. The plan was to overpopulate the planet and farm the wildlife drops for the rare Tech Duinn Essence." Ogma paused in his story and looked at Jophi sadly.

The moment stretched, and Azrael realized this was information he had never told her.

Is he resigning himself to his fate—given up on saving himself and his brother?

After a few moments, Jophi shrugged, "Yeah, Cathodiem already knew that part before I got sent to you."

Ogma nodded but held up a finger. "Oh, it gets worse, I'm afraid. Oberan was in charge of the hunter teams who were collecting Essence from wildlife. They founded a few Territories to house themselves and placed some Cardinal Dungeons to add some challenges for their days off. Well, one of the Cardinal Dungeons was the Arena Pit in Samheim. During a run, Oberan killed a few of his guardsmen who had been stealing bottles of

Essence. Instead of normal loot, the Pit presented Oberan with bottles of Essence for every second kill."

Jophi held up a hand and asked the question on Azrael's mind, "Dungeons are part of the infrastructure that help planets filter Ether to Essence. Why would this dungeon help him?"

Azrael turned back to Ogma, who answered, "Turns out that the Planetary God isn't communicating with his dungeons like he should. The lack of communication is a huge confirming factor for why I believe Dagda is in trouble. He isn't able to handle being a Planetary God."

Azrael scratched his head, "Is that why they push people to the arena?"

"Not only that, Azrael, why do you think the system allows people to loot all gear off of a corpse? The Tech Duinn system doesn't even lock the equipment after a kill. They encourage murder now, anywhere on the planet. Danu is pillaging Tech Duinn to gather enough Essence to create another broken Planetary God. If someone doesn't stop her, one day the Tuatha De Danaan will have thousands of broken, unstable Planetary Gods. Then no one will be able to stand against them."

The sight of the Black Pyramids of Samheim came into view behind Ogma and Jophi. They followed Azrael's gaze and the conversation stopped. The pyramids were small things on the horizon but the reminder of their destination and his fate didn't leave him in the mood to continue. Azrael was likely to end up in the Arena Pits. A slow death certainly, but a death all the same. Jophi had some protection still from her family but ran the risk of also being converted to a bottle of Tech Duinn Essence.

Ogma wasn't going to die. No, his mom was going to turn him into a planet—yay for family, right?

CHAPTER THIRTEEN

Welcome to the "The Pit Arena".

This Arena Dungeon has an Ether Contract with the Territory. You must have the leader's permission to enter here. This dungeon cannot be cleared, only challenged. Step onto the sands to compete.

Good luck.

Level: Unknown
Age: 3155 days
Best time: N/A
Clears: N/A
Ether Concentration: High
To exit the dungeon, leave through the entrances.

Azrael jerked as the prison transport stopped. "I wish you luck in the arena," Ogma said as he stood.

Azrael sighed. He just needed to survive and gain strength. To hold out long enough to find a way out—honestly, those aspirations were only slightly better than hare-brained.

The guards opened the back and politely removed Ogma and Jophi. Azrael stood, expecting to be taken out as well, but was largely ignored. One of the guards escorting Ogma shouted, "The last one is a recruit! Make 'im feel right at home, boys."

Azrael closed his eyes and breathed. He needed to be in control of his racing heart. He opened his eyes to find a barrel-chested orc, wearing cheap leather armor, approaching the back with a long polearm. Something bounced at the top of the shaft. The movement was a loop of rope tied in a noose.

Oh, come on! The other two weren't treated like animals.

He used Analyze.

Torin Tarzac
Master-Warrior
Level 8

Moderate Analyze failed to provide additional information.

Torin barked, "Don't resist, and this ain't got to be hard on ya."

Azrael stood still after the warning. He let the rope slide over his head like he was a dangerous pet. His body stiffened when the rope scratched down the front of his face and settled in place. Torin wrenched his end and dragged Azrael from the center of the prison transport. A small pop sounded from his neck as it protested the whiplash. "What? Ow, man! Was that totally—"

Torin yanked on it again, completing Azrael's extrication from the back of the prison vehicle. Azrael bit his tongue as he fell the five feet from the bed of the hovering transport to the stone floor. He braced the collision with his palms and the gray stone peeled back skin. Pain blossomed along both his hands, forearms, knees, and chest. Instead of trying to talk again, he quickly got to his feet, hoping to minimize the orc's poor treatment.

His compliance didn't help. No matter how fast Azrael moved, there was constant pressure on his neck from the rope. They moved towards a doorway out of the courtyard and Torin jerked the pole, forcing Azrael to collide with the stone doorframe. He managed to avoid slamming into it face first, but only barely.

Azrael slid along the wall of the hallway before careening across to the other wall. It was like a grotesque puppet show. They ignored passage after passage before Torin yanked him back into one he had already walked by. Azrael was beyond the door frame and collided first with the wall, then was dragged back over the corner, and into the passage Torin wanted to take.

It took every piece of training he had to avoid being knocked out in one of fifty collisions.

They entered a well-lit room. Azrael got a look at his hands and knees. Both body parts were burning from the constant abuse, and a glance showed them to be bloody and raw.

He checked his interface during the reprieve, and his health points were even down twenty-two points!

Torin guided him to the center of the space and commanded, "Strip!" Azrael breathed in his first full breath in minutes. At least there wasn't a wall immediately beside him to be wary of. His hesitation cost him. The orc flicked a switch.

Instead of Azrael being able to remove his tattered clothing, a jet of water exited the wall. A spike of intense pain tore through his ratty shirt and ripped it right off his back. The jet of water, now on his bare skin, began to tick away at his health points as it flayed him. Azrael screamed in pain and shock, but Torin just maneuvered the polearm and, by association, Azrael into turning around, so his back got torn as well.

His health points hit one hundred, and Torin hit another button. The jet of water fell to his stomach. The process repeated. The button clicked again, forcing Azrael to protect his manhood with his hands, which soon were painfully red and chafed. He didn't dare remove them, or he might become a eunuch.

He felt the Ring of Holding on his right hand and covered it with his left. He didn't think Torin would notice it, but wanted to be cautious anyway. He considered pulling out his sword and attacking Torin but realized in his weakened state that was certain death.

Another side effect of the spray, making its way to his lower body, was the loss of what remained of his tattered garments.

The torture finally ended. Azrael was only standing on his feet because of the rope and polearm. Around him, red water swirled into a nearby drain. His health points had dropped to a dangerous ten points, and he had numerous debuffs on his interface.

Torin didn't let him rest long and steered him back out of the chamber.

He kept his hands cupping his exposed manhood, and tried not to let the lump in his throat morph into tears. He locked onto his anger and mentally began plotting all the ways he would hurt Torin in the future. He would gain power, and Torin would pay for this casual abuse.

Azrael stumbled into another well-lit room. A massive Bearman stood in front of stacked shelves. His jerky entrance heralded the man to turn, pick up a bundle of assorted cloth, and shove it into his stomach. The bundle knocked the air from his lungs while simultaneously pushing him backward. Of course, his hands came away from his 'jewels' to catch this package.

Torin jerked the pole forward towards the new abuser. Azrael's neck dragged his upper body forward as his ass and stomach were pushed back by the Bearman. Intense pain flared at the base of his skull, threatening to turn out the lights.

He bit his lip to combat the blackout with pain and growled. The Bearman growled back at him louder. Mocking him. Torin and the Bearman laughed. Azrael clenched his teeth and Analyzed his new tormenter.

Papi Vears
Journeyman-Grizzly
Level 43
Moderate Analyze failed to provide additional
information.

Gallows humor. It had no meaning. But Azrael stacked logs on his inner fuel source. These two would one day burn if he had his way.

Azrael was *directed* through an exit. The only upside was that Torin stopped abusing him, due to his low health points. The width of the path opened up, and Azrael breathed in a full lungful of air. There were no close walls to bounce off. Then he noticed the two stories of cells with leering faces. He was paraded naked and bleeding past hundreds of angry eyes.

He was without a stitch of clothing, barely able to cover his manhood, and being frog-marched. This scenario had never even crossed his mind. Not even in his nightmares. Now he knew he would be reliving this moment in his worst dreams the rest of his life. He stacked more logs inside of his heart. He refused to allow this to break him.

Torin stopped rushing him too, instead reigning him in whenever he tried to speed walk. This orc was a toad, and Azrael's fingers dug into the fabric bundle he held, imagining the cloth as the orc's neck.

Without warning, he was wrenched sideways into an empty cell. The cell didn't have any windows. The light in the hallway was the only illumination, but even that was dim.

Torin jerked the rope, which loosened it, and then pulled it over his head. It might have been unintentional, but Torin managed to hit Azrael in the face with the rope. The threaded fibers caught his nose, and Torin chose that moment to pull. His nose cracked, and a debuff image of a broken bone joined his interface. Azrael roared.

Another image of a red teardrop joined it, and hot liquid spilled down onto his lips and chin. He tasted salt and iron. He cut off his roar, clenched his jaw and turned around. Torin met eyes with him. The toad was smiling, and Azrael glared back. They stood there for a brief moment facing each other before the orc chose to slam the cell door and turn away.

Torin turned over its shoulder. "Battle Royale tomorrow morning at dawn. Sleep well." As if that was an afterthought. The toad howled with laughter and continued its strut away.

Azrael glared at the orc's back, hoping an iota of his rage transferred into the action. That toad was going to die one day.

He dropped his bundle to the stone floor and twisted his storage ring on his finger. They hadn't thought to take it from him. Not that they could have, thanks to its Soulbound nature, but he still had a weapon and the desire to kill—to survive.

Too bad he had left all those spare clothes tied to his portable tent and not in his ring!

CHAPTER FOURTEEN

Torin strode out of the cell block. The toad's exit signaled Azrael's brain to stop emitting pure static and allowed him to begin to use the organ again. He remembered the dropped bundle of assorted cloth. He picked it up and sorted through it. He groaned when he found only a rough woolen bed sheet, blanket, and some sort of scratchy towel.

After numerous failed attempts, he at last managed to wrap the towel around his butt, waist, and privates. Tucking it in on itself. The end result was a very uncomfortable loin cloth. He took a deep breath; he needed to continue thinking. Anger would only hinder him now.

There was a life or death free-for-all battle tomorrow—he needed to prepare. Despite everything he tried, a part of him was still seething. Roiling like magma. He couldn't wall it off or cool it down and decided to run through his martial katas one by one.

His erratic heart fell into line first. His muscles demanded the organ's appropriate action to supply oxygen. His brain was next as his movement grew more complex, and the neural capacity being used to throw a temper tantrum shrank. Sweat broke out on his skin and, with it, an occasional cool breeze as he moved. The magma calmed but the volcano below it remained active, rumbling its displeasure at his treatment.

The cooling heat sharpened into a blade that he was more comfortable using. Azrael went through some stretches to reduce stiffness after his exertions and studied his character sheet.

He was a bit unbalanced now towards Stamina. But it may have saved his life. So, while it was slightly high for what he would have wanted, he was able to come to terms with it.

He had mostly ignored Charisma and Luck. Charisma represented external beauty, the ability to convey emotion through speech, and general likeability. A person's charm, per se. It might be helpful in the arena to gain the favor of the crowd, but he was praying to never be in the precarious hands of that mob. The blood crazy entity that reduced all sapients to their basest natures.

Luck, on the other hand, could be the most useful or useless stat. In many ways, Luck was a multiplier. The more points in Luck, the higher chance of finding rare situations.

Those rare situations could be finding a dropped money pouch in a massive city or running across a mighty and deadly creature. After arranging this *fateful* encounter, Luck seemed to not play into the picture. It was a literal crapshoot that played with chaos theory, tugging on threads in a woven tapestry. Sometimes creating something better, but often destroying the entire work.

He wanted no part in Luck's dubious results. He needed high *combat* stats, first and foremost. They were concrete— tangible.

His points in Stamina increased overall health and added to his body's recovery rate. A point in Strength increased one's physical ability to maneuver heavy objects, cut through opponents' inherent Ether, and increased bone density. A point in Agility was a point in synapse speed, muscle response rate, and explosive power. Dexterity added nerve endings, creating heightened awareness to sensory inputs, more exceptional motor control, and in some ways, speed to precision actions.

After that, you were out of physical and into the two spiritual attributes. Intelligence was a *no brainer,* his teacher used to say. A stat point placed in Intelligence increased brain synapse response, information recall and, of course, the body's ability to encapsulate personal Ether. Wisdom was also linked to the brain, but simultaneously the body. Wisdom was the speed of information recall, the efficiency of brain usage, and the body's ability to absorb external Ether.

His sheet came across like a melee class. Not horrible, but from this point on he was going to need to balance out the spiritual stats. The more skills he unlocked in his custom class, the more he believed his strength lay in a balance. His class was shaping up to be something on par with how people described the Sovereign class: a threat from anywhere on the battlefield.

He continued to twirl his ring and briefly considered pulling out his sword to use in training. No. That was too high of a risk to use for a prolonged period. If he lost the blade, he would be at a severe disadvantage tomorrow. Instead, he looked around his cell for the first time. There was a cot in the corner, made from old and cracking wood. He had a hole, right at the foot of the bed. Theoretically that hole was the perfect toilet to relieve himself.

That was everything the cell contained.

Azrael's eye twitched. He turned towards the only structure that might work for his plan. Surreptitiously, he began a downward strike and pulled his sword from his ring's inventory into his hand. The sword sheared through the old dry wood of the bed with ease. The blade exited the wood and he dismissed it back into the Ring of Holding.

He waited as the bed collapsed in the destroyed corner, acutely listening for any reaction. The boom of the bed was loud in the silence, followed by the leg he had cut, falling and bouncing hollowly on the stone floor. Each bounce echoed a pang through the cell block, but other than some angry hissing, nothing else happened. Perfect!

He got to work. For the next few hours he went through every sword form and kata he knew, using the bedpost as a training sword. Pushing himself hard. After each form, he took a break to stretch.

His skill in swordsmanship climbed, but he knew this was playing with fire. Two issues existed in his strategy. First, he wasn't going to sleep tonight, which could cause him problems in combat. Second, other than a small water pouch and some dried rabbit meat in his ring, he had very little else to sustain himself.

The more he exerted himself, the more his body needed to recover.

Azrael stretched out and sighed. He was counting on breakfast before the event—a last meal for the combatants. He didn't think it would be fancy. In actuality, he assumed it would be gruel. He just prayed they would let him eat his fill!

Hours later, he succeeded and clicked the rank up option on swordsmanship.

Swordsmanship
- **Swordsmanship skill will help you better wield any weapon classified as a sword.**

Weak
- **Chance of being disarmed reduced by 12.5%.**

Moderate
- **100% more accurate with strikes.**

Strong
- **10% increase to penetration power of the edge of any blade you hold.**

Greater
- **Increased damage by 1% per level in the skill.**

Current Rank: Greater level 1.

Azrael smiled, and stretched out again. As he elongated muscles, he ate his single piece of dried rabbit meat and sipped his water slowly, attempting to make the dry meat more palatable.

His rank up gave him a chance, now he just needed to increase it. Azrael stood up, swallowed his mouthful, and got back to work.

CHAPTER FIFTEEN

The noises of people waking up and moving around began to echo through the cell block. Azrael stopped training with his makeshift practice sword. His body was drenched in sweat, but he had one final task to accomplish before too many eyes would be on him.

He pulled out his Sovereign Blade. Surreptitiously, he charged the edge with his max Ether pool and released the skill into his Soul Storage.

He managed to drop the sword into his Ring of Holding before collapsing. Azrael felt like a puppet with no strings. The ground rushed to slap him in the face, and he couldn't even lift his arms to protect himself.

After training all night, with little water and practically no food, the one hundred percent drain of his Ether pool in a single go was debilitating. He gained back a semblance of awareness a few desperate heartbeats later. He tried to remove his cheek from the stone floor. His attempt caused his rear end, currently sticking up into the air gracelessly, to crumple to the side.

He focused on his Ether bar as it slowly ticked up. Was it slower than usual? That could be his imagination—he didn't often make a habit of watching paint dry.

Slowly he managed to get into a seated position. His tired body fought him the whole way. He performed slow stretches, trying to avoid his body stiffening up in any way. Azrael's current predicament reminded him of a lesson from Politics class.

Individuals on Gaia were protesting for a change to the way the system worked. If they succeeded, which large complaining crowds often did, then the system would automatically protect individuals from situations like his current one. The notion was to create a small, protected reserve of Ether in the body. In essence, protecting the idiots who couldn't protect themselves.

I probably am not one to talk. Considering I am planning to do that again in the future.

Would a change mean he couldn't use ten stacks of Soul Strike? His ability stated ten percent of his Ether pool, so perhaps it would adjust accordingly. The theoretical outcome of the bill was challenging to comprehend, and he gave up.

Once his head stopped throbbing and his body felt less rubbery, Azrael got to his feet. He used the rest of the morning to go through slow stretches and keep his body flexible. The cell door slammed open, accompanied by echoing crashes, indicating many nearby cells were opening. He stood up and placed his hands above his head. Not wanting to give a guard an excuse to abuse him. Again.

No one came into his cell.

He moved slowly to the door and peeked out. Sapients from every race he knew, and some he didn't, were exiting cells and forming a line in the middle of the hallway.

He followed suit with a deep breath. He walked into a gap between a satyr and a mudcap. Neither one spoke to him. The cell block was silent. Azrael cleared his throat and confirmed that sound did still exist. A door slammed shut in the distance. The boom was loud in the stillness. That loud crash was followed by three more in quick succession.

Azrael stuck his head out of line and saw guards checking cells on both levels. Each time they got through with a cell they slammed the door. He had to assume a slammed door meant they were empty.

Peeking to the other side, he saw Torin on the ground level slamming a door and moving onto the next in line. Azrael expelled his air through his nose in a hiss, as he tried to control his disgust. Torin slammed the next cell, and a cry sounded. Someone was still inside, as evidenced by a pleading, "I can't see well, mister. I can only see in a five-foot dome. If you lead—" A strange blue-skinned man came to the bars of the cell and was unceremoniously punched by Torin, which cut the prisoner's pleading short.

Torin laughed happily and moved onto the next cell. That interaction told Azrael a lot, especially when combined with the subservience of the people around him. Something desirable, or good, came from this portion of the day. If they were lining up to fight, Torin would have dragged the blue humanoid creature out by his large wing-shaped ears. This was probably the line for breakfast.

Soon all the cells were closed, and the lineup began a slow march. The lineup was filing through the same doorway Azrael had entered through the previous night. Off to the side of that doorway, Torin stood leering at each prisoner as they filed past. Azrael dreaded each step, as it brought him closer to the toad. His body wanted to lash out and release his Soul Storage skill. If he caught Torin by surprise, the toad would be torn apart. Unfortunately, he needed the skill for the upcoming fight later in the morning, and he was pretty sure he would die a split second after the orc in that scenario.

Azrael walked by the Warrior, holding his breath, every part of himself on edge. He stepped through the archway and breathed out, his body relaxing. A glob of something warm and sticky landed on his scalp and neck. The viscous liquid was accompanied by a throat clearing sound. As it dribbled down onto his shoulders, he shuddered.

Torin called, "Looks like I missed a spot yesterday, noobie!"

What was it about Azrael that provoked the orc? He hadn't done anything different than the others here. He wiped the mucus from his hair and neck. He shuddered again and threw it to the ground with a sickly plop. His eye twitched and he wiped the remnants from his hand onto his loincloth. His body convulsed when his eyes registered the yellow smear his hand left behind on the fabric. He clenched every muscle in his body to stop the shuddering.

You have been through worse. Bide your time.

Azrael's tensed muscles drew him to an unintentional stop. The line kept moving, and he received a jostle from behind. Sweat broke out on his skin and he leaped forward to close the gap. He was dangerously close to holding it up.

Too late—Torin barked gutturally.

"Noobie! Out of line," Papi, the Beastkin, shouted, from somewhere in front of the slow parade. Azrael hesitated a moment before his shoulders slumped. He better follow Papi's order. No point giving the imbeciles an excuse. He stepped to the side. A few people gave him sympathetic looks, but most just sneered at his misfortune. A few even spat on him. He marked those that did. He may not be able to kill a guard yet, but fellow slaves in a battle? No problem.

A Goblin, an antman, an elf, a faerie, and a satyr. He would remember their faces.

As more people streamed by him, he felt his chest tighten. He knew who would be at the end of the line—Torin.

The yellow fangs grinned at him from the back of the slow-moving group. He considered running, of joining the line again, of prostrating himself, but assumed the Warrior would react worse or the same in all scenarios. His weakened body tried to shiver, and Azrael fought with it.

How dare his body betray him.

Torin grabbed him by the back of the neck, and half led, half-carried Azrael through the halls. Like he was a tiny kitten. He was glad he hadn't tried to release his skill on the orc; this show of strength was terrifying. He had earned Master rank, after all. Torin didn't bang him into anything—this time. Azrael's toes did drag along the rough stone floor, though. He could feel the skin peeling away as the slow trip continued.

Azrael bit his tongue and furrowed his nose. He would not scream or react. This ugly gorilla wouldn't break him. His resolve hardened, and that small shift of thought did it. He would make anyone who wronged him pay. He was likely the most highly-trained combatant in here. He would be the first to make it out.

The reason for the lineup's slow speed became obvious when they entered a cafeteria. Each individual waited to be scooped a bowl of porridge and took a seat to eat it. Torin stood to the side, still holding Azrael with ease. Once everyone had a bowl of gray sludge, the angry orc shoved Azrael through the area, and he received the remnants. A gray sludge, with blackened flecks adorning its depth.

Torin let him go. "Enjoy your last meal. It's missing something, I think," the orc moved to spit into the porridge.

Azrael jerked his bowl away, barely keeping the meal from being spoiled further. Torin walked away laughing. Azrael began breathing in and out rapidly. He could drop the food and attack it from behind…

No, he would wait.

He looked for a place to eat and got his first unimpeded view of the cafeteria. Near the two exits stood guards. Torin walked to one of the groups and joined Papi. They began chatting energetically, and Azrael thought he saw some Crystals change hands. Afterward, Papi walked away.

The rest of the massive chamber contained metal tables and metal benches—nearly every available surface in use. Azrael scarfed down his bowl standing, instead of attempting to squeeze into a seat. Row upon row of seating existed, but at a casual glance, the occupants seemed to grow agitated. Better not to risk it. Azrael had a Battle Royale to compete in later that day.

He almost spit back out his first bite, as it was burnt and spoiled. A debuff floated onto his interface. It had a picture of flies on red meat. He forced himself to swallow a second bite as he read.

Slightly Spoiled Food
- **The food you recently consumed was spoiled. While it wasn't bad enough to poison you, it was still detestably bad.**

-1 Stamina, -1 Strength
Time remaining: 3 hours, 59 minutes.

He continued mechanically. Spoonful after spoonful until his bowl was empty. He didn't have a choice after his night's activities. Without food, he would suffer the Weakened debuff in the upcoming battle, and Weakened was a far worse debuff than Spoiled Food. According to his teachers.

He placed his bowl onto a growing stack and joined a line-up that began forming near the far doorway. Torin barked again and servants began clearing plates. It didn't matter if a slave was finished eating. A few refused to give up their bowls willingly. Torin quickly rid them of their resistance.

Azrael was pretty sure the orc accidentally killed one of them. A neck just didn't bend that way. The bodies were carried out of the room and he thanked his choice to eat quickly.

A lady then separated the line-up with a clipboard and two guards. She would either nod or shake her head as she passed. The guards responded in one of two ways—a nod meant physically maltreating the individual out of line. The shake meant a shove backwards.

Azrael was a nod and felt the guards grab his shoulders, lift him, and deposit him in the new line. After the woman finished this sorting, she checked through the room and shouted, "I am missing a few. Where are Bat, Goran, Heph, and Lito?"

Torin, who Azrael hadn't seen leave, jogged into the room as if on cue and threw a bruised and beaten blue-skinned creature with the funny ears onto the floor. "Bat, ma'am! The others were disciplined for insubordination," it reported.

The woman sneered at Torin. "Why is this one so beaten up, Guard? Have you been betting again? Wanting to skew the results in your favor, maybe?" The woman pointed her clipboard at Torin then the combatants all around them. "You heard the warning last time. You want to be one of them?"

Torin smiled at the woman and two guards. "No, ma'am! I bet on that scrawny runt near the front!" Torin pointed its yellow nailed finger at Azrael, and he felt himself stiffen. Why would Torin treat him like crap and then bet on him?

One of the guards beside the woman chimed in, "To die in the first one-hundred, ma'am. We saw Papi place the bet ourselves."

Yeah, that made a whole bunch more sense. The bag of mucus was trying to hedge its bets after all.

His line started moving, so he missed the rest of the conversation. Azrael now had a goal and knew how to inconvenience Torin. All he had to do was survive. Since that was his original goal anyway, this knowledge fed him resolve. His skin broke out in goosebumps and he prayed to be able to see Torin's face after the combat.

The line moved fast. Azrael filed into a circular room with a domed ceiling and numerous enchanted wood grates. One massive grate let in actual sunlight, and the sounds of the mob beyond.

In the very center of the room stood a handsome elvish man, wearing gold-brocaded leather armor, two beautiful gladiuses, and a red cape. His stance told of confidence using the weapons, and his threaded leather kilt told of his lack of a fashion sense. Azrael scanned the room to find numerous posters adorning the walls. Mr. Gladiator, in the center of the room, was featured prominently on one. He instantly disliked the elvish man.

"My name is Octorian, and I am the highest-ranking combatant, currently! I just passed the eleventh challenge for the eighth time. One day you can all grow up to be strong and— yeah, I am not reading this garbage!" the man exclaimed as he looked over everyone's heads. Azrael followed his gaze to find a script hanging from the ceiling.

Octorian looked back down at the scared thousand or so individuals below him and stated, "You can never be as good as I am. I don't see the point of lying. However, if you're one of the last two-hundred surviving members in this *entertainment*—you will live until supper time. I would wish you luck, but if you don't die here, you will likely die tomorrow, or the next day." He pointed to a picture of a massive black mammoth covered in scars. "If you don't die from the lesser mobs, you will one day face him."

Octorian jumped down after his *motivational speech* and walked from the room. Well, that was melancholic. Even the strongest person here feared the final challenge of this place.

Azrael adjusted his earlier plans. He would find a way out of here, even if he had to dig every centimeter with his bare hands.

Chapter Sixteen

The thousands of different races stood around, shifting from foot to foot after the champion left. Azrael took the opportunity to look around the circular staging area. His entrance gate wasn't the only one, as multiple other entrances and exits dotted the domed walls. Octorian walked through the only open one, and a grate fell from the ceiling behind him with an ominous crash.

Azrael's eyes fell on Jophiel across the room, and he blinked. His heart crawled into his throat. He thought she had some form of diplomatic immunity. But she was going to take part in the Battle Royale as well?

He threaded towards her but noticed a guard strangely close to the woman on the other side of the nearby gated entrance. The two were clearly talking through the grate of enchanted wood. He had never seen this man before, but he looked to be a member of the arena guards. Their interaction made his feet stop and he froze. He backpedaled a bit, choosing to keep his distance and observe instead.

Jophi made an indication to the man in his direction, and Azrael felt his eye twitch. Was she talking about him? He hoped she knew better than to tell others about his heritage. Oberan already knowing was bad enough.

He tried to fade back into the crowd and stopped again. His heart began trying to break out of his chest. He growled at himself to reduce his body's reaction. Verimy stood at another grate, waving both hands at him. Azrael slowly moved to the entrance to join his former trainer. His heart refused to calm down.

Verimy could be the one who betrayed you. Trust no one.

"How is it that you are here?" Azrael asked. Looking past Verimy to find numerous combatants behind the man.

"This is where they brought Dara and I after they captured us. Still can't figure out why the army was out there."

Azrael thought about telling Verimy about Ogma and Jophi, but figured it was less important than surviving the upcoming battle. "Why did they let you all out of your cells?" Azrael asked.

Verimy shrugged and pointed to viewing ports set along the wall behind him. "They let us watch the combat, it seems. All the new combatants go through a Battle Royale. Dara and I went through ours a day ago. More importantly—do you have a strategy, kid?"

Azrael checked the people behind Verimy again. No Dara. He scratched his forehead and looked at the floor. "Kind of an obvious one. Try not to die!" He felt terrible about being flippant as soon as the words left his mouth, and he moderated, "Sorry I wasn't there when you and Dara got taken."

Why are you apologizing? He knows that. Idiot.

Verimy waved his hand dismissively. "Don't be stupid! There was nothing you could do—we were glad you were away at the time. But in the end, you got caught anyway. Ignore that for now; we will talk later. Right now, you need a strategy to survive what comes next. My suggestion is to clear an area of combatants and hold that ground. Preferably a space near a wall."

Azrael looked at Verimy. Something looked off about his eyes. "Where is Dara, Verimy?"

A shadow crossed Verimy's face before he waved his hands in front of it. "Sorry, she isn't dead. I am upset because she is in a different cell block from me. We worked together during our Battle Royale, and the Arena Master didn't like that. Skewed the odds I guess."

Azrael nodded and turned at the sound of a massive sucking-grating noise. The initial noise faded to reveal a slow clanking chain as the massive main gate rose into the roof.

"Good luck! Remember my suggestion," Verimy shouted over the din.

The more confident combatants started filing out, while the others stayed put. Azrael hesitated, and Verimy added, "Don't stay in here—they release mobs to force you above!"

Azrael hopped forward thanks to the warning. Verimy gave him a *super helpful* thumbs up as he turned to go.

The passageway echoed the din from the cheering crowd, amplifying it to a nearly overwhelming decibel level. The explosion of noise made him falter for a brief moment before he steeled his nerves and continued. He only needed to be one of the two hundred who survived. An approximate odd of one in five combatants.

At the top of the ramp, the pathway opened into a colossal Coliseum. The crowd had tiered seating encircling the sands. Azrael scanned the seating, seeing metal benches closely spaced on the lowest levels, that gave way to individual leather chairs and finally massively carved wooden boxes filled with important-looking people. Azrael scanned the outer rims of the construct and found screens everywhere, many filled with advertisements. Others proclaimed, 'Battle Royale,' in bold flashing letters. Directly above the center of the sands, a jumbotron dangled. Its screens currently read, '1104 Combatants Alive.'

That seemed like a large number. Still, Azrael recalled the change in Mur. He wondered, was Oberan forcing the enslavement of combatants to speed up Danu's plans?

Azrael shivered, then shook his head. This wasn't the time. He placed his hand on the nearest wall and continued to walk around the massive open space, reaching the side furthest from the entrance before he chose to stop. He agreed with Verimy. He should start somewhere like this—and work to clear a safe zone.

His observation revealed that all combatants had chosen to hug a wall. Over a thousand bodies currently ringed the sands of the arena. Everyone eyeing their neighbors warily, bodies tense.

He glanced at his neighbors; none of them stood out, but a few seemed to be assessing their current situation as well.

Azrael Analyzed them first, wanting to categorize his most significant threats.

The first sapient was an antman.

Cochtid Ferg
Apprentice-Spearmaster
Level 23
Moderate Analyze failed to provide additional information.

The next wary combatant was a rock giant.

Gurg Boulderhand
Journeyman-Mountain
Level 11
Health Points: 1100/1100

The final unshaking individual near him was a tiger beastwoman.

Dhalary Sharpstripe
Journeyman-Boxer
Level 8
Moderate Analyze failed to provide additional information.

The others he Analyzed and categorized but then ignored for now. He did see one combatant that made him smile, though. One of the individuals who had spat at him, when Papi and Torin had worked together to pull him out of line.

I will get to you, soon enough!

First, the three threats needed to die. He hoped that when the battle commenced, they wouldn't all gang up on him. He had seen a few assess him but thought they might have dismissed his threat status due to his lower level. Perhaps that would save him off the first bell.

In a true one on one contest, fighters often dumped all of their skills or most powerful trump cards fast. Attempting to overwhelm opponents. However, this wasn't a one on one, and instead people would try to conserve Ether to use on larger opponents. Azrael was lucky in some ways, as his skills weren't particularly showy. Unless he released a ranged Soul Strike...

An announcer's voice boomed over the crowds' enthusiasm. "Today, we have a spectacular event for you! Another welcoming Battle Royale! Please join me... in saluting our combatants this day!"

The boom came from the entire arena, thousands of voices intensely chanting, "You are the brave, the strong, and the true. We salute you!"

Yeah, sure. You just want to see the fountains of blood as we die for your entertainment.

Azrael felt his skin crawl as silence descended after the unified chant. The combatants around him breathed into the hush it left, making goosebumps rise on his skin.

It was about to begin! His heart began to steady and his mind sharpened. It was always this way for him during combat exercises. Nerves before, but ice cold during. He activated his Soul Cloak.

"Begin!" the announcer intoned, and he saw one of his neighbors' fists glow red as it attempted to sucker punch him. His cloak warned him of the approach as well.

He smiled wickedly—his first attacker was one of the idiots who spat on him.

He brought his hand up beside his head and turned. His elbow connected with the elf's wrist and deflected the skill-infused sucker punch away from his face. Azrael used his other elbow to swipe upwards and connect with the chin of the combatant. He watched the elf's pretty eyes flutter, but not extinguish.

Not so weak and vulnerable now, am I?

Azrael followed up his advantage by leaping off his plant foot, performing a flying knee. He felt the crack of his quad on the elven sternum and watched the body of his foe topple to the sand. Azrael landed astride his enemy's chest, finishing the fight by crushing its heart with the pressure of his knee. He rolled off the dying elf instantly as his Soul Cloak warned him of a strike from behind.

His other neighbor had hesitated at the 'begin' signal, but once the Troll saw him engaged, it attempted to strike him from behind. Its haymaker cross swished through the air where he had just been. Azrael regained his feet.

He turned to face the Troll and in that short spin, assessed the nearby fights. He had been right in his earlier assessment. Two of the three he had marked were laying into opponents. Other small patches of combat existed, but many more chose to hug the wall, thinking it might save them. Azrael shook his head in disappointment. He wasn't kind enough to allow that, but first, the Troll.

Trolls often had health regeneration skills and increased inherent Ether. Based on this Troll's lower level, it may not possess an offensive skill. Or it might be holding it in reserve.

He waded forward, shooting out a quick jab and a shoulder fake meant to look like the second in a one-two combination. The Troll reacted, slapping down his jab and overextending a block for his fake right straight. Snarling, Azrael retracted his jab and launched it again, scoring high on the larger creature's shoulder. The confusion of the unseen blow caused the defense of the Troll to overextend to its left side. Azrael stepped into the opening that made and torqued his abdomen. His right fist dug painfully into the hard, gray skin and connected just over the kidney.

The rocklike texture cut Azrael's knuckles, but the damage caused his opponent to crumple to a knee. Azrael swung his leg over his opponent's head and locked his hamstring and knee under the Troll's chin. His other knee pressed firmly into the cervical spine. The Troll's body began to glow and Azrael made a jerking twist with his lower body. The action broke his foe's neck, and he released, rolling over its dying body.

That Troll would have been terrifying if it had been higher level.

He came to his feet and stared at Dhalary finishing off the dying elf. It obviously thought the elf hadn't been dying fast enough. He met eyes with the tiger beastwoman as it stood back up.

It exposed its fangs and taunted, "You shouldn't leave your prey unattended, cub!"

Azrael didn't bother to retort. Jibes were for a spectacle or to unsettle an opponent. He didn't expect either here. The Boxer closed the distance with him in a skill-assisted dash, and Azrael pulled his sword out of his ring and layered a single Soul Strike onto the blade. He had left it there for just this type of surprise, and as Dhalary's glowing fist ascended in an uppercut, he swung down using Headman's Bloodletting.

His technique required a triangle step, a pivot, and a backstep. He performed all three actions using his Soul Cloak to help avoid its wild skill-assisted uppercut and felt his own skilled steel bite into the fur of its elbow. His downward chopping strike combined with the reciprocating Soul Strike removed the limb at its elbow, and the blink Dhalary made told him of its surprise. He didn't let it recover and reversed the blade, spinning into Wind's Etching to sever its spine and end its life.

He moved on, hoping to come back and loot the bodies later. He wasn't sure what he would receive, but noticed many of his opponents wore gear far less revealing than his scratchy loincloth. His next few *opponents* were those who had chosen the wall. He mercilessly cut through them, not wanting to leave potential enemies at his back. Or free Etherience for others.

With nearly six hundred fighters left, these ones would die either way. This way at least they help me.

Once he cleared the wall, he turned to find four battles raging in his safe zone. It was time to make it as reliable as its namesake. He chose Cochtid, the antman, next, marking the rock giant and its smashed foes as a possible stumbling block. He checked his stat page and saw he had gained a level. He placed the skill point into Soul Storage and attempted to ambush the antman.

The creature somehow sensed his approach and kicked sand backward into his path. Through the sand screen came two tiny balled insect arms. They attempted to hit his face and shoulder simultaneously. Azrael had seen four appendages on the creature and chose to roll backward. He regained his feet in a back handspring and saw the two unaccounted for limbs wrap around the air where his feet had been. Clever.

Good thing the Spearmaster is without a spear!

He darted forward, performing Boulder Roll, reversing his blade with each steady step. The antman moved well, dodging each strike by inches. It attempted a sideways step and fired its top limbs in simultaneous jabs. Azrael's Soul Cloak warned him and he performed the 'Roll' of his current technique, sliding his heel in the opposite direction. He adjusted his weight, letting his other leg's forward step become a balance, and spun. His sword swished over the ducking head of the ant and Azrael 'Bouldered,' crunching his core hard and headbutting the hard chitin forehead of the Spearmaster.

Both he and his opponent reeled from the collision. The strength of the chitin had been stronger than expected. Azrael recovered first and entered Dancer's Finale, attempting to pierce the chest of his opponent with a thrust. The point of his blade clicked into the chitin then twisted out as the antman's skin glowed dark black. Azrael growled but changed his blows to Troubadour's Act, which contained large actions. Cochtid easily dodged each swing, and began recognizing the timing of Azrael's technique.

Cochtid stepped into one of Azrael's backswings, its mandibles clicking excitedly and all four appendages firing forward as if they were spears. This was a skill. Instead of worry, Azrael felt the corner of his mouth pull upwards as he pulled his feet together, removed his hand from his pommel, and placed it on the blade as he released his Soul Strike skill into its ranged version. This action doubled or even tripled the speed of his strike, and his departing skill sliced Cochtid's skull in half. The four blows lost their Ether but still connected with Azrael's chest, and his hand was cut badly on his own blade—but he had beaten his foe.

Had his Soul Cloak redirected those attacks slightly?

He checked his debuff bar to find he had broken ribs and was bleeding. He struggled to take the deep breaths his body insisted on and stepped back to his cleared wall to recover. He glanced at his hand and saw white bone in the cut—that wasn't good.

Unfortunately, just as he made it to the wall, the rock giant crushed its current foe like a water balloon filled with blood and bone. The stony face turned to regard him.

Azrael glanced around and found no other opponents or distractions remaining for the massive giant. He breathed through his nose while simultaneously forcing his injured hand to close on the sword pommel with clenched teeth.

Azrael fell back into his training and controlled his breathing to purge the pain as he entered a fighting stance.

CHAPTER SEVENTEEN

Azrael stepped out from the wall, not wanting to be between concrete and a rock giant. They squared off, but a stumbling form in Azrael's peripheral vision drew his attention. He tilted his head and took a deep stuttering breath through his nose. That blue-skinned, bat-eared blind thing practically fell directly into the combat angles between Azrael and Gurg. Azrael seriously considered letting the rock giant stomp over the creature during the fight, but the thought made him feel sick.

Get over it. Wait, maybe you can use the thing? 'A chess master uses all pieces to their best effect.'

It was already a miracle that the poor creature had lasted this long. Should he use it to force Gurg's hand? He should get it to move at the least. "Over here, this way. Go towards the wall," Azrael called.

The sad pitiful thing began crawling towards his voice. Azrael Analyzed it.

Bat
Apprentice-Sonar
Level 8
Health Points: 40/60

Now if Gurg took the bait he would know which direction his opponent would attack from and he could counterattack. That was why he was helping. "The only reason I am helping," he mumbled to himself.

Gurg blinked slowly. Its bulbous head looking at the skinny blue-skinned rat thing and then to Azrael. Finally, realization crossed its stupid face. It attempted a grin, showing its square stone teeth. The action only accentuated its stupidity.

Think you have it figured out now? Or do I need to draw you a picture?

Azrael came at it from a blind angle.

He charged his Soul Strike on the edge of his sword and struck at his ten-foot tall opponent. rock giants had abnormally high inherent Ether—higher even than Trolls—and Azrael knew that without the skill, he would likely never injure it. Using

Wading Bull, Azrael jogged by his opponent with his blade out and braced against his chest. The sword clicked and rattled off the blueish-gray stone skin, yet his skill split a few large rock protrusions.

Azrael heard a roar and a crash behind him. He instinctually activated Soul Cloak during his stop and turn. He couldn't afford to get hit by this opponent. A single strike could crush the impact point, likely leading to Azrael's death, in all painful cases. He hoped if a blow did land that it was a critical strike and instantly fatal. He would prefer not to die in a slow, pain-filled way.

His depressing thoughts caused him to scan up to the jumbotron; a count of three-hundred and eighty still lived.

He dropped his eyes back onto his enraged opponent as it got back to feet. It was now facing him and ignoring Bat.

Smarter than your average rock giant, I guess.

He could try to bait and run, kiting the creature, but that tactic could lead him into other areas with even stronger combatants. Better to stick with the known quantity his safe zone presented.

Azrael inched forward, his knees springy and loaded. It was a good thing, too, because the giant leaped twenty feet into the air, probably using a skill. It began to descend right on top of him. He sprinted and dove, both feeling and hearing the impact behind him.

He slid to a stop and turned again. Gurg was in a sand crater smiling at Azrael. The stupid grin was back. As if big stupid expected him to be intimidated by its show of this skill. Quite the opposite, the action told him just how much his opponent underestimated him.

Azrael checked his Ether and found it to be three-quarters full. His sword still had a charge on it, and so he doubled the Ether, adding an additional stack of Soul Strike. Time to get serious.

He rushed forward, attempting to keep Gurg in its self-dug pit. The depth was probably only two feet, but that made the ten-foot-high head of the creature more accessible.

Sliding to a stop a foot back from the loose sand, Azrael entered Dancing Flame, sword held vertically above his head. Gurg blinked and stood still, unused to prey coming to it.

Do you think I am going to jump into your mouth next? Attack me already.

It reached out a massive stone-encrusted hand, trying to crush Azrael. He countered by slicing his sword down the palm of the beast. Two stacks of Soul Strike parted hardened skin, and Gurg roared. It pulled its hand and waved it around as a gray sludge leaked from the wound.

Azrael returned his blade to the top of Dancing Flame as Gurg clenched both fists and its eyes went wild. It swung its uninjured fist in a boxer's hook. Azrael countered, striking down at the back of the wrist and swaying back.

Again, the strike drew blood, and Azrael returned to ready. For the next scant seconds, Gurg swung wildly at Azrael, and each blow he met with Dancing Flame. Gurg became wounded all over its hands and arms, but finally used its tiny brain and took a step towards Azrael, which forced him to abandon this tactic.

Azrael shuffled backward, but a different type of shout exited the giant's mouth, freezing his feet in place. In horror, Azrael watched a debuff float onto his interface, a stun debuff that lasted two seconds.

2

Gurg laced its hands together above its head and stepped out of the pit. Its arms stretched even higher as its back muscles elongated fully, and it smiled triumphantly.

1

Come on! I don't want that dumb face to be the last thing I see!

It took another step forward, its front foot now only a few feet from Azrael. Its bodyweight shifted, and its upper body followed the foot. Azrael watched its abs contract, reversing its elongation for the killing blow.

0

Azrael removed a hand from his sword and slapped his injured palm onto Gurg's chest. He shouted, "Soul Release!" and his Soul Storage emptied a Soul Strike with ten charges.

A bass drum boomed following a massive shrieking crash, and Azrael stood eye to chest with Gurg. Slowly Azrael saw one arm of the giant fall limply to its side, then the other. Azrael glanced up and pulled his hand back. Gurg crumpled to its knees, and Azrael could see a hand-sized hole in the giant's chest.

He backpedaled, realizing its upper body was going to collapse on top of him. His rush landed him on his rear end, where he continued to crab away from his deceased foe.

With a thundering crash and spray of sand, the heartless corpse fell the rest of the way to lie face down mere inches from Azrael's scrambling feet. He stood slowly and dusted himself off. He couldn't tell what was missing, but then heard the absence of the fighting. He glanced at Gurg's back and saw it was entirely gone. His eyes tracked up from the creature and saw a swath of destruction with numerous dead or dying strewn around it.

Leading away from Gurg's body were ten neat grooves in the sand. Almost like a massive creature had dragged claws through the Coliseum for fifty feet. The claws had sliced through anything in their path, and in some cases sprayed the corpse in all directions. Azrael swallowed his rising bile and looked up at the scoreboard. '225 Combatants Remaining.'

Some sort of forcefield separated the crowd from the fighting. Behind it the crowd was animated and clearly loud. In here? He couldn't hear them.

The fighting resumed, so much louder after the silence. Azrael surveyed his safe zone and found a few individuals had chosen to inch along the wall into it. They hurriedly retreated under his scrutiny. He found Bat, leaning against the wall and shaking in the middle of that zone. Bat's arms raised into a mockery of a combat stance.

Instantly, Azrael felt sick of killing. This creature wasn't a threat, and he didn't need the tiny amount of Etherience from it. He surveyed his surroundings to ensure he wouldn't be attacked, scratched his head, and walked over to the sorry excuse for a combatant.

"What's your story, Bat?" His approach went unnoticed in the din of the combat and Bat jumped.

Bat tried to orient its pathetic combat stance towards Azrael as it offered, "I am a powerful warrior! If you come close to me, I will eviscerate you. Don't let my lack of eyes fool you. I have other methods of sight."

Azrael felt his tension break slightly as he chuckled and retorted. "I heard you this morning in your cell. You can only see five-feet around you, and probably not at all in this ruckus."

Bat's head fell, and its ears twitched. After a few moments its head came back up. "You aren't planning to kill me?"

Azrael glanced at the screen. It would be a waste at this point. This pathetic creature barely held any Etherience for him. It had suffered under Torin's abuse as well. Perhaps he was feeling a warped comradery because of that? Either way he had no desire to kill the creature. "Nope, not today. Don't worry Bat, after only ten more people die, we are both going to walk out of here. Care to tell me what race you are, at least?"

Bat licked his lips, seeming to hesitate before he said, "I'm a batman!"

Suddenly the noise of the crowd bounced over the sand, deafening Azrael. Bat seemed to almost go catatonic. "Congratulations to the victors. Collect your loot and exit the arena."

Azrael stored his sword into his ring and then froze; he had forgotten about loot. In a panic, he rushed from corpse to corpse. For the most part, the individuals he killed had nothing of value on them, but he shoved everything into his ring to sort through later.

His storage ring gave him a unique advantage when it came to his sword. The guards might want to take the sword from him for example. But because they wouldn't know about the storage device, they would likely jump to the conclusion that it was a Soul Blade. The ring's Soulbound nature made it even more impressive, as people couldn't take the ring from him unless he died.

He thought about the powerful item and even had a fleeting thought of thanks for his *father*. All the loot and his sword wouldn't be taken away today...

After he finished looting, he moved toward the exit with a glance behind him. Bat stood against the wall, slowly inching along it. He closed his eyes, and sighed. He moved to assist the batman. He announced his intention before guiding Bat below into the staging area. Once they were out of the ramp, Bat began to walk more confidently. Azrael let go of his hand after a time and looked around at the two-hundred other survivors.

His eyes immediately met Jophi, who looked back at him. She made a motion at her hand and then symbolized an explosion. Azrael pursed his lips, still not sure who she had been talking to before the combat began. He gave her a shrug and continued to inspect the room. Verimy gave him a quick thumbs up from the grate before he got escorted out of the gallery with the other combatants that had been watching the melee.

Within a few minutes, every exit door opened, and arena guards streamed in. Azrael waited for instructions. A moment was all it took, and someone shouted, "Everyone stays still and waits to be collected by a handler!"

Azrael glanced around to see Torin striding angrily towards him. He groaned, the anger on the orc's face promised punishment but also forced Azrael to hide a smile. He had wished to see this expression after all. Small victories...

The warrior punched him in the side, which broke a few ribs. Torin hissed, "You lost me my pay, noobie!" He looped the rope over Azrael's neck and began dragging him across the stone ground. Azrael attempted to get to his feet, but each time he tried, a particularly angry tug laid him out.

By the time Azrael made it to his cell, he had fourteen health points remaining and a laundry list of debuffs. Torin, who hadn't spoken once, shouted, "Your injuries from the combat prevent you from having lunch!" He then slammed the cell door and spat on Azrael, adding further insult to the injuries.

Azrael let his smile show then. Small victories...

CHAPTER EIGHTEEN

The full night of training, intense battle, atrocious food, and Torin's abuse combined to drop Azrael into unconsciousness. He would have slept through dinner if Bat hadn't shouted, "There is someone still in his cell!"

Azrael started awake, sweating and hot. He had the wherewithal to grab a set of bloodied clothing from his ring and change. The clothing was missing a sleeve and he assumed it was from the tiger beastkin he had *disarmed*.

He stumbled out to join the line of prisoners. Torin scowled at his appearance from the second floor, where he was checking and closing each cell. Azrael breathed a sigh of relief and wiped his forehead with his forearm. It came away very wet and he checked his debuff bar. He was running a high fever and hadn't eaten enough food. Bat was about ten people in front of Azrael, and he nodded exuberantly when Azrael joined the line.

Glad I saved that particular pawn. He may have just saved my life.

He squinted and checked distances as they stood to wait for the line to start moving. Based on Azrael's assessment, Bat had increased his range on Sonar quite drastically. Azrael currently stood over fifteen feet away, and his cell probably doubled that distance.

The evidence of Bat's increase reminded Azrael to look through his notifications.

Azrael Level 15
    Class: Revenant
Class Skills: Soul Strike (V), Soul Cloak (V), Soul Storage (II)
    Health Points = 135/270 Points (-50% Fever)
    Ether Pool = 80/160 Points (-50% Fever)
You have 3 stat points and 3 skill points to distribute.
    Stamina – 27 (-13.5 Fever)
    Strength – 19 (-9.5 Fever)
    Agility – 29 (-14.5 Fever)
    Dexterity – 30 (-15 Fever)
    Intelligence – 16 (-8 Fever)

Wisdom – 16 (-8 Fever)
Charisma – 16 (-8 Fever)
Luck – 12
Skills:
Analyze – Moderate 28
Combatant – Moderate 29
Endurance – Moderate 16
Martial Arts – Strong 38
Obfuscate – Strong 3
Sneak – Weak 18
Swordsmanship – Greater 15
Tracking – Weak 12

Three levels—how many combatants had his stored Soul Strike killed? He placed his new skill points into Soul Storage and unveiled the fourth tier of skills.

Despite the heat radiating off his skin and feeling extremely weak, Azrael felt a flutter in his stomach. Soul Storage upgraded and gained the ability to have two attacks stored within. This miraculous change in his skill tree sure seemed powerful. He would immediately refill his trump card when he returned to his cell. The talent had saved his life against the rock giant, after all. But now with two slots, it would probably be good to have some versatility.

Tier 4 Skills
Bloodletting
- **Widen a wound, while simultaneously preventing most healing from taking hold. This Skill will increase damage dealt when blood is drawn by 20% and add a bleeding debuff stacking 20% of the initial damage every three seconds until the wound closes.**
   Passive Skill gained at 1/5, "<u>Bloodletter</u>."
   0/5

--

Soul Siphon
- **Successful attacks return a small portion of Ether and power to the user. This Skill will**

return 1% of the opponent's maximum Ether Pool to the attacker and transfer 1% of the user's statistic points. The buff is stackable up to five times.
 Passive Skill gained at 1/5, "<u>Soul Steal</u>."
 0/5

He didn't have skill points to place. So, he put off making a decision on what to pick for later. He tried to subdue a round of coughing but failed. He should stop hoping for a Soul Blade skill. He recalled the unrivaled pain he had felt when he realized he wouldn't get the Sovereign class. This fever paled in comparison to that disappointment, and each time the Fog of Discovery rolled back, he felt a muted pang of that same anguish.

He finally managed to control his coughing, and he checked through his final notifications. Azrael found where a large amount of that Etherience came from. To his surprise, he had been given and completed another quest!

Congratulations! You have completed a quest.
Dungeon Quest
  Survival Quest
   Battle Royale
- **Azrael, you are one of the surviving members of the Battle Royale. The TechNet system realizes that you had no say in participating, but since you made it to the final 200 living participants, you will be rewarded.**
Rewards:
  200,000 Etherience
  Advancement to Initiate Combatant
--

Summary of Etherience from recent kills:
44 kills. 252,312 Etherience rewarded.
305,688 remaining until level 16.

He couldn't recall how many cowering combatants he had dispatched, but knew that it wouldn't be over fifteen. His ten stacked Soul Strike had killed at least thirty combatants. For some reason, he was instantly glad Jophi hadn't been in the path. He quashed the strange bubbly feeling in his chest. She likely had betrayed him to that guard anyway.

Does it matter? Oberan already knows you are a Sovereign Son.

The line started moving, and Azrael closed his windows. He kept his eyes forward and wobbled along as best he could. He wasn't going to miss food again if he could help it. Torin was stationed at the door, and Azrael narrowed his eyes, thinking sluggishly for a way to avoid the stupid orc. Obviously, he came up with nothing.

With his stats impaired, it was like his head was stuffed with cotton wads. Inspiration finally struck as he tried to force his feet onto a straight line.

He activated his Soul Cloak skill and instantly felt the combatants behind and in front of him encroaching on the zone. He thought he felt the bright green Martian in front of him stumble and could time the combatant's foot scuffs behind him with the image of the creature in his mind.

Torin made disgusting throaty noises, warning Azrael of the incoming spit wad. He swayed instinctively and almost fell as he bumped into the wall. He need not have bothered with the sway. Soul Cloak actually adjusted the course of the mucus projectile, causing it to miss by more than a foot.

So, it did adjust the ant's strikes in combat!

He steadied himself on the wall and got back into line before he disrupted the flow. He watched the mucus drip down the wall with satisfaction. He could feel a continued glare from the toad as he hobbled away. It was a small victory, but only his second against the guard. He released his skill and followed the others, his fever feeling slightly better. Despite the debuff telling him it wasn't.

Tonight, they were brought to a vast dining hall instead of the cafeteria of their morning meal. Many tables spanned the floor in a tiered system, and each tier had a decor. It was like the arena seating all over again. The highest raised tier had a single table, made of shining, well-polished, dark wood. The piece was surrounded by individual chairs that were closer to thrones.

The sapients around this single table helped themselves to monstrous platters that littered the center of the polished wood. Octorian stared despondently at his plate. Picking at his food with a lackluster energy, Azrael could only describe the man's demeanor as a death row inmate. Other individuals from a multitude of races were talking jovially as they ate. Azrael recognized most of them from posters in the antechamber before the Battle Royale. They all contrasted Octorian's mood like marble to obsidian.

Azrael clutched his bicep and flexed as his body shivered. Ogma sat sullenly amongst them. He, like Octorian, stood out. Ogma's shoulders were slumped and his plate was empty. His eyes were fixed on someone Azrael couldn't see in the crowd. He jerked his eyes away from the Firbolg as he felt waves of ice shoot over his shoulders.

*I can't believe he just let himself and **us** be captured!*

Just below that, on the second highest tier, were beautiful wooden tables that still shone but looked less vibrant to Azrael's eye. The individuals at these tables looked healthy and happy but didn't converse with their neighbors. No, there was a subtle hostility in the air around each person on this tier. A space around each person eating. Every so often a set of eyes would shoot up to the head table, glaring with hate and jealousy. There were no platters on this tier, and Azrael had to assume the people upon it had gotten their own food before sitting to eat. Still, the food looked delicious and Azrael's mouth watered.

On the third highest tier sat wooden tables and benches that were stained and cracking. This group avoided looking at any of the higher tiers as if the people there would take offense. Instead, the hateful glances were at the lineup. Azrael could feel the individuals on the third highest tier sizing him up. Based on the height, decor, and those hateful stares, he assumed these were one step up from his current initiate status. The food on the third tier was still delectable but the portions seemed smaller.

At ground level, metal tables formed long, segmented seating and two long metal benches were snuggled along the sides. This lowest tier took up most of the room's floor. The setup of the room told him how few made it through the Combatant ranks. The most bedraggled of the room's occupants sat on the benches of this lowest tier. These individuals didn't meet eyes with anyone and ate hurriedly, like they worried someone would take what little food they had.

Another lesson that Azrael chose to learn as he watched them.

The portions on this bottom tier were the smallest by far and looked like they would barely satisfy a child.

He felt his stomach growl hungrily when the *chef* slopped a mixture of potatoes, meat, vegetables, and gravy onto his tray. He hadn't gotten a good look at what people were eating on the lowest tier, but this was a far better fare than he had expected. The portion size was small, but at this point he would take any food he could get. Especially if it looked this good!

There was no cutlery in sight. He hurried to a seat beside Bat, and prepared to devour the small portion of food with his hands.

Azrael began shoveling the food into his mouth, using his dirty fingers and saw Bat not following his lead. Mouth full, he sprayed, "Eat, Bat. Or someone will come to steal—"

His heart stopped as a tray slammed down, cutting his instructions off. He looked up to meet Jophi's eyes and he narrowed his. But continued to wolf down his meal. He couldn't afford not to eat every morsel of this tiny meal. He needed to regain some strength. Especially with his fever and lack of lunch.

Eventually he gave up the glare to focus more on his slop. His dish was empty with a few remnants clinging to the sides. He began cleaning it as best he could, not wanting a single scrap to go to waste. No debuff for bad food showed up this time, and he breathed a thankful sigh.

In fact, he noticed that his Fever debuff had decreased and was about to elapse, thanks to the meal.

Bat had commenced eating once Jophi sat down and finished his own meal a few heartbeats after Azrael. Jophi ate a bit more daintily. No one assaulted her for her food, but a few did eye it. Azrael wasn't sure if it was her beauty or if Ogma's constant stare kept the would-be thieves at bay. At least he knew who Ogma had been staring at in the crowd earlier.

Once she finished eating, she leaned forward and whispered, "I can't believe you didn't tell us your heritage and now I am stuck competing to survive!"

Azrael blinked and saw Bat's ears begin twitching animatedly. He met her eyes. "I already told you that this was going to happen with or without me. Also," he looked around meaningfully, "not exactly the best place to bring up those sorts of things."

Bat didn't say anything, but Azrael could feel his attention. Clearly, his sensitive ears could pick up Jophi's whisper. Azrael hadn't noticed anyone else react, but luckily, she hadn't let slip anything either. At least, not yet.

Jophi clenched her jaw, not liking being rebuked. Then she shook her head and conversationally added, "Everyone is talking about the Guild's campaign against the Sovereign Empire. In fact, most of the people on Tech Duinn are captured serfs from recently-conquered worlds."

Azrael tilted his head, now curious where this conversation was going. He then frowned and matched her tone, "It would seem that the Sovereign Empire is stretched too thin. Everyone knows that the Sovereign himself and his elites are the real power."

Jophi intensified her pointed glare. "The captured Empire citizens talk about the Sovereign coming to rescue his people. They believe he will not stand for this any longer and will come personally with his entire retinue to exact justice."

Azrael heard the unspoken question. He shook his head and frowned. There would be no rescue sent for him. He countered, "You would think that one of the *other* Guilds would step in to curb the Tuatha, or one of the powerful Guilds' higher ups would disagree with the Tuatha's current path."

Jophi looked to the head table, sneering at first, but her look softened when she saw Ogma. Azrael watched as she slowly turned back and shook her head. No rescue would be coming for her either. Silence stretched and he changed the subject. "This was much better cooking than this morning. I missed lunch, were you two there?"

Bat nodded and finally chimed in, "I unfortunately missed breakfast—" Azrael had somewhat forgotten the mournful pleading he had witnessed, however Bat continued, seeming unbothered, "—but the snake and mashed turnip of this meal was delicious! Lunch was a simple stew with bread."

Of course it was a snake. Azrael closed his eyes and tried to mentally force his stomach to calm down—he had never loved snakes. Still, food was food, and he couldn't complain as long as it kept him strong. If his broken fever was any indication, he needed to eat anything and everything they served him.

Bat's jaw dropped open. Azrael was about to ask him what was wrong, when a collar fell over his head and settled on his neck. Azrael flinched his shoulders, moving them towards his ears and shortening his neck. He expected the rope to pull tight and wrench him from his chair. But an extremely well-dressed guard stepped up beside Azrael. "Oberan would like to have a word with you."

He stood up and extricated himself from the metal bench. It was awkward with the collar around his neck but he managed. Once standing, he allowed another guard to place enchanted chains on his feet and hands. Then, in a strange shambling walk, he was escorted out of the room. All eyes focused on him as he moved through the crowd. He was sure the special treatment would not go unnoticed—he saw Torin's darker than usual green face out of the corner of his eye. Torin's eyes twitched continuously as it ground its teeth together menacingly.

Azrael amended his final thought—or unpunished.

CHAPTER NINETEEN

Azrael wasn't jerked around or abused on the pathway the guards led him down. On the contrary, the well-dressed guard guided the way and even indicated turns before he had to make them. Thinking back, Torin originally had picked him out as a loser of the Battle Royale, and so hadn't hated him, but was strategically attempting to undermine his chances. His making it through alive had given birth to the toad's intense dislike. Torin blamed him for the lost money and wages. Losers were often like that. Always someone else's fault and never their own.

The guard behind him with the polearm, whoever he was, seemed almost gentle in comparison. Azrael wanted to Analyze the man but didn't dare to turn around or stop. He knew that his treatment could change in the blink of an eye. That was also why he didn't ask any questions. He did Analyze the well-dressed guard in front of him.

Laith Farr
Master-Steward
Level 61
Health Points: 700/700

Not a guard then. A non-power class, if Azrael's guess was correct.

The smart-looking steward motioned up a set of metal stairs and Azrael felt his stomach lurch. Higher altitude clearly indicated better ranks to the Tuatha. As he climbed, the pattern he had seen elsewhere repeated itself. Metal morphed into simple wood after a single story of stairs, then polished wood after another, and when Azrael stepped onto the fourth set of stairs—made of hand-carved, highly polished wood—he knew this was a serious meeting.

What would Oberan want with me?

The guard maneuvered the pole to the top of the stairs and gave the lasso a firm but gentle tug. He stopped, which seemed to be what the individual wanted. Two very well-geared guards approached and nodded to the guard behind him. The steward came and gently removed the noose from Azrael's neck and walked back towards the stairs. He chanced a look backwards but only saw the retreating back of Laith.

He faced front again and quickly Analyzed his two new guards.

Gyr Hoff
Master-Bulwark
Level 44
Health Points: 4500/4500

Gyr was a strange creature. His head was level with Azrael's, but he was hunched over, and he used his incredibly long arms to help propel him over the floor. His skin was mottled brown, and his legs were muscular and bunched beneath him. Azrael was forced to assume he was looking at a sapient Plains Troll. His race would be outstanding as Bulwarks if the rumors of Troll regeneration were true.

Yonel Getz
Master-Swordmaster
Level 73
Health 1400/1400

Yonel, on the other hand, was red-skinned, tall, and wiry. He was extraordinarily well-muscled and wore only loose-fitting high-end clothes. The way he carried himself told of his supreme level of confidence. Azrael would have guessed that his lack of armor was because he specialized in Agility and Dexterity. Especially when he saw the health numbers. One of these guards alone would be challenging to contend with for most combatants. Both were a nightmare to his combat training. Even if he put himself on par with the level gap, he couldn't see a viable winning strategy.

The two didn't talk but efficiently frisked him, then took positions beside him and simply waited. They didn't indicate he should move forward. So Azrael stood still, attempting to keep both in his peripheral vision. Not that seeing an attack coming from either of them would save his life, but his training wouldn't allow him not to try.

After five minutes, he started to feel uncomfortable. After fifteen, he was sweating from keeping his body tensed and ready for movement. It was at the twenty-minute mark that the stalemate broke, and a voice made him jump. "Azrael. That was quite the display in the Battle Royale. Let me tell you, I don't think I have seen such a promising new recruit since Octorian. Isn't that right, Gyr and Yonel?"

Neither of Azrael's guards answered the figure that approached. Azrael took the opportunity to Analyze him.

Oberan Faedon
Epic-Houndmaster
Level 21
Health Points: 9000/9000

Azrael's mouth dried up like he was standing in the desert at noon. He tried to hide his reaction and stood straighter. He would never be presentable in his bloody and stolen clothing, but he refused to look like a mouse in front of this powerful man. His slight movement clinked his leg and arm irons together, reminding him of their weight and presence.

Oberan seemed to still be waiting for an answer, and he wasn't looking at Yonel or Gyr. Azrael glanced at the guards. They stared ahead and showed no signs of speaking. He coughed. "Thank you?"

"The compliment was earned, young man. I am truly surprised by what I saw. Of course, I would expect nothing less from a Sovereign Son. Gyr, remove those chains, he won't be needing them."

Gyr moved forward using his long arms and bunched legs. Using strength alone, he ripped the enchanted chains to pieces and dropped them to the ground. Azrael felt his stomach flip at the Troll's casual show of strength.

As soon as the restraints were removed, Oberan continued, "It is an honor to finally meet one of the fabled sons of the Sovereign. I brought you here today to ask you a few questions. Your pale face makes me believe you fear reprisal, but quite the contrary, young man, I plan to reward you."

Oberon's smile didn't reach his eyes. It was wolfish. A Houndmaster eyeing its prey. Oberan let the silence stretch.

Azrael took the hint. "What do you mean, reward me? I haven't done anything."

They were playing a game now. Azrael knew it. He only hoped Oberan underestimated him.

Oberan tilted his head and pursed his lips. "You are quite right, young man. It is more what you are going to do. You see, I have a high enough Perception to see through your Obfuscate, and I am also high enough ranking amongst the Tuatha to know the Sovereign's secret.

"I want you to unhide your surname and change your class to that of your father's. I wish to have you fight under his banner. The crowds will love it. If you win, you will gain your father much in the way of reputation—at least amongst the common folk."

Azrael picked out the unsaid. If he lost, the common folk would lose hope. Did he believe that Azrael harbored some sort of loyalty and love for his father, who he had never met? Other than the ring, scroll, and sword, his father had never given him a thing. They were definitely playing the game now, though. "I am sorry, but I would rather not. There is no benefit for me. Maybe if you offer me a way off this rock…"

He let his offer hang in the air. It was his turn to make the silence stretch. He was playing a dangerous card to act this way. Still, he was staring death in the face no matter how this played out.

Oberan could kill him by breathing on him, yes, but he couldn't force Azrael to remove Obfuscate. Azrael understood what it was that Oberan could gain from a budding arena combatant who was a son of the Sovereign. But the people's hope wouldn't be crushed unless Azrael kindled that fire a bit.

The rumor of a *dead* son of the Sovereign would only be a quickly spoken of and discarded topic. The rise of a Sovereign savior would bring hope to the people, have them believe in something more. Then came Azrael's inevitable death—that was the real blow Oberan desired. It would likely quell the masses, and send people to the arenas in droves.

Azrael had no intention of dying, but he knew there was a very high chance of it happening anyway. He might as well milk this situation for everything it was worth. He hadn't had time to consider concessions from Oberan, and so now was scrambling desperately trying to find something. What did he need that this man could provide?

In a word? Privacy.

"I could have either of my guards kill you right now." Yonel shifted his feet, and Azrael jumped. "You dare to ask me to provide passage off my planet. I would have believed that a son of the Sovereign knew when he had no ground to stand on."

Azrael's heart was racing, but the overreaction told him everything he needed. Oberan was desperate for something. He needed to crush the people and have more combatants in the pit. The reduction of slave ships to the planet likely meant that the Tuatha were falling behind on the amount of bodies needed to continue to farm Essence.

The raise in taxes suddenly made sense as well. It was like a thin bandage on a massive wound, though.

Oberan must believe Azrael was heroic, loyal, and strong to ask this. Azrael felt his mind focus and sharpen. Time to steer the conversation. "This son of the Sovereign knows that if you kill him now, you gain nothing. The people of Tech Duinn and the others that you enslave will hear a passing rumor of my existence. Even if you parade my corpse through the streets, it won't matter. Obfuscate holds after death."

Oberan made a noise of pure ecstasy. "Oh, how wonderful to talk to someone with education. I have been on this mud swamp for years, with only Yonel and Gyr." Both men shifted, and Oberan shook his head and indicated them with a gesture. "You see what I mean. Great sparring partners, and combat trainers, but conversationalists—not even close!"

Why would Oberan change tactics so drastically in the game? He didn't believe for a second the man was actually starved for conversation. He smoothed his features and asked, "Oberan, why do the Tuatha have you here? You are so strong, and running a planet could be done by others, I am sure?"

Flattery never hurt.

Oberan over exaggerated fanning himself as he pretended to swoon. "And he cares about me. If I didn't know any better, Azrael, I would think you were hitting on me." Oberan's smile told a dual story. Azrael knew from that wolfish grin that Oberan was joking but would need minimal prompting to take up the offer to bed.

He stored that particular piece of information in his pocket for later consideration. "Your lack of *good* company aside, I have already told you, I won't do as you ask for nothing." Azrael held his breath, hoping he was right about the direction that claim would take them.

"You think you have nothing to lose then?" Oberan seemed to grow weary and studied the back of his hands. "Perhaps, instead of killing you, I should have Yonel here head down to visit Bat or Jophi? Maybe Verimy or Dara?"

Azrael intentionally flinched after Verimy and Dara. That was the direction he wanted. Now to close.

Oberan saw his reaction and pulled back his lips to show his canines. "Have a soft spot for your former trainers, do you?"

Azrael didn't respond, needing it to go one step further. *Come on, Oberan, you're so close.*

Just like that, Oberan stepped into the conversational trap. "Yonel, please go fetch Dara and Verimy."

Yonel saluted and turned.

"No!" Azrael shouted. His voice cracked perfectly, thanks to his recent puberty. "I will do it, but you can't hurt my friends," he whispered and let his head fall.

That was the start, now to water it and get the second seed planted. Azrael shook his head and mumbled, "Only I should have to fight. Trainers of a Sovereign Son won't get you much at all. I will do as you ask if you can guarantee no harm comes to my friends."

Oberan studied him. Scrutinized his body language.

To give that final push, Azrael dropped his head and whispered, "No, he will trick you. How would you know if they are alive? Unhurt?" He shot his head back up to meet that wolfish grin and stared into Oberan's eyes trying to give a sense of false bravado.

With Oberan being in the Epic ranks, Azrael knew he would hear his whisper. He just hoped Oberan didn't realize that he knew that. Oberan seemed to grow thoughtful and held up a hand to stop Yonel. Yonel did stop and turned but the guard didn't return to neutral, indicating that this was more of a hold on the execution. If Oberan dropped that hand, then Azrael had lost. Oberan would bring his *friends* up here one at a time to be slaughtered in front of his eyes.

For some reason his stomach and chest tightened at that thought. Was it because he would lose bargaining chips? He didn't care for them—did he? His training wasn't supposed to allow personal connections. So, was the emotion he was feeling a personal connection?

They are your trainers. Nothing more. Chess pieces. Just like Bat, you can discard them whenever it gives you strategic advantage.

Ten long seconds passed.

"I can offer you a place on the second level. We could move you and your friends into a single cell. That way you would know they were safe. I will be keeping one on the third level as insurance. I think Dara would work best."

His stomach and chest got tighter. He forcefully ignored it and acted his part. He looked at the floor. He had perfectly orchestrated this result. His friends could look for a method to escape while he fought.

Putting them in the same cell was an added victory to Azrael. Instead of answering right away, he waited in his defeated posture for an equal ten long seconds.

Then Azrael nodded.

"Good," Oberan said and then stared directly at Azrael's hand and his ring. Azrael felt his chest tighten in a particularly uncomfortable way. "That ring must be quite powerful for my guards to not have removed it. I will expect you to use the '*Soul Blade*' you have accordingly—to add to the show."

Azrael stood frozen. Oberan had noticed the ring and was going to let him keep it? Oberan turned and left, which finally freed Azrael's mind. Gyr tapped him on the shoulder and motioned to the other door out of the room.

Confused, Azrael stood up and followed the Troll out of the room. On the way back down the stairs, he could only think—*that had seemed too easy.*

CHAPTER TWENTY

The powerful Troll led Azrael back to a gate he vaguely recalled. Was this the same gate the prison transport had brought him, Ogma, and Jophi into the Pit through? He studied the courtyard. It definitely had space for a transport and the gate was large enough as well. It had been the middle of the night when he arrived, and the twilight of the setting sun currently shone through the massive iron bars.

Gyr stood off to the side near the entrance to the room. Azrael continued to try to figure out why he was back on the ground floor and waiting five feet from an exit. Did Gyr want him to try to escape? He studied the impassive Troll for a hint. Nothing.

Echoing footsteps came down the passage he and Gyr had entered through. Then fellow combatants dressed in ragged clothes streamed out from it. The guard near the front of the line stopped to speak with Gyr. Azrael wished he had stood closer. He couldn't hear a syllable over the tromping feet. Papi was at the back of the line and joined the conversation.

Azrael caught a glare from the Bearman and looked away hastily. Soon the two guards had fitted each one of them with enchanted clankers. A quick head count told Azrael there were exactly thirty other slaves. Papi connected a chain to a ring on his chest and the other side to the second guard's back. Azrael Analyzed that guard to discover he was a Journeyman rank. His white skin, white hair, red eyes, and gauntness meant he was likely a vampire.

The guards attached each prisoner in pairs on both sides of the enchanted clankers and then the vampire led them out of the gate. Out of the dungeon? Azrael could feel the change in the air when they left. He took in a deep lungful of air, smelling the city around him. Remembering the town that had formed around the Sovereign Halls. Where could they be going that was outside the dungeon?

Azrael filed down a cobblestone street following the slave in front of him. The buildings immediately surrounding the arena were merchandise shops. He could see Octorian's gear replicated in display windows or hanging on walls. As they continued, the arena specific shops gave way to restaurants, live music bars, grocers, and even a few populace-accessible shops. You could tell these clearly because of the Arbuckle. Azrael tried to find the seed shop that had to be connected to it, but didn't see it.

He got a hint on the second Arbuckle shop he saw. The back of the rare metal merged with another building made of concrete bricks. An Arbuckle warehouse stood behind that building and also merged into the concrete. Oberan was keeping the seed shops hidden from the populace of Samheim. An interesting solution to keep citizens disconnected from outside forces.

Soon they were passing into an industrial quarter of the city. The banging of blacksmiths' hammers, the grinding of automated sawmills, and the hiss of boiling vats filled the air.

The group of combatants was observed a few times by citizens of the city but usually were dismissed. A few people pointed to different combatants and whispered to each other, though. Azrael heard two young men who had pointed at a werewolf a few links in front of him. "That's Dincarn. He destroyed every combatant during his Battle Royale. No one even saw him release a skill. He was like an Assassin. I bet he becomes a champion."

Azrael Analyzed the combatant the young men whispered about.

Dincarn Abylos
Journeyman-Ripper
Level 31
Health Points: 350/350

Dincarn's level was a stark reminder that Azrael was a small fish here. Each slave with him had survived a Battle Royale. Every person chained to him was dangerous. He doubled down on his focus and worked on being attentive to all the combatants he was chained to. It was a great exercise and could save his life if someone tried to surprise him.

The werewolf began sniffing the air pointedly. Azrael tested it himself. Maybe there was a faint iron tinge to it. But they were near a great number of blacksmiths. That smell of iron grew stronger and was joined by the putrid scent of decay as they approached a massive gated complex. The complex's double steel doors opened to admit the parade of slaves into a butcher's yard.

Of course the city would use the combatants as a free labor force. Why not have them perform the tasks that few others wished to? They didn't need to pay slaves, and this would likely recoup some of the costs for the Arena Pit. Feeding thousands of mouths was likely very pricey.

He scanned the perimeter of the complex and found numerous guards on walls and walking routes inside. Was this group of guards always on duty? Their guards disconnected the thirty combatants. Papi shouted, "Shift change." The thirty bloody and dirty slaves currently working dropped their last piece of meat into red-stained plastic barrows.

His group moved to fill the sections that the current workers left. Azrael joined the werewolf at a massive corpse. Two people had been working on it before, and he figured someone would correct him if he shouldn't be there. The creature he began butchering could have been a gigantic pig, if the white color of the meat was an indication. That or a terrifying bird. He Analyzed a piece he had cut free, out of curiosity.

Warhog Loin
Cooking component

He added it to the barrow.

"You'rrre a noobie?" Dincarn, the werewolf, growled at him.

Azrael looked around. Dincarn's voice definitely carried to the guards who walked by. But they just continued their patrol. Talking was permitted, then. Definite bonus to being in a group of two. Azrael continued to work. "Yeah, I just went through my Battle Royale today. You?"

The thirty slaves followed the vampire back out of the complex and the doors closed again behind Papi at the back.

"I completed the second challenge alrrready. I have seen the fifth stage. I will not live long."

Azrael nicked his finger and hissed. He refocused on his butchering task. "How did Octorian and the other champions survive?"

Dincarn chuckled deep in his throat. "The crrrowd favorrred them. If you *lose* and still live, the mob chooses yourrr fate. Combatants that arrre given a chance to live go back to the firrrst challenge. I hearrrd Octorrrian was sparrred eight times. It helps that he is Elven. The crrrowd favorrrs those that look like them."

"You're worried that a single loss will cost you your life? Those boys we passed were enamored by you. They want you to become a champion."

"Cubs arrre purrre. Rrregarrrdless, I won't leave my fate in the hands of the mob. I have alrrready made my decision."

Dincarn's growling intensified and Azrael could practically feel the anger of the werewolf behind him. The powerful combatant saw no way out. The feeling of inevitability tried to settle onto Azrael, and he fought it. Shoving down the oppressive weight and looking for a logical reason for the werewolf's feelings. "Why won't you get past the fifth challenge?"

"Disease," was the short one-word response from the werewolf.

Dincarn clammed up for the next few hours. They finished butchering the monstrous creature and it got replaced by a freshly-skinned corpse which had red meat. Azrael got back to work and Dincarn finally whispered, "I need you to prrretend nothing happened. When we switch shifts. Prrromise me."

Azrael blinked and looked around. Dincarn was begging him to act naturally? The only reason he would need to do that was if Dincarn was attempting to escape. The hundred strong military guards in the complex weren't going to allow that to happen. He searched his feelings and realized he didn't care about Dincarn, but he did care about what his plan might be...

"You won't make it out of here, Dincarn," Azrael switched to a whisper as well, hoping he could get the werewolf to share his strategy.

"I have a powerrrful stealth skill and can even crrreate a duplicate of myself, so thirrrty of us will still leave."

Azrael looked around and considered his Ripper class. The kids had assumed he was some sort of assassin but even

Azrael's assassination instructor couldn't get out of here. "Your Ether will run dry if you try to move through this place undetected. I know people with Superb level Stealth that wouldn't even risk what you are suggesting."

"Do not fearrr. The guarrrds will move me to the rrrefuse pile."

He looked over to see their last corpse's bones, guts, and sinew get dropped onto a massive decaying pile. As soon as it was added, the grate exploded into a bonfire. The background noise changed to hissing and crackling as the bones and sinew caught ablaze. Azrael scanned the area to find six other grates all filled with refuse. A guard shouted, "Get to work. Or I will get my whip out," thanks to his distraction.

He returned to butchering and stayed silent. The guard was now closely watching him and Dincarn. Dincarn was planning to load himself onto the corpse of the creature they were currently slaughtering. Azrael would never consider an escape plan so reckless. If Dincarn was added to one of those piles, he could be burned alive instantly. It was even more likely because they worked on some of the largest corpses in the complex.

The guard moved on and he whispered, "That is extremely dangerous. You would have to hope that you get added to a fresh pile with the size of corpses we are working on."

"Do you have a betterrr idea? I can't fit onto the smallerrr corrrpses and I prrrobably won't get placed on butcherrr duties again beforrre the fifth challenge."

Azrael gave up trying to convince him not to try. His question did kick-start Azrael's mind, though. If the hare-brain was going to commit suicide, it would be best for him to gain some valuable information. His current plan would only succeed for someone who had stealth and some sort of clone ability. The fact that thirty slaves entered and left the complex made the clone skill a necessity to escape from this particular compound.

With those skills, how would Azrael escape?

At a glance, Azrael had no chance of escaping this place. Their current barrow had been replaced when their carcass was changed. The cooks likely didn't want white meat mixing with red. Azrael had seen it wheeled through a side door in the complex. Likely into a freezer or straight out into the town. He hadn't been here long enough to study all of the intricacies. But if he was going to escape right now, that was the best shot he saw.

Riding in the bucket would allow Dincarn to focus on controlling his clone, while simultaneously lowering the strain on his stealth skill. This method could also theoretically work for him in some way. All he would need was a clone ability, as stealth wasn't particularly necessary for this plan.

Azrael could summon a clone and hide in the bucket. Be away before the guards did a headcount. Add to that Dincarn's stealth ability and the wolfman had an even better shot. "Have you considered the barrow?" Azrael asked in a hushed whisper.

"I don't know what is thrrrough that doorrr. It could be a cold rrroom with only one exit," Dincarn admitted.

Azrael nodded while looking at his blood-covered arms and stolen clothes. He wanted to convince Dincarn to try this escape plan. It gave Dincarn a better chance to escape but also provided valuable information to Azrael.

"Fresh meat is more likely sold to the vendors immediately. Or at least brought to merchants to pick through." Azrael Analyzed and then held up a piece of meat he had just cut. "This could be a choice cut of Devil Duck. A smart merchant would be able to tell, and a smart leader would let people buy the expensive meats from the town at a profit."

Azrael had said his piece, and now it was up to Dincarn. Either way, Azrael would get information. He likely wouldn't have turned in the werewolf anyway, but the benefit of this information made it a certainty that he wouldn't.

They both continued to work and then Dincarn rumbled, "Tell me when the coast is clearrr."

Azrael did so, and watched as a second Dincarn suddenly popped up. Before one of them vanished. Azrael held his breath, but no guard began shouting. He saw the bucket shake a few times and smiled as he continued his work, throwing pieces on top of the now-concealed Dincarn. The werewolf had chosen to go with Azrael's plan.

He Analyzed the clone.

Dincarn Abylos
Journeyman-Ripper
Level 31

Health Points: 150/150

Dincarn's health had drastically changed. Azrael hoped that none of the guards would notice. Or if they had stronger Analyze they didn't have other information that would alert them.

The clone worked away beside Azrael and together they made their way to the line when the change in shifts happened. Unfortunately, they hadn't finished butchering the corpse or filling their barrow, but they were extremely close. Azrael crossed his proverbial fingers for the werewolf. If this worked, Azrael would have found a method of escape on his second day.

It was a dark night, the stars providing a low level of illumination which allowed the guards to guide the prisoners on the pathway back to the Pit.

Halfway back to the Arena Pits, Dincarn's clone vanished. The two guards heard the clank of chains and began screaming at all of the captives. They ordered everyone to sit down in place. Within thirty seconds, more guards arrived. Torin was among them. They conducted a very thorough search of the surrounding area.

A military runner approached Torin. "The Obliteration Enchantment destroyed a barrow of meat. The guards assume a slave was hiding inside."

One of the guards chuckled. "At least this rumor will spread through the noobies, and no one will try to escape again for a few months. It seems to happen every third month, like clockwork."

Torin sneered. "Oberan is still going to be pissed. A combatant and a barrow of meat…"

CHAPTER TWENTY-ONE

Azrael and the group of slaves were brought back to the entry chamber of the dungeon. Once back in the dungeon, Torin rushed out of the room, mumbling about having to tell Oberan. Azrael felt the tension in his shoulders drop and he was able to breathe normally again. The toad hadn't even acknowledged him because of its own stress.

The slaves around him were collected as a group and led away, but he was told to wait.

Gyr knuckle-walked into the room and led him to the second floor. Azrael exited the metal staircase and waited for more instructions, unsure where to go from here. Gyr made a gesture left, and Azrael started down the raised platform in that direction.

He peeked over the rickety railing and found the hallway he now knew led to the courtyard dungeon entrance. He began tracking how many doors and turns they might take. A rock wall made up the other side of the walkway he followed. He counted each passage carved into it. Gyr grunted at the fifth passage, and Azrael turned down it.

It was much more pleasant to be escorted without the dog leash and polearm, and he was hoping that good behavior here might bring more such treatment in the future. Not likely, but he sincerely didn't wish for Gyr to get physical. Torin may have been intense, but he doubted that the toad could come anywhere near the strength of Gyr or Yonel. Oberan sparred with the two regularly. If they could keep up with an Epic ranked individual, then they were beyond dangerous.

Azrael's hallway had branching pathways, and on the third carved path to his right, he heard another grunt. He turned and exited the tunnel. The room was another dual-leveled cell block, but strangely these cells were made from wood that contained glowing symbols. Azrael wasn't an expert at any crafts but could tell that these symbols carved into the wood were Enchanting glyphs. He wondered why they had been cut into the bars, as most enchantments were invisible to the naked eye.

Gyr motioned to the first cell, and Azrael entered a dual gate. The outer gate clacked shut loudly behind him and the inner door opened in front of him. Now he was in a large compartment that contained eight wooden beds, a wooden harvest table, and a spare cave with an open door. Azrael moved to the door and found a full bathroom, complete with shower, toilet, and sink. He turned to check on his escort, only to find the Troll gone.

He looked down at his blood-stained arms and clothes and smelled himself. He shuddered and entered the bathroom— it was time to empty his ring of the *loot* and take a much-needed shower.

Then I can fall asleep.

He dumped everything within his Ring of Holding onto the floor of the room and began sorting through it. The vast majority were ragged clothes of the people he had killed inside the arena. However, he had managed to loot a few rings, earrings, necklaces—and a glowing stone? He picked it up and was shocked when something stabbed into his mind, "I have been in that stupid alternate space for what felt like months! How dare you ignore me! I let you live to spread my greatness—wait, where are we right now?"

Azrael had completely forgotten about the dungeon core. His cheeks flushed red and he ran his hand through his hair. He remembered the blood on his hands too late and removed the hand with disgust.

"We are inside the Pits. I think it is an Arena Dungeon," Azrael said.

"Really? Put me down onto a surface." Azrael raised an eyebrow but lowered the dungeon core onto the stone floor. It shrieked, "Pick me up, pick me up!"

Azrael jerked it off the ground. "What was that about?"

Apep flashed brightly for a moment before responding, "I wasn't ready for it to realize I was inside its depth. It will likely devour me if I don't capture an area for myself. Where are we in the dungeon?"

Azrael looked around, bemused by the question. "A washroom, off of a group holding cell for arena combatants."

Apep's pink center flashed rapidly, and Azrael could swear he felt pulses of power coming off the stone. "Do you think people would notice if I started consuming their refuse?" the dungeon asked.

Azrael looked at the toilet. "Do you mean our poop?"

Apep began pulsing so quickly that Azrael could feel the stone vibrating. Just before Azrael could ask a concerned question, Apep stated, "Put me down again."

"Not so fast, Apep. What do I get out of this?" Azrael questioned the dungeon core.

Apep's stone seemed to illuminate and darken in time to Azrael's breathing. Silence stretched and then Apep spoke into his mind again, "We could come up with a binding agreement. You did complete my quest after all…"

Azrael squinted before nodding hesitantly.

Ether Contract
By agreeing to the contract, Azrael Sovereign and Apep will be linked.
The dungeon core will:
- **Attempt to help Azrael escape the Arena Pit**
- **Provide any other reasonable help that Azrael asks for**
- **Follow Azrael's commands where reasonable**

Azrael will:
- **Place the dungeon core on the ground within The Pit**
- **Bring Apep sustenance where possible**
- **Allow Apep access to excrement of his companions**

   Agree to Ether Contract terms?
    <Yes> | No

Azrael's stomach knotted and he swallowed a nervous lump in his throat. Was there anything within this contract that could hurt him? He could demand more from Apep, but that would likely increase his own stipulations. Right now, both his and the dungeon's terms were loose. This was preferable to something concrete. Breaking a contract could put you entirely in the power of the other party.

His body broke out in a cold sweat as he mentally clicked yes and did as instructed. This might not even work—was he going to watch Apep get consumed by the Arena Dungeon?

A purple wave pulsed through the bathroom, and Apep's core sank into the stone. Azrael tried to grab the stone before it fully submerged but was too late. Damnit, he should have figured out a way to increase Apep's chances. Of course it would lose to a much older and more powerful dungeon.

"I have successfully set up this room, and most of the cell outside as my territory!" Apep said.

Azrael jumped and felt his heart begin to beat rapidly. "Wait. Can you dig us out of here?" he asked.

Apep didn't answer, and Azrael growled. After five minutes of waiting he chose to do something else. For all he knew, the dungeon had just escaped on its own. Hopefully the contract prevented that, though.

He looked through the rest of the gear from his ring. Only one of the earrings and a single ring held any enchantments. The other gear was mostly junk.

Most civilized systems enforced a locked status on gear. Those systems only allowed a certain number of enchanted pieces of equipment to drop as loot from sapient kills as well. In essence, this was to promote peaceful relations. Instead of killing someone to gain what they had. On Tech Duinn, the system had no such restrictions.

Ring of the Cow
- **This ring looks like multiple woven strands of grass. It is cast of some mixture of alloys and is poorly formed. This will affect its ability to hold enchantments.**
    Ether Pool: Small
    Current Ether Pool: 25/25
Enchantments: Strength I (+1)
--

Earring of the Junior Sorcerer
- **This ring has a chipped amethyst as its focus and can store a single spell in it. The spell cannot cost more than 20 Ether to cast.**
    Ether Pool: Small
    Current Ether Pool: 20/20
Enchantments: Spell Storage I (Minor Heal)

He put on the ring and felt it adjust to his finger size as it crossed his knuckle. The earring he punched through his ear and winced at the pinching sensation. A small bleeding debuff joined his bar, and he shrugged it off. It would heal quickly, and if he must, he could consume the minor heal to fight infection.

Azrael looked around himself and prompted, "Apep?"

No response so Azrael jumped into the shower and began cleaning himself. The water was freezing cold and he was forced to jump in and out of the stream, shivering. There was a soap dispenser hanging on the wall which he used liberally.

He was just about to jump under the stream to rinse off the suds when Apep spoke. "No, I can't dig us out of here. This whole place is another dungeon, which far outstrips me in ranks. I am hoping I can tap into a few Ether veins... Got it!"

Azrael cleared the soap from his eyes. Then sputtered, "Wait – you were doing that right now? What if it caught you?"

"I would have been destroyed, absorbed, and he likely would have collapsed this area on top of us."

"How do you know that it didn't sense you tapping its vein?" Azrael shrieked, looking at the roof. This stupid dungeon core was going to get him killed.

"Obviously, I am still talking to you—aren't I?"

Azrael ground his teeth together. The core had just played chicken with his life, and he wondered if he should try to dig it out and kill it himself.

The noise of people approaching sounded down the hall. Likely his friends were being delivered to the cell after their own labors of the night. He made a quick decision. "Never do something like that again without my permission! Don't talk to anyone else. Only to me and when I am alone in this bathroom. Can you do that?" Azrael asked.

Apep huffed, "I'm magic, I can do anything I want."

Azrael jumped back under the shower and rinsed off. Shivering, he began cleaning the clothes he had looted. He needed something to wear in the cell.

Shivering even more, he looked critically at the hanging wet clothes. Inspiration struck. "Apep, can you absorb these and make me a clean set?"

"I can't absorb anything when you are that close to it. Move to the door." Azrael did so and saw a single shirt dissolve into the stone. Apep continued, "That's the max distance away I can absorb, and create. Toss everything there and get back to the door."

Soon all the clothes were gone, and a fresh set of dark gray trousers, undergarments, and a shirt appeared for Azrael. He looked disgustedly at them and asked, "Can't you do color?"

To his delight, Apep absorbed the clothes again, and a new set emerged. The new collection was yellow and black in a stripe pattern. Azrael hissed, "I am going to look like a giant bee! How about just black? Apep. Apep! Oh, come on!"

Azrael was forced to wear the bee suit and pulled each piece on sourly. Once he was fully dressed, he turned to the doorway and exited the bathroom. He froze and gnashed his teeth together. Verimy and Jophi stood nearest to him. They cast glances at each other and outside the cell continuously. Outside the glowing wooden bars, Torin was leering at Azrael. Bat was on the end of Torin's collar. The creature was battered nearly to death.

Bat had clearly pissed himself.

Azrael's eye twitched.

Shouldn't you be happy it wasn't you? He's just one of your pawns, after all.

Torin guffawed. "Is that the cleanest you found after the battle? You look like a giant Bumble. Careful everyone, don't let him sting you." The toad guffawed again, loudly.

Azrael looked around. The cell block was empty, so Torin's raised voice seemed unnecessary.

Is the moron playing to an audience?

Torin pressed a whimpering Bat into the grate bars. Bat began to convulse violently as soon as his bare skin touched them. His mournful howl sounded like a tortured cat. Azrael involuntarily stepped forward; that was his—his—the thing he saved. Torin pulled him off the bars as Azrael advanced to them. Still laughing, the toad approached the entrance to the cage, dragging Bat's body over the stone floor.

Torin deposited Bat inside the first door and closed it with a resounding bang. Azrael grabbed his nose as Torin pulled the loop aggressively over Bat's face, remembering the same rough act breaking his own. The loop caught on Bat's large ears. One of the fragile pieces of skin tore, and Azrael's arms shook. The toad spat towards him, and he sidestepped the mucus to allow it to land on the wall. Their eyes locked together for a heartbeat.

Torin showed off his massive yellow teeth. "I think I'll volunteer ta watch over this floor. What da you think, little Bumble? We could become great friends."

Its maniacal laughter echoed down the hallway as it walked away. The second gate opened to allow the group access to Bat. Azrael rushed over and Analyzed him.

Bat
Apprentice-Sonar
Level 12
Health Points: 5/90

Verimy must have Analyzed him too. "He is in pretty rough shape, but doesn't seem to have any life-threatening injuries. What are we all doing here, Azrael?"

Of course, Torin wouldn't risk killing Azrael's people. Oberan was counting on them as bargaining chips. Azrael turned to Verimy and told a half-truth, "Oberan wants me to fight as a Sovereign Son. I told him if I was going to do that, he needed to ensure that you all won't be fighting."

Verimy squinted his eyes at Azrael. Did his trainer not trust him?

Jophi jumped on the hole in his story, "What does that matter? If you die, he will just go back to using us as combatants—if he doesn't kill us outright. Next time you should let the grown-ups do the planning."

Azrael glared at the woman. Adults? She was a teenager, at best!

He'd already had enough of others making plans for his life. These *adults* wouldn't be making the plans going forward— he would. They just would have to slowly learn that fact.

If he could be sure they had no traitors amongst them, he could start coming up with an escape plan immediately. Unfortunately, Verimy or Jophi, or both, could be feeding information to Oberan.

Azrael snarked his response, "Well, I asked to be let off this rock first, but he said no. At least now you have a washroom to do your hair." Azrael motioned to the door of the bathroom.

Jophi deflated and looked around the cell. After a cursory examination, she admitted, "It is quite the step up from the last hole in the wall I was in. I just don't see how this helps us with getting out of here."

Clever. If she was a spy, that was a dig for his plan. Well, he wasn't going to let her know, even when he did figure it out. Right now, it was best to test the situation. Azrael smiled and asked, "Do you have a plan, then?"

Verimy stepped in front of the red-faced Jophi, interrupting her glare and asked, "Where is Dara, Azrael?"

It was Azrael's turn to deflate.

CHAPTER TWENTY-TWO

"Just to recap our conversation from last night. Jophiel, you were brought to a laundering complex yesterday. Bat, you did some unloading of shipments in a warehouse. Verimy, you have done a few different tasks, but last night you were skinning?" Azrael paused as they each nodded after his summary.

"The other chores we know of are wood cutting, stone gathering, and farming," Jophi added.

Azrael had left those off intentionally. They were the three they knew about that offered the best chance of escape for combatants. As the guards brought people outside the walls of Samheim. They were escorted by the military and in such high numbers that escape still seemed impossible, but it removed an obstacle if you succeeded in getting away.

Azrael stood from his cot and moved to the center of the room. The cot was made of wood and had no pillow or padding. He would prefer something softer, but it was a definite step up from the rickety bed he had destroyed in his first-floor cell. He began going through stretches to remove some of his stiffness that had formed from sleeping on the planked bed.

The others continued to plan as he went through his warm up, almost as if he wasn't there.

"Asking around, I haven't heard of a single person escaping," Verimy stated.

"Azrael said that his butchering partner was destroyed by an enchantment. Or at least discovered by it. There are likely similar enchantments in each of the complexes within the city. We need to focus on the three I mentioned," Jophi insisted. Like the night before, she was trying to take over the escape plans.

They don't even realize that I steered them to these plans. In time, they will realize I make the final decisions here.

Azrael stood from his stretches and moved into his katas. Verimy saw his face and stood up to begin correcting him in the manner he used to as he continued, "Jophi, every slave will think the same as you do. The bigger question will be how to all get assigned to the same work duty."

The room went silent. Just like the previous night, no one had an answer to that problem.

They needed to come up with a solution to that problem first. After that, he needed to be placed at one of those three chores to assess the security for himself. He wouldn't trust any second-hand knowledge. Any one of them could be a spy for Oberan. He considered Jophi, or Ogma.

A gnome walked down the hallway, interrupting his thoughts. The gnome balanced four huge trays. Azrael stopped his sword practice and watched the amazing feat of dexterity. The gnome stopped dead and squeaked, "If you attack me, you won't get any food! Just stay back and let me set it down in peace!"

Azrael stared at the gnome, not understanding the change. Verimy sorted it. "Put your sword away, stupid student."

"And go stand on the far side of the cell please," the gnome said while staring at Azrael. The four trays were rattling around, and Azrael let out a defeated sigh as he went to stand in the washroom doorway.

Sadly, the gnome still wasn't comfortable entering the cell, even after Azrael stood far away. It would seem that most combatants weren't allowed to keep weapons outside of the arena. That was a definite advantage in Azrael's favor. Oberan spreading his class around made everyone assume it was a Soul Sword. No one would try to take it away. Theoretically, if they noticed his ring, they could have hung his Ring of Holding outside the cell, but he could still access it. Soulbound items couldn't leave a person's side and would always be close to the owner. Unless the thief spent an exorbitant amount of resources to break the bond—or killed the individual.

Before the gnome got out of view, he Analyzed it.

Louis Darft
Journeyman-Saucier
Level 37
Health Points: 190/190

Azrael shouted after Louis' retreating blue hair, "We wouldn't ever hurt you. I promise. Thanks for the food."

He wasn't sure if it would help, but if it stopped spit from floating in his soup or porridge, he would be more than happy. To everyone's surprise, the food was much better than the breakfast in the mess hall. Not quite on par with the champions' opulent spread, but better than the standard. They ate yogurt with granola and some fresh fruit. There was more than enough to feed everyone and even have some leftovers. Azrael even got a small buff for being well-fed, which awarded him plus-one Stamina for six hours.

Bat had fully recovered from Torin's abuse but still seemed a little twitchy to Azrael. Even as Bat ate, he chose to sit on the floor with his tray. That might be the downside for Azrael's group. Bunking with him meant that Papi and Torin's hatred transferred to them.

Jophi sat quietly as she ate and flushed red each time he looked at her. Was this a sign of her betrayal?

What had the woman chosen to reveal about him to that guard? Maybe he should have let her stay in the cells below— Ogma likely would have found a way to protect her, after all.

A small part of him wanted to ask her that right now, but a tightness in his chest stopped him. It felt like someone was gently squeezing his beating heart.

He closed his eyes as food stuck in his throat. Why was his mouth so dry? Did he not want to know the truth?

Why is my body reacting this way?

After breakfast, he got back to his katas as he considered that very question.

***

It had been three hours, and Azrael was pacing. He had expected there to be chores for them today, but discovered that the group was scheduled to fight this afternoon. Normally, there were three days between fights, from what he had been told, and combatants didn't have to do chores on days that they fought. The fact that this was only day two of his schedule left him walking back and forth while he sweat.

This could be nothing. They could have used Verimy's fight schedule. Or this could be why the negotiations with Oberan were so easy.

He heard approaching footsteps down the hallway. He watched the entrance to the cell block and saw something blue bobbing down it. Sure enough, Louis came walking into view, trays balanced. He approached the cell and muttered, "Lazy service guards—look, I don't want any trouble. I am supposed to drop the food off on the table to finish the quest. Last time I failed because not all of the trays made it to the table. Who ate on the floor?"

Azrael moved to place Bat's tray onto the table and Louis took on a blank look. The gnome smiled before continuing, "Thank you. I'm going to be level with you. None of the guards or runners want to bring the food to an empty cell block up here. They don't think the Etherience will be worth it. If I don't run this food myself, you won't be fed—"

Azrael chose to help Louis out. "If you place the trays on the ground between the double gates, we will grab them and place them on the table for you."

Louis' eyes widened comically, and he rushed to do as suggested. Once the trays were down on the ground, and the gate closed, his excitement seemed to dry up. He eyed the morning dishes and began to wring his hands. Sighing, Azrael went to the harvest table first and picked up the empty trays. He brought those trays to exchange them with the new ones.

Once crouched, he motioned for Verimy and Jophi to help. His Dexterity likely wasn't as high as Louis' and he had no chance of balancing all of them. Verimy and Jophi came and together they placed the trays laden with lunch on the harvest table.

Louis waited to collect the empty trays but then squinted at them. "Wait a minute! Where are the plates, the cutlery—the leftovers? I'm going to have to report this! You can't make weapons or hoard them." Louis held up a tray that was missing a corner. It looked like someone or something chewed on it.

Azrael squinted and noticed that it wasn't one large bite but thousands of tiny ones. He glanced back at the washroom, and then Bat. Thinking fast, he sputtered, "I'm sorry, our friend has a strange appetite! He isn't hoarding them, just eating them…"

Bat yawned, putting his small sharp fangs on display. Louis squeaked and stepped back, "Well, you tell that… thing…

to stop eating the serving utensils or you won't get any more food—eek!" Bat stood up, and Louis fled.

Bat sniffed loudly and then three times in short succession. He seemed to follow his nose towards the table before exclaiming, "There's rat meat! I haven't had rat since I got captured from Berstrand!" Bat clumsily found a seat and sat down, his ears twitching as he turned his head left and right. "You all coming?"

Azrael moved to join Bat and felt Jophi and Verimy eyeing him. They likely knew he had just lied, and his head fell when Verimy called, "What in the Broken Sanctum was that about, Azrael? Where are the plates and cutlery from this morning?"

Bat interjected, "I am sorry, guys. I got famished. Azrael must have seen me eating them." Azrael blinked and saw one of Bat's ears almost fold in half. Was that a wink? He couldn't believe that Bat would follow along with his ruse, but he'd just done it again.

As confidently as he could, he motioned to Bat and then gave both Jophi and Verimy a 'told you so' stare. "You two ready to eat now?"

Verimy raised an eyebrow. "Fine. What functions do sapient beings serve for Planetary Gods?"

Azrael groaned. Guess they were going back to the old routines. He would play along for now. "Sapient beings perform multiple functions in the eyes of a Planetary God. First, they are a filter for Ether, calming its wild nature and converting it to a new form of energy upon death. This new energy is something that Planets can use." Azrael left off the name Essence, which had been a hotly contested point at the Sovereign Halls. He now knew for certain that it was the name of the second tier of energy, but didn't plan on sharing that. "Second, sapient life can protect a Planetary God from marauders and pillagers."

Jophi jumped in. "Yes, but theoretically, a Planetary God can just create a powerful monster, mutate and evolve it, to serve the same goal."

Azrael widened his eyes at her interruption. Had she just chosen to make his explanation harder? She smiled and took a bite of rat. From their smug expressions, Azrael assumed they both knew he was lying and Jophi wanted to get in on Verimy's revenge.

He coughed and looked at Verimy, who was laughing and eating himself. Grumbling, Azrael stated, "That is true, but historically, large unintelligent monsters create larger and larger hunting zones until very few creatures live within that space. In those cases, the Planetary God that created them loses the accumulated filtering of all those living beings. Instead, those Legendary beasts consume land and Territories that could house millions of pieces of Conversion Ecostructure."

He wolfed down what he could after Verimy nodded at his answer. He stopped his shoveling when Verimy asked the next question. "Where do dungeons, like the one we are in now, fall into the Conversion Ecostructure?"

This one was a bit easier at least, but Azrael glanced at the bathroom, wondering how Apep would answer this question. Turning back to Verimy, he rattled off the Sovereign Halls answer, "Dungeons are larger filters for Planetary Gods, but also use the secondary energy themselves. The theory is that they are actually the next step in the filtering process, creating some third level of energy that sapients are yet unaware of. Dungeons also provide challenges for sapient growth and can combine with Territories."

Verimy allowed him to eat another portion of his food before he followed up with the demand, "Elaborate on how dungeons combine with Territories."

That one was a substantial theoretical debate, and Azrael felt himself roll his eyes. *Was all this really necessary?* "All that is known for sure on the subject is that each Territory can house four dungeons. Those 'Cardinal Dungeons' regulate the wildlife and land within the Territory. Territory leaders can create zones for hunting, farming, and gathering. The Cardinal Dungeons also provide four unique dungeon Dives for those permitted entrance. The adventurers often attempt to clear all four challenges so that they can access the Prime Dungeon. Also known as the fifth challenge."

Jophi chimed in again, "The Prime Dungeon is a mutual creation of the four other dungeons, each one adding portions to it as they expand it. My father told me that people must clear the challenges of each floor before the dungeons can add another."

To his horror, Jophi reached over and snagged a piece of his toast. Azrael growled at her as she chirped a laugh. He quickly shoved what remained of his food into his mouth, not giving Verimy time to ask for a longer answer. He was done with this game.

When Azrael looked up, Verimy had a vacant expression on his face. Azrael glanced over his shoulder, trying to find out what had taken Verimy's attention. A moment later, a notification popped up.

A Tournament has been arranged for the pleasure of our viewers!

Tournament of the Beginner Combatants

- **Team Sovereign Son will fight against Team Phoenix Rebirth at 4:00 pm today. This will be a single-elimination tournament and begins in the round of 64.**

Rules:

1. **Each team will contain four combatants.**
2. **A combatant can be eliminated, withdraw, or forfeit a fight. Once the combatant has taken any of the above options, they will be considered a victory point for the opposing team.**
3. **The first team to three victory points wins the round. If the bout ends in a tie, then a battle between surviving combatants will commence to break it.**
4. **A combatant can continue to fight multiple opponents until they are eliminated, have withdrawn, or have forfeited.**

The current order of combatants for Team Sovereign Son:

Azrael – Verimy – Jophi – Bat

Is this correct?

<Yes> | No

Good luck, Team Sovereign Son!

Azrael clicked his cheek. That wasn't precisely the agreement he had made with Oberan. However, he saw the cleverness in the maneuver. Azrael could essentially stop the others from fighting by winning three contests for each fight. However, if he chose to let someone else fight, then he would have already lost, which likely meant his death.

The other option was for Azrael to select someone else to fight. But if he chose someone else to fight, he might give away his hand. He needed to appear heroic.

Clever. But he wouldn't fall for it.

CHAPTER TWENTY-THREE

Azrael waited in a much smaller antechamber than the Battle Royale starting room. Jophi threw both of her hands above her head as she exclaimed, "Fighting until you are injured is sensible, but trying to fight all of the battles is just stupid. We don't even know the strength of our opponents. I don't care how strong you think you are. I can fight, and it looks like Verimy is a combat class too!"

Azrael had grown tired of arguing with her. Why was she so against his leadership?

Oberan had made Azrael the team leader. He turned to Verimy instead. "I am going to use this as a training exercise. Did we all get the Dungeon Quest?"

Verimy and Bat nodded. Jophi screamed at the ceiling, and both Bat and Verimy flushed, seeming to either be embarrassed for her or themselves. Azrael didn't care and opened the quest they had received on entering the antechamber.

Arena Chain Quest
Single Elimination Tournament
Win the Round of 64
  • **The dungeon created a competition for new combatants. Win the round of 64 to gain benefits and concessions from the arena. The better the score during the contest, the higher the rewards!**
Rewards:
Etherience
Points to buy Class-Appropriate Gear
Failure:
May result in death

Azrael filled the silence that followed Jophi's frustrated scream with a question, "Does anyone know exactly how the Combatant rankings even work?"

Verimy, who had been here the longest, answered, "You move through the ranking systems to obtain longer breaks between fights, better food, and lodging. From my perusal of the mess hall, there are four ranks – and I only know two of the names. The bottom is Initiate, and the third is Champion. The top rank only exists after you defeat the fifteenth challenge, and I don't know the second rank."

Azrael nodded, glad to have that answered. His group hadn't moved up in rank, but was being housed in a cell for combatants of the second tier. If the treatment he had seen so far was the benefit, he wouldn't complain. He looked over to Verimy. "Do you know how long of a break between fights Initiates normally have?"

Verimy shrugged. "I fought when I first got here and was scheduled to fight three days after, which would have been today. So my schedule is the same. But all three of yours changed because of this tournament and your deal with Oberan."

Azrael had already been aware of that timeline. Maybe moving through the arena ranks may give them a longer break, and more tasks, but to beat the fifth challenge Dincarn couldn't defeat seemed like a long shot. Since those tasks were their best option to escape, Azrael needed to consider it, but doubted it would help them.

He looked at his status page to ensure that he had stopped hiding his last name. He then Analyzed his sword.

King's Tide – Soul Blade (*Click here to see actual information*)
- **Level 10**
  - **A soul sword of the Sovereign Class.**
    Current Ether Pool: 210/210

Enchantments: Strength X (+20), Stamina X (+15)

With Verimy and Jophi's help, he had Obfuscated his sword to look even more like a legendary Soul Blade. He hadn't been Obfuscating it during his Battle Royale and hoped that most people who had seen it up close were currently dead. Or hadn't Analyzed it. He also knew that his Strength and Stamina would possibly give his ruse away to his opponent or an intelligent combatant. But there was only so much he could do. There were a lot of things to think about when attempting to create a ruse this complex, and he hoped he had gotten them all.

According to Verimy and Jophi, he seemed to pass the test when they Analyzed him. Bat strangely could see right through everything he did. Azrael asked Bat, "What level is your Perception, again?"

Bat's ears twitched. "Me? It's part of a Class trait, and mine is currently Greater level five."

Wow. This pawn is turning out to be very valuable—maybe a rook? I am sure we can use that to some advantage, right?

Verimy had Strong ranked Perception and couldn't see through the Obfuscation skill. As a hunter, his skill was higher than average as well. Azrael figured he would use him and Jophi as the standard to fool. A countdown timer flashed into the corner of his interface, and a notification opened simultaneously.

Preparation Time
5 minutes of Preparation Time has started. Your first fighter is required to enter the entrance gate before the timer elapses. This time is to talk about strategy and adjust equipment.
Good luck!

Azrael checked his Soul Storage to find a ten stack and a five stack of Soul Strike stored. Then he walked into the double gated entrance and smiled—finally, it was starting. He did get a bit of a knot in his stomach. Some of it was nerves, but most of his fears were legitimate worries. This preparation time would become more useful at each level of competition. It made Azrael's plan of fighting straight through more difficult as opponents learned his identity and current skills.

Looking through the grate, he found two blind spots in the circular expanse of sand. Far to his right and left had the view mostly blocked from where he currently stood. That's where he would try to fight. As long as he killed his opponent, then the next challenger would gain no advantage. That meant he couldn't leave the decision up to the crowd.

Jophi came to the door and vehemently stated, "Good luck, Azrael! Don't overdo it—please?"

Her demand to take over leadership failed. Is this a new avenue of attack?

He looked at her with his head tilted. She seemed so sincere—and beautiful. He just couldn't understand why she would talk to that guard—or what she had said. The timer continued to tick down.

The possibility of death gave him courage. Azrael asked, "What did you tell that guard?"

She blinked, and her eyebrows drew down, then a look of recognition crossed her face. She looked around and whispered, "The guard you saw is a member of the Cathodiem Guild stationed here. I asked him to get a message back to my father. I told him about my capture with you and Ogma."

She studied his face and must have seen something there because she added, "I didn't tell him you were a Sovereign Son."

Her reaction seemed genuine. He rubbed his shoulder and feigned a shrug. "How can he get any communications off this rock?"

They stared at each other, and her eyes narrowed further. She released the bar and turned away. "He can't, Azrael. That's why I know my father isn't coming. None of our agents can get communication off this world. At least he doesn't know of any way to," she mumbled.

With her back to him and her soft voice, Azrael had barely heard her. As she walked away, he watched her go, and blinked at her retreating back. She clearly wanted to pin her hopes on a rescue of some sort. That was why he would never count on others to save him. He recited his lessons in his head. He could only count on himself.

The counter dropped to zero, and the gate sprang open. Azrael blanked his mind with a centering breath and stepped into the arena. The other gate had been far enough away that he had only seen a shadow of someone within it for a moment, and it now stood empty.

He searched the sands and then narrowed his eyes. He didn't find anyone immediately, which told him the opponent was using Stealth or Invisibility. Azrael activated his Soul Cloak and sprinted to the right, wanting to get out of view of both doorways. He continued surveying the sands, looking for a sign of movement. His eyes caught flying sand in his peripheral, and he reacted instantly by dropping into a roll. Two daggers flashed in the space his chest had been. A black-wrapped individual wielded the serrated blades. Two strips of cloth hung in the air behind the form and Azrael Analyzed his attacker from the bottom of his roll.

Caxir the Silent Wind
Apprentice-Stalker
Level 22
Health Points: 135/135

Azrael shot his body into a rigid position using his shoulders as a springboard and catapulted himself to his feet. He landed and turned to find the air empty again. Still, with an area to concentrate on, he could see shifting particles of sand that gave away the position of Caxir. He continued to sprint into the blind spot of the arena, keeping an eye on the shifting sands that followed.

Once he felt comfortable where he was, Azrael swung his sword in a patterned backhand whip, entering the form of Mages Fanning. His blade clanged against something in the air, and Azrael turned his wrist, changing his blade's course downward. He changed the direction again in a flourish, making the edge a diagonal attack at the invisible Caxir. His sword clanged again as Caxir attempted to trap it between both of its serrated knives.

Azrael smiled and released a single hand from his hilt. Mages Fanning wasn't a combat form, but more of an artistic rendering of what sword fighting could look like. Each blow was exaggerated and flowing. Azrael's instructor told him never to use it in combat. In sparring, Azrael found that his opponents often underestimated him in this form or tried to catch and hold his weapon. He extended his arm and opened his palm, shouting, "Release five."

A Soul Strike exited his palm, this one with five stacks of the skill. All he had needed was to know Caxir was standing still. The blades tore through something in the air, and he saw black wraps falling to the ground. Without warning, a blast of wind hit him along his entire front. His feet left the ground, and his body careened into the center of the arena. He landed on his heels and allowed the momentum to take him onto his butt, back, and then hands before springing to his feet again. Was that a spell?

The announcer who had been silent behind the enchanted dome called out, "And there goes Caxir, one of the Windfolk. His wind has been set free forever." Suddenly the garb and the final moments made complete sense. The Windfolk were bodiless. Instead, they formed from a strange collection of the element of wind. They often wore Ether Wraps to help keep their element under pressure, which gave them more of a standard shape. This allowed them to wear other pieces of equipment on their forms, as most of the universe had physical bodies.

Azrael knew his attack had been overkill, but ensuring the death of his opponent should protect his skills from the next combatant. He hoped he had been out of sight like he calculated. Azrael went over and touched the rags to loot them.

Dancing Cloak
- **This cloak will move around and strike at opponents as you fight. Its pieces of fabric attempt to confuse the enemy.**
    Ether Pool: Medium
    Current Ether Pool: 12/50
Enchantments: Attacking Dance V
--
Body Wraps of Wind's Grace
- **This five-foot length of wrap will increase the wearer's grace.**
    Ether Pool: Small
    Current Ether Pool: 5/15
Enchantments: Dexterity I (+1), Agility I (+1)

After looting the *body,* he moved back to his team's entrance. As he approached, the doors opened and he could see his team pressed to the grates. Jophi exclaimed, "What happened? We couldn't see you at all over there." That simple statement made him content. He had been successful in his plan.

Before Azrael forgot, he turned away and charged his blade five times, and then released his skill, whispering, "Store," as quietly as he could. His skill didn't fly off into the air, and he smiled again. That dropped his Ether pool to fifty percent but it began refilling based on his Ether regeneration. Perhaps he had a real chance of being the only combatant.

Azrael entered the gate and heard the mechanism reverse, as a five-minute timer began to count down again. He looked to Jophi and answered, "That was the whole point of going over there. As for what happened, I won against a Windfolk Assassin. Just let me put on this new equipment."

He wrapped the cloth around his left forearm from his wrist to his elbow and then placed the cloak over his shoulders. Again, these weren't exceptionally helpful pieces of gear, but were more than he currently wore. Next, he checked his Etherience gains and found that he had been awarded just over two-hundred thousand from the Windfolk.

The Etherience placed him under one hundred thousand away from a level up, and he hoped the next opponent would get him to level sixteen. He began thinking of what his next skill choice might be, and then stopped himself. The next opponent had to die first.

Azrael looked at Verimy, who just nodded at him as if to say, 'Your strategy is a good one.'

Is that him finally acknowledging that I have some idea what I am doing?

Azrael glanced at Bat, and his blue-skinned companion flicked his ears in what Azrael was calling a blink. A mental button was available to change combatants, which likely would raise the inner gate to allow a switch. Of course, that wasn't what he wanted to do.

Jophi looked like she wanted to say something, but their last interaction probably held her tongue. Azrael knew it was still rattling around in his head, and he looked to Verimy, his long-time trainer. Someone he had known since he was a kid. Was he wrong not to trust anyone?

The time ticked away, and the gate opened again. A glance showed his Ether recovered to the eighty percent mark. Azrael took off out of the entry chamber. This time pumping his legs to the left of the opening as he tried to get out of view. A centaur charged from the other side and course-corrected towards him. Its hooves kicked up sand in a dust cloud behind the horseman, and it leveled a lance towards him. Behind the lance, Azrael saw the sleek brown fur, crossed with white accents. Its upper humanoid body was bare-chested and well-muscled.

A few strides later, Azrael was in range to Analyze his opponent.

Jaten Brendil
Apprentice-Jouster
Level 24
Health Points: 150/150

Azrael needed to get just a little farther to remove himself from sight, but based on the closing speed of Jaten, he wouldn't have time. Azrael slid to a stop and entered the high guard of Trellis Lily, named after a type of flower with a long stalk and a drooping flower that only looked beautiful from below. This stance was extremely effective at fending off downward strikes from taller or higher opponents.

Azrael caught the tip of the lance and began to push it to the side. A lance was a cumbersome weapon and only held by the wielder at a point far away from the target. This unbalance made it a threat that could be maneuvered off-target with relative ease. Azrael's blade and Jaten's lance pulsed. In time with that pulse, Azrael felt the force on his arms from the lance increase drastically as the point tried to correct course.

Two things stopped the point from skewering Azrael. One was his flexing arms, which held the lance slightly away. The greater of the two reasons was his Soul Cloak skill. This normally moved the attack away from Azrael, but because the attack was Ether-assisted the skill actually slid Azrael's body infinitesimally across the sand. The two skills warred with each other, and the tip tore into his left deltoid, and then quickly out the other side. He felt the muscle sever, and his hand let go of his hilt as the centaur body flew by him and began turning a large semi-circle.

Azrael clenched his jaw against the pain and moved further into the blind spot, hoping to release his Soul Strike skill from cover. He didn't want his last opponent to have an advantage. Unfortunately, the centaur used a second skill and blurred around the turn. Azrael caught the motion and spat on the ground, attempting to force the hand of his injured arm back onto his hilt. The hand refused to respond, and Azrael gave up on trying to hold back information from the final opponent. He loaded his blade with a single Soul Strike and released a vertical slash at the blurring form of the charging centaur. The reciprocating blades cut through the sand, and Jaten ran into them with skill-assisted speed and momentum. For a split second, the blur continued as blood streamed behind it, and then the entire body parted.

The announcer called again, "Another victory for Azrael of Team Sovereign Son. Jaten Brendil hadn't seen his opponent's Blade Projection skill in the previous fight and pays the ultimate price: bisection!"

He minimized the notification that told him of his successful rise to level sixteen. He moved to the bloody remains and looted, tuning out the announcer. Another opponent he hadn't given the crowd the opportunity to spare. Success.

Lance of Kyron

- **A lance which increases momentum transfer to its targets while also providing extra power to the wielder.**
  Ether Pool: Medium
  Current Ether Pool: 45/50

Enchantments: Momentum II, Strength II (+2)

--

Centaur Child's Doll

- **This is a child's toy and has sentimental value to the owner.**

Azrael felt a pang in his heart, and he left the doll on top of Jaten to be absorbed with him. If that was a family member's or a keepsake, it deserved to travel with him into death.

He walked back to the entrance and cast Minor Heal from his earring on himself. He would ask his team if any of them had a spell he might be able to place within the gem. Immediately, he felt his shoulder begin knitting together. The blow must have hit a nerve because he felt a pop, and then he gained back control of his arm. He moved it experimentally in a few circles and, while still stiff, he was satisfied that it was now functional.

The Etherience from killing Jaten had brought him to level sixteen, but he would probably wait to place the skill point. It would be better to weigh out the pros and cons of both of his tier four skills. Five minutes just didn't seem like enough time to consider everything.

The gate opened again on his approach, and Verimy called out this time, "Your next opponent will know your primary skill now. Someone should switch with you."

Guess his nod and acceptance was only temporary. These two will have to begin accepting me as leader soon, right?

The gate began to close as the timer started again, and instead of answering, Azrael asked, "Does anyone have a spell that costs under twenty Ether? I want to store it in my earring."

Jophi blinked and looked at the earring before offering, "What do you prefer? Fireball, Arctic Breath, or Barrier? Mind that, for only twenty Ether, they will be pretty weak versions of the spells."

Azrael looked at Verimy, who shook his head. "Only skills here, no spells."

Bat just shook his head and Azrael turned back to Jophi, somewhat hesitantly. Did he dare trust her? If she was the traitor, she could load a blank into the earring and get him killed. He moved closer so she could touch the gem, telling himself that Oberan wouldn't want him to die in his first fight. Oberan needed his legend to spread before that happened, which was what Azrael was counting on.

Jophi smiled a moment later, and Azrael felt the wattage of the gesture in his chest, somehow. He shook his head, and she stated, "All done." Then after a moment's hesitation, she leaned in and whispered, "I actually tossed a once a day Fireball in there. I can double the size for half the cost. Figured it would be the best option for you. Good luck..." She looked at his pink shoulder and grimaced, then looked across the arena.

He turned back to the exit and waited as the timer elapsed. His Ether was nearly full and he had both slots in his Soul Storage full. When the gate opened, he didn't bother attempting to get out of the line of sight and instead stepped straight out onto the sand.

As if a funhouse mirror ran down the center of the arena, a massive creature stepped out from the other entrance. It flexed all of its muscles and roared, which caused a fire to dance across its skin.

Azrael's next opponent was a fire giant.

CHAPTER TWENTY-FOUR

Azrael seriously considered surrendering and sending Jophiel in to deal with this opponent. Unfortunately, he didn't think surrender was possible, but a class like hers with access to Frost spells would have a much easier time. Of course, then Oberan may separate the group and there would go any escape plans.

I wonder if Apep will be able to follow me if my cell changes?

He shook his head, dispelling the distraction. fire giants weren't exactly common, at least not anymore. If his lessons were correct, they were an extremely aggressive race. Their coming of age ceremony involved a small dropship to another planet where they took on a local Territory by themselves. There were very few success stories, and the ones who got captured alive got sold to places like this.

That didn't mean that they were weak. No, the fact that there were a few success stories amongst fire giants at all told the tale of just how terrifyingly powerful they were. Azrael immediately felt his blood cool. That Fireball spell Jophi loaded wasn't going to be very helpful. If anything, it was likely to heal his distant, roaring opponent. Had she known? Had she betrayed him?

Azrael charged his Soul Strike with five stacks and held the attack ready. Closing with the creature was his last resort. Supposedly, the air near their bodies during combat rose to temperatures that rivaled Dragon's fire. Azrael checked his Ether bar and saw he was at around forty-five percent, after the fifty percent he had just pumped into his sword. He felt his mouth sour and hastened to assign his skill point from level sixteen.

He had not wanted to make the decision in five minutes, feeling that it would become a hasty one. Now he had a split second.

Lesson learned—always assign skill points when you have time.

Tier 4 Skills
Bloodletting

- Widen a wound, while simultaneously preventing most healing from taking hold. This Skill will increase damage dealt when blood is drawn by 20%, and add a bleeding debuff stacking 20% of the initial damage every three seconds until the wound closes.
  Passive Skill gained at 1/5, "Bloodletter."
  0/5

--

Soul Siphon
- Successful attacks return a small portion of Ether and power to the user. This Skill will return 1% of the opponent's maximum Ether pool to the attacker, and transfer 1% of the user's statistic points. The buff is stackable up to five times.
  Passive Skill gained at 1/5, "Soul Steal."
  0/5

Azrael dumped his point into Bloodletting. Both skills seemed compelling. But with his upcoming opponent, Azrael needed the extra damage. He also didn't have the time that he would have liked to sit down and consider the options. He crossed his metaphorical fingers that the increase to striking and bleeding damage would make a difference.

The selection had taken him less than a second, so he caught the end of his opponent's roar and watched as the behemoth locked its eyes onto his position. The fire giant began to charge, each step eating up the distance as its feet splashed into the sand. Azrael took a deep centering breath and waited for his opponent to come into range. He really needed to Analyze it for a strategy.

Angr Sotd
Journeyman-Berserker
Level 11
Health Points: 550/400

His eye twitched.

The creature even had temporary hit points that Azrael would have to chew through. Angr bunched its tree-trunk legs and launched into the air. The closeness of a moment ago allowed Azrael to estimate his opponent's height at fifteen feet and its weight at over a ton. To see Angr jump forty feet into the air froze Azrael for a fraction of a second.

His battle training kicked in, and he sprinted away. As expected, Angr had used some sort of skill, likely a variant of Heroic Leap common in giant classes. The sand exploded out from its landing and he felt the super-heated air that surrounded the giant rush by him.

Azrael blessedly took no damage. He turned and let his five stacks on his sword fly—the blades actually became visible as they brought a colder wave into the air around Angr. Azrael watched them slow down before colliding and attempting to saw through the fire giant.

To his horror, only two of the blades connected with his opponent, who stood thirty feet away. He had known that the edges grew further apart the farther they traveled, but with such a big target he had hoped—no matter. He would have to use it from a closer range. Despite the inherent danger in that tactic.

He Analyzed the fire giant—four hundred and ninety. Sixty points of damage for fifty percent of his Ether was not a good trade-off, but the blades were still grinding away, attempting to dig deeper. To his relief, the skin parted, and dark red blood welled forth, which would trigger his Bloodletter passive. But that was the end of the good news. With a mighty twist and elbow blow, Angr countered Azrael's Soul Strikes.

He began sprinting away, tactically retreating.

He needed to keep a buffer between himself and the furnace-like air that surrounded Angr. The fire giant charged after him, and its long legs closed the distance. Azrael clenched his jaw as the heat ratcheted up a few degrees with each step. Just as the heat cracked his skin, he held out his palm behind him and croaked, "Release five," from dry lips.

The skill shot from his palm and closed the twenty-foot gap. Due to the distance, all five of the blades made contact with Angr's chest and arms. The skill shook the ton of bulky muscles and flaming skin, slowing its advance but not stopping the behemoth. As Azrael watched, it took a terrifying step forward.

The reciprocating blades began to cut layers of thick gianthide away, and Angr fought to get his palms around the invisible Soul Strikes. Two drew blood before Angr threw this skill away—again! Three hundred and forty-two health points remaining. As he watched, the health ticked down another point from Bloodletter but this still wasn't looking good.

He only had one further skill stored, this second one with ten charges, and his final trump card. He checked his Ether pool and noticed it contained just over fifty percent, and he added one more skill use at the fifth level to his calculations. That would lay him out though.

This just kept getting worse. If he wanted the ten Soul Strikes to connect with the target, he likely needed Angr even closer. Did he dare? He glanced at his entrance as he continued his sprint—this fight would have been much more manageable for Verimy or Jophi.

Azrael was already committed, though. Oberan wouldn't win. Oberan *couldn't* win!

The heat began to climb. Angr was closing in once again. The heat suddenly vanished, and Azrael chanced a glance behind him. No flaming giant.

His sweat chilled on his forehead and back. He planted his feet hard and reversed. His reaction was just in time, as Angr crashed into the sand ten feet from him. Right where he would have been. Azrael, now well within the accompanying shockwave, was blasted violently away to bounce over the sand.

In his spinning tumble he caught a glimpse of a screen. "Sovereign" flashed continuously across it. Guess that meant Oberan was getting what he wanted.

Azrael careened a few feet further and pressed himself to his feet. A massive fire-ax descended from twenty feet above the head of the already fifteen-foot tall Angr. Azrael dove and heard the whoosh of displaced air beside him. The blade cleaved into the ground, and a wave of fire registered on his Soul Cloak. He felt the heat blister his left side. He clenched his fist and teeth to dispel the agony that accompanied the burns. He glared at the fire giant, planted a foot and patted out a few flames that clung to his bee suit.

Each touch caused him to wince from the rawness of the skin underneath. He tried to cling to the anger at himself. Use it to ignore the wounds and motivate him to win at all costs.

Angr was charging towards him. If fire giants had one weakness, it was their abysmal Intelligence and low Ether pool. How many more skills could Angr unleash? Azrael began hobbling away, attempting to maintain some buffer, and simultaneously lure Angr into the ten foot radius for his trump card.

Angr closed, and Azrael's sweat wicked away. His burns began screaming at him as the heat ran over the raw nerve endings. His breathing grew difficult as the air started drying out his throat and lungs. He clenched his jaw and began breathing through his nose, hoping the extra few inches of travel would cool it just a little more. Soon he felt like his skin was paper and ready to combust.

He reached back and hissed, "Release ten."

The skill exploded out, and Angr roared in unison. A wave of fire shot out of the giant's mouth.

Sovereign Hell! Another skill?

Azrael's blades struck, which forced Angr's mouth to bang shut. Still, an eight-foot-high wave of fire rushed towards Azrael. It spanned thirty feet across, and he sighed in resignation. It was going to hit him.

He had one option left, and he wasn't even sure it would work. Azrael charged every ounce of Ether he had remaining into his blade. He felt his brain protest, and his legs wobbled. As a final act of defiance, he stepped forward and thrust his sword forward, releasing six charges using the form Dante's Needle.

The Ether exploded outwards in a pointed cone-like front towards the giant as he collapsed to the ground face first.

This time his head collided with hot sand, and he felt a wave of all-consuming pain begin eating away at his back. He failed. So much for the strength of a Sovereign Son.

Azrael got one last blurry view of Jophi screaming something from the gated entrance. Angr's roar continued and ushered him into darkness.

CHAPTER TWENTY-FIVE

Azrael managed to crack open an eye. It took far too much effort. His vision blurred so severely he could only see black shadows on a white background. Someone shouted, "Azrael, hang on. The healer is coming to patch you up after Angr." He scrunched his eyes as the voice caused his head to ring. "Get over here now! I don't care how much more Angr cost to purchase, Azrael was the victor. He needs healing!"

"Live. Live. Live." An unmistakable chanting from the crowd rattled around his skull.

Did I win? Or is the crowd chanting to save me? I hope I haven't left my life in the mob's hands.

He shifted in the sand infinitesimally. His body was hit by a wave of nauseating pain. It reached his brain, which wasn't ready to handle any more and turned out the lights.

***

Again, he managed to open an eyelid with effort—not as much energy as the last time, but it still wasn't easy. A feminine voice cooed, "Here, drink this."

He moaned, and she shouted excitedly, "Can you hear me? Are you awake? Drink this. The healer said you need food!" Some sort of salty liquid poured into his mouth and he sputtered. The following cough sent his body into spasms and he promptly passed out again.

***

The third time he woke up, he didn't bother opening his eyes. He could feel someone pressed to his hip. And a bone from the individual's body pressed painfully into his abdomen.

A squeaky voice whispered softly, "I know you are awake. Drink this if you have the strength. I am going to drip it into your mouth."

Drops of salty liquid touched his tongue, and he swallowed whenever they fell to the back of his throat. This continued for a time, and then the squeaky voice asked more of him, "Now it will be water. We are going to try slightly more. Here we go."

This time small splashes of blessedly cold liquid touched his tongue, and he flinched at first from the temperature change. His mouth stung all over, and he almost choked from the sensation overload, but managed a quick swallow. Once in the routine, he got more liquid into himself. After eight swallows, the voice squeaked, "Go back to sleep now. Recover, I will be here when you wake."

This pattern continued for what felt like an eternity. The world was still slightly blurry, but he could make out colors and shapes at least. The blue-skinned Bat sat beside him, Jophi paced behind Bat, and Verimy sat cross-legged in the distance.

They were still in the preparation room, and it would appear that his waking up triggered something. All people stopped and looked at the space in front of them. Then fixed their eyes on him. He saw the blue notification screen pop up and would have read it, but the letters were just white blobs to his sensitive eyes.

Azrael attempted a question, "How—out," but failed to moisten his mouth enough to do more.

Bat answered in a whisper anyway, "It has only been a few hours. They refused to crown you the victor until you survived. The fire giant would have died but the healers closed his wounds. So, it would have died first. The healers did everything they could for you but said you were suffering a burn debuff they couldn't cleanse. You had to ride it out. One of them came by occasionally to heal your skin, though. They just weren't sure if the internal damage to your lungs and organs would come around."

"Seemed like a piss poor healer to me," Jophi muttered.

Azrael started to sit up, felt lightheaded, and laid back down, head resting on a mound of sand. Well then, that was good news. He had lived through the round of sixty-four. Jophi continued, "Wow, the Etherience gain is huge! I just gained two levels from it. What multiplier is the quest talking about?"

Verimy responded, "I think it awarded us six points. Each win is a single point, but if a combatant wins two battles in a row the second battle is worth an additional point. If that same combatant wins all three battles, then the last win is worth three points. Essentially, little Azrael and his stubbornness got all of us the maximum. Look at the available equipment, too. You must be able to save points to purchase more expensive things."

Azrael didn't bother to try to comprehend what they were saying. His brain was starting to fog again. He motioned for Bat to give him more water and—broth? Bat did so, and Azrael felt himself slowly fade.

Maybe Bat is worth more than even a rook?

This time he fell into actual sleep, unlike the unconsciousness of the previous fits.

***

He woke up again to the clatter of trays and sat up in his bed, startling Louis. Louis was placing the dishes between both gates to their cell. Azrael had shot up rather abruptly to a sitting position, so held a hand up, and groaned, "Sorry, sorry. I didn't mean to startle you, Louis."

The others traded the old trays, with the plates and plastic intact, for the new trays. Louis still commented, "You know rat bones can puncture your stomach lining? Be careful. I don't want to get charged with poisoning you lot."

Azrael didn't bother answering and instead got to shaky feet and limped over to the table. He checked his Ether and health to find them both at fifty percent. That wasn't right; he should easily have been full in both by now. His eyes traced up and he checked his debuff bar.

Recovering
- **You are recovering from a near-death experience. Due to the Ether damage to your heart and lungs, your maximum Stamina and Intelligence are limited to 50% until they fully heal.**

Time remaining: 6 hours, 14 minutes.

Sovereign Hells!

Azrael had been told that this was a danger in exhausting his Ether pool while already physically injured. It would seem his teacher hadn't been making up the danger.

Combine his Ether exhaustion with the super-heated air he breathed and the burns he had suffered, and he was lucky to be alive.

He ate his meal in silence, not wanting to tax his throat and lungs too heavily.

"How come we are eating dinner up here instead of the mess hall?" Azrael croaked after he finished.

"We missed dinner when you were dying in the antechamber. We likely got special treatment for it today," Verimy answered, then scratched his chin. "I have to wonder if all combatants on the second level get breakfast and lunch delivered to their cells?"

Azrael shrugged, not seeing a need to respond. They had their meals delivered, which probably meant the others did as well. Then read the quest the others had spoken of.

Congratulations! You have completed a quest.
Arena Chain Quest
Single Elimination Tournament
Win the Round of 64
- **You have won the round of 64 with a solo combatant. This earns your team 6 points and four times the Etherience.**

Congratulations!
Rewards:
2,000,000 Etherience
Six points to spend in the Tournament Shop – Click for Access
342,312 Etherience remaining until level 18.

He was slightly disappointed that he hadn't gained two levels like Jophi had, but she was currently in the low levels of the Journeyman rank.

He clicked the shop and looked through the list. His mouth fell open. There were a few Skill Scrolls near the top. They were, of course, the most expensive to purchase, ranging from fifteen points all the way up to twenty.

Some of the skills were truly valuable too. The one for fifty points was a scroll to learn Heal. He doubted he would get enough tournament points to make it to a scroll, though. He had almost died in the round of sixty-four after all.

Next came equipment that ranged in price from one point to six points. Azrael scanned the gear, trying to determine its actual value in Crystals.

He found an Ether-Tech Helm for six points. He tilted his head and clicked on the item to enlarge it.

Halo Helm of the Martian Commando
- **Mass-produced Ether-Tech Helmets are made for the most common infantry unit in the Martian military. This Commando helm has three-hundred and sixty degrees of vision, filtering, environmental monitoring, and up to eight hours of the air source of choice for the wearer.**
    Ether Pool: Medium
    Current Ether Pool: 50/50
Enchantments: Resistance III (9% all Elements), Intelligence V (+5)

He didn't even hesitate and purchased the piece of gear on the spot. An Ether-Tech Helm with filtering capabilities was ideal. It would mitigate certain skills and likely even be able to highlight enemies in different spectrums. Like ultraviolet or infrared.

If the shop had a full set, he might just buy it. Ether-Tech was a relatively new form of equipment. It was a great combination of technological marvels and enchantments. He didn't buy into the hype that it was the best equipment possible, but it was fantastic at increasing stats in a way that opponents couldn't Analyze.

Nothing happened when he pressed the purchase button. He searched the cell. Everyone looked back at him, but he ignored them as he kept looking.

"What are you looking for?" Verimy asked.

"I just purchased the Ether-Tech Helm. I expected it to materialize nearby."

"Did you read the message on the front page of the tournament shop?" Jophi asked with a raised eyebrow. At his blank stare she continued, "All gear purchased appears in the team antechamber and can't be used in other fights. We actually were waiting to talk to you about that. Do you plan to do all the fighting on your own still – even after nearly dying?"

Verimy answered for Azrael, saving him the lie, "Azrael was always stubborn, so I am sure he does. I've suggested we all purchase gear that you can use."

"What would be in it for all of you?" Azrael asked, his breathing slowing, and his eyes narrowing.

Verimy held up a hand. "I don't plan on giving you more than these first points. Just to give you a leg up in the next round. It is entirely self-serving, Azrael. If you keep winning all the fights alone, we get more points *and* Etherience. I doubt any other team is willing to hand over gear to a single individual. That makes their Etherience gains and probability of getting six points very low."

"I will let you purchase anything you want with my points," Bat added.

Azrael, for some reason, found Verimy's response more comforting than Bat's offer. His willingness gave Azrael pause. Was Bat just trying to buy his freedom? No one did anything without motivation. Another hard-earned lesson from the Halls. Yet, wasn't the batman the one that helped tend to Azrael, or was that all a dream?

"I think it better if we each purchase something, and Azrael lets us fight," Jophi said, crossing her arms over her chest. "It's not like we can take any of this gear with us when we escape, though. So, I am willing to purchase you a piece with my points if you guarantee you won't overdo it again!"

That was a strange request—that he wasn't going to agree to. He nodded, hoping she would take his action as agreement. She did.

Verimy smirked and gave him a look that told Azrael his trainer had noticed his omission. Their eyes met and Verimy nodded again, very much like he had in the arena. A nod of respect and acknowledgement.

Azrael kept his expression flat but nodded back. He was the leader here—they would all realize it sooner or later.

He now had the helm, chest, legs, and boots waiting in the antechamber. Those four pieces completed the set from head to toe. That made it so the mechanical parts could work together to increase his speed and power. Without the boots, he had been told he would have to lug around the legs and chest with no structural support.

The helm by itself wouldn't have caused that problem. It would likely be slightly heavier than a hoverbike helm.

He read over the pieces, memorizing each of them.

Halo Chest of the Martian Commando
- **Mass-produced Ether-Tech Chest pieces are made for the most common infantry unit in the Martian military. This Commando Chest has filtering, environmental monitoring, as well as muscle and structural support.**
   Ether Pool: Medium
   Current Ether Pool: 50/50

Enchantments: Resistance III (9% all Elements), Strength V (+5)
--
Halo Leggings of the Martian Commando
- **Mass-produced Ether-Tech Leggings are made for the most common infantry unit in the Martian military. These Commando Leggings have filtering, environmental monitoring, as well as muscle and structural support.**
   Ether Pool: Medium
   Current Ether Pool: 50/50

Enchantments: Resistance III (9% all Elements), Agility V (+5)
--
Halo Boots of the Martian Commando
- **Mass-produced Ether-Tech Boots are made for the most common infantry unit in the Martian military. These Commando Boots have filtering, environmental monitoring, as well as muscle and structural support.**
   Ether Pool: Medium

Current Ether Pool: 50/50
Enchantments: Resistance III (9% all Elements),
Stamina V (+5)

Azrael rapped his knuckles on the harvest table. "Tomorrow, each of us will be placed on chores. We need to each record our tasks and our best guess for escape plans. When we return here, we will go over them one by one. Let's start compiling our options."

Jophi squinted her eyes at him, but didn't contradict his plan.

Azrael hid a smile.

They would all realize who the leader was in time.

He went to sleep after that thought. He still needed to recover from being torched alive. Unfortunately, Bat beat him to it.

How could a whip skinny creature snore so loudly?

CHAPTER TWENTY-SIX

Upon waking, Azrael moved to the washroom and took a shower. He really should have showered the previous night, but just hadn't been able to work up the energy. This morning, with the Recovery debuff gone, he felt good. He was up before anyone else, so had the shower to himself.

He turned on the shower and threw his burned and bloody clothing into the corner. Azrael then ran under the ice-cold water, getting himself wet. Standing outside the water, he lathered up and ran back into the shower. He wondered if the higher levels got showers with hot water. He missed relaxing in a scalding shower. He left the shower running. "Apep, thank you for not eating the food trays anymore."

"Why do you shake and shiver like that? Are you scared of me?" Apep asked.

Azrael chuckled then cut off. He gave the question some serious thought. Actually, he was scared of Apep, though not as much as before with the contract in place. "I'm not shaking because of my fear of you. I am currently shaking because of the glacier water from the shower."

"Glacier water? This water comes from a stream running through the dungeon. I can assure you it wasn't from a glacier."

"Sorry, turn of phrase. I meant that it is very cold water and is causing shock to my body's core temperature. My body reacts by shivering."

Steam began to rise from the floor in the shower. The temperature in the room spiked up a few degrees. Sweat broke out on Azrael's skin. "Apep, if you are controlling the water temperature, can I make a few suggestions?"

Azrael explained to Apep how showers normally worked, and the dungeon created a knob to change temperatures. The problem was that the others would question the sudden appearance of a temperature knob in the shower, as he had heard them all complain about the temperature. Together Azrael and Apep placed a small rock protruding from the corner of the shower. Once the temperature was perfect, Azrael lounged under the stream of hot water and let some of his problems melt away.

The door shook. "Is that steam? Azrael, are you in there?" Jophi's voice pierced his period of pure bliss.

Azrael whispered, "Apep, I am going to let the others take hot showers in here too. Remember, don't talk to them."

Apep had helpfully formed a set of black clothing for him and a towel to dry off. He used the towel and placed it back in the absorption corner. After a quick thought, he placed the dancing cloak and Kyron's lance in the corner as well. Dungeons could remake items they had absorbed or make others with enchantments they learned. Azrael needed to keep the dungeon core growing and have a plan B, if escape through the slave labor failed.

If the others ask about the items, I will have to tell them they are in my ring.

After the items vanished, he exited the washroom. He shared his *discovery* of the temperature stone, claiming he tripped over it. Jophi practically threw him from her path to get into the bathroom.

Louis hadn't come by with breakfast yet. So, it was still early morning.

He checked his Status page.

Azrael Sovereign Level 17
    Class: Sovereign (Revenant)
Class Skills: Soul Strike (V), Soul Cloak (V), Soul Storage (V), Bloodletter (II)
    Health Points = 270/270 Points
    Ether Pool = 160/190 Points
You have 0 stat points and 0 skill points to distribute.
    Stamina – 27
    Strength – 20
    Agility – 32
    Dexterity – 33
    Intelligence – 19 (+3)
    Wisdom – 18 (+2)
    Charisma – 16
    Luck – 12

Skills:
Analyze – Moderate 42
Butcher – Weak 21
Combatant – Moderate 49
Endurance – Moderate 33
Martial Arts – Strong 38
Obfuscate – Strong 6
Sneak – Weak 21
Swordsmanship – Greater 31
Tracking – Weak 12

He had placed four of his points during the fight with Angr the fire giant. Three into Intelligence, and one into Wisdom. He placed his newest free stat point from level seventeen into Wisdom and his free skill point to Bloodletter. The skill had probably saved his life in the previous fight.

It would be easy to say he needed more health after nearly dying in the last fight. But that was flawed logic. With higher Ether, and Ether regeneration, he would have finished off his foe sooner, with more powerful skills. This would have saved him from a great deal of damage.

Defense is for the weak, one of his teachers used to say. The woman was a barbarian who could run through walls. And had probably hit a few too hard, as well.

Louis came bobbing down the hall with breakfast. Azrael preemptively placed the trays from last night's meal in the entrance cell. Louis exchanged them and then cleared his throat, which resembled a rat squeaking. "I have been informed that I am never to serve you dinner again. Even if your injuries are severe. Torin has forbidden it."

Torin has more power than I expected. This toad grows frustrating.

Azrael took in a deep breath and let it out, as heat suffused his face. "Thank you for letting us know, Louis."

"There is a sheet on one of the trays that tells you who your next opponent in the arena will be, as well as some other information. Good luck," Louis said before walking away again.

Louis seemed much more comfortable than he had been yesterday. Maybe they could mine him for a bit of information in the future. The fact that the chef could open their cell sparked several ideas for Azrael.

Azrael approached the table. Verimy and Jophi had carried the new trays over. They were huddled close together, reading a slip of paper. He joined them and had to read over their shoulders.

Bat's singing in the shower carried through the door to the group. "All sail, there's a new Bat in town. Pups and Elders gather round…"

This afternoon, after Combatant chores, Azrael Sovereign will begin the challenges. His first fight will take place immediately against the dreaded Frost Rabbits. In the future, no chores will take place on combat days.

In three days, Azrael will fight against the Doom Wolf Pack. This fight will take place at nine in the morning.

No gear purchased from Tournament points will be allowed in the challenges.

In the afternoon on the same day, Team Sovereign Son will fight against Team Blue Blood.

All the best,
Arena Coordinator

Reading the paper generated a quest.

Dungeon Quest
    Apprentice Combatant
        First Level Survival Challenge
Frost Rabbits
- **The dungeon will pit your skills against its first level mobs, the Frost Rabbits. Defeating the first challenge will unlock the second challenge. Completing these challenges will increase your rank in the arena and offer rewards along the way. Every fifth challenge will be a mini-boss, until the 20th round, at which point you will compete against the Arena Champion spawn.**

Good luck!
Rewards:
            Etherience
            Looted reward
      Progression through Combatant Ranks

Azrael felt his head fall. This started the timer much sooner than he wanted. He would have to fight again today. Even after his near-death experience from yesterday.

"Verimy, have you started your challenges already?" Jophi asked.

Verimy shook his head and looked to Azrael. "As I said before, I was to start yesterday, but your intervention stopped those fights. The first challenge is a joke from what I have heard, and you're supposed to get longer breaks at higher ranks. But I can't tell if this is faster than normal or not, Azrael. Though it does seem that way."

Azrael sighed. He should expect to fight as often as possible. If Verimy was right, the time between bouts would increase the higher up the ranks he went. The tournament would add a layer of unknown to that. Regardless, Oberan wanted Azrael's fame to grow, and then to snuff him out. This made it a priority to learn the rules Oberan was going to play by.

He ate in silence before Bat exited the shower. Still humming his ridiculous high-pitched tune. He sat beside Azrael and whispered, "Who are you talking to in the bathroom?"

Azrael froze and looked at his blue-skinned acquaintance. He didn't seem to be anything other than curious. So, as discreetly as Azrael could, he made a shush symbol in front of his lips. Bat ducked his head by a small margin, and Azrael went back to eating.

I really need to find out more about his abilities. They could prove very useful.

Within fifteen minutes of Louis delivering breakfast, guards arrived to escort Azrael and his friends, one by one, out of the cell. Azrael was last. His guard thankfully wasn't Torin.

He was brought to the launderers complex this time.

In his group of thirty slaves, he didn't recall a single face. He also realized with discouragement that it was entirely possible for multiple facilities to exist. He and the other slaves were brought into a complex that smelled strongly of lye and chemical soaps. Then brought down to the basement, where they began sorting through dirtied linens.

Jophiel had said she was cleaning clothes at the launderers yesterday. This added an entirely new dynamic to the escape plans. Was Verimy at a skinning section within the butcher's yard? Was there a planking area for woodcutting? He felt his mood sour further because he had already considered the likelihood of getting them all onto the same work team near impossible. But to get the work duty they planned their escape around and be on the same team was statistically impossible with so many potentially varying tasks.

He sorted colors of clothes into buckets already set out. The task was so monotonous that he didn't have to pay it any mind. He studied the surroundings, trying to find escape options. A cloth bag easily the size of a small vehicle thumped to the ground loudly. The weight suggested it was stuffed full of fabrics. He read the label, "Gulliver?"

An identical bag held the buckets he was currently sorting his pile of clothes into. He read that bag, "Hansil." These must be the linens from noble houses in the city. Likely, that chute led up to a shop on the street, which servants dropped soiled and picked up laundered linens from. Theoretically, if he could climb up the chute into that shop, he had a chance to escape.

His werewolf 'friend' made him very wary of that method. If there was an enchantment halfway up, it could obliterate him in the enclosed space. The climb could also be longer than the two stories he had descended. He checked the stairs the slaves had come down. Some form of metal bolted into the concrete wall. Another set of stairs was near the chute. On the landing of both sets of stairs, two guards stood surveying the workers. Another ten guards patrolled the floor he was on. There was very little chance of escape from this basement. Azrael mentally checked it off as impossible.

He went through the rest of his tasks until lunch time. They were brought back to their cell to eat. This time it looked like Verimy *lucked* out. His trainer was bruised and bloodied, lying on the ground and breathing hard when Azrael returned. Bat was cleaning a few of the worst scrapes. "Torin?" Azrael asked.

Bat continued cleaning the wounds and nodded. Honestly, that angry toad was getting really frustrating. Jophi arrived last. Lunch had already been delivered by Louis while they were out, so the group sat down to eat.

Verimy broke the pragmatic silence, his injuries still not fully healed, which was indicated by the strain in his voice. "What did you do to that orc, anyway?"

"I didn't die in the Battle Royale like I was supposed to," Azrael replied.

Verimy laughed then groaned from the pain. "Oh, that's all?"

The silence now broken, the group chatted as they finished lunch.

"Ogma might be able to get Torin let go as a guard if I tell him about all this."

Verimy flinched. "How do you know Ogma?" Azrael jumped at the volume of Verimy's voice. Verimy modulated it. "Sorry, we all barely know each other, and I think it's time we at least know some basics."

Jophi told her story, which seemed to bother Verimy, but instead of confronting Jophi, he indignantly turned to Azrael. "You have brought a member of the Cathodiem Guild into the cell with us? All Guilds are scum and have no loyalty!"

Back to questioning my plans, huh?

Jophi shook her head, seeming to convey a world-weariness that was far too old for her young looks. In a low voice, she retorted, "And where do you come from, Verimy?"

Verimy pushed his chest out, "I was a trainer at the Sovereign Halls—"

Jophi's laughter cut him off, causing him to glare. "You question Guild loyalty but trained unwitting bastard sons of your Emperor King? Once they left your care, did you ever see them again?" At Verimy's head tilt, Jophi's eyes widened, and she looked at Azrael. "Does he not know?" She laughed louder. "You poor imbecile! Azrael, do you want to tell him the whole story—why your class reads Sovereign now, but didn't before?"

Verimy's clenched jaw and flushing face demanded an explanation. And fast. So, Azrael gave a quick summary of what he had learned when he read the letter. Verimy's face faded from red to pale white. After Azrael finished explaining that there was no Ancestral Sovereign Class and that it was all a ruse, Verimy didn't speak. He just looked to the table and shook his head, over and over again. As if he was trying to wake himself up from a bad dream.

Bat looked around as the silence started to stretch. His jaw tensed and his ears folded in half. "I was an envoy to Gertid, one of the many planets of the Sovereign Empire, when the Tuatha De Danaan attacked. Even though there was an entire battalion led by Sovereign Sons in residence, the Territory I was in stood no chance. But after hearing your tale, it is making more sense.

"The batman race lives on a planet that is nearly perpetually dark, called Nosferat. The planet has six moons that circle it and only a distant Sun God. We had been trying to join the Empire, but hadn't yet heard about the Guilds' campaign against it. Perhaps it was best that I failed the negotiations? Or maybe that was why they sent such an untrained low-level negotiator with only a token guard," Bat chirped into the silence.

Everyone's head fell after Bat's tale. Verimy continued to shake his head, and Jophi frowned, seeming to feel bad about her part in everyone's current mood.

Azrael looked at his small group and hoped they could successfully escape just as footsteps echoed down the hallway.

His guard was here to take him to the first challenge.

Chapter Twenty-Seven

A wolf leaped at his throat, and Azrael swayed back, using Praying Mantis to score deeply into its back. The blow severed the spine and the wolf crashed heavily into the ground. Its back legs were now useless.

He rotated his wrists and thrust the point of his sword at a low-lunging member of the pack's eye. It sank home and a small bit of pressure scrambled the brain of the beast. Lunging forward, he rolled over the back of gray fur to avoid two more of the pack that attempted to hamstring him.

He executed Feldman's Retreat and released a double stack of Soul Strike. Both invisible skill blades struck home with yelps of surprise and pain that echoed off the walls. Most noise absorbed into the sands, and Azrael fought against the remaining three healthy wolves. With only three to track, he dealt surgical blows, killing them easily.

Azrael exited his fighting crouch and took a deep breath. The arena barrier came down and the sounds of the crowd washed over him. "Sovereign. Sovereign. Sovereign."

He cleaned his sword on the fur of a nearby wolf and looted each corpse. Only a single item dropped.

Necklace of the Wolf Fang
- **This is a necklace made of a string of wolf hide and has a canine tooth as its pendant.**
Ether Pool: Small
Current Ether Pool: 20/20
Enchantments: Strength I (+1), Agility I (+1)

Azrael slipped the cord around his neck and walked back to the arena entrance. The cheering never stopped. He waved at the crowd and made his sword disappear mid-motion. The decibel level spiked and he exited into the antechamber with his ears buzzing. It would seem the arena wanted more showmanship, and he was sure he would hear a demand for it from Oberan.

He opened the quest notification.

Congratulations! You have completed a quest.
Dungeon Quest
>**Apprentice Combatant**
>>**Second Level Survival Challenge**

Doom Wolf Pack
- **You have completed the second challenge of the dungeon: the Doom Wolf Pack.**

Congratulations.
Rewards:
>>**100,000 Etherience**
>>**Access the Third Level Survival Quest**

The first challenge had been even easier than the second one. It had only awarded half the Etherience and no loot had dropped. The rabbits had only been level five of the apprentice rank, too.

Today, Azrael had luckily been escorted to the arena by a guard that wasn't Torin. Now that same man escorted him back. Azrael considered what his best course of action would be. He knew that the second level of the challenge had also been *easy*. But, he had seen the betting odds displayed on the jumbotron. Making it past the fifth challenge was listed at a ten percent chance.

He still had the tournament this afternoon. Oberan chose to have Azrael fight a double header every third day, from now on.

He could allow the others to fight in the tournament on his behalf. Of course, doing so had its own repercussions. Azrael needed to appear like an idiotic hero to keep his group together. To keep the escape plan, albeit a slim chance, a possibility.

In the three days of slave labor, his friends had confirmed that the highest chance of escape were the three tasks outside the gates. So many unanswerable questions still needed to be discussed. Both Jophi and Verimy had mostly accepted his leadership at this point, but there was a sticking point for each of them.

Jophi wanted to know how they would save Ogma. Verimy wanted to know how they would save Dara. And Azrael knew that some people would have to be left behind. There was no way to take everyone in an escape. Unless he brute forced it. And that was a very stupid idea.

Regardless, this all came down to his timeline. In nine days, he would face the fifth stage. In all likelihood, that would end in defeat. The crowd might save him, but counting on something that changed with ticket sales of the day was extremely distasteful to him.

The guard dropped him off in the double gates. Jophi, Bat, and Verimy stood up. He entered the room and immediately sat down, wanting to take the weight off his legs. The system would help you recover from muscle fatigue. But loading stone the previous night and then fighting this morning had taken its toll.

He looked around at his group. Each of them regarded him back. They had the day off today to fight in the tournament that afternoon. He tried to think of the best way to bring up the escape planning. Each time he had brought it up recently, the conversation devolved into bickering by Verimy or Jophi. Or both.

"We need to start planning an escape. We have about nine days before I face a boss creature in the arena. I am listed at nine to one to lose. We need to have a plan and work out the rest out as we go."

Bat's ears flicked, and he bared his sharp teeth. "Nine days?"

Verimy punched the stone wall. Jophi spoke up, "I agree, but we don't know how to get ourselves onto the same crew even. Let alone have Ogma and Dara out there with us. Thanks to Louis, we found out that Octorian, or the current Arena Champion, makes the schedule. How are we going to get him to place us on the same team?"

Azrael did have a thought on that, but it required Jophi to ask her Cathodiem guard to talk to Ogma. He worried that she might not do that, as it would risk her family's spy.

She looked around. "Does anyone have an alternative idea for escape?"

"There are many unused tunnels all around—and below us. With my sonar, I found an enchanted vent in our team's waiting room—we could likely use it to access the lower levels and attempt an escape. Unfortunately, we would need to know how to disenchant the bars, and I think the area below belongs exclusively to the dungeon, as well. I couldn't sense any guards down there."

Azrael leaned back and narrowed his eyes. "Why haven't you said anything before, Bat?"

"I am pretty sure the floors below are filled with monsters. I see them coming up the stairs at the end of the air vent," Bat responded.

Azrael blinked and looked at the others, finding their looks of shocked surprise directed at Bat as well. It would seem everyone was starting to notice the value in the batman. He smiled at Bat and quipped, "That is certainly a good option. Can you investigate further this afternoon during our match?"

Bat nodded simply, but Jophi spoke up, "Can we save Ogma? He knows enchanting!"

Verimy growled at her and spat, "Ogma? Ogma is a member of the Tuatha De Danaan. He is not even at risk. Let's save Dara, she also can enchant!"

This was Azrael's cue that the conversation was mostly over. Perhaps he could find an escape option that didn't require anyone's help. Dara and Ogma were likely kept in the upper tiers of the complex. How these two couldn't understand that infuriated Azrael. And yet both of them had begun treating *him* as a child. They both needed to come to terms with leaving their friends behind. Maybe in time they could come back and try to liberate them, but to do that they had to escape first!

Jophi was red in the face and opened her mouth to respond.

Azrael stood up and slammed his fist on the harvest table. The crack of the wood startled everyone. "We have no chance of rescuing those two. Stop bickering. Our only option is escaping and coming back for them. To have any chance of saving the others, we must first save ourselves. We will need to come back to find a ship off this rock anyway. I am going to go shower and calm down."

Everyone went silent and Azrael walked into the bathroom. He needed to speak with his dungeon core. The shower was just an excuse. He closed the door and turned on the shower.

"Apep, could you hear what we were saying outside?" he asked.

Apep stated, "Yes, I heard. Do you speak of escape through the hypogeum? I would not suggest it. I used mine to keep all of my creatures. It is part of our system instructions to do so. You would essentially have to battle through every creature this dungeon can spawn."

Azrael dunked his head under the hot water. "It's currently our best plan. Do you have a better idea?"

Apep didn't respond, and Azrael stood under the tap, letting his muscles soak in the heat. He jumped and banged his head on the nozzle when Apep whispered in his ear, "I could tap more of the Pit's veins. With enough power, I could dig a way out, while also seizing control of some of the Pit's body."

Azrael rubbed his head, trying to change the pain to a different sensation. "Didn't you say that was dangerous to do the first time? Do you think you can do more without getting caught?"

"Something is severely wrong with this dungeon. It should be fighting me for the space I have seized, but it hasn't even seemed to notice. I think I can steal more from it without worry."

Azrael shrugged. "Go for it when we are out fighting this afternoon, then." This way they wouldn't be caught up in the collapse if something went wrong.

***

Torin held Azrael at the end of its polearm noose. A wad of spit landed on the wall beside Azrael and he rolled his eyes. That was at least the tenth attempt. Soul Cloak wasn't going to let any projectile mucus land on him. The toad was clearly as stupid as it looked.

Torin growled at its latest failure. Then tried another tactic. "You and your team dan't have long now! Other groups are allowed ta watch the competition, but you lot are all dolled up on the second level. Alone."

Torin dropped Azrael into the antechamber and removed the noose. "Good luck. I've got some bets to place."

Azrael spun and glared after the orc as his friends were led into the antechamber one by one. Jophi was already inside and studying the Ether-Tech gear when Azrael was deposited.

Of course, Torin chose to drop that bombshell just before the fight.

"They know your fighting style, Azrael. If one of us takes the armor and gear, we will be just as capable of winning three fights in a row," Verimy said.

If they did that, Oberan would take it as Azrael breaking their *contract*. "Verimy, try to help Bat if you can. More options for escape are better than pinning everything on one."

Azrael didn't believe for a heartbeat that facing a fire giant in the first round was *random*. He had to wonder if he was about to walk into a death match. He put on the new armor to hide his nerves. It was a massive gamble no matter how he played this. He slid the helmet over his head. "Bat, try to find a way into the hypogeum. I will slow the fight and try to buy you time."

Jophi looked at Verimy and then Bat before realizing that they too hadn't understood the word Azrael used. Azrael's face got hot under the helmet and he closed his eyes.

That was a slip-up. Do better.

"What is a hypogeum?" Jophi asked.

Azrael didn't even bother trying to make something up and instead boldfaced his way through it. "My apologies. A slip of the tongue. Bat, just try to find a way into the floor below this. Jophi, you stay near him too, perhaps together you can all plan a destructive way to gain access."

Jophi looked like she wanted to pursue her initial question, but Azrael entered the smaller double gated entrance. The timer began and it saved him from her further inquiries. The gate behind him thudded into place and a trumpet assaulted his ears.

Through his Ether-Tech helmet? The animalistic horn blared for a whole ten seconds according to the timer.

What in the Sovereign Halls was that?

He looked behind him to see Bat shaking uncontrollably. Verimy stared wide-eyed, and Jophi knelt with hands over ears. It would seem the helmet had even filtered the decibels of the horn. But it had still been terrifyingly loud.

Azrael swallowed hard and got to his feet. If that was his opponent, he was in trouble. The arena shook, and he fell back to the floor but quickly sprang back up. What could cause the entire dungeon to rock—just how big was his next opponent?

He was slick from sweat when the timer reached zero. He stepped out of the entrance and watched a silhouette opposite him exit to face him. The silhouette, while large for a humanoid, wasn't large enough to have shaken the arena. If that was his opponent—what had made the noise? A grunt and rumble turned his head slowly to the right. Caged by a gigantic square forcefield in the arena wall was a nightmare.

The creature's skin was black, crisscrossed with red scars. Its ears were shredded skin flaps, and its tusks seemed to have holes drilled into them. The eyes of the creature bore down on the arena, red and pulsing menace with each blink. The beast rose onto its back legs and dropped its powerful front hooves onto the forcefield that separated it from the sands. The chain around its neck clanged taut and the sands quaked. Not as severely as the last rumble, though.

Is that an elephant? Could it have caused the arena to shake?

He sighed and jerked his head back to check on his opponent.

His opponent had been frozen as well, and Azrael took the opportunity to charge forward. There was no use hiding his skills now. The other teams likely already knew all about them.

His opponent was a Draugr, which was troubling. All of his teachings dictated destroying Draugr with numerical advantages. Not one on one.

Draugr were large humanoids that stood upwards of eight-feet tall. Their blue skin and awkward gait often had people compare them to shambling undead, but they were far more terrifying than a walking corpse. Draugr underwent a ritual at birth to sever all nerves in their body that conveyed pain signals. The nerve severing was likely the reason for their abnormal movement, but the benefits outweighed the consequences. If you asked them, at least.

The Draugr that faced him wore massive plate armor and shouldered a dual-headed battle-ax.

Azrael used Analyze.

Ragdulf Ironhead
Journeyman-Mountain
Level 33
Health Points: 1100/1100

Theoretically, the high health points likely meant Ragdulf was slow and tanky. However, the fire giant had possessed high stats across the board, and Azrael wasn't sure what average starting stats would be for a Draugr. He recalled a teacher mentioning it once, but the exact lesson escaped him.

He chopped down in Headman's Fall and connected with the armored shoulder of Ragdulf. Azrael's sword sent a reverberation through his hands and arms. The mechanical nature of his new armor added massive power to the downswing. The sword cut deeply, then clanged and bounced back out of the wound. The sword squirmed out of his hands and vibrated through the air down to the sand.

He leaped back as the Draugr stopped staring at the elephant. Ragdulf roared while swinging the ax one-handed. It bit into the sand mere inches from Azrael's fallen sword. Ragdulf was already injured in one arm and couldn't pick up the weapon but noticed its advantage immediately. It entered a defensive stance while straddling the sword between its feet.

Azrael considered his options. If his hands couldn't withstand the added strength his new equipment seemed to place on them, then martial arts were out as he would only end up with broken fists.

He disengaged with two backward leaps, knowing he needed to draw Ragdulf off of the weapon. Ragdulf didn't follow, and Azrael realized the rumors of Draugr stupidity were unfounded.

He began circling, trying to think of other options. Azrael could always try to throw sand and pick up the sword or release a stored skill. A notification interrupted his planning.

Timer to Musth
- **Your inaction for a minute in this fight has triggered the countdown on Musth's release.**

Finish the match in 5 minutes, or the Arena Boss will go on a rampage.
Time remaining: 4 minutes, 58 seconds.

Azrael's eyes tracked over to the elephant.
Hello, Musth.

Chapter Twenty-Eight

Azrael roared. What did the tortured elephant have to do with this fight? Would all tournament battles have this feature, or just his? Musth was probably one of the boss creatures from the Pit.

The red eyes of Musth created an oppressive thickness to the air. He knew instantly that if that monstrosity was released, he would die. He shook himself like a wet dog. Mentally commanding himself to ignore the pressure of the timer. The Draugr was beatable—he had to focus there.

Alright, a five stacked stored Soul Strike then. The skill would at least get the Draugr to move. He stepped forward into a palm strike. Ragdulf reacted, its ax descending. Azrael dug his toes into the sand to perform a stop. Spun, shuffled, and lunged forward with the opposite leg and palm, whispering, "Release five."

The skill exploded from his palm and began to expand. The Draugr brought its feet together and then rolled forward, Azrael's sword rolled with it, caught between its heels. Azrael snatched at his weapon but missed because of an upward chop of his opponent's ax.

He followed Ragdulf's roll, sliding over the sand with a shuffling sprint. As soon as Ragdulf gained its feet, Azrael attempted to knock it down. He shot his palms into the Mountain's chest. They hit the armor and a bell dinged loudly over the sand. The ringing elicited an ear-shattering trumpet by Musth, and Azrael flew backwards, his own strike rebounding into him.

He landed on his butt and turned his motion into a backward roll. Coming back to his feet to find his opponent still standing above his sword. Was Ragdulf not worried about Musth? Something was off in this fight. If that nightmare was let out, they would both die. But Azrael's opponent had just ignored an opportunity.

Oberan is up to something.

He wanted to spit but his helm enclosed his entire head. Instead, he checked Ragdulf's health and found it was at nine-hundred and eighty, which was where it sat before this last strike.

That rebound skill had transferred all damage back on Azrael. His health had dropped ten points, even with his Ether-Tech armor.

He roared again and tried to think. If he wanted to hit the Draugr, he needed to get close and attempt a blow with his trump card. But that reflect skill complicated that tactic. If his trump card reflected against him, he would die instantly.

Was there another option?

His only truly offensive skill was Soul Strike, and he had just tried using it at five stacks from his Soul Storage. He wondered why Ragdulf hadn't reflected his initial Soul Strike? With the distance that had been between them Azrael likely would have dodged as well, he supposed. Maybe the reflection was the Draugr trump card or could only reflect non-skilled strikes?

Too risky to gamble on, right now.

Ragdulf had easily dodged the blow from range, though. With the Draugr's higher level, it would continue to dodge most ranged skills. If Azrael closed and used his Soul Strike, it could possibly be reflected—killing him instantly. He roared his frustration into his helmet's interior. He had two ranged skills left. Fireball and Soul Storage—wait. He revisited martial striking as an option. He recalled his martial arts mentor cutting through thin paper with his palm. Could he charge a Soul Strike into his hand?

Azrael envisioned the edge of his palm as a blade. He had never successfully managed to cut through paper like his mentor Bee could. He had broken many boards and bricks. He pictured the edge of his palm sharp like a sword and charged it with his Soul Strike.

The Ether infused, and he did the same with his other palm. "This might actually work," Azrael whispered as he moved his hands through the air.

He struck using the Shuto Uchi method, in a martial style called Balanced Top. The first blow was rebounded by the Draugr's skill. This was why Azrael had chosen Balanced Top. He lifted his front foot and allowed the strike to spin him. Halfway through the dizzying move, he planted that front foot again and switched his planted leg. The spin continued on the new leg. Effectively moving Azrael away and reducing the rebounded damage. Blood flew from his hand onto the sand, though, telling him his strategy was only partially effective at dumping the rebounded skill's damage.

His opponent's ax cut through the air, just missing him as he spun away. Seeing the strike miss, Azrael dragged his raised foot to dump the momentum. And waded back into battle.

The spinning was his best option to dump rebounded strikes. Azrael just hoped that the Ether from his skill infusing his hands would help protect them enough to keep them functioning.

This was a duel of Ether pools, now. Azrael gambled on his being higher, due to the high health of Ragdulf.

Again and again, he struck, and Ragdulf began to reflect random strikes, attempting to catch Azrael off guard. None of Azrael's Shuto Uchi strikes budged the eight-foot-tall massive Draugr, but they began to tear his skin and armor apart. Azrael checked his Ether pool and found it to be falling from fifty percent.

I have lost all feeling in my hands too.

He ignored that tidbit with force of will and Analyzed Ragdulf. The Draugr's health ticked down from five hundred. He blinked. He hadn't hit his opponent, so why was its health dropping?

Azrael disengaged, trying to understand what was causing Ragdulf's health to decline so rapidly. Azrael noticed the puddle of blue blood on the ground and the massive rivers of more that continued to flow.

Right! Azrael's Bloodletter skill was stacking.

Four hundred health remaining.

Azrael waded back in, wanting to ensure that any debuffs for bleeding that fell off the Draugr got replaced with a new one. He checked the timer. Just over a minute left before Musth would be released.

One of his strikes staggered Ragdulf, which allowed Azrael to pick up his sword. Or attempt to. His hand refused to close onto the hilt. He forced his hand to obey and cried out when it creaked around his sword hilt. He forced worry about his hands to the back of his mind.

I will deal with it later.

Azrael's Ether was only thirty percent, and he dismissed his Soul Strike skills to regain approximately thirteen percent of his Ether. He began striking lightly with his blade. Attempting to stack more bleed debuffs and not jar his unprotected hands more. The armor's damage assisted him as he layered cut after cut on Ragdulf.

The timer counted down, and just as it reached twenty seconds, Ragdulf fell to the ground motionless in a puddle of its own blood.

Healers rushed onto the sands as the domed protective enchantment fell. "Death. Death. Death," the crowd chanted. And the countdown timer vanished.

I left it up to the crowd. I wasn't supposed to do that.

The crowd cheered louder when the jumbotron flashed "Death" in oscillating rainbow-colored strobe lights. Azrael felt sick to his stomach.

The healers let the final health points of his opponent vanish. He wondered if he was supposed to have decapitated the Draugr for sport. He surveyed the crowd as he looted the corpse, placing its gear into his ring. He would drop the gear in the antechamber for the others to study. The crowd didn't seem upset with the lack of showmanship.

Best to keep them on your side from now on. Either kill your opponent outright or give them a spectacle at the end.

His shoulders slumped but he built up the resolve to look at his hands. He almost threw up. There was practically no skin visible under the blood. He took in a deep stuttering breath. He had a grip of his sword and he could move his fingers. That was good news. Likely he sustained multiple fractures but no breaks. His muscles still worked as well. That was something at least.

He received a notification to return to his starting zone. Azrael made a slight detour and Analyzed Musth.

Musth
Epic-Raging Bull Mammoth
Level 71
Health Points: 23000/26000
Boss

Correction, that is the final boss of this place!

The crowd continued to cheer, and the announcer broadcast the intermission. He entered the waiting area.

"Show me your hands!" Jophi practically screamed at him.

Azrael ignored her. He wasn't sure he could close them onto the sword again if he let go. Instead he turned to Verimy, "Do you have any bandages or cloth to wrap my hands?"

"You imbecile," Jophi shouted, holding up a roll of white linen.

He looked at her. She probably couldn't see his face behind the helmet, but he scrutinized her severely. He still wasn't sure if she was an ally, but they had come too far together. "Fine. But I need the sword wrapped in my hands. Can you do that?"

Jophi clenched her jaw and her eyes began to water. *Were those tears for me?* He let her do the wrapping while still watching her. "Bat, any luck with the air vent?"

Verimy looked backwards at a seated Bat. "He has been meditating since we arrived. I think he is using his ability to look deeper into the tunnels."

Azrael nodded. They could discuss it later at dinner in that case.

Time for the next round. Jophi finished wrapping his hands and he checked his Ether pool. It was above fifty percent, which meant he could recharge his Soul Storage. But that would start the next round with a near empty pool.

He decided quickly that his Soul Storage was too useful. He recharged it with a five stacked Soul Strike. Then sat down. The others left him alone, knowing that this was increasing his Ether regeneration. He began to meditate and even picked up the Meditation skill. Meditation was a skill that was taught at the Sovereign Halls, which also made the skill acquisition and levels go faster now.

I probably should put some time into increasing its level, if I can find some.

He stood back up when the timer reached ten seconds and moved through the door, this time consciously thinking about how to moderate his striking strength so as to not lose his sword. Or further damage his hands.

It turned out that he needn't have worried. The next two rounds were against fast-moving, leather armor wearing fighters.

Azrael, with Ether-Tech gear, easily kept up with them despite both being Journeyman rank. His sword strikes, with the added penetration, parted their armor with little effort.

Azrael made short work of them both and never triggered Musth's timer. He used showmanship whenever possible, ensuring that the kills were bloody. That they were spectacular.

Each time the protective dome came down, the crowd chanted, "Sovereign! Sovereign! Sovereign!" and Azrael raised his sword. Oberan was getting exactly what he wanted from him. But Azrael also needed the crowd on his side.

Just in case…

He only hoped Bat had gathered enough information during these short contests.

He dismissed his sword. And the others helped him remove his equipment at the behest of the guards. The gear was left in one of the lockers for the room. He checked his quest as the guard collared him. His hands were rewrapped in fresh bandages in front of him. He hoped there wouldn't be any permanent damage and his debuff bar seemed to confirm the lack of it.

Congratulations! You have completed a quest.
Arena Chain Quest
　　　　Single Elimination Tournament
Win the Round of 32
- **You have won the round of 32 with a solo combatant. This earns your team 6 points and 4 times the Etherience.**
　　Congratulations!
Rewards:
　　　　　　4,000,000 Etherience
Six points to spend in the Tournament Shop – Click for Access
5,797,712 Etherience remaining to level 20.

Azrael purchased the gloves for the Ether-Tech set as he walked back towards the stairs. With the full set, they likely had a real chance to win this tournament—if he lived that long.

After reviewing his most recent battle, he was convinced no other team would share points like his did. So, that full set was a huge advantage. At most, another fighter would have two strong pieces or many weaker ones. Still, his timeline to escape needed to stay based on the arena challenges, because he couldn't wear this gear in them.

He started to turn off on the second level and was jerked back onto the stairs to continue upward. His brow furrowed. He glanced back to see his group collared and also marching up to the higher level. Where were they being taken?

Any noise would get them disciplined; even though Torin wasn't in this group of guards, they were still vicious if combatants began to converse outside of the cells, the mess hall, or the arena waiting rooms.

Azrael climbed past the third level and was led into a posh meeting room on the fourth. His noose was removed, under the eyes of Gyr and Yonel. The two powerful guards caused him to swallow hard as he took a seat. The others followed, huddling near him at the end of the table.

Bat turned his head in every direction, probably trying to hear sounds from every angle. To get a better 'look' at the room. Jophi looked at Azrael, and Verimy stared at the table in front of him. Azrael looked at his bound and bandaged hands and chose to hide them under the table.

Ogma and Dara came into the room from a different entrance. Azrael, Jophi, and especially Verimy perked up. Verimy opened his mouth, ready to speak until Oberan followed closely after them. His trainer's mouth snapped shut with an audible click.

Dara and Ogma both sat, and neither wanted to meet the eyes of the group. Could Dara have broken? Seeing her now, it made sense, but why wouldn't she meet Verimy's eyes?

Oberan sat down and smiled. "It's great to see everyone." His tone carried such thick sarcasm, Azrael felt he could pull out his sword and cut it. Oberan looked around the people sitting at the table and chuckled before leaning forward and growing severe. "I will give freedom to the person who tells me what happened to the cell block you resided in."

Oberan looked around. Azrael's mouth had fallen open. He was genuinely shocked at first. But quickly remembered

Apep. He attempted to hold that initial expression and emotion, doing his best to act the part. Apep must have failed to tap the veins and been destroyed by the Pit. That didn't bode well for the backup plan, but Azrael was confident he was the only one who knew about the dungeon core. So he held his look of confusion as the surprise of the accusation came down.

Oberan sneered. "The dungeon claims that there was a disruption in the power flow through that area. However, I find it extremely suspicious that it happened in your cell block and when you were all conveniently out of the cell. I want to know how you all accomplished it, and I want to know now!"

There was something in his voice this time that went beyond authoritative. Was Oberan worried about something? Azrael began putting pieces together in his head. The Pit didn't know what had happened, or wouldn't tell Oberan the truth. Did the Tuathan leader have full control of the arena?

Azrael ventured, "How would we know more than the dungeon? I have read that dungeons reorganize their interiors all the time—" He cut off from the glare Oberan bestowed on him. Azrael knew when speaking more would undo what little he had just gained and stayed silent. Oberan transferred that glare from person to person. Did he linger longer on Jophi; on Verimy? He barely glanced at Bat, that was for certain, dismissing the blue-skinned, long-eared batman as inconsequential.

Little does he know that the batman is so useful.

They were all escorted from the room after a few more minutes of awkward silence and locked in individual cells on the third floor. To Azrael's surprise, their group now included Ogma and Dara. Those two were in cells that looked lived in. Azrael was left to conclude that this had been their place of *residence* for a while.

He entered the double gate mechanism of his new cell and studied the bars. These weren't the cheap wood fixtures of the second floor. No, these cells each appeared to be carved from a single piece of wood. The enchantment runes were artistically added, creating spirals and loops so beautiful Azrael felt he was in an apartment more opulent than his quarters in the Sovereign Halls.

On the flip side of the beauty was the sheer power he could feel coming off of the bars. This floor definitely had added security as it put his group closer to Oberan. Was he trying to keep an eye on them? Nothing he could do about it, either way.

The bed frame in the cell seemed to grow out of the ground, and the interior had memory nanobot gel. A glance told him the washroom looked like an elven treehouse, with living tree branches providing water faucets and the floor so perfectly elegant Azrael couldn't decide if it reminded him of an artist's walking cane or a luxury carved yacht.

Verimy and Dara were across the hall and had immediately begun talking through the use of their hand gestures that Azrael had never fully mastered. Still, from what little he knew, love got conveyed as well as anger and disdain on both sides—typical lovers?

Jophi and Ogma spoke openly, and Azrael tuned in to Ogma, mid-sentence, "—did the Cathodiem Guild respond? No, Jophiel, they have ignored every missive I've sent. Your father is absent from every news article out of Atlantis. I can't tell if they are making a move or if he is still at court."

Jophi's mouth formed a small smile, and she looked at Azrael, before mouthing, "My father is coming."

That seems like a bit of a stretch.

CHAPTER TWENTY-NINE

"Ogma, do you think you can talk to Octorian? Convince him that having groups on a single task everyday will be more efficient?" Azrael asked, after deciding to be open with their plans of escape.

Ogma might betray them, but without the help of the Firbolg Tuatha De Danaan Guild member, they would fail, regardless. It had taken Azrael listening to Jophi and Ogma talking for an hour before coming to the risky decision to include him. Dinner in the mess hall would be very soon, and if he could get Octorian to adjust their tasks, they could begin planning.

Ogma looked to Azrael, then Verimy, Dara, and Jophi. "Jophiel, is this child the leader?" he asked.

Dara glared at Verimy and made some hand gestures that conveyed her own outrage with that point. Azrael shook his head. Here it goes again...

To his surprise, Jophi smiled and shrugged sheepishly. "Despite my original misgivings, he has proven to be quite apt."

Verimy indicated Jophi with an open palmed gesture to Dara. "I agree with Jophiel. Dara, Azrael has proven he should lead."

Well, that's a surprise.

Ogma nodded to himself a few times. "What task specifically do you think has the best chance of a successful escape?" Ogma asked. Azrael hadn't yet mentioned an escape. The man was quick to see through what was left unsaid.

"Hypothetically, woodcutting and stone gathering. They are never in the same area, so no permanent deterrents have been set up," Azrael responded, not bothering to hide the current consensus.

"We should just wait for my father to arrive. I am sure I can convince him to take everyone out of this place," Jophi interjected.

"Jophiel, honey, don't be a fool. You have no idea if your father is en route to Tech Duinn. I have failed to provide you with any political protection at all. Oberan treats me like a prisoner. If you can escape, then you should," Ogma stated. His voice dripped with world weariness.

Maybe she will listen to Ogma, at least.

"Are you two taken out for slave labor, fights, or anything? Or do you just sit up here in these cells?" Azrael asked Dara and Ogma.

"Dara and I are honored guests. I am allowed out to eat dinner and watch fights," Ogma said.

"I have been eating with Oberan on the fourth floor every night," Dara added.

Verimy stood up, face red and fists balled. "You what? Why?"

"Honestly, he has many women at his table. None of them speak. It is a very depressing affair. I think he is lonely, and the others are prisoners as well. But I truly can't say. Haven't seen any of them outside of that room," Dara responded.

The two began speaking in angry hand motions, turning the conversation private in a way Azrael envied. "Enough! Guards will escort us to dinner soon. Do you think you can convince Octorian or not?" he asked.

Ogma shrugged. "I have never spoken to the man. I will test the waters tonight."

***

Azrael, Verimy, and Bat sat together at a table on the first level. Was it Azrael's imagination or were they getting a great deal more stares? Had something changed?

Jophiel and Dara were both escorted from the cells by Gyr. Azrael assumed it was to join Oberan at his *dinner* on the fourth floor. He disliked being split up, but from his first read of the man, Azrael assumed Oberan was into other men. Perhaps he didn't have a preference? More likely the large gathering of women at dinner was a bit of a show. Azrael wasn't worried for the two ladies, because he was pretty confident in his initial read.

Azrael watched Ogma at the head table and he didn't see him talk to Octorian once. Rather, Ogma spoke to others. Which was a huge improvement from his sullen disinterest of previous meals. Was he playing the slow game? Azrael couldn't afford the time that would waste. He only had nine days.

Azrael checked his character sheet while he ate quietly. He had dropped his two skill points into Bloodletter but still had to place his stats.

Azrael Sovereign Level 19
> **Class: Sovereign (Revenant)**

Class Skills: Soul Strike (V), Soul Cloak (V), Soul Storage (V), Bloodletter (IV)
> **Health Points = 270/270 Points**
> **Ether Pool = 190/190 Points**

You have 2 stat points and 0 skill points to distribute.
> **Stamina – 27**
> **Strength – 21**
> **Agility – 35**
> **Dexterity – 35**
> **Intelligence – 19**
> **Wisdom – 18**
> **Charisma – 16**
> **Luck – 12**

Skills:
Analyze – Strong 4
Butcher – Weak 21
Combatant – Strong 31
Endurance – Strong 12
Martial Arts – Strong 44
Meditation – Weak 12
Obfuscate – Strong 12
Sneak – Weak 22
Stone Cutting – Weak 18
Swordsmanship – Greater 43
Tracking – Weak 12

Octorian stared into his plate. At past meals, Octorian would be charismatic and bold at the head table. Tonight, he was disconnected. Azrael glanced up the top table for a hint at why the elf was checked out. Each Arena Champion who sat at the table had defeated the tenth challenge, a Treant mini-boss. Octorian was the only one to have challenged the fifteenth, some kind of massive horse creature. The Goblorc to Octorian's left was the next highest and had failed to complete the fourteenth challenge. The mob saved his life and he was working his way up the challenges again.

The Goblorc was tall and muscled like an elf. It had pointed ears and teeth but carried with it a beauty that the orc race and the Goblin race failed to have on their own. Goblorc's were that perfect combination between the two, bringing an Elven appearance to two races that many people found terrifying. Regardless, the body language of this particular Goblorc seemed strange. Today, he was acting the way Octorian often did. False benevolence dripped from his gesturing arms and half smiles. He acted like he was the current champion.

Octorian looked up and his mouth twisted into a sneer. Then he went back to eating sullenly. Something was strange, and Azrael couldn't place it. Ogma carried on conversations with anyone who would listen, but Octorian continued to ignore everything around him right up until the end of the meal.

***

Azrael's luck finally ran out and the toad noosed him onto the end of a polearm. He waited for torture, waited for Torin to slam him into walls, the floor, or to attempt to humiliate him. Instead, Azrael was directed calmly to a cellblock at the back of an orderly line of arena initiates. He wondered if the angry orc was going to lock him up in a cell and pretend to have misplaced him. Instead, he was directed to the center of the room.

"Is that the *Sovereign Son?*" one of the initiates yelled from a second story cell.

"The initiate who traded his name for a spot on the second or third floor?"

"The Katydid that pretends to be better than the rest of us. Oberan's little pet?"

The stares at dinner began to make sense, as the insults continued to fly. The rage built and pieces of broken beds were lobbed at him and Torin. The toad knocked the poorly-aimed projectiles out of the air with its hands, and Azrael's Soul Cloak effectively stopped any from hitting him. However, the sentiment carried through.

Torin brought Azrael to ten other blocks on the first floor and *showed* him the general feelings towards him and his group. Did Torin expect the insults about Azrael's parentage, his looks, and his morals to hurt him?

There is no shame in living at any cost. That's the first lesson of the Sovereign Halls. Does this warty toad fail to understand that?

On the way back up to the cells, Torin added its customary physical torture to the mental one it had attempted. Azrael barely felt the pain this time. If the moron was stooping to mental attacks and name calling, then the toad was already desperate.

He wouldn't be broken by such a weak creature. He watched his health drop below one hundred and spat out a mouthful of blood from his severely ravaged lips. He wouldn't lose this way.

Dara, Jophiel, Verimy, Ogma, and Bat were already in their cells when Azrael was dropped into his. His health points and hamburger skin told the story for everyone.

"What happened to him?" Ogma asked, clearly unfamiliar with such treatment.

"That orc guard has taken it into his head to torture Azrael and our group whenever he can. I think Azrael told us that the guard bet against him in the Battle Royale and still holds a grudge. Luckily, he holds himself back from severe injuries, only stacking minor wounds in his torture," Jophi responded, her voice worried.

A growl escaped someone, and its depth and bass made Azrael think it was Ogma. He couldn't sit up right now to check, though. "Give me a sign you can hear me, Azrael," Ogma said, the growl cutting off and confirming its origin.

Azrael raised an arm and forced a thumbs up on his heavily-skinned hand.

"All right. I promise to try to make someone aware of this guard if I can. Still, we must discuss Octorian and my attempts tonight," Ogma continued after Azrael's confirmation.

"Octorian will face the Enbarr again tomorrow. No one, not even himself, expects a victory. After being saved by the crowd eight times, many of the other champions think his luck has run out. This was the reason for his somber attitude and distance tonight. I did manage to get all the champions to reminisce about their days doing slave labor and how inefficient it was to do varying tasks. Whether Octorian heard that conversation is anyone's guess. Frag the Goblorc is technically next to the position if Octorian dies tomorrow. I can only promise to try again," Ogma intoned.

Azrael let his frustration and weariness with that answer pull him into unconsciousness and slept right there on the cold stone floor.

CHAPTER THIRTY

The following day, Azrael woke covered in sweat. He shouldn't have spent the night on the cold floor, especially after the abuse Torin had put him through. He took a shower to avoid getting any unsavory debuffs. There were some bad debuffs out there, that took quite a while to dissipate even with the system's help.

He was even more disappointed to see the damage and blood on his clothes. He didn't have Apep anymore to provide new garments. He wondered if there was a way to transfer Torin's dislike from him and his group. His current clothes were practically rags again, and he had fed all of his backups to the dead dungeon core.

After his shower, he dressed in his dirty rags again and promised to find an opportunity to stock back up on gear. Louis happily brought breakfast to each individual cell, actually handing the trays off of a cart to each occupant. Somewhere along the way, his fear of Azrael had vanished. "You've done pretty well out there, lad. Are you excited to watch the Arena Champion versus the Enbarr tonight?"

Azrael stepped back—a single eyebrow raised. "What do you mean, Louis? Do the combatants get to watch this contest?"

"Tradition is to allow everyone to watch the Champion's fights. Your group should be included this time. Who knows though?" Louis said as he handed Azrael his tray of food. To his surprise, it was overflowing with much more food than he had expected. He gave the gnome a questioning look and got a smile in return.

I will take any benefit I can get!

"I have been brought to watch every fight in the arena," Ogma stated as he looked around at the others. "I don't think combatants get to watch every fight. Mostly because of the labor crews, but you should have been taken to see the other Initiate tournament bouts if nothing else. You weren't?"

Azrael shook his head. "Our *best friend* Torin told us that the other teams are watching our fights, but that we won't be brought down."

"That doesn't sound like Oberan at all," Dara stated in her motherly way. "He always brags about the fairness of his competition at his dinners. I am not saying he isn't a horrible, greedy man. But he truly believes he is fair in his own way."

Azrael felt his heart stutter—another unknown out to get him?

"What's the name of the team you're fighting in the round of sixteen?" Ogma asked in between bites of breakfast.

Arena Chain Quest
Single Elimination Tournament
Win the Round of 16
- **The dungeon created a competition for new combatants. Win the round of 16 to gain benefits and concessions from the arena. The better the score during the contest, the higher the rewards!**
Sovereign Son VS. Plotz
Rewards:
Etherience
Points to buy Class-Appropriate Gear
Failure:
May result in death

Verimy supplied the name to Ogma as Azrael read over the quest. Ogma tapped his chin in response. "I think I remember them. They have lost two fights so far, but won both matches. One of their combatants was killed by crowd decision after their loss. The second combatant was saved.

"The one that was saved is a werewolf assassin. His combat is terrifying to watch. He has some sort of teleport or shadow step ability. The other fighter I saw was a templar. He used his fist blades in efficient martial forms. The fourth and final combatant we haven't seen yet. My guess would be he is the strongest of the group. At least based on what I have seen of the escalation of their fights."

Azrael took that in. At least he knew what he would be facing. He looked around at his group and considered if they were any closer to an escape. No, they weren't. If he saw an opportunity to get out of here, he needed to take it. At least they would still have the gear for the tournament if they left through the team room and the tunnels Bat found.

The guards came shortly after, and Azrael was escorted back to the stone gathering yard. Bat and he had already been here and together had theorized a few escape options. Azrael reassessed it now, looking for anything they might have missed. The task was simple from a mental standpoint. But absurdly challenging physically.

Using a pickaxe, they were to break off a stone from the nearby crag. Carry it over to a station, and with a mallet and chisel, chip it square. Once square, it was loaded onto a transport truck and taken to be finished by laser cutting somewhere in the city. Bat had been horrible at breaking rocks from the wall, according to the batman. But had been very skilled at chipping the block square thanks to his ability to *see* cracks and minute details in the stone.

Both Bat and Azrael had concluded that the group could force their way out by defeating the guards. The vast majority of the guards were near the transports, with few ranging at the edges of the compound. Azrael noticed something new in his current appraisal.

On the shift change, the guards escorting the group Azrael's replaced allowed them to ride on the transport. Was that just a lazy group of guards? Bat would have notified Azrael if he had been allowed to ride the transport back. Even blind, he couldn't have missed being loaded onto the hover vehicle for a ride. Azrael hadn't received a ride back on his last shift, that was certain. Maybe the truck was full—so the opportunity existed?

Azrael scanned the load of the truck as it floated away. His goal for today was to test out if the transport would give his group a ride back if the truck was full. He worked at a feverish pace that day, loading what felt like half the transport by himself. Still, at the end of the shift the truck was as full as the one before.

No group came to replace Azrael's. Likely because of the fight that afternoon. They were all chained together again when one of the guards said, "Wow, this group filled this truck. Guess we don't have to walk back either!"

Another guard, some sort of Lizardfolk, blinked and his mouth broke into a huge smile. "What luck! When the lassst group took a full load, I thought we had misssed the ride back by a ssshift. Thisss group mussst have worked hard."

Azrael stepped onto the transport and studied the interior. His two guards were joined by two others in the back. Two more loaded into the front seats to drive. There was a door from the truck bed to the cab. This could work. He had seven obstacles, with a variable twenty-nine. How would the other slaves respond?

The seven obstacles, not including the other slaves, were the six guards and his enchanted handcuffs. Six Master ranked fighters versus a single Apprentice were horrible odds. Add in the variable of the other slaves and his restraints and he would die, even with his sword. Could he sneak the Ether-Tech gear out in his ring?

Maybe.

Having his group with him would skew the odds towards his favor much more. He just needed to convince Octorian to place Dara, Verimy, Jophi, and Bat with him in this task. If Octorian survived today, they would have to come up with multiple arguments for Ogma to use.

***

Azrael peered through a grated slit at sand level into the arena pit. A fight between a massive white Liger and a combatant was currently underway. Unfortunately, he had missed what challenge level this was. The levels of the combatant were clear, but the skill was severely lacking.

He could already predict the ending of the fight. The combatant was managing to damage the Liger with very powerful and showy Class Skills. Unfortunately, he didn't have a sound strategy. He Analyzed both again.

Liger
Journeyman-White Claw
Level 44
Health Points: 1215/1540

--

Jack Fan
Master-Master Mage

Level 15
Health Points: 450/450

Jack's low health points, combined with his class, likely meant he had high Intelligence and Wisdom. Still, the massive ice spikes, fireballs, lightning storms, and other skills were failing to damage the Liger enough. Azrael predicted that the current stalemate would end shortly when Jack was forced to conserve Ether.

Azrael shook his head; Jack chose to go big instead of conserving Ether. He summoned some sort of Area of Effect spell that pulled the Liger to the ground, almost sticking it in place. A swirling black cloud began coalescing on top of the downed white beast. Red embers flashed inside through the dark smoke and a roar sounded from within. Jack held both spells, his hands outstretched in front of him as his jaw clenched and sweat broke out on his skin. A slow count of ten seconds and Jack fell to a knee. Ether exhaustion.

The smoke cleared to reveal nothing where the cat had been. Jack's face sported a small smile, right before a sooty black monstrosity flashed into sight behind him. Claws raked his back as the paw holding those claws batted Jack like he was a ball of yarn. His broken body bounced over the sand, careening to a stop in a tangled jumble of blood and rags.

Guards with bloodied slabs of meat approached the entrance gate and the Liger went to lie down in front of it. Silence stretched for a heartbeat, but then the force field fell, and the crowd's noise roared into the space. "Live. Kill. Live. Live."

Something Azrael couldn't see happened, and a mixture of jeering and polite applause echoed across the sand. "Jack Fan lives to fight another day. The healers are heading out to his mangled remains now. This is his first time failing at the ninth challenge, and we will see this Master Combatant again in four days, starting back from the first challenge. A brief intermission before the main event! Hurry back to your seats though, because you won't want to miss the Enbarr and Octorian!" the arena announcer boomed out of speakers.

Azrael turned away from the grate. He had never noticed the sand height grates when he was fighting in the arena. Perhaps it was his focus or the enchanted shield that sprung to life around them once combat began. From the way other combatants began talking, watching fights was common enough. Why this was his first time he wasn't sure, but he had a suspicion. In fact, he recalled Verimy had watched his Battle Royale.

"Verimy, were you allowed to watch fights before I arrived?" he asked.

Verimy nodded. "Well, I was brought to your Battle Royale and saw people watching mine. I think they try to schedule important fights when all slaves can watch. We haven't been to another Battle Royale or any other fight, though. It's extra odd that other teams are being allowed to watch you in the tournament, but we aren't being allowed to watch them. Someone is preventing our team from watching fights..."

One of the other combatants turned towards Verimy. "The fact that your team is a group of people who knew each other outside the Pit is complete centaur poop. All the other teams were randomly selected, and not a single team pooled points from wins. Oberan has clearly rigged this tournament for an easy victory for you!"

Azrael shivered—he had considered that an advantage for his team—but was it a concession? He Analyzed the adlet who had spoken.

Rex Woofer
Apprentice-Pit Fighter
Level 22
Health Points: 140/140

An adlet was often mistaken for a beastkin. Their dog-like appearance made others assume that they were one of the tribes. adlets were far older than the moon folk though, and originated on a small Planetary God called Pluto. Rex was white-furred on his snout and his chest. The white merged into a brownish-black as it approached his eyes and his back. The eyes were an intense blue and conveyed a disdain for Verimy and Azrael.

"We didn't choose our team either, Rex," Azrael commented, meeting the adlet's icy glare.

"You're still far better off than the teams who choose the order through combat in their antechamber. Many of the teams initially placed their weakest combatant first, and never even sent out their strongest. That fire giant you fought lost to the fourth member of its team, and you barely survived. So, don't go complaining about the advantages other teams are given to even out the rigged Initiate Tournament. Everyone knows Oberan favors you."

Verimy turned to Azrael and subtly shook his head, conveying that this conversation wasn't worth it. This solidified the hatred from other combatants in the mess hall. When people have nothing, it was very easy to pick out someone in the same situation with a minor benefit and pin hatred on them. Azrael agreed with Verimy, but telling Rex that he was being set up to have a glorious death wouldn't gain him any sympathy. Death still awaited every slave in here.

Just because Oberan had a purpose for his death didn't make him special. Rex continued to glare at Azrael, though, so he retorted, "What exactly makes you think extra work duty is a favor?"

Verimy's head dropped and Rex's face morphed into a wolf grin. "Torin told us your whole team is allowed the use of cells reserved for Champions. You're delivered food for breakfast and lunch, but you are all Initiate Combatants. Even if you win this tournament and advance to Combatant, you should only be moved to the second level," Rex spoke loudly, which drew the attention of the other combatants sharing their viewing port.

Angry muttering broke out and Rex raised his furry arms to emphasize the discontent. "You have been handed everything, Sovereign Son. But you falsely think that because you are a slave like us, that you are one of us." The combatants began grouping up into a buzzing mob. "I think we should exact some revenge right here—boys?"

"Behind us as well, Azrael," Bat whispered into his ear. The batman had remained silent the entire time but warned him of the smaller group at their backs.

Verimy entered into a ready posture and came to stand shoulder to shoulder, facing the opposite direction towards the group Bat had indicated. Azrael pulled out his sword from his Ring of Holding. With a grin on his face, he barked a laugh. "All right! I was just thinking I needed some extra Etherience. Rex, would you like to go first? You are the instigator, after all. Why don't you lead your fellow Initiates into battle? I will show you why I am given the quarters of a champion!" Azrael infused his words with as much disdain and confidence as he could.

The mob quieted and looked to Rex. The pup deflated and even took a step back, and just like that the tension broke. The larger group on Rex's side muttered to themselves and moved back to the viewing grates. Azrael turned to the other group. "I think you guys had a better view than us. I think we would like to have it. Move!" he commanded.

They didn't have a better view, but they did have a much safer area of the small room. Azrael was now acutely aware that they were essentially in the middle of the viewing room. He vowed to never allow such a strategically disadvantageous situation to occur again. He felt his heart pounding against his sternum and tried to hide the shake in his hands. They were lucky bluster had worked to dissuade the mob. Azrael was sure he could have killed them with his Soul Strike and Soul Storage skills, but in tight confines with his own allies nearby? Those skills were essentially sealed. It would have proven difficult to fight and keep Bat and Verimy out of the line of fire. Fighting without the skills, Azrael would have killed a few of them he was sure, but they likely would have overwhelmed and killed his group in turn.

This had almost turned into a disaster, all because he had wanted to try to find some more information. Definitely no point in looking for help from any other combatants was his conclusion.

Never rely on the help from others.

The announcer called, "Take your seats for the main event!"

Thirty seconds later, Octorian strode out onto the sand. Azrael studied his gear. He wasn't bare-chested anymore, and instead wore a suit of studded leather armor, a Pteruges skirt of leather, gloves, bracers, and even leather sandals. He almost appeared to be themed, all of his armor chosen partly because of how it looked together, rather than for strength.

"I stand before you yet again to face the terrible Enbarr! Is the equine nightmare invincible? Today I will prove to you that together, you and I can beat a creature of any strength!" Octorian shouted to the crowd.

The stands erupted with noise. Most of it was raucous cheering but mixed in were some jeers and catcalls. "You have failed eight times… today is your last… your blood will stain the sands…"

Azrael cataloged the interaction as a charismatic appeal to the crowd for their support. The sounds of the masses were silenced by an echoing whinny. A horse the size of a transport truck slowly rose into the cage that Musth had occupied during Azrael's last tournament battle.

Enbarr
Master-Flowing Mane
Level 88
Health Points: 11500/11500

The horse was large, but it was the long mane of hair that drew Azrael's eyes. It seemed to slither and move as if it were a pile of snakes. Groupings and strands of the hair moved in all directions, coiling and whipping about.

The protective dome enchantment sprung up and muffled all noises from inside the arena. Azrael took a quick glance around and found all the combatants in his cage glued to the bars. "Warn me if anyone gets closer," he whispered to Bat.

A fight between two Master ranks was fast enough that any distraction could mean you missed something. Octorian began to glow. Subtle but noticeable as an outline of brighter yellow surrounded him. He spun his gladius in his hand, and it split in two. He brought the two together in a clash of sparks just as the cage released the Enbarr.

The horse shot forward, running a foot above the ground. At first, Azrael thought it was running on the air but then realized it was just moving so fast that he couldn't see its hooves hit the sand. The spray of the sand behind it assured Azrael that the creature was touching down though. All of its mane reared up like a cobra ready to strike as the distance closed.

Octorian stowed his swords and moved his hands in seals. Azrael tried to discern what skill was being used but couldn't see anything except the continued glow around the man. A single stride of the horse later and a massive glyph formed in front of Octorian. It hung suspended for a split second before the Enbarr crashed into an invisible wall. The whole arena vibrated, and the creature's hair attempted to strike at a foe that wasn't there.

Where the coiled mane hit, the air seemed to crack. Spider web fractures appeared and highlighted the invisible wall, which was moving forward. A mound of sand built in front of it and because of that effect Azrael noticed three other walls closing in on the Enbarr. It was a box of some sort. Was Octorian attempting to crush the Enbarr, like a garbage truck?

Octorian shook from the effort and the sun glinted off a clear sheen of sweat that broke out on his skin. Azrael tilted his head; if the hair had cracked the rectangle already, the chance of this construct holding the Enbarr wasn't good. Wait—where had the cracks gone?

The spider web cracks had vanished, which meant that this spell could repair itself. That gave Octorian a small hope. But Azrael would never have gambled in such a way. Octorian's trembling intensified as the invisible box-pressed in on the Enbarr. The black hair of the horse had formed five pillars and fought back. The hooves of the Enbarr sunk into the sand. A knee collapsed. Maybe Octorian could—the entire mane of hair joined together and formed a huge battering ram, which punched forward.

Two things happened in near unison. The invisible wall in front of the horse and nearest Octorian exploded. But the other four walls crashed down, pinning the Enbarr to the sand. Azrael followed the massive mane as it lashed out at the gladiator. Octorian made some hand motions as he ducked and dodged the strikes from the beast. He clapped his hands together and placed his palms on the ground. The arena lit up with a glowing glyph that formed on the sand, centered on the man's touch.

He pulled out his swords again and waded forward, deflecting blows from the mane of hair as he walked. The gladiator's skill with the swords was phenomenal. Azrael would rank him near a Swordmaster. The mane split into smaller sections and began striking faster. Still, Octorian waded forward, almost arrogantly approaching his trapped foe.

"Is he going to be able to damage it?" one of the slaves in Azrael's nook exclaimed.

"What was his last record? He got it to ninety percent health, right? At least he has already beat that number and reduced its health to eighty-five percent. But he has no chance of winning," another slave replied, his voice filled with a tone that turned Azrael's stomach.

Azrael glanced over to find the owner of the voice. A whip-thin fae sneered out between the bars, its mouth forming a delighted smile.

Azrael turned back to the fight. Octorian parried each strike from the Enbarr and continued to close the distance. Ten feet. The strikes were coming faster than Azrael could track but Octorian had no problem. Perhaps he was at the level of a true Swordmaster after all.

Once in melee range, the glow around Octorian pulsed, growing brighter until it eclipsed the sunlight and forced Azrael to look away. He blinked spots out of his eyes and turned back, trying to figure out what had happened. The golden glow was fading, but in its place a fiery blue shimmer was growing. Octorian stepped back slowly from the burning body on the ground. Had the Champion won?

The fire stood up and through the enchantment, a muffled, angry whinny sounded. Azrael Analyzed the blue flickering flames.

Enbarr
Master-Flowing Mane
Level 88
Health Points: 3750/11500
Boss

In one strike, Octorian had dealt more than fifty percent damage to the creature's health. The airborne sand settled, and the view resolved itself. Octorian was stumbling away from the Enbarr. The four-sided box that trapped it moments ago was gone, and the Enbarr was on fire all across its body. The mane was a bright blue, which ebbed and flared in the wind, like the hottest of fires.

In a blink, the hair and hooves of the horse lashed out and Octorian vanished from view. The crater that formed sprayed more sand into the air, but the Enbarr kept stomping down. Its mane kept flinging strands like a thousand whips. Octorian never had a chance.

After ten long seconds, the Enbarr calmed down, moving to the elevator and the enchanted dome fell. "Octorian lies broken at the feet of the Enbarr. The legendary horse that has never lost. Today, the champion enraged the beast and was utterly destroyed for his folly. We apologize to the crowd, but there was no saving him today!" the announcer added.

The mob seemed to draw in a collective breath. Then it exploded in jubilation. Azrael assumed that they had never seen the Enbarr pushed that far. The bloodthirsty didn't care about the death of the champion. They were ecstatic to see something new...

Azrael's lungs screamed at him and he let out a breath he didn't know he was holding. His heart stuttered and his stomach flipped. This was why he wouldn't leave his fate up to the crowd!

CHAPTER THIRTY-ONE

Bat, Jophiel, Verimy, and Azrael were all assigned to the stone gathering crew the next day. Azrael wondered if this was a permanent change to the work crews or if this was pure happenstance. If this was luck, they might have their highest chance of success right now. Of course, if Frag, the new Arena Champion, was making permanent changes...

Well, then they had time to plan. Azrael wasn't normally in the business of hoping—but with all the lobbying that Ogma was doing and Octorian's death? He had to believe this was not chance.

After the fight yesterday, dinner had been a very subdued affair in the mess hall. Frag practically bounced in his seat. "I'm the new champion! That windbag finally went all out against the Enbarr. He must have been feeling the pressure from the rumors and the crowd's displeasure," the Goblorc crowed.

Azrael couldn't speak to the rest of the room's dejected state, but he couldn't stop thinking about what a deathtrap this place was. The strongest combatant couldn't even face the third mini-boss. How could anyone hope to defeat Musth?

The truck was already half full today and so the group spread out and worked sedately. He extricated a chunk of stone with distracted swings from his pickaxe. When he placed it on the table to shape, he overheard the nearby guards talking. "Do you think Frag will have what it takes to get to the Enbarr? Octorian was the closest I have ever seen or heard of. He had it below fifty percent!"

"I think everyone just wants to see Musth fight! I would even accept it getting released during the tournament! That's pretty much the most we're ever going to see of it," his fellow guard responded.

"I heard it was the pet of a top member of the Tuatha De Danaan, and it was getting too unruly to control! Can you imagine controlling a creature that powerful!"

Their patrol took them out of hearing range after that. That little nugget of conversation gave Azrael an additional backup plan. It wasn't for an escape, but it may get the crowd further onto his side if he was ever in danger.

***

"Frag is making the work crews more efficient. From now on, you will all be placed on the same job. Frag can't reassign Dara, as she is a *maid* for Oberan. There is an unofficial ranking of the duties. It seems that the stone crew is by far the most hated, which made it easy to convince Frag to place you all there. Seems most of the other combatants don't like you. Dara, as a guest of Oberan, can't do the 'harder' tasks," Ogma confirmed Azrael's suspicions from earlier this morning.

"We need to find a way!" Verimy exploded from his seat. They were all eating lunch in their cells on the third floor. "Would bad behavior relegate her status? Can we change the opinion towards the stone crew?"

Azrael shook his head. He had always found it odd that two trainers from the Sovereign Hall were so close. The students were taught to never count on anyone else, to see people for the value they added, or took away. Here was the reason. Irrational thoughts that led to stupid actions. He wouldn't let himself do the same.

"Sweets, you must escape and then come back for us. There is no other way," Dara attempted to soothe Verimy. They quickly broke into hand gestures to continue the discussion privately.

He couldn't speak for anyone else, but Azrael would likely leave everyone behind if it meant escaping. Last night's fight had highlighted just how screwed they all were. Piercing blue eyes met his. He shook his head. Why was he staring at Jophiel?

He felt his cheeks heat up and spoke to cover his confusion. "What do you guys think of trying to take a transport truck? It is easy to control the pace of the work to ensure it is full at the end of the shift. This has worked twice now to get a ride back. Once onboard, there are only six guards with us."

"What about the other twenty-six slaves?" Bat asked.

"If the team is the same going forward, we could recruit them to our side," Jophiel suggested.

Azrael considered that as he chewed. Verimy just stared at him, his look oscillating between dismay and a paternal pride that made Azrael uncomfortable. Once he swallowed, he responded, "With the reaction we evoke in the others, I doubt it. Even if we can convince them, we can't pull them in fully. It is far too risky. One may turn us in to gain favor with Oberan. I think the best bet is to try to befriend them a small amount. Since they are also on stone gathering, they must be hated as well. This way they won't go against us when the time comes. But don't tell them a thing about the plan."

"How do you plan to get out of the enchanted restraints?" Ogma asked, his voice dripping with humor.

Azrael hadn't thought that far ahead, but gave Ogma a weary stare to show he didn't care for his tone. Dara and Verimy rejoined the others only to further disrupt the planning. "How do we plan to come back?" Verimy interjected, skipping the whole section where they had to escape first.

Azrael glared at his former trainer. "They sell tickets to the events, don't they? I am sure we can use that to gain access back into the Pit. Still, we have to escape first, so let's focus on that…"

Verimy flushed and went silent. Azrael hoped he would stay like that for the rest of the discussion. "We don't have a lot of time left. Ogma, based on your tone, I assume you have a way to neutralize the restraints?"

"Yes, but it takes some practice. You essentially have to learn enchanting, so you can disenchant the runes. We can work on it starting now. How many people know meditation?"

All but Bat's hand went up. "All right, everyone else get into a meditative state and I will give Bat a crash course."

Azrael sat down and began meditating. He cleared his muddled thoughts and immediately felt his shoulders relax as his breathing calmed. He had practiced meditation for his entire life, and had missed using it for its calming effects deeply this last week. For the first time in days, he felt like himself again. He calmly analyzed the current escape plan and acknowledged its few flaws. Without emotions, he could see a few other sticking points. Where was the best place to go with the transport? Could they dump the stones to be more efficient? Would the other slaves follow his group's orders once extricated?

Ogma interrupted his musings. "All right! Within your meditation, I need you to feel inside yourself. Find your Ether pool."

Azrael sunk deeper into himself and did as requested; he had learned to do this at the Sovereign Halls. The pool rippled as it expanded and contracted, lapping against an invisible shore. Almost like his stomach lining was sand that held the pool in place.

"Bat, the pool is usually below your heart, in the area of most races' stomachs. The heart is actually the primary filter for external Ether. It converts the external to internal and allows you to use it. Found it? Good. Next, try to mentally grab an edge of the shore. Picture it like sand on a beach. Right now, you have a hole dug in the sand filled with water. Begin digging a path in the sand away from the pool."

Taking a deep breath, Azrael attempted what Ogma suggested and felt his Ether pool stretch in the direction he indicated with his mind. In shock, he stopped concentrating and felt the pool snap back.

"Make sure you keep holding that picture in your mind. I want you all to dig a path to the palm of your left hand," Ogma continued before waiting a moment. Azrael's face began to sweat but just as he neared his palm, Ogma gave further direction. "Now round it in the palm and return the path to your pool. *Do not* merge the streams you have created!"

Azrael had been about to do that and felt his breathing quicken at the tone in Ogma's voice. It suggested that connecting the pathways wouldn't end well. He wondered what would happen but heard someone scream and collapse a moment after the errant consideration.

"Dara, you are okay. It only rebounded into your pool. You will have a headache, but when you are ready, try again. Good, Bat, let's let the others catch up," Ogma instructed.

Once Azrael connected the river to his pool, he felt a pull and then Ether flew down the first path and back, creating a loop.

Congratulations! You have learned a new skill.
Ether Channels

- **This skill allows you to increase the regeneration of Ether in your body.**
  - **Weak – Increases your Ether regeneration by 1% per level.**

Each rank of this skill will increase Etherience awarded due to increased filtering capacity by 0.1% per level.

Current Rank: Weak level 1.
--
Congratulations! You have learned a new skill. Internal Ether Manipulation.
- **This skill will allow you to form spells faster based off of your skill level.**
  - **Weak – Increases casting speed by 0.5% per level.**

Current Rank: Weak level 1.

Azrael dropped his meditation and looked at Ogma. Those two skills were insane. Anyone could learn them? Why hadn't the Sovereign Hall taught him about them? Would they have taught him after his eighth birthday? No, Dara and Verimy were learning them right now too.

He narrowed his eyes at Ogma. The Firbolg smiled and shrugged, "It is best to know these two to become enchanters. You can become an enchanter without it, but it is not as effective. Also, these are just the low levels of both of these skills. The real secret and power come much later. Now, get back to it, we are going to create a few more paths."

Soon Azrael had five, one to each limb and one through his head. He couldn't believe how good it felt. Almost like he had only been breathing through pursed lips and finally discovered how to open his mouth and take a deep breath. His whole body tingled and from a few glances at others' faces, they all felt the same.

That was when the guards arrived to take them to their next shift at the stone yard. Ogma nodded to himself before sitting down. "Good, after dinner tonight we will do some more work."

***

After dinner, Azrael excitedly entered his cell and immediately entered meditation in preparation. There were deeper secrets to these new techniques, and he wanted to find them!

Ogma laughed when he saw Azrael sit down as if in preparation for a riveting lesson. "Let's let everyone else get into meditation. For now, Azrael, just try to adjust the pathways you already have. Send more or less Ether along them to cycle back to your pool, things like that."

He followed the instruction and soon was able to speed up or slow down the amount. His pool swirled almost like it was a whirlpool. The pattern mesmerized him. If he got the speed of the channels right, it promoted the spin. It required his two arm channels moving at full speed, and varying adjustments on his legs and head. Still, the swirling pool of Ether didn't seem to gain him any benefits.

He opened his eyes and saw Ogma regarding him. His eyebrow raised. The others were all meditating. What had happened to the lesson?

Ogma shook himself and coughed. "Sorry, I got distracted. Next is to create smaller channels that branch off of the large ones. Think about it like arteries and capillaries. Wait!" Azrael had started branching off his streams near his pool and assumed the shouted exclamation by Ogma was directed at him. "Consider where you want Ether to congregate more heavily. You already have a pool in the center of your body, so no need to create vast networks there just yet. Start with the channels in your hands. Create a thin strand for each finger."

Under Ogma's directions, they had small branching streams in all of their extremities. Azrael thought it had been a quick process but checked his interface clock and realized it had taken a large amount of time. As soon as he opened his eyes, a wave of exhaustion crashed over him. He found the others asleep on their beds and looked around. Ogma was regarding him. He held a finger to his lips and made a pillow symbol with his hands. It was time for sleep.

Azrael laid down in his bed. Tomorrow he had to fight the third Arena Challenge and Team Plotz.

CHAPTER THIRTY-TWO

Azrael watched his opponent hop towards him. The third challenge—was a warren of rabbits? He looked at the quest again.

Dungeon Quest
      Apprentice Combatant
            Third Level Survival Challenge
Basher Colony
The dungeon will pit your skills against its third level mobs, the Bashers. Defeating the third challenge will unlock the fourth challenge. Completing these challenges will increase your rank in the arena and offer rewards along the way. Every fifth challenge will be a mini-boss, until the 20th round, at which point you will compete against the Arena Boss spawn.
Good luck!
Rewards:
                  Etherience
                  Looted reward
           Progression through Combat Ranks

The rabbits had a shining white, flat protrusion on their foreheads. It was oval in pattern and surrounded by brown fur. Instantly, he could tell that it was bone meant to batter opponents. Each rabbit came up to his knee in height but had powerful enough legs to clear heights higher than his head. Their strength, combined with the sheer number of them, was going to make this fight difficult. Getting hit could easily break a bone or, if a vital area was struck, cause severe damage. The dozen bunnies were already spreading out and surrounding his position. Azrael jogged back and put his back to the wall. Dealing with them in one hundred and eighty degrees would be hard enough.

Activating Soul Cloak, Azrael prepared by dropping into Wind's Etching. His sword wouldn't have time to stop spinning after the first attack. He charged his blade next, trying to determine how many stacks would be ideal. Some quick math landed him on three stacks. With his current Ether pool and regeneration, that should last for a minimum of ten opponents. The first bunny bounded at him from the direct front and he batted it out of the air. His blade turned the creature into a bloody mess that his swinging sword flung away. He continued the motion of the slash and turned both thumbs down, attempting to conserve most of the momentum in the weapon.

His wrists rotated and he brought the hilt above his head to swat at another rabbit that was already airborne on his right. The power of the blow pounded the corpse of that rabbit into the sand, cratering the surface as more red blood sprayed. At the bottom of his swing, he absorbed some momentum into his knees and levered his right elbow into his chest, turning the rest of the force into a cross body slash again. He pushed off with the toes of his back foot and rotated on his front heel to turn his body. This sent another bunny corpse into the rounded wall behind him. He drew the blade close to his body and continued to spin.

He stepped with his front foot, stretching his groin muscles, and snapped his arms back out, slowing the rotation and striking another rabbit a few feet from him. He pushed into the opening that strike created, making a small step and then a leap to the right of his original position. He tucked into a roll over the sand and his Soul Cloak told him that three Bashers had barely missed him. He regained his feet and restarted his spinning sword. Five down—seven to go.

The fight continued to go his way until he killed his tenth critter and lost track of the final two beasties. His Soul Cloak screamed at him.

Great, I know where they are, at least.

He arched his back, trying to avoid the one careening at his floating ribs. The second one was unavoidable and crunched into his knee. He heard the impact and felt the limb buckle in a direction he knew it shouldn't. The momentum of the Basher that had just broken his knee stopped, and Azrael took a hand off of his sword to reach down and pin it to the sand using the scruff at the back of its neck. He rolled on top of it, grunting as his knee protested in pain. The Basher began bucking and attempting to escape just as he skewered it with the point of his sword.

The one that had aimed for his ribs jumped off of the wall, directly toward his head. He rolled farther and barely avoided having his head caved in. Then he held out a hand and whispered, "Release five!" The final Basher was obliterated in a cloud of sand and blood. Azrael unsheathed his sword from the bunny corpse and looked at his crooked knee. He sneered—this next part was going to hurt.

He took a deep breath and put his sword hilt between his teeth, then gripped both sides of his mangled right knee. On his exhale, he jerked it back into place and screamed against his gag. His broken bone debuff morphed into a red highlighted joint.

Tendon Damage
- **Your tendons were never meant to bend that way. Minus 50% Agility and Dexterity until the end of the debuff.**

Time remaining: 2 hours, 59 minutes.

That was going to be cutting it very close to his next combat. Maybe eating would help speed up recovery, though he doubted it. He limped to each corpse or patch of fur that remained of his opponents and looted them. He received one item.

Lucky Rabbit's Foot
- **This foot will grant the carrier no luck whatsoever. It is simply a grisly trophy that reminds you of your barbarism. Why are you still holding it?**

Azrael threw the item to the sand in disgust. At least he had finished the quest, but if he was struggling this badly on the third challenge, he doubted he could live past the fifth. This made it even more important to follow through with his plan to win the crowd over, just in case.

Congratulations! You have completed a quest.
Dungeon Quest
> **Apprentice Combatant**
>> **Third Level Survival Challenge**

Basher Colony

You have completed the third challenge of the dungeon: the Basher Colony.
Congratulations.
Rewards:

400,000 Etherience
Access the Fourth Level Survival Quest

He limped into the antechamber and the announcer began preparing the crowd for the next fight. Instead of taking Azrael back upstairs, the guard just moved him to the team waiting room. He informed him that food would be delivered. Which meant everyone got gruel and not Louis' deliciously prepared foods.

Azrael ate it and equipped his full suit of armor. He considered the group's next move as the timer slowly ticked down on his injured tendons. They had six days left, and then he would face the first mini-boss. He had been told that most champions failed at least a single time on each boss as they climbed the ranks, and the crowd didn't actually save all the champions who failed to complete a stage.

Ogma had assured him that the crowd was on his side. Oberan's plan to publicize him was a double-edged sword in some ways. If Azrael stayed and kept fighting, he may in time become the most popular champion within the Pit. On the other hand, all final decisions could be overruled by Oberan, as the Arena Moderator. He likely wouldn't turn Azrael into a martyr but he still shivered—he truly didn't enjoy feeling as though his life was being entirely controlled by others.

His team arrived at the waiting room when he had forty minutes left on his tendon damage debuff. That likely meant that he would have to fight the first combatant with highly diminished Dexterity and Agility. If he hadn't had the Ether-Tech suit, he wouldn't have considered it.

"How did your fight go? Ogma couldn't recall what the challenge was. Now that you fought it, what was the third challenge?" Jophi asked as she came in and sat down near him.

Azrael had the Ether-Tech helmet sitting on the bench next to him. He picked it up and stood with it under his arm. "It was a Basher Colony. Bunch of rabbits with battering rams for heads. Twelve of them. I really wish Ogma would have told me more. Regardless, at least he could tell me a bit about Plotz."

Why does my stomach flutter now? Does this next fight worry me that much? I still have the armor's advantage, after all.

Azrael moved to the double gated entrance to the sands. The werewolf assassin would likely be first, if Ogma's information proved accurate. He didn't like the idea of fighting a speed-based fighter with his injury, but giving the gear to someone else and having them fight still created problems he wasn't ready to deal with. His agreement with Oberan was quite possibly the reason he would escape. Then again, all of his backup plans until now had failed. He really hated pinning all of his hopes on hijacking a transport truck filled with cut stone.

At least his plan today should give him a higher chance of having the crowd on his side.

"Az, do you have a plan for this first opponent? Assassins are dangerous when they are hidden. If you survive the first strike and can force them out into the open, their risk is usually mitigated," Verimy suggested from his crossed-arm lean.

That was common knowledge and Azrael didn't need to be told, but he nodded to placate his former trainer. He glanced up at his debuff bar again—still thirty minutes remained. The five-minute timer for the beginning of the match popped onto his interface and he swallowed. Guess he would have to face these opponents injured.

Is it even worth it? Oberan may not even care if I let one of the others fight.

He shook his head, and placed on the helmet to hide the sweat that began to bead on his scalp and neck. He went over his plan again and shuddered. He was certain the mob mentality of the crowd would appreciate it. The only question was—

The timer cut off and went red. What had just happened?

Azrael shifted his attention back to the drawling announcer.

"Team Plotz has forfeited the match. The group got into a fight inside of their own team room. All of them are severely injured and we even have the footage to show the crowd. Enjoy this unplanned spectacle!"

The gate behind Azrael opened and the grinding sound of stone on stone sounded simultaneously. The sound was echoed over the entire arena as well as inside his team's antechamber. A viewing screen was revealed behind the stone wall inside and an image flickered to life, showing three men.

"You saw his last fight. He was only missing the gauntlets. He probably completed the Ether-Tech set already!" a werewolf covered in black cloth spat into the room. "I refuse to go first!" It finished by drawing two silver daggers from the folds of its fabric. The werewolf crouched low and bared its fangs at the other two.

"I agree. We should meet their strength with our strength!" a blue-skinned creature concurred. The creature had a smooth, beautiful face but didn't appear to have a mouth. The features made the creature look mystical. Strapped to each wrist was a gleaming silver short sword, which left the creature's hands free. Its glowing blue eyes stared at the third member. It shifted its steel-clad feet minutely, setting itself into a better position to respond to battle.

The final member in the room was sitting down. It cracked its long neck and slowly stood. Then hissed through a fanged mouth at the other two, "Don't you remember the resssultsss of lassst time?" A book and a gavel appeared in the green-scaled hands of the snake-like man.

"Together?" the werewolf asked.

The templar didn't respond but lunged at the snake. The camera did a pretty poor job of capturing the intricacies of the combat, but Azrael could tell that the snake creature had the upper hand. If the two other members hadn't attacked together, they both would have been defeated soundly. The others in Azrael's team room looked to him a few times throughout the contest.

This is only going to make the rumors of the rigged tournament worse.

Finally, Jophi spoke, "This means they will likely change the rules for the next contest."

Azrael replayed the beginning of the altercation. The werewolf had mentioned his Ether-Tech gear. He clicked his cheek and pursed his lips as he considered. This definitely meant they would adjust the tournament.

Congratulations! You have completed a quest.
Arena Chain Quest
      Single Elimination Tournament
Win the Round of 16
- You have won the round of 16 with a 'solo' combatant. This earns your team 6 points and 4 times the Etherience.

      Congratulations!
Rewards:
                8,000,000 Etherience
Six points to spend in the Tournament Shop – Click for Access
10,504,912 Etherience remaining until level 21.
--
Congratulations, you have gained a new level. Level 20!

CHAPTER THIRTY-THREE

It was crunch time. They had five days to plan and execute their escape. Otherwise, Azrael would risk his death. His backup plans had all failed and he was left with this single option to pin his hopes on.

He felt his hand twitch as his nerves sent a shiver of sensation into his toes, starting from his neck. Azrael hated feeling desperate. Still, it was unfortunately the only plan for escape left after his near constant failures. He used a physical action to dispel some of his own stress and shook his body like a dog.

He desperately tried to think of some other plan but failed there as well. What other option did he have? They still had the hypogeum, but that was suicide. Or as close to it as he knew. There was a better chance out in the wilderness of Tech Duinn that they might lose their pursuers or defeat them. Down under the arena floor, they would encounter the Treant, the Enbarr, and Musth. Not to mention the Wendigo from his upcoming fifth challenge.

"Do you think they check the rooms after we leave, to ensure we left the purchased gear behind?" Azrael whispered as he pretended to blow on a spoon filled with green soup. He took the bite right after and savored the flavors. It was pea soup, with some sort of white meat inside. He would guess pork based on the texture and salty flavor.

Verimy met his eye and made an unmistakable nod with his lips pressed tight together. Of course they would check the team rooms. It was going to be really hard to leave the Ether-Tech gear behind, though. They could really use it during the escape.

He dipped his spoon again and jolted, causing a wave in his bowl that almost exited the container. "Wait. How many points do you two have right now?" he whispered again using the same tactic of placing the spoon and his hand in front of his mouth.

"We have been discussing it quite a bit. We each have twelve points and need to figure out what to get you for the next contest. I have a feeling that the other teams will be allowed to pool their points from now on. Or, at the very least, something is expected to change," Bat squeaked into the conversation.

Azrael nodded and smiled. That meant Jophi also had twelve points. Maybe they could buy a second set of gear to leave in the room and fool the guards. Was there a ledger that told the guards exactly what they had purchased?

He nodded and continued eating in the silence. The group had decided to talk about their escape plans only at dinner from now on. The camera being placed in Team Plotz' room made them all acutely aware that they were likely being watched.

It was plausible that their only saving grace so far was due to the fact that no one had studied the tapes of whatever had been recorded. If every area was under surveillance, his guess was that video was monitored but not audio. Still, in a large open room like the dining hall, they could talk with very little chance of audio being picked up. Other than from nearby combatants.

That put the hypogeum even farther behind in his estimations of a successful escape. How would they be able to escape a monitored room? Had security already noted Bat's meditation near the grate?

***

Azrael slept fitfully that night, waking up repeatedly in cold sweats. Each time he startled awake, it was because in the dream their plan failed, was found out, or he got assassinated by faceless shadows. On his fifth such heart-pounding episode, he chose to meditate for the remainder of the night.

He circulated his Ether and felt himself relax as his mind methodically began to compartmentalize his worries. If they had been recorded discussing the plans and found out, Oberan would have already reacted. Additionally, Oberan would have known about Apep and why their old cells collapsed.

Instead, Oberan didn't know, and Frag had been allowed to alter the work crews. That didn't mean that the new cell block wasn't being monitored, though.

Azrael began absently spiraling his Ether inside one of his channels as he continued to think. The planet was small, certainly, but not so small that there weren't areas outside of

Oberan's control. There must be a rebel faction that existed outside of the arena.

His heart stuttered and he grabbed his chest. What in the name of the Sovereign had just happened? He calmed himself and entered back into his meditation. He felt nothing out of place. Was that a heart murmur? No, his heart didn't hurt or feel abnormal to him.

He saw a small black spot in one of his channels that was slowly refilling with the unmistakable blue of Ether. The spot was moving away from his heart. The outer edges of the space still had a small swirl from his absent-minded spiraling.

He watched it hit the capillaries in his foot and vanish. He considered what he had just done. The areas on the outside of the small patch of blackness were much denser. More vivid. He mentally narrowed the flow near his heart and felt the tightness return. It was almost like he was underwater and in desperate need of fresh air. He immediately widened the flow back out. That was not comfortable in the slightest. Still, he experimented with narrowing the channels leading away from his heart. No immediate pain.

He held it for a time, wanting to ensure no problem existed with the Ether that returned to his heart. The capillaries diluted the Ether back to normal by the time the Ether traced back towards his center. Azrael ground his teeth. What if he changed the flow of the entire leg?

He narrowed the side returning to his heart. The swirling pattern that existed at his pool intensified, but he felt no pain. Was it similar to water and pressure? Did a narrow channel move the Ether faster?

He worked to refine each channel and watched in fascination as his center became a true whirlpool. He touched it with his mind and intense pain shot through his head.

***

He woke up to the sound of Louis placing a tray on the floor nearby. Azrael clutched his head, a massive headache invading his thoughts. His hand found sticky, cold sweat drenching his brow. Had that been a dream?

At least I was meditating in bed this time.

A peek at his channels told him they were normal. Maybe it had been a dream.

A quick glance at his character sheet told him it hadn't.

Azrael Sovereign Level 20
      Class: Sovereign (Revenant)
Class Skills: Soul Strike (V), Soul Cloak (V), Soul Storage (V), Bloodletter (V)
      Health Points = 270/270 Points
      Ether Pool = 190/190 Points
You have 7 stat points and 0 skill points to distribute.
      Stamina – 27
      Strength – 21
      Agility – 36
      Dexterity – 36
      Intelligence – 19
      Wisdom – 18
      Charisma – 18
      Luck – 12
Skills:
Analyze – Strong 11
Butcher – Moderate 21
Combatant – Strong 35
Enchanting – Weak 5
Endurance – Strong 21
Ether Channels – Moderate 12
Ether Manipulation – Moderate 14
Essence Conversion – Weak 3
Martial Arts – Strong 46
Mediation – Moderate 18
Obfuscate – Strong 15
Sneak – Moderate 4
Stone Cutting – Moderate 11
Swordsmanship – Greater 45
Tracking – Weak 12

He had jumped up in Ether Channels and Manipulation quite a bit, which told part of the story. Still, it was the new skill that made him scroll back through his minimized notifications. Essence Conversion?

Congratulations! You have learned a new skill, Essence Conversion.
Essence Conversion
- **You have made your body a better vessel for converting Ether to Essence. Your body's ability to act as a filter increased fractionally. Planetary Gods always need more Essence; since you stand out in this regard, you will be awarded 1% more Etherience per kill per level in this skill.**

Current Rank: Weak level 3.

Azrael stared at the notification—this skill was beyond rare. If he took a guess, this skill would be worth millions of Crystals if purchased as a scroll. How had he never been taught this skill in the Sovereign Halls? If this was the weak effect of the skill, how powerful were its effects at the moderate ranks?

Let's make that a priority to practice then. Should I ask Ogma about it?

He glanced at the Firbolg, who was eating slowly, lost in his own thoughts. Maybe after they managed to escape from here.

Azrael ate his food mechanically and opened his Class Skills. Trying to plan what he would do with his twenty-first point.

Tier 5 Skills
Call of the Soul
- **All Soul abilities will increase in potency by 10% per talent point.**
    Skill gained at 5/5, "__Unknown.__"
                    0/5
    Each skill will be updated per talent point.
Call of Blood
- **All Blood abilities will increase in potency by 10% per talent point.**

Skill gained at 5/5, "<u>Unknown</u>."
0/5
Each skill will be updated per talent point.

The fifth-tier skills didn't give him any new offensive or defensive options. He knew that a fifty percent increase in skill damage and effectiveness would be strong. However, for the ultimate tier of Apprentice rank? He looked into the Fog of Discovery. To his surprise, there was still a filament leading to another tier. Azrael had never heard of a class that offered a sixth tier before.

He wondered; would this class offer a rank up at level thirty instead of twenty-five? That wasn't exactly a benefit. In fact, that would mean that he had a longer 'grind period.' He heard his teeth clacking together in his inner ear. He forced himself to calm down with a breath—at least the class had proven powerful so far. Choosing a custom class, as he had, could have turned out very badly.

As Azrael ate, he got his pool spinning as he had the previous night. This time he avoided touching the whirlpool. He vowed to keep the speed of circulation for the rest of the day as he worked and ate.

When Azrael looked up, Ogma was staring at him with narrowed eyes and a distinctive frowny shape in the hair that surrounded his mouth.

Chapter Thirty-Four

The next three days went by in a blur as the group planned the escape from the stone cutting yard and, before Azrael knew it, the next day of fights dawned. He was currently sitting in the antechamber getting ready to fight the fourth challenge. He checked his quest again.

Dungeon Quest
> **Apprentice Combatant**
>> **Fourth Level Survival Challenge**

Armored Rhino
The dungeon will pit your skills against its fourth level mob, the Armored Rhino. Defeating the fourth challenge will unlock the fifth challenge. Completing these challenges will increase your rank in the arena and offer rewards along the way. Every fifth challenge will be a mini-boss, until the 20th round, at which point you will compete against the Arena Boss spawn.
Good luck!
Rewards:
> **Etherience**
> **Looted reward**
> **Progression through Combat Ranks**

His fight was scheduled to begin after the current combatant finished its fight with the Doom Wolf Pack. Azrael paid the contest no mind, instead meditating and circulating his Ether. He would have watched if the individual was higher ranked, but he had already fought the wolves himself and would be able to pull from first-hand experience if he faced them again.

He had managed a discussion with Ogma about the upcoming fight and learned the rhino's greatest weakness was also its strongest attack. It moved in straight lines and had potent charging skills. This had led Azrael to store two fully charged, ten stacked Soul Strikes in his Soul Storage. This wasn't going to be a fight of subtlety. He would brute force it.

The combat ended with the combatant having its throat ripped out and its vibrant green blood spraying the sands. The crowd roared their approval and the announcer shouted, "There goes the dryad, who confounded her opponents in the most recent Battle Royale. Guess you can't hide from the Doom Wolves. Next up is the much-anticipated rookie sensation. The child mercenary, the savior of the people, the Sovereign Sons' team leader, Azrael Sovereign!"

The crowd cheered as the wolves were led back to the elevator with appetizing meats. The corpse of the dryad and associated blood sank into the sands, and then Azrael's door opened. He stood up and walked out. The crowd boomed its approval and he waved, summoning his sword into his hand mid-motion. He could hear gasps and people calling to neighbors, "There it is. His Soul Blade!"

Oberan has definitely gotten what he wanted.

When it reached the bottom, the elevator clunked noisily, and the crowd quieted infinitesimally. The hush grew in intensity until the elevator began whining mechanically as it reversed direction. The contraption was definitely lifting something heavy.

The horn of Azrael's next opponent came into view first and he felt himself swallow hard. The sun reflected off of the black protrusion, casting iridescent rainbows across the arena. The crowd rumbled back to life as more of the creature came into view. Huge obsidian bone plates covered the creature, making Azrael's breath catch. The creature was on par with the Enbarr in size, but where the Enbarr had looked graceful and exotic, this creature looked muscular and warlike.

He checked his earring of spell storage and knew he had a once a day Fireball loaded within it. He Analyzed the creature as its legs came into view.

Armored Rhino
Apprentice-Battering Ram
Level 24
Health Points: 2000/2000
Skills: 5

He clicked to examine the skills more closely.

Skills List:
Charge (V), Hardened Skin (V), Pierce (V), Trample (V), Beastly Health (IV)

Azrael was happy to have more information on his opponent. Two of the skills sounded passive while three sounded like ones he wanted to avoid. The elevator clicked into place, giving him no more time to contemplate. The forcefield fell.

The rhino didn't hesitate and began to lope out onto the sand. It slowly picked up speed as it ate up more ground. Azrael felt the sand quivering beneath him with each hoof that fell from the beast. He took a deep breath and held out his hand. He hadn't come up with any better strategy than what he planned to do. He began jogging in a circular pattern away from the line of the rhino.

At this distance, the creature was able to make changes as it ran but it continued to close. At around one hundred feet, its hooves glowed red and Azrael released everything. Starting with the Fireball, and then calling, "Release ten," twice in quick succession as it increased its jog to a full out sprint.

The rhino blurred forward and Azrael's skills exploded from his palm. The collision sent out a wave of sound like a thunderclap and the sand rippled out as if it was water. Azrael felt the wave hit him and his feet left the ground as he was bombarded by sand. It was almost like his first day in the Pit when Torin had abused him with the high-pressure water.

He landed five feet away, digging his toes in and coming to a stop. Azrael studied the smoke and sand, looking for movement, but couldn't see anything. The sand slowly filtered back to the ground and a broken obsidian horn was the first thing to come into view. Then the sand settled on top of the collapsed bulk of the rhino. An Analyze confirmed it was dead, and Azrael breathed a sigh of relief.

He wasn't sure what would have happened if it was still alive. The protection dome fell and the crowd's raucous cheering assaulted his ears once again. "Did you see that? How powerful was that skill? Could he beat the Enbarr?"

"The Sovereign Son has defeated the Initiate wall of the fourth challenge on his first try! Can this phenom take on the

Wendigo? Join us in three days to see the Sovereign Son try his hand at the first Boss!"

Azrael ignored everything as he moved to loot. He received a crafting component. A black Rhino Horn. He stored it in his ring and walked out of the arena, waving to the crowd. He planned to be out of here long before the crowd got a chance to see him face off against the Wendigo, at any rate.

Once he was back in the antechamber, he was escorted to the team room to have lunch and wait for the others. To date, no one had heard any plans to change the rules around the tournament. Presumably, most combatants had made purchases from the shop now that it was the quarter-finals.

He continued to meditate and work on his extremely powerful Essence Conversion skill. He felt that there was a secret to the technique just outside of his grasp. He needed to ask Ogma.

***

Azrael looked across the sands at his disabled opponent as the timer to Musth counted down. The Lizardman had been a capable fighter, but unrefined. Its skills had also been all over the place. Azrael had managed to remove the tail of the creature and cripple its legs. Then he had dragged the body over to the front of the forcefield.

Someone must have realized what he intended, because the protective enchantment fell and the crowd began to chant, "Musth! Musth! Musth!" The air in the arena was so thick with electrical currents of excitement, Azrael could feel himself jittering. Or maybe that was because he couldn't guarantee that Musth wouldn't trample him right after the Lizardman.

He had planned to use this tactic during his previous fight, but the team had forfeited. Now, against his first opponent in the quarterfinals, he managed to set it up perfectly. The announcer called, "Azrael has proposed a sacrifice to the Arena Champion, and the crowd agrees. Will the Arena Coordinator agree with the Sovereign Son?"

Azrael inspected the upper decks looking for Oberan, but couldn't find him. He must have been set back in a box seat. However, his voice crackled out over the sands a moment later,

"Let's release the leash on Musth. Azrael Sovereign, I suggest you return to your team room."

The crowd ignited with some of the loudest cheering Azrael had ever heard as he jogged off the sands. As soon as he was into the team room, the protective dome went up and Musth was released. The elephant didn't even bother with the Lizardman and charged straight at an enchanted wall. The collision rattled Azrael's teeth with the vibration the impact caused.

Next, the elephant rose up and stomped down onto the sand which seemed to bounce all the seated watchers out of their chairs. For the next ten minutes, Azrael watched in horror as the beast went berserk. Somewhere in that ten minutes, the Lizardman had been trampled. Just a piece of collateral damage to the rampaging bull elephant. Musth continued to display its strength and his group watched on in abject horror.

This creature is coming close to breaking the enchantment! How in the Halls do they plan to get it back onto the elevator?

A grating sound revealed the screen in their rooms and a message.

"You have been given the win in the quarterfinals. The continuation of the match has been canceled due to the rampaging Musth. Best of luck in the semifinals. Congratulations."

CHAPTER THIRTY-FIVE

At dinner, Azrael and his team finally received no glares. Whether that was because everyone was contemplating the sheer power they had just witnessed, or because Azrael had defeated the fourth challenge, he didn't know. Regardless, he and his team ate in silence.

Everyone is finally seeing how much of a deathtrap this place is.

Bat broke the silence with a squeaked, "Where did the guards take you three this morning?" His question was clearly directed at Verimy.

Had the guards taken Verimy, Jophiel, and Dara out of their cells this morning? That seemed strange. Every other time Azrael had been fighting a challenge they had been left in their cells. Azrael paused his eating to listen to his trainer's response.

"Oberan wanted to question us individually about the collapse in the dungeon. I am sure you and Azrael will be taken in the next couple of days," Verimy responded, sounding a little too casual about the experience.

Azrael squinted at him. "And?" he asked.

Verimy shrugged. "Nothing. I still have no idea what happened to our old cell block. Do you?"

The flip of the question made Azrael pause. He knew he wasn't going to say anything to Oberan, but what did Bat know? He had definitely heard Azrael speaking to someone or something in the bathroom. Azrael looked at the blue batman and received a minute shake of the head.

The good news is that Oberan underestimates and dismisses Bat. Glad he doesn't realize how helpful and strong he is.

It wasn't like Bat knew much about it anyway. Just that Azrael was talking to someone or himself while showering. Though it could lead to more directed questions by Oberan if it came out. Either way, Verimy and Dara couldn't know about Apep. Jophi might be able to put the whole puzzle together, but it was a bit of a logical leap. Azrael shrugged, reflecting Verimy's casualness. "No clue, Verimy."

Bat smiled at the man as well and shook his head more emphatically, conveying his lack of knowledge. Regardless, they were more or less ready to make an escape from the stone cutting yard. They planned to go tomorrow morning. Azrael looked at his completed quests and went to assign his free stat points in preparation for the escape.

Congratulations! You have completed a quest.
Dungeon Quest
> **Apprentice Combatant**
>> **Fourth Level Survival Challenge**

Armored Rhino
You have completed the fourth challenge of the dungeon: the Armored Rhino.
Congratulations!
Rewards:
> **800,000 Etherience**
> **Access the Fifth Level Survival Quest**

--

Congratulations! You have completed a quest.
Arena Chain Quest
> **Single Elimination Tournament**

Win the Round of 8
- **You have won the round of 8. Since the contest was deemed incomplete, the rewards have been adjusted.**

Congratulations!
Rewards:
> **2,000,000 Etherience**
> **One point to spend in the Tournament Shop – Click for Access**

7,701,412 Etherience remaining until level 21.

He placed his stat points, attempting to keep a balance. Of the seven free stat points, Azrael had placed one into Wisdom, one into Intelligence, and the final five into Strength. He needed to keep Stamina and Strength relatively close for the future. He would likely breakthrough in Agility and Dexterity at the same time, as long as he kept the two balanced. While he could instead push his mind stats for his second breakthrough, he first wanted to ensure all of his linked stats were close to even.

Being forced to place my points in Stamina early on has made my stats lean heavily towards a close combat fighter. Still, my class does balance that out a bit with the percentage cost of Soul Strike, Soul Storage, and Soul Cloak.

All in all, his class had become a goldmine of powerful skills and he thought back on the Bottle of Tech Duinn Essence. Was there a class change that occurred or had it just powered up his current tree? The answer didn't matter much for his current problems, but it would be a great piece of information for others in the future. That thought panged against his heart, and he viciously quashed the feeling of loss. The other students at the Sovereign Halls were just other chess pieces, nothing more. Just because he didn't have anyone to share the information with right now didn't mean he wouldn't have them someday.

***

Azrael was escorted to the fourth floor right after dinner, along with Bat. Turned out Verimy's words were a bit prophetic, but inaccurate about the time.

They were left in a meeting room with only Gyr watching them for a few hours before Oberan finally strode in with a giant smile on his face.

"Azrael. What a treat it has been to watch you grow in the Pit. The skill of a Sovereign Son doesn't disappoint! And to come up with the idea to sacrifice to Musth? Pure genius! Too bad it took most of the night to get him back onto the elevator, but the fans will be talking about it for years," smarmed Oberan.

He looked at the man, trying to figure out what game it was they were playing now. Was he going to ask them questions about the collapse, as Verimy suggested? Then was the man buttering him up? The silence stretched. "Thank you?" Azrael interjected into the uncomfortable moment.

"Not at all, not at all. I couldn't have asked for a better figurehead. Your greatness spreads more and more each day. I can't wait to see what you have planned against the Wendigo…" Oberan let his last words hang in the air like a threat.

Not if I can help it.

Oberan continued a few moments later. "I think you are just too valuable to be used for slave labor. I think from now on I will have you watch all the matches from somewhere visible. After all, people will pay good money just to catch a glimpse of you. In addition, I think splitting up your matches for better admission sales is a must. Are you okay if I adjust your rest schedule?"

His eye twitched. Azrael felt something squeezing his heart. He tried to keep his breathing smooth but failed, and instead sounded strange as he pulled in a breath through constricted lungs. Oberan's smile deepened upon seeing his distress. "Oh, don't worry, your team will join you in the box seating. So, you won't be starved for company. And I am sure two days of rest is plenty…" Oberan said, his eyes twinkling deviously.

Had he been outplayed? This couldn't have been a coincidence—could it? His three *friends* left their cells this morning, and now Oberan had taken them off of work details with the plan of escape tomorrow?

He entered meditation and sighed out a breath, bringing his body back under his control. He put on a smile and directed it at Oberan. "Of course, *we* can't let the *crowd's* favor go to waste," Azrael said.

Oberan's smile faltered just a bit, and Azrael counted it as a small victory.

I'm still screwed.

Chapter Thirty-Six

For the next two days, Azrael, Bat, Verimy, and Jophiel sat in the box seat the entire day. Oberan even had their breakfast and lunch delivered to the box, only allowing them to leave to sleep. To his surprise, Ogma and Dara joined them as well. This did give them the opportunity to watch matches, but that soon became very boring. The Pit seemed to never stop. Every minute of every day had a scheduled match. This gave Azrael the opportunity to see his next opponent—the Wendigo.

He wished he had never seen the creature. Bloodletter wouldn't be helpful against the Wendigo, since the creature was considered a type of undead. Ogma claimed that Soul skills would also become far less effective against an undead, soulless monster.

The other matches of the Initiate tournament were already finished and so he didn't even get new information on the next team. To his surprise, there were also Combatant ranked tournaments occurring simultaneously with the Initiate one. Based on the announcer's commentary, the teams stayed together whenever possible through the ranks. After the Initiate rank, there were Combatant and Champion ranks, but there were too few of the latter to have a tournament.

Another piece of information—no one had ever made it past the fifteenth stage and into the fourth rank of combatants. So, no one knew about what rank came after Champion.

He did manage to find a single moment of privacy with Ogma in the box seating, though. Azrael was delivered to the open box first and about ten minutes later Ogma arrived, escorted by the same two guards as Azrael. That likely meant they were ferrying Azrael's group back and forth. Azrael approached the strange Tuatha De Danaan member.

"You looked at me strangely during your lessons on Ether Manipulation and channels—why?" Azrael asked bluntly, wanting to get right to the point in the brief time they might have. Before the others were escorted into the booth by guards.

Ogma gave him a perusal. "You're too young to be messing around with your channels the way you did. It is very dangerous and could easily have killed you," the Firbolg said after a time.

"Well it didn't kill me, and I got a new skill," Azrael retorted, slightly peeved that Ogma would warn him off the skill. Did the man want to keep it for himself?

Two massive hands lifted him off the ground and pinned him to the wall beside the entrance to the box. "You received the Essence Conversion skill?" Ogma hissed, his face a few centimeters from his nose. Azrael could feel the beard hair scratching his clothes.

His mind caught up to the actions and words of the Firbolg and he nodded. If Ogma wanted him dead, Azrael wasn't likely to stop him. Ogma took a deep breath and put Azrael back down on the ground. Even going as far as to smooth his tattered clothing. Then he breathed out and said, "That skill is something that took me over a hundred years to discover, and you did it at the age of eight. I am not sure whether I should be angry or impressed.

"Look, my warning still stands. From everything I have learned, Essence is dreadfully powerful. Literal wars are fought over the stuff. Don't tell anyone else about this and be careful," Ogma added to his earlier warning.

Azrael tilted his head. "Is there anything concrete you can tell me about it?"

Ogma sighed. "I am discovering things as I go myself. But it is what allowed me to break the system stasis. There is something deeper to it all, but I am not quite able to figure it out yet. I can almost sense the converted Essence, but it leaves my body before I have a chance to study it."

"Leaves your body? To where?"

"It flows into the planet as far as I can tell…" Ogma trailed off as noise came down the hallway leading to the box.

That was all Azrael was going to get out of the man, it seemed. Should he share this knowledge with Verimy, Dara, and Bat? What about Jophiel?

***

It was the following day and Azrael was sitting in the antechamber, preparing for his upcoming life or death fight.

He shook his head and began stacking Soul Strike into his sword. There were a few minutes left before the fight started, so he sat to meditate and recoup his Ether. If he kept the skill active on the blade, he was able to regenerate half of the infused Ether. He managed to infuse three stacks before the timer reached zero.

Azrael got to his feet as the gate opened to the arena. He walked out onto the sands, his sword glowing faintly, and waved to the crowd. To his surprise, the protection enchantment was already active. His eyes caught movement, and his head snapped to lock onto a gray-skinned, smiling horror charging over the sand.

He hadn't even stepped out of the gates fully, and the Wendigo was already a quarter of the way across. Azrael Analyzed his opponent.

Hannibal
Journeyman-Wendigo
Level 12
Health Points: 1550/1550

The smile became more evident, and Azrael shivered. It was such a gleeful expression, from a mouth of razor-sharp teeth, that he just couldn't help the reaction. It was like a rabid animal, who was finally unleashed to tear something apart and eat the remains. Seeing the speed of his opponent, Azrael entered Dancing Leaf's defensive forms and began a split step.

The claws of his opponent were four-inch blades, the teeth two-inch saws. Azrael knew that one blow could end his life. He needed every advantage he could manage, and to use every lesson he had ever learned.

He activated Soul Cloak just as the creature closed to twenty feet and wasn't a moment too soon. Hannibal activated a skill, and its claws shot from the right hand. Azrael had seen this skill before and batted two from the air with quick slashes as he maneuvered away from the others. The Wendigo left the ground with an inhuman leap, aiming its landing right on top of Azrael.

Azrael reacted by instinct and released his triple charged Soul Strike at the creature mid-air. The greatest weakness of a non-skill-assisted leap attack was that it gave the user no real opportunity to adjust course. Hannibal, being an undead, didn't use tactics—more animal instincts.

The Soul Strike struck the gray skin of the undead mid-air and bounced his opponent away. The reciprocating saws of the skill failed to gain purchase on the lightweight body of his opponent. Still, the ability caused one-hundred and fifty points of damage, according to a quick Analyze.

Its body isn't as strong as the Rhino, but it is ten times as fast.

Hannibal didn't leap into the air again, instead charging at Azrael with its dog-like run. Azrael used his split step to shift right. As Hannibal course-corrected, he moved his weight further right and then flicked his calf and pushed back left. All of the Wendigo's instincts made Azrael's stance work, and he slashed down at the ribs of the undead as it passed by a few feet away. He placed a single charge of Soul Strike around his sword, and this time saw the skill gain a bit of purchase before he was forced to leap away in shock.

His ribs burned excruciatingly, and he glanced to find five vicious claw marks, two claws still embedded in his left side. He followed the retreating form of Hannibal, and scrutinized his opponent. There! The back-left leg was missing two nails. Azrael had focused on his strike and somehow missed his opponent's counter. A disease debuff climbed onto his interface. He pulled out the two claws as Hannibal stopped and began stalking in a slow circle. Azrael lost ten health from the initial slash and would lose one health a minute for thirty minutes according to a quick read.

I can't let this debuff stack. No more mistakes.

Azrael had noted it could stack those debuffs from watching the Wendigo's previous fight. Hannibal stood up on two legs, changing its dog-like form to something more human. Azrael found the sight disturbing as the emaciated body stretched out. Instead of another charge, his opponent continued to circle him. It was slowly closing in with its manic smile and flexing fingers, claws extended.

Just as Azrael landed from a split step, Hannibal shot two of its finger claws at him. Azrael twisted his body to avoid one and blocked the other with his sword hilt. The defense and his shift of focus was clearly the Wendigo's intention, because it shot forward.

Azrael released Jophi's Fireball from his earring. The creature somehow anticipated the attack and dodged as it closed the remainder of the gap. The Fireball exploded on the sand behind it. The Wendigo began swiping at him with lightning-fast jabs. His Soul Cloak blazed and began to help him avoid the blows, but only slightly.

He struck at each limb, trying to sever the hand, but only scored cuts and slashes on his opponent—even with Soul Strike's help. The Wendigo scored four more hits on him, and he swore. This couldn't continue, or the debuff alone would kill him regardless of the outcome of the battle. He dropped one hand off his hilt and continued to dance around strikes as he reached out and whispered, "Release ten!"

Hannibal bit into his hand, its mouth encompassing Azrael's pinky finger and ring finger. The razor-sharp teeth pierced into his palm. Simultaneously, the skill exploded out. Azrael blinked in the aftermath of the confusing moment. He was staring at his hand, which was still pierced by the Wendigo's teeth – but only the back?

The top of Hannibal's head still sat on the back of his hand, its eyes glaring at Azrael. He stared in disbelief as something slumped down and bumped wetly into his thigh. His trump card had torn through Hannibal's jaw, neck, and most of the upper torso before exiting and careening across the sand. Azrael checked his debuff bar and saw he had ten stacks of the disease, and as he watched, it ticked up to eleven.

He pulled the head off of his hand and hurriedly threw it away, stepping away from the rest of the body. Blood sprayed from the holes in his hand and he checked his health to find it at ninety points. The debuff had renewed itself, giving him thirty minutes to survive. Azrael had one chance to live without the crowd's help, and so he sat down and began meditating on the spot.

This was a race now between his regeneration and the debuff. Azrael tried to calculate his chances and kept realizing his regeneration would likely not be strong enough. He entered meditation as deeply as he could. Sweat began to form on his brow—his health regen was going to fail; if the crowd didn't save him, he was going to die.

He felt each minute tick by. Not in the cliché way he would use to describe boredom. No, every few seconds, his gut clenched, and his world spun as the debuff ravaged his body. After the fifth such 'attack,' he felt his body begin to weaken and numb.

That could be a good thing, or he might be so close to death that his body was shutting down. He didn't know and couldn't afford to look.

"Live! Live! Live! Live!" A chant began to reverberate over the sands as the protection shield receded.

"The Sovereign Son is close to succumbing to the disease of the Wendigo. Could this spell the end of our rookie phenom?" The announcer overrode the chant for a moment. "What is the Coordinator's decision?"

A wave of cooling relaxation washed over him and he felt himself almost collapse at the euphoria his body felt. The healers had arrived, helping to save him in the nick of time. The crowd had clearly decided to save him, but had Oberan waited to acquiesce to add to the suspense?

"The Sovereign Son lives to fight another day. He will return to the first challenge. Come see him face off with the Frost Bunnies once again, in three days!" the announcer boomed.

Azrael cracked an eyelid with great effort. They were stuck shut. He needed to reach up and physically help the action with his fingers. Scabbed blood fell away onto his palm as the eyelid finally opened. He repeated the work on the other eye.

Azrael found his health sitting at five points and his debuff bar clear. The crowd had saved him—he had lived.

His mind screamed at him. His life had just been placed in the hands of the bloody mob!

He had sworn not to let that happen.

CHAPTER THIRTY-SEVEN

Azrael awoke the next morning to his sphincter clenching as a familiar voice echoed down the hallway to their third-floor cells. "I heard they changed the rules of the tournament and have allowed the contestants ta get a one-time refund! Now Azrael will have ta face opponents equally geared! I bet the next month's salary that today that skidmark loses!"

There was a brief silence as footsteps continued echoing down the entry hall. Then the growly voice of Papi responded, "Torin, didn't you say that you would pay back your debt with your next two paychecks?"

The sound of spit splattering on the wall had Azrael out of bed and activating his Soul Cloak in a heartbeat. He watched as the Bearman, Torin, and four other guards entered the area with loop poles. That number was odd, but Papi stayed close to Torin—both of them approaching his cell.

I guess Oberan no longer wants to take any chances. Six guards for four of us?

The number of guards gave Azrael an idea, and he called over to Ogma, "Looks like they put two guards on me and none on you, big guy. Guess that confirms Gyr is more worried about me than you!" Azrael threw out Gyr's name, hoping he had guessed right. Someone had to be in charge of the guards in the complex, and he knew it wouldn't be Oberan himself.

Ogma's eyebrows drew together, and he frowned slightly. Azrael smiled broadly, then shrugged, "Looks like they aren't going to even put a guard on you for this escort because you are a member of the Tuatha."

Azrael moved to his double-gated entrance, and Papi elbowed Torin, who shrugged, looking at Ogma and then back to Azrael. The ugly orc frowned, making its face even uglier before asking one of the other guards, "Did Gyr want us to escort everyone here down to the team antechamber?"

The other guard was a fair-skinned, pointy-eared, very skinny elf. He responded haughtily, his voice carrying a great deal of disdain, "Can't you count, orc! There are six prisoners and six of us. It seems pretty obvious to me. We have been bringing them all to the box, haven't we? Still, you were given the orders, not us."

Torin narrowed its eyes and searched them one by one. Azrael wasn't sure what it was looking for. It wasn't like anyone would yell out 'Fooled you!'

Papi elbowed Torin, "Look, man, you get the big guy. You are closer to his level. I will take the kid and lead the way." Azrael smiled as Torin began to scratch its scalp. This had gone farther than he ever thought it would, and he crossed his fingers behind his back.

Torin spat to the side and turned its glare on Azrael. *Does it suspect me of something?*

"Don't worry, Azrael. If you survive today, I will make sure I am the one to escort you back!" Torin sneered as it turned to walk over to Ogma's cell. It pointed to the double gate mechanism angrily, seeming irritated with the Firbolg for not yet being ready.

Ogma complied, looking at Azrael suspiciously but willing to let this play out. The rest of the group was already noosed, and Papi slipped the collar over Azrael's head, which stopped any further conversation. The group was led, by their necks, to the waiting room, and all deposited one by one into it.

As soon as the entire group was in, Azrael cheered, "Welcome to the group, Ogma and Dara."

The others smiled at Ogma, and a few even looked hopeful. Jophi gave the big Firbolg a huge hug, and he returned it. This was an interesting development. Azrael may have a second option for escape. Ogma was an enchanter, which meant Bat could show him the area they needed to disenchant, and they could figure out if it was possible together.

Bat was the farthest along, by far, in the enchanting training they had been performing every night. He just seemed to have a knack for seeing the flow of Ether. While Bat could definitely have disenchanted the clankers, Azrael wasn't sure if he could manage the enchantments out of their room.

Azrael saw the countdown timer start. He equipped the set of Ether-Tech gear and thought back to Torin's conversation. Based on the orc's betting habits, he knew something would be different this time around, something that would disadvantage him or even the playing field at least. Returning equipment meant that the group might be allowed to pool their gear on a single fighter—just like Azrael's team had done.

The question was, would they? Should they use up the extra points to buy more gear for him?

Azrael looked at the gear. He didn't think they needed more and instead turned to the group. "Buy another set of Ether-Tech armor. If you have any more points left after that, get some more armor or weapons. Whatever you think is best. We are going to have to try to escape from here…"

For once, the group just nodded at him. He had assuaged both Verimy and Jophiel by tricking Torin into bringing Dara and Ogma down to the team room. He pressed his lips together. They were headed to the hypogeum and the Enbarr, though. So, instead of freedom, he had likely bought everyone a sure death. At least Musth would be up here…

He put the armor on and stood in his space between the two gates. He turned back and nodded to the group with the Ether-Tech helmet under his arm. He reminded them, "Don't forget that this inner gate needs to open as well, if you gain access to the hypogeum." They all nodded and looked over to Bat and Ogma, who knelt in the far corner over what looked like a cold air return. Bat was making gestures with his hands, seeming to describe a route through the walls to Ogma.

Azrael smiled, put his helmet on, and whispered to himself, "Try to give them as much time as you can."

As soon as the door opened, Azrael recognized that something was different than the last round of fighting. He looked around himself, trying to understand what had changed. He saw his opponent exit the far doors and the sun glinted from some brand-new equipment set. However, that wasn't what was giving him pause. He scanned the cage that should have held Musth and froze. Where was the nightmare elephant?

The cage wasn't empty. No, inside the forcefield were five Wendigos. Ten pairs of red eyes and crooked smiles raised goosebumps all over his skin under the Ether-Tech suit. Had they changed the prod precisely because of his last near-death experience? He tore his gaze away and locked on his opponent's slowly advancing suit of armor. Or was it because of Musth's rampage during the last match?

Or were they aware of his last plan of escape? There was no other option, though.

The heavy suit of armor kept approaching. The opposing team must have watched his previous fights and assumed he had the most trouble with tank classes. The humanoid moving towards him was covered from head to toe in thick metal. In one hand, it held a long-handled single-sided ax and strapped to its other arm was a massive tower shield.

Azrael bit his lip. That suit couldn't be as expensive as Azrael's Ether-Tech gear, which meant he still had the advantage. He Analyzed his opponent and started a charge.

Craterface
Journeyman-Metal Knight
Level 31
Health Points: 3200/3200
Strong Analyze has failed to provide additional information.

Azrael wasn't sure how he was going to chew through that much health. His immediate goal was to make sure the timer for the Wendigo release didn't start. He closed in and began weaving in a pattern, attempting to force Craterface to turn the awkward tower shield. It wasn't hard, and as soon as it lifted the cumbersome thing, Azrael planted and changed direction. He charged in, gaining the side of the Metal Knight, and began slashing at its armor with just his sword. This was his first experiment. He needed to know if his sword combined with his technological and Ether strength could penetrate this armor.

Loud screeches sounded as the edge of his sword etched deep grooves into the thick armor. It failed to penetrate, and the swinging ax forced Azrael to step back for a moment. This gave Craterface the chance to reorient the tower shield and trigger a skill. The shield glowed yellow for a split second and jumped forward. Azrael leaped into the air, and the Shield Bash passed several feet beneath him. This Ether-Tech gear was something else.

He landed behind Craterface and charged a single Soul Strike into his sword.

He cut at his opponent's back using the aptly named form of Rock Cutter. This form used his body weight and core to attack with hefty sword swings. He wouldn't have been able to use this form without the full Ether-Tech set; the opposite reaction of his strike contacting the armor would have broken his wrist at a minimum. Still, with his current set of gear on, an ear-piercing screech vibrated the air as his blade scored deeply into the metal. Azrael estimated that his cut was at least half an inch deep, but it still didn't make it through the thick metal.

Craterface activated another skill, and its ax crashed into Azrael from the side. Azrael hadn't seen it coming and flew away from the massive blow. He bounced over the ground but managed to gain his feet as he took stock of his armor and found a deep cut in his shoulder. It hadn't made it through the mechanical armor. But he could see some exposed wires within the metal. He moved the arm and didn't feel any loss of strength.

Next, Azrael set eyes on his opponent, who was currently spinning in lightning-fast circles. Almost like a toy top. This could only be the Whirlwind skill, which would be an abysmal decision in most fights. However, Azrael glanced at the Wendigos and sighed, "If I don't attack soon, the timer will likely begin."

He counted to thirty seconds slowly and then released his single charged Soul Strike at his opponent. The phantasmal blade bounced off the Whirlwind, and Azrael began another slow count to sixty seconds. A notification popped up.

Timer to Wendigo
- **You and your opponent's inaction has triggered the countdown on the Wendigo release. Attack your opponent or finish the match in 5 minutes, or the Arena Bosses will go on a rampage.**

Time remaining: 4 minutes, 58 seconds.

That was a subtly different message than the last time. First was obvious, as the timer would trigger the Wendigos' release. The other was that he could cancel the timer with an attack against his opponent. He shrugged and shot off another single Soul Strike at Craterface. Something with that high of health wouldn't be able to sustain the skill for much longer. His blades dinged as they bounced away from the Whirlwind and careened over the sands.

The timer didn't reset. Did ranged attacks not count? He analyzed his opponent and noticed something – Craterface's health was down about three hundred points. Azrael knew he hadn't gotten through the armor.

The timer ticked as he considered what was going on. If damaging the armor hurt the individual, that would mean the armor was, in essence, the body of the individual. That explanation fit, but only partly. The other option was that this was, in fact, a construct made of the armor, and his actual opponent hid somewhere in the arena. He scanned around himself. His eyes locked onto the jumbotron, and he read the matchup: Azrael Sovereign versus Nathaniel Sprockethand.

He hadn't attacked his opponent at all, just his opponent's construct. Azrael sprinted to his opponents' entrance and found no tracks in the sand other than the Knight's. The Knight stopped spinning and dropped the tower shield. This increased the speed of the construct, but not enough to keep up with Azrael in his Ether-Tech gear.

He combed over the sand. The timer counted down as he played hide-and-seek with a stealthed Nathaniel.

When the timer reached two minutes, Azrael made a split-second decision and ran into the center of the arena. Craterface followed closely, and Azrael waited until the creature closed in before leaping straight up in the air. Once he reached the peak of his ascent and began to descend, he allowed himself to enter into a face-first dive.

He reached out both hands in front of himself and said, "Release ten!" His skill blasted out of his hand. His nearness to the ground created a reverse action that stopped his descent and spun him back up in the air. Craterface was directly below his skills, and Soul Strike crashed into it with the screech of a starship's collision.

Two thunderous drum beats reverberated over the entirety of the arena before a massive boom. Then, just as in Azrael's fight with the rhino, sand flew up in a gigantic cloud. The center of the arena was so thick with it that Azrael couldn't see. Still, he could study the outside edges of the arena. Azrael saw what he had been hoping to find. A humanoid shape was clinging to one of the walls directly above his opponents' entrance.

The falling sand highlighted its position, and Azrael charged in Nathaniel's direction as soon as he landed. Azrael saw the outlined humanoid fall from its location and begin fleeing, but Nathaniel didn't have the speed to outpace Azrael.

Azrael slashed his sword across the area Nathaniel's sand-coated form resided. A loud yelp echoed over the sand. The body of a small gnome came out of stealth and fell to the ground. Nathaniel turned over onto his back, and held up both hands, "No, please. Don't kill me! I didn't even want to fight against you. They forced me!"

Azrael checked the timer, which was no longer counting down and sighed in relief before responding. "That isn't my decision, unfortunately. That is the decision of the crowd – now admit defeat and submit to their judgment!"

CHAPTER THIRTY-EIGHT

Azrael flicked his sword, sending blood droplets into the sands of the arena. He also looted the now-collapsed suit of armor in the middle of the arena. He summoned what he could into the ring and then carried the tower shield, ax, and chest piece to the gate. He didn't bother examining the set yet because he assumed that it would get taken away from him. It seemed looting gear that the dungeon made for the tournament was not allowed. However, he had looted it from the middle of the arena, and not the dead gnome, which had somehow forced the dungeon to enable him to do it.

As soon as the gate closed and the five-minute timer began, Jophi pulled open his inner gate door, smiling. She put her finger to her mouth and whispered, "Think we can set up that new armor of yours to look like a person?"

He shook his head before whispering back, "No, it fell to the ground as soon as Nathaniel died. Probably best to just leave it in some sort of pile to cover that hole in the wall." As Azrael spoke, he had noticed the gaping hole in the corner of the room. It was just big enough for Ogma to crawl through, but the Firbolg was double the size of any of them.

Jophi pursed her lips and then walked to the exit and crawled inside. Azrael followed her move and dumped the armor from his ring into a pile in front of the space. He took a few seconds to stack it to cover the blackness at a first glance. Then he crawled after Jophi on the rough stone floors.

Azrael caught up to her a few moments later and asked, "Where is everyone else?"

Jophi made an exaggerated point at the floor and turned a corner. Azrael followed closely, but when he turned the corner, she was gone. His heart stuttered, and he wondered if she had tricked him. He reached out his hand to crawl forward and found no stone surface to place it on. Luckily, he was still in the Ether-Tech gear, and it helped him rebalance himself. Had she jumped down this chute, then?

He turned around in the confined space and went into the chute feet first. A feeling of weightlessness came over him before his feet collided with something. The technology in the suit absorbed the impact and automatically bent his knees for him. The suit had some minor form of night vision, but the change from the tunnel to wherever he was now was drastic. All around him was dar—no, wait. There was some light.

Azrael followed the distant flicker and walked down a hallway until it opened up into a massive cavern. As soon as he stepped inside, he heard Bat call, "You made it! We didn't leave until we were sure you were going to win. The escape became much easier with Ogma here; there was no way I could have disenchanted those bars. It took everything out of Ogma to do it."

Azrael felt his heart almost stop. Ogma wasn't at his best? He looked around and noticed that Bat wore the second set of Ether-Tech gear, Dara had a bow, and Jophi had a staff. However, Ogma was leaning heavily on Verimy. Azrael tilted his head. Tactically, Bat wearing the gear was poor. Yet, the creature would need increased protection if he was going to make it out of here.

He isn't a pawn, and I think we are going to need him if we have any chance of escape.

The room they stood in was lit by a burning trough that ran around the entire perimeter of the cavernous construct. In the center was a huge staircase that spiraled up and further down. From his current position, Azrael could see mechanisms with gears and pulleys in various areas of the gigantic chamber, but he had no idea what any of them did.

Azrael asked, "Are we in the hypogeum?"

Ogma croaked from Verimy's shoulder, "No, this is the staging floor, which is directly below the arena. Come, we have to get down those stairs, so I can recover below. Can you still see the timer, Azrael?"

Azrael nodded and said, "Yeah, it's counting down from one minute and fifty-four seconds."

The group moved towards the stairs but were only a few steps in when Bat stopped. Azrael and the rest took a few more steps forward before realizing. Bat whispered, "There is an ambush just up ahead!"

Azrael felt his heart speed up, and he glanced around at his friends. Everyone looked shocked by this revelation, except for—Verimy? Dara was the first to catch his mood change, and she hissed, "What have you done, V?"

He looked at her and looked away, then looked at Azrael, eyes watering. He cried, "Azrael, Oberan had Dara. He threatened to feed her to Musth. I didn't want to tell him anything, but since the beginning, he has been threatening me with her life. I can make this right—we just need to make it to those stairs!"

Ogma pushed himself off of Verimy and nearly fell over from whatever Ether exhaustion he faced. Azrael caught the Firbolg and looked at Verimy sadly. It was already too late. Verimy's shout and their hesitation had alerted the ambushers to his group's knowledge of the impending attack. Guards began pouring down the stairs as a group of ten came out from behind the back of the circular staircase. One of the guards sneered at them. "Gyr and Yonel are on their way with Oberan. You all might as well give up now."

The guards formed up at the bottom of the stairs and Verimy fell in beside Azrael and quietly commanded, "Give me the armor, Azrael. Promise me you will get Dara out of here!"

Azrael nearly began removing the armor immediately. Verimy's tone was that of his instructor. The man who had saved his life on the day of the invasion. The man who had taken care of him for the trip to Tech Duinn and ensured his survival in its wilderness. He did manage to hesitate, though. One hand twitched at his side, as he held Ogma with the other, and he studied Verimy's face. In his trainer's eyes, he could see a deep hurt, but he also saw the man who had never led him astray. That same man who would protect him at all costs—unless it risked the only thing more precious to him, Dara.

Azrael glanced over at Bat, but he wore the new undamaged armor. If Verimy failed here, they could lose the set of armor given to him. Azrael lowered Ogma to the ground and began removing the armor. He handed Verimy the helmet first and asked, "What are you going to do?"

Verimy looked to Dara, who sidled up right beside him. She had tears in her eyes as she asked, "Are we going to use it?"

Verimy smiled back, kissed her, and then struck her with a Shuto Uchi chop at the base of her skull. Her body ragdolled into his arms, and he held her lovingly for a moment, whispering, "I love you, Daramelia, with all of my heart."

Another guard crowed, "Perfect! Just remove your armor and surrender. If you don't fight back, no one will get hurt." One of the other guards tilted its head, seeming to grow suspicious, and trying to find the true motive behind his group's strange actions. Not a single guard moved towards them, yet. A few narrowed eyes stared at the seated form of Ogma, which told the actual reason the guards hesitated. They hadn't expected him to be here! But they didn't know how terribly weak the Firbolg was.

Once Azrael had removed his armor, Verimy handed Dara to Jophi before stepping into the pile, which began affixing itself in place. The clicks and whirs of the resizing armor alerted even the densest guards of a problem.

The same guard from before shouted, "If you don't stand down right now—"

Verimy nocked two arrows to his bow and crowed, "Demon Hunter!"

Azrael thought he was blind for a split second. He had been looking right at Verimy when his friend had uttered those words. Now he saw nothing and blinked his eyes. The blink didn't even register as a change. He looked around, and his eyes picked up on the light from the wall track fires. His other friends were looking at Verimy, each one making a different face. Bat seemed to be the only one who wasn't affected when he said, "Why are you all looking at Verimy like that? Did something happen?"

Black patches began firing out of the darkness. They were so fast that Azrael missed the first few, but when Jophi tapped him on the shoulder and he moved away, they were easily noticeable. Like black streaks of death that began burying themselves into guards. Each guard struck cried out in horror. Darkness began spreading from the wounds of the injured, and Azrael watched in awe. Verimy was only targeting the guards who were between them and the stairwell. Each dark black— arrow?—perfectly aimed regardless of cover.

The guards began using anything they could find as cover, even each other.

A voice in the blackness intoned, "Go now! Keep Dara safe!" The sound was so deep and menacing that Azrael would never have said it was Verimy.

Jophi began carrying Dara towards the stairs. Azrael grabbed Ogma and started following. Without the Ether-Tech armor, the Firbolg was insanely heavy. As he moved, he shouted, "Verimy, you have done enough. Come with us!"

A disturbing laugh was the only answer he got, and then the darkness flew forward into the injured guards, scattering them like a boulder tossed into a puddle. Bat charged into the gap Verimy made. Jophi followed, Dara held over her shoulder. Azrael struggled with Ogma's weight and fell in behind the line of friends. The dark form of Verimy allowed him to make it to the stairs. He and Ogma began to descend.

Azrael approached the stopped form of Jophi holding Dara midway down the stairs—should he put Ogma down and go back up for Verimy?

He looked back and felt a hand on his shoulder. "He isn't coming, Azrael. That skill… it was a Last Stand," Ogma croaked.

Azrael blinked and looked around at the group, which had stopped as well. Only Bat looked shocked by the revelation. Verimy's strike against Dara made a lot more sense in hindsight. He felt something knot up in his stomach and try to climb up his throat. He didn't understand the feeling and was more confused when Jophi gave Dara to Bat and wrapped Azrael in a huge hug. She cried, "I'm sorry," into his ear.

Was he supposed to cry as well?

You have failed a quest.
Arena Chain Quest
    Single Elimination Tournament
Win the Round of 8
    • **You have failed to appear for the contest during the round of 8.**
Your failure to produce a combatant for the second round has initiated a forfeiture of the match. Upon further review, the contest was forfeited, as your team seems to have no intention of fighting.

Consequences:
All gear will be forfeited
Demotion of Combat Ranks
Gruel for all meals until further notice

The notification shocked him out of his confusion. It was rather ironic. The only thing he was slightly sad about was the Etherience they would have gained.

The consequences didn't mean anything if they could get out of the Pit.

Chapter Thirty-Nine

The bottom of the stairs had come out into a wide stone hallway. The oil wall trough continued down here but wasn't lit. Ogma managed to get his feet under him and he limped over to touch his finger into the oil, commanding, "Flame." With a whoosh, fire sprang out from his finger and raced away down the hallway. With a jerky motion, Ogma removed his finger, which burned like a torch, and flicked the flaming oil that coated it into the trough on the other side. The spark caught, and fire raced down the hallway, lighting up a rough stone corridor in a subdued intake of air.

Ogma sat down heavily after this act, almost looking like a man who had just run miles. Sweat dripped down his face and his breathing was labored.

Azrael was preoccupied with trying to console Jophi, as she seemed upset. He patted her arm, and she came in to squeeze him tight. Strangely, his heart clenched more with that action. Soon she let him go with a whispered, "I am so sorry."

What was there to be sorry about? She hadn't forced Verimy's hand or killed him personally.

Azrael nodded and looked over at Bat, who was placing Dara on the ground. If Verimy had used a Last Stand skill, he would be near death when it elapsed. Unfortunately, without a healer, that meant he would undoubtedly die. Still, Azrael recalled Dara's words before he had knocked her out. She had known and had been ready to join him. If someone was going to be upset, it would be her.

Azrael looked up the stairs and heard muted sounds of combat, then asked, "Should we not move a little farther away from the stairwell? Just because smart people don't want to come down here because it's so dangerous doesn't mean they won't peek in to see if we are just standing around."

The group nodded, and moved away until they turned the first corner they came to, Bat placing Dara back onto the ground. Ogma surprised Azrael by managing to make the walk around the corner without assistance. It seemed that the Firbolg would recover on his own in time. Ogma smiled tiredly at him, "That was rather clever. I didn't expect you to maneuver the guards into taking me with you. Those enchantments took nearly my entire Ether pool to remove. Now I wish I could have kept more strength to handle the guards. Still, with Verimy's Last Stand, here we are."

Ogma leaned against the wall and looked at each of them. "Not like we can get out of the hypogeum, but at least we aren't under the control of Oberan anymore."

Azrael squinted at Ogma and then Jophi, who was glaring at the Firbolg. She spoke first. "What do you mean we can't get out of here now? You are a Master rank, with high levels to boot! Are you planning on not fighting again?"

Ogma wheezed a laugh and shook his head. "Oh, I will fight with you all certainly, but Musth was my brother's pet. I have known him since we were children, and I also know that we will not be able to defeat that elephant. Even if Oberan and I tried to take it on together, we would probably lose!"

Azrael felt his mouth fall open. How had Ogma not mentioned this before? Oberan using the Wendigo as a prod made a lot more sense now. He was ensuring they had no chance to escape, even if they did manage to get this far. Musth was just too strong!

Other people would likely get extremely mad with Ogma for not telling them all of this earlier. Azrael just got cold, and began to look at all the options.

Obviously, they could just go back up the stairs and turn themselves in. That wasn't a great option, but would keep him alive for a few more days. They could continue through this floor and fight Musth, but by the sounds of it, that was a sure death as well.

Azrael shrugged and chose the final option. Continue forward and wait for some other opportunity to present itself. It wasn't like going forward closed the doors on the other options they had. As Verimy had told him in the forest, 'Improvise!'

Bat, still wearing the other set of Ether-Tech gear, stepped forward. "Do one of you want this set of armor? I am sure it will be more effective with someone else. I can only tell you what is around each corner as we go forward. Will Musth be walking the hallways down here, or does he have an area?"

Azrael looked at the group. Ogma was likely too powerful already to have the armor be anything other than a hindrance to his speed—once he recovered. That left him, Jophi, or Dara for the armor. The two ladies were both ranged fighters though, and that meant the one who would benefit most from the Ether-Tech gear was him. Still, taking the gear would likely spell the death of Bat.

"Hold on to the armor for now, Bat. I may take it from you later," said Azrael.

Bat nodded but looked unsure. "Okay, well, I agree that we should move away from the stairs. I will let everyone know what I see before we reach it."

Azrael looked at Ogma, "Can you recover as we walk?"

Ogma nodded and pushed himself off the wall in response.

Every tunnel was likely a death sentence but maybe they could avoid some of the stronger creatures. Azrael nodded and looked back to the entrance hallway. Verimy had given his life to buy them this chance; they needed to move forward.

Bat went to go pick up Dara and had his hands slapped away. Dara looked around herself, her eyes fogged over but clearing quickly. She shot to her feet and shouted, "Where is Verimy?"

Azrael understood her anger at the man. Verimy had taken away her choice. Perhaps saved her life, but she had been ready to die by his side. Verimy had robbed her of that decision. Azrael pointed above them, "Verimy is keeping the guards busy with his Demon Hunter skill."

He expected more anger, perhaps for Dara to rush back down the hallway. Azrael did not expect her to fall back to the floor and cry. Crying wasn't even the word for it. She hugged her knees to her chest and bawled. Azrael watched as Jophi went to sit beside her and hugged the woman close. Similar to what she had done with him. Azrael had been taught not to create strong connections with people. Again, he was reminded why. Dara, one of the strongest women he had ever known, was a puddle of worthless on the floor. A lesson he had never fully understood finally made complete sense. Be grateful for the people around you, enjoy their company, and respect their contribution to your life, but in the end, they were just chess pieces.

The main point of that lesson had been to make sure you can drop any person out of your life and leave when it becomes necessary. Azrael finally saw the reason why close attachments were a weakness, and felt sad to see Dara hadn't taken that sage lesson to heart.

Azrael felt a huge knot form in his stomach and wondered when the last time he ate was. They had breakfast that morning, hadn't they? Yeah, it was gruel, unfortunately, and not Louis' great cooking. That was probably where the knot was coming from.

Azrael wondered why he had forgiven his trainer so fast. His anger at the man flared and banished his hunger. Verimy had been weak and likely was up above sacrificing his life to make it right. That was the warrior's way.

Strangely, no one disrupted Dara in her floor puddle. They appeared to want to allow her to regain her composure by herself. No one broke the silence that seemed to surround them like his Soul Cloak could. Azrael had examined his feelings and come to his conclusion. Perhaps that was what everyone else was doing now for Dara?

Azrael shrugged and moved away down the hallway, catching Jophi giving him a look out of the corner of his eye. Somehow the look conveyed a deep sadness that he couldn't explain. Dara and Jophi had barely known each other and still Jophi felt for the other woman. Bat followed Azrael, and wrung his hands as they walked.

Azrael asked, "Do you sense something nearby?"

Bat shook his head, his long-ears almost slapping him in the side of his face. Then reached out and patted Azrael twice on the shoulder before squeaking, "I am sorry for your loss. Also, I never really thanked you for keeping me... umm, alive. Thanks for taking me with you through all of this."

Azrael rolled his eyes and shrugged. "Don't mention it. Let's keep exploring for now. Tell me if you sense anything, okay?"

Bat tilted his head, but when Azrael turned on his heel and left, he heard the blue-skinned man follow. A couple hundred meters further, Bat hissed, "Tigers patrolling up ahead. They are coming this way. Can we go back to the group?"

Azrael smiled and charged forward. He had wanted to fight something. For some reason, he just felt it would make him feel better. He pulled his sword and loaded it with Ether. The roar that echoed towards him only caused him to bare his teeth. When he heard the creatures begin running towards him, he felt something inside him catch fire.

The striped cats came into view, and Azrael entered Threshing Wheat. A stance designed to make low strikes that connected together but left many openings for retaliation. His blade connected with the first tiger as it leaped at him. The attack caught it in the chest and its reciprocating nature tore into the tiger's body before flinging the corpse away into a wall. He reversed and pivoted on his front foot, contracting his abs and reversing his sword direction in a full spin. He struck the second tiger mid-air as well. This sword form was dominant in an enclosed space, with a limited hitbox. He turned again and felt claws dig into his back—and there was the weak point in this style.

Azrael turned on Soul Cloak, crouched low, and jumped back into the wall while driving his sword under his arm and into the abdomen of his enemy. He heard the tiger yowl loudly behind him and shrugged his shoulder to dislodge the claws and move his sword simultaneously. Azrael smiled at the final tiger that approached him, then opened his mouth wide and roared.

His sword had impaled the now-dead tiger behind him and sunk partway into the stone behind. Azrael abandoned the sword and rolled forward, below the last enemy's pounce. He shot back to his feet still roaring, somehow fueling the continued cry with an anger he hadn't known he held. His roar cut off as the last tiger collided with Azrael's art deco installation. A moment after the collision, Azrael landed on the creature's back, both hands charged with a Soul Strike. He performed two piercing strikes and felt one hand hit a rib just as the other destroyed a lung.

He stood over the corpses of three tigers and felt himself shudder. Azrael looked at his shoulder, where the second opponent had bit and clawed him deeply. What had he been thinking? He knew how aggressive Threshing Wheat was. He knew it had a glaring weakness. Why had he chosen it?

He clenched his bloody hands together and then relaxed them before cleaning them on one of the dead cat's fur. He stood back up and retrieved his sword with a vicious pull. As he turned to look back down the hallway, he saw his group standing and looking at him. An armored Bat looked worried and hunched over. Had he run to get the others?

Dara had tears running down her face, but she had the same look on her face that Jophi held. They looked like two bookends, heads tilted away from each other, eyes large and glinting with water. Ogma had his arms crossed, and he seemed to be surveying the scene indifferently, but he wouldn't meet Azrael's eyes.

Azrael shrugged and turned to continue down the hall, leaving the looting to others. He didn't know how to respond to the silence the others offered and chose to keep going. That fight had helped him decide, at least.

He would keep going. He would never stop fighting for a way out. Going back was certain death. Moving forward had only a chance of death. Dara fell in beside him a moment later and nodded. Jophi took up the other side but stared straight ahead. He felt his back straighten, and his breathing grow more even as they moved down the hallway. He heard more than saw Bat scrape his feet as the batman joined him.

Azrael didn't look back to find out if Ogma followed. He didn't care. If dying down here would take away something from Oberan, then he would die in the hypogeum. He remembered a quote his Swordmaster had lived by, "The right to choose how to die is the one thing all living creatures are entitled to."

CHAPTER FORTY

Ogma had followed Azrael and continued to recover, which made the next creatures they ran into easy fights. Often a single punch from the strengthened Master was enough to end the life of the mobs. The group followed along behind him and discovered numerous open cages built into the rock as they passed. Ogma explained, "A hypogeum usually keeps monsters spawned in cages and transports them above for fights. Now that we are down here—maybe the dungeon has opened all the cages to eradicate the intruders?"

Azrael considered his statement and found a few oddities. He pointed them out, "Some of these cages look broken, though. Why would the monsters break out if the Pit released them?"

Ogma shrugged and admitted, "I have never been down to a hypogeum before. It is typically a bad idea. It could be that it removed the enchantments on the bars to release the monsters."

Azrael didn't respond to that and pointed at the cage they were passing. The bars had ascended into the roof and still glowed with an enchantment. Ogma gave him a shrug but didn't comment further. Bat called out, "The next hallway holds a horse."

The group stopped, and Jophi turned to Ogma, "The Enbarr?"

Ogma nodded and spat, "There isn't any other horse in the challenges. Is there a different route, Bat?"

Bat pointed back the way they had come, and the group turned around. Azrael asked the question he assumed some of the others were thinking, "Most of these creatures don't seem native to Tech Duinn. What is the Enbarr?"

"Well, as you know, it's the fifteenth challenge of the Pit. It is from the planet of Neptide and is considered to be the fastest horse ever found. According to my cousin, Manannan Mac Lir, they can even run on the wind. I would rather not challenge the beast if we don't have to. We might have a slightly better chance than Octorian because we are in a group, but the creature is strong," Ogma responded as he passed Azrael.

Azrael glanced back once and swallowed. If the Enbarr concerned Ogma this much, avoiding it was pragmatic. The group retraced their path and took a different turn they had skipped before. This led them to some Phooka, which were a kind of bunny rabbit. However, they were more massive than the wolves and tricky. Another issue was they attacked the group in a large open hallway, and with numbers.

He used Devilish Dance and caused the bunnies small injuries with each attack they attempted. This tactic worked well against creatures that shied away from pain and usually worked for evolved herbivores. Dara sunk arrow after arrow into the twenty or more who stacked six or seven deep on Azrael's side. He left Jophi and Ogma to deal with the others, and Bat stood in the center, offering whatever aid he could. Azrael thought Bat was just cowering until one of the leaping bunnies dropped unconscious at his feet – eyes rolled up into the back of its head.

Azrael finished off that creature with a quick stab between its eyes. The fight continued, and Azrael and Jophi had managed to kill five animals when Ogma arrived to help. Azrael kept fighting, but immediately felt the weight of the combat lift from his shoulders. With Ogma's strength beside him, he could forgo the small cuts meant to caution the Phooka and changed to killing blows.

The group took a break after the Phooka were dealt with and Jophi sat beside Azrael. She explained, "Those Phooka were the sixth challenge. They would be slightly easier than the Wendigo mini-boss according to Ogma. I never saw forty of them at once, though. Do you think the dungeon is scaling up the numbers to eliminate us?" She asked the final question while turning to Ogma.

Ogma pursed his lips and shook his head, "While I do believe the dungeon would spawn more creatures to kill intruders, when Jophi and I watched the sixth challenge, there were only five of the creatures. To go from five to forty would take far longer than the Pit has had."

Dara, who hadn't spoken much, murmured, "Maybe they were scaling up the difficulty for Azrael's attempt at the sixth challenge?"

Bat stroked his chin then shook his head. A dull slapping came from inside the helmet as his over large ears likely slapped him in the face. "No, that would create unrest and a platform for martyrdom. Everyone knows the strength of the challenges. So, making Azrael fight harder opponents would just give people an excuse to revolt. No offense, Azrael, but you didn't even make it past the fifth challenge. Scaling up challenge difficulty would seem excessive."

Azrael didn't take offense to the comment; he had thought the same thing. He did ask, "We never did see the tenth challenge in our two days up in that box. What is it? Some sort of tree?"

Ogma clenched his jaw. "Yewman. Similar to a Treant, but more demonic and aggressive. Truly a terrifying opponent."

Azrael turned and tilted his head as he looked at Ogma, who realized the unspoken question and continued, "This creature is from Tir na n'Og, another planet, and was donated by another relative of mine, Morrigan. She has some very bizarre tastes. She keeps the Yewmen as guards on her private Territory on the planet."

This whole dungeon seemed like a nightmare menagerie put together by Ogma's family. Azrael could see why this place upset the Firbolg.

After catching their breath, they continued to follow Bat's directions and even managed to avoid a pathway that led to the Yewman. However, a little farther on, they ran back into the Enbarr. "Did it move?" Azrael asked.

Bat shook his head, "Unfortunately not, it is planted at an intersection of four paths. We came up a different one this time. I am not sure we can avoid this fight. Retracing our previous route put us on a new path, and I assume we will just discover the third one if we go back."

Ogma nodded. "Alright, then let's come up with a plan. I will be up front—the rest of you attack from range."

Azrael blinked. That wasn't a plan. That was a tank and spank. He opened his mouth, but Jophi gave him a look that told him to let it go. He shrugged, knowing Ogma was their best chance of getting through this fight alive, but he asked, "Any weaknesses that might help?"

Ogma looked at him and shook his head. "Don't let it get around me. It will close the gap to you all in a split second."

Yeah, if they made it out of here, Azrael would be coming up with plans from now on. He wondered if Ogma had really chosen to stay in the Master ranks or if he was just stupid.

Azrael shook his head and shrugged. It wasn't like he had a better idea.

Before they moved forward, Azrael asked Bat, "Do we have some time to stay here for a bit?"

Bat nodded, and Azrael continued, "I am going to need that armor, Bat."

Bat took off the Ether-Tech set, and Azrael put it on before he checked his Soul Storage. He had a single ten stack of Soul Strike still charged from the fight with the Wendigo. He recharged the other slot in his Soul Storage, which caused him to fall flat on his helmeted face.

This opponent was unlikely to feel even those, but it was best to have it ready just in case. Jophi checked his earring and recharged it with a regular Fireball. She kept her powerful doubling skill for herself this time.

About ten minutes later, his headache finally receded as his Ether topped back up.

Ogma stood from meditation, looking fully recovered as well. "That storage skill is powerful, but sure takes some preparation time. I assume everyone else is ready?" The group nodded, and he held up a hand, which glowed blue for a moment, then red, and finally a golden yellow.

Strangely, Azrael felt a drop of liquid on his tongue during each flash. The first tasted of glacial water, the second of hibiscus berries, and the third was sweet honeyed beer. Three buffs jumped onto Azrael's bar, and he blinked when reading them.

Beverage of Glacial Strength
- **This beverage has increased your Strength and Stamina by 5.**
  Duration: 5 minutes.

--

Beverage of the Power Berry
- **This beverage has increased your Wisdom and Intelligence by 5.**

Duration: 5 minutes.

--

Beverage of Nectar
- **This beverage increases your health and Ether regeneration by 10%.**
Duration: 5 minutes.

Ogma didn't wait after his skill assisted buffs were added and charged around the corner. Azrael assumed they weren't adding much for a Master ranked individual, but for him and the others, these were extremely beneficial. Azrael charged around the corner behind him and nocked an arrow into a spare bow the group had purchased.

It wasn't anything fancy, but it would add some damage. He only had twenty arrows and no skills to imbue them with. His current plan was to act as the second line tank if the creature bypassed Ogma. His twenty arrows were only meant to hinder the creature, and so Azrael picked his shots carefully.

His first five arrows struck joints, and his next five landed in an even spread on the ground between Ogma's back and the group. If his markers were accurate, they were standing and firing from fifty feet away. Dara and Jophi held their skills, waiting for Ogma to hit, and hopefully anger the horse. Azrael hadn't worried about his non-skilled arrows. They were just pinpricks meant to irritate and maybe slow down some of the Enbarr's movements.

After his markers were in place, he charged Soul Strike five times on his sword and stood ready.

Ogma smashed into the creature with a resounding boom. Azrael felt a wave of air buffet him, and his brain absently tried to calculate the force that collision must have held. Ogma's fists glowed with light, and he moved quickly, connecting each strike with a knee of the twenty-foot-tall horse. The mane of the Enbarr took up the entire hallway, but the horse itself was only a quarter of it.

As Ogma dodged the striking hair whips, Azrael Analyzed it.

Enbarr

Master-Flowing Mane
Level 88
Health Points: 10734/11500
Strong Analyze has failed to provide additional
information.

Dara and Jophi joined in and began peppering the horse with blindingly fast skills. Green, black, red, orange, and yellow arrows started to strike the Enbarr. Some got caught in the mane of the beast, but others sank home with a sizzle or percussive boom. From his other side, ice, fire, wind, and the chipped stone walls themselves became weapons that hurtled towards the Enbarr. These magical missiles would collide with hair and break up into small strikes.

Azrael was just a bystander here. A second line of defense, but he didn't mind as long as it worked. Just as the health of the Enbarr dropped below seventy-five percent, it started to glow. Then the glow began to blur as the hair and horse started to charge back and forth in a jaw-dropping display of speed. Ogma managed to only lose five feet in the first minute but Azrael could tell it was everything he could do to keep the creature contained. The Firbolg was extremely skilled at holding the Enbarr's attention, which was the job of a tank.

Azrael felt his eyes widen and stomach drop as a massive glowing hair fist punched Ogma into the wall. Ogma had been holding the Enbarr right up until he landed from the punch and the ground under him broke. Azrael released the charged Soul Strike he had held in reserve for this possibility. He had stacked only five within the blade. The combat until now, and their short wait before battle, made sure he had seventy five percent of his pool still in reserve.

The five Soul Strikes struck the creature and slowed it down at the thirty-five-foot mark, but it continued to plod forward. Like a workhorse pushing the mill instead of pulling it. It was enough to let Ogma break free of the hair and begin his assault from behind. Azrael's skill wouldn't last long, and he held his hand up ready to release a stored ten from his Soul Storage.

The Enbarr's health dropped below fifty percent and the slight glow became iridescent blue and began to smoke. The effect transformed the glow into a fire, like they had seen with

Octorian. Azrael loosed the skill, shouting, "Release ten!" The skill shot forth and collided with the horse between the thirty- and twenty-foot markers. Spells continued to pepper the beast, but Azrael couldn't find Ogma behind it.

He watched its health continue to drop and its pace towards the ranged attackers increased even though his ten stacks of Soul Strike now assaulted it. Twenty feet. Azrael released the Fireball in his earring and heard it whoosh from his hand as it grew to the size of a dropship. The black smoke of its explosion blocked the creature from view for a time. Azrael saw a hoof plod forward to the ten-foot marker. It was close enough now that the hair was beginning to strike at Jophi, Dara, and himself. Bat stood back, keeping himself as safe as he could manage.

Azrael shouted, "Release ten," and simultaneously charged his sword with eight stacks of Soul Strike. Dara and Jophi couldn't do max damage anymore with the mane striking at them. He saw it cross under twenty five percent health and the flame became bright red. Real fires broke out onto the body of the Enbarr, and Azrael released his eight stack of Soul Strike with a thrust. He had just drained his Ether pool nearly dry. He smiled, though, as the hooves of the horse were pushed back, causing dirt to be dug up and begin piling behind it.

The health continued to drop but Azrael saw that it wasn't going to be enough. His skills were going to run out. He charged a single stack into his blade and saw a skill up notification pop up. The accompanying headache nearly made him pass out, so reading the minimized text was impossible. He glanced at his Ether pool. Only two points remaining.

They were going to die.

If Ogma has any powerful skills, now would be the time to unleash them!

If they failed here, at least they had chosen their own way to die. A vast blue fist careened the Enbarr into the wall. Azrael followed the trajectory back to see Ogma pressed into the opposite wall, the skill connected to him and literally pinning both him and the Enbarr to opposite walls. Ogma didn't look good; his body was scored with cuts that dripped blood down the wall under him. His outstretched fist began to smoke and blister from the heat the Enbarr gave off. Azrael still wasn't sure it would be enough. The Enbarr had just under ten percent health.

Ogma collapsed, and his skill retracted as Azrael watched him slide down the wall. He began to charge forward, Ether-Tech-assisted legs pumping. He was willing to try to remove the last eight percent in any way he could. As he approached, two massive branches burst from the recovering Enbarr's side, causing the creature to shake and shudder.

The glowing stopped, and Azrael blinked at the creature.

Bat's voice trembled as he called, "The Yewman is now at the place where the paths meet!"

CHAPTER FORTY-ONE

Azrael followed Bat's pointing finger and saw a massive black tree standing in the distance. It had sunk two branches into the ground, and Azrael looked at the Enbarr, which had two dark black branches protruding from its chest. Why would the Yewman attack the Enbarr? Weren't they on the same side?

Azrael turned to Dara and Jophi, who both looked badly cut up along their arms and scalps. He made a motion at Ogma, who was unconscious, and said, "Retreat. I will grab Ogma!" Everyone began moving away as Azrael leaped forward and began dragging the bloody form of Ogma away from his slumped position on the wall.

The Yewman didn't move, but as they passed the Enbarr's corpse, it received shocks of electricity that emanated out of the branches. Each shock twitched and spasmed the legs of the beast. His group picked up the pace and were almost around the corner when the Enbarr shot back to its knobbly knees and spoke, "Azrael, is that you?"

He blinked and looked at his group, wanting to know if they had spoken or heard what he just had... coming from... a horse? They were looking back at him with wide eyes, except for Bat, who had his ears spread as wide as a hang glider. Azrael dragged Ogma around the corner before peeking back out and calling, "Who is that?"

The branches removed themselves from the horse, and it trotted back down the hall to join the Yewman. However, from the floor near where the Enbarr had lain, a voice responded, "You can't tell me you forgot me already."

The combination of the talking space and the voice finally clued him in, and he exclaimed, "Apep! I thought you were dead. What happened?"

Azrael rounded the corner and approached the bloody stone where the voice emanated. Apep sighed and responded, "I tapped the three veins, and the level of power they held was far more than I anticipated. I kind of lost myself in the moment, and when I regained my senses, the cell block you had placed me in had fallen apart. With each passing day, I gained more strength as I leeched it from the Pit. When I reached the hypogeum, I managed to kill and capture more and more of the Pit's creatures. However, I couldn't beat that stupid horse!"

Dara and Bat peeked out from the corner, and he motioned them over. Azrael pointed to the wall and said, "Apep, these are Dara and Bat. You two, this is Apep. He is a dungeon that I fell into, and Ogma captured. He had been working on a plan B for escape. Speaking of—can you get us out of here?"

Apep had the Yewman shake its head before his response, "I tried to, but other dungeons reinforce the Pit on all sides but one. That side is the one down that hallway." The Yewman pointed a branch down the fourth hallway. As if on cue, a massive trumpet reverberated through the corridors. It wasn't as loud as it had been above, and Azrael assumed it was more distant based on that fact. Still, if Apep was right, it had come from the only direction of escape.

Azrael made a motion back to where they had dragged Ogma. "Our friend is injured badly, and we will need him to continue. Can you do anything for him?"

Jophi shrieked from around the corner, "Guys, come quick, a huge spider is coming to attack."

He remembered the insect theme of the core's previous dungeon, and looked to the wall for confirmation. The Yewman nodded, and Azrael shook his head. Apep was the dramatic type, it seemed. "It's one of Apep's," Azrael shouted.

Azrael did run around the corner to see what the spider would do and watched as it began creating bandages from its silk webbing. If it stopped the bleeding, it would drastically increase Ogma's recovery. Azrael returned to the wall and asked Apep, "Do we have a chance against Musth?"

"Normally, I wouldn't have even gotten this far but something is strange about the Pit. It has so much power, but is sluggish and slow in its responses. Almost like it is a child, or unintelligent. So, normally I would say we have absolutely no chance." Apep cut off at an odd spot.

Bat encouraged, "But...?"

However, it seemed Apep was gone. The group dragged Ogma into the fork of paths, and they all sat down under the Yewman and Enbarr, waiting for Ogma to recover. A massive trumpet sounded again, but this time from closer than the last call. Azrael tilted his head and looked at the Yewman. "Is it coming this way?"

Both the Yewman and Enbarr stood statue-still. Perhaps five minutes later, Apep said, "Oberan has joined Musth, and is riding the elephant down the halls. We could retreat to the central area. It is a large underground space, much like the arena above. That would allow me to use all of my minions and the captured ones as well."

"Wouldn't it allow the Pit to do the same?" Azrael interjected.

Apep had the Yewman pick up Ogma and begin retreating down the central hallway, as it shook its head. "No, I don't think it will. Still, I could be wrong."

Dara, Jophi, and Bat looked at him with concern, and he blinked back. Jophi spoke up, "Hold on there, Apep, when did you become the leader?"

Apep didn't answer, and Azrael looked to Dara, who shrugged, and said, "I hate to say this, but this is likely our only option. I don't think we can take on Musth, especially with Ogma injured. Definitely not Musth and Oberan. We need this core's help."

They entered into a massive chamber with a flat ceiling that only cleared the twenty-foot tall Yewman by a few feet. Once they reached the center, Apep's voice reverberated all around them, "I am going to try to capture the entirety of this space. This will force the Pit to send reinforcements from farther away—if it is even present. It should also allow me to spawn creatures and reinforce faster."

The trumpeting grew more frequent and louder as creatures began flowing into the room. The Yewman placed Ogma against a wall and stood slightly ahead of the center of the room. The other exit from the room slammed shut, and Azrael hoped that meant Apep had control. He asked the air, "Was that you, Apep?" and the Yewman nodded once. Okay, at least the retreat was available if they needed it. Azrael hesitated and then added another ten stacked charges of Soul Strike to Soul Storage. Once he picked himself off the floor, he turned to Jophi and indicated his earring.

Jophi came over and whispered, "Stalagmite, this time. Underground like this, it will have a bit of added power. I used my doubling skill in the fight with the Enbarr and can't boost the stored spell in your earring this time."

He waited for his Ether to tick up to fifty-five percent and managed to forgo an Ether drain headache when he put another five stack into his Storage skill. He was more or less bottomed out on Ether, but he was hoping that Oberan would want to try to preserve his plans instead of outright attacking them. Plus, they had the time it would take for the man to get here.

A door slammed shut on the other entrance they had retreated down, and Azrael smiled. It would seem Apep succeeded in capturing the area, and that was also a way to buy more time!

Apep whispered from right beside Azrael's foot, "There is something above us, and I think it's the other core. I am going to try to dig it out. I won't be able to provide more reinforcements, though."

Azrael hissed, "Don't do it now!" but it was too late. Apep was ignoring him. Just great! Azrael surveyed the troops and noticed wolves, rats, wasps, ants, beetles, and even a large number of holes in the floor, which likely signified the bees. At the head of their formation were the Enbarr and the Yewman. He hoped it would be enough.

A massive boom sent spiderweb cracks through the stone doorway into the room. Dara cried out in alarm, and Jophi held up a hand, bracing it with the other. The air of the room shook with the next strike, and a few pieces of stone fell away on their side of the stone door.

The third strike crumbled the door and a black elephant stumbled into the room, eyes red and angry. Oberan walked in casually behind the beast, and he had brought Gyr and Yonel. The odds just kept getting worse.

Luckily, Oberan seemed to want to preserve his plans and called out, "Azrael, you have surprised me multiple times today. However, this is the end of this hare-brained escape attempt." Oberan held up a gloved hand that held a sword with something glowing pink at its pommel. "It took me some time to gain control of Musth, but I control this dungeon, and so have very little to fear down here in the hypogeum. I am not sure how you have managed to wrest control of these spawns from the Pit, but I assure you, Musth and I do not need to worry about them."

Azrael watched Oberan gesticulate and include the whole room in his gesture of disgust. He also saw Oberan's eyes alight on Ogma, and a cruel smile played across his lips as he sneered. "Good, my cousin still lives and conveniently can't try to perform any heroics…"

Oberan looked up and saw Azrael was also looking at Ogma. "Did he get you this far? Is it one of his skills that controls my Pit's creatures?" As he spoke, he caressed the pommel of his sword. The item pulsed pink and Azrael blinked at the crystalline heart, trying to recall if he had ever seen anything like it. The shape wasn't circular, and Azrael doubted that it was a functional counterweight. It vaguely reminded Azrael of a dungeon core, but its form and glow were different. This thing flickered like trapped fire, and the pulsing was from some sort of enchantment that surrounded the piece.

Trying to stall for more time, Azrael tried negotiating, "If you give us a ship and let us go, I will give you full control of your Pit again. Otherwise, you will continue to lose what little control you have over it until it turns against you."

Oberan stepped back and looked around him, then glared at Azrael, "You lie. You don't possess that kind of power!"

Azrael was bluffing, of course—he didn't possess that kind of power. Still, Apep might be able to pull it off. The dungeon core had put up a good show this far. "Think about it, Oberan. You started losing control long before we entered the hypogeum. Probably right around the time my cell block collapsed."

Oberan looked to Gyr and Yonel, then to Azrael. He continued to stroke the pommel of his sword. Azrael took the opportunity to look around at the massed forces on their side of this conflict. He tried to calculate their odds and knew it wasn't good. Even without Gyr and Yonel, they would have lost to Musth and Oberan. The addition of the latter two just added to the opposing scale.

Oberan murmured, "I can let your three friends go free on the surface, but you and Ogma must remain here."

Azrael blinked seriously, stunned that he had gotten anything out of Oberan. He wasn't going to take that offer. He wasn't a hero, despite what he had led Oberan to believe. He responded coolly, "That doesn't work for me. You can keep Ogma—your family is none of my concern—but the rest of us get to leave."

Oberan smiled wickedly, turned to Gyr, and cooed, "Do you think you can torture the information out of him?"

The silent, stoic Gyr smiled for the first time Azrael could remember. He wished the man would take it back. The look sent shivers running through his body—starting at his scalp, arching over his shoulders, and down the backs of his legs. Gyr didn't say a word. His look was enough confirmation, and Oberan's eyes crinkled fondly around the edges before he commanded, "Musth, destroy them."

Azrael had just enough warning to brace himself inside the Ether-Tech suit before a trumpet blast shook the roof and walls of the room.

CHAPTER FORTY-TWO

Musth charged forward, its eyes glowing pink for a brief moment before morphing into a deep red. Each loping step shook the ground, and each bounce hit the ceiling, causing the entire room to shake and rumble on its approach. The shaking seemed to wake Ogma, who sat up and shouted, "Danu!"

Azrael didn't have time to process the shout because the Yewman shot its branch arms into the ground. The ends exited shortly after, right in front of Musth, and were subsequently batted aside by the elephant's massive trunk. The thick branches weren't out of the fight, though, and began to wrap around Musth's feet. At first, the elephant was able to pull its massive legs out of the bindings, but then the Yewman seemed to grow thorns that bit and scratched the hide of the legs. Musth fell to the ground in a colossal heap that bounced Azrael.

The Enbarr was holding back Oberan, Yonel, and Gyr—its mane segmenting into single strands in some places and vast collections in others. Oberan and Yonel both slashed expertly at the hair, cutting off pieces of the whips that then fell around them. Damaging the Enbarr simultaneously. Gyr moved in and out, scoring hits against the legs of the powerful mini-boss. Within a few seconds, the Enbarr began to smoke, and Azrael felt himself grow cold. They already had it reduced to seventy-five percent health.

Musth flared red, and all of the restraining vine-like branches withered and died around it. The Yewman convulsed and pulled back what remained of the branch-like arms, severing the damaged parts in the act. Musth trumpeted again. Azrael fell to the ground, the Ether-Tech suit failing to stop the stun debuff this time. The other skills that had been peppering the massive elephant ceased immediately, and Azrael assumed his friends had also been stunned.

After a few seconds, he stood back up and relocated Musth, who was now violently stomping on the Yewman. The bottom of each foot glowed red before impact and flattened the demon tree where it contacted. The tree must have come out of the stun at the same time though, because suddenly it became a flurry of movement. Each whip-like appendage was growing twelve-inch thorns and striking Musth. Azrael checked his Ether pool to find it at seventy four percent. He shot his hand forward and readied all of his attacks when Ogma's massive phantasmal fist rocketed Musth off the Yewman.

Azrael made a perusal of the battlefield, looking for any area he could help. The stun had affected everyone in the room. The Enbarr and its opponents had resumed their fighting, but now the three humanoids were being mobbed by all of the fodder. Ants, beetles, wolves, and wasps began dying. Still, they distracted the three enough for the Enbarr to score numerous hits on them.

Azrael turned back to Musth and released the Stalagmite spell. Jophi must have cast one as well, because two massive spikes grew up from the ground and fought against the thick skin of Musth's underside. They lifted the elephant and even drew a small amount of blood before the tips broke off from the strain. Next, Azrael repositioned and called, "Release five!"

His Soul Strikes screeched as they attempted to dissect Musth. Dead skin patches fell away, but his skill wasn't powerful enough to breach the inherent Ether of the Pit boss. Ogma added his fist to the blades, and together they shot Musth into the wall, causing it to crack. The crack extended into the ceiling and floor. Azrael watched on in horror. Musth slapped its trunk on the ground, then rose onto hind legs, hitting its head and causing the cracks to spread further. Was the ceiling going to bury them all?

Musth's front two legs landed back on the ground, and Azrael Analyzed it.

Musth
Epic-Raging Bull Mammoth
Level 71
Health Points: 12880/26000
Skills: Opponent's level is too high.

It was already at half health. They had a chance. As he thought that, the elephant's front feet landed, and Azrael saw a green glow surround it. Then its health rose to seventy-five percent. The green light morphed to brown, and armored plates grew all over its body. Azrael cursed himself for his naivety. Of course it wouldn't be that easy.

The group continued to bombard Musth with everything they had, and Azrael felt rather useless. The Yewman was still collecting itself into shape, and Azrael checked its health to discover it was below twenty-five percent. He checked in on the Enbarr fight to see it glowing blue. This wasn't going well on any front. While there was still fodder launching into battle, Azrael didn't hold out hope for any of the four powerful opponents to fall.

He ran over to a hole in the ground and shouted, "We need you up here now." Nothing happened. Cursing, Azrael yelled to Jophi while pointing at the hole, "Hit one of these with a Fireball!"

Jophi didn't question him and launched a Fireball to splash over and into one of the spaces. Worker and Drone Bees launched out from the holes. Azrael hoped that the Queen was mixed in amongst the swarm. A glowing light confirmed the Queen's presence as it began charging its spell attack. The blast hit Musth on one of its armor plates and an explosion displaced the air with a resonating whoosh. The elephant reeled back into the wall, cracking it further, causing a good quarter of the ceiling and floor to become more unstable.

The attack phase of the Worker Bees followed, and they attempted to pick up Oberan, Gyr, and Yonel. The Enbarr got a break as its opponents fought off the aerial attacks. The Workers died by the hundreds before the Drones shot forward, attempting to skewer the three and Musth. They pin-cushioned Musth, whose armor did very little against their sharp stingers. Azrael watched as the thoraxes of the Drones pumped methodically.

Musth stumbled, and Azrael saw it was back under fifty percent. It glowed red again, and all the bees shriveled and died as it got to its feet. The flying swarm got decimated during its attack on the four opponents, but none of them came away unscathed. Light began to glow again, and Azrael fixed his eyes on the Queen as it charged another ball of light. Spells pelted into Musth, and its exploding shot of white light blasted the elephant again. The ceiling began to leak stone dust, and Azrael shouted, "The ceiling, guys! It's growing too unstable!"

Musth's health dropped to twenty-four percent, and an ominous, oppressive feeling came over the entire room. Elephant blood began to form little balls where it had fallen. Then all the blood spheres shot towards the massive Bull Mammoth. Azrael and his team dodged the projectiles but the Yewman wasn't so lucky as it had been mid-attack on Musth. The blood balls tore its remaining health away, and it fell to the ground in a lifeless heap. The balls collided with Musth, and its health began to climb again.

It climbed right back up to eighty percent before a red mist began to surround its massive body. The armor plates began to shine and morph into spiked armor—transforming Musth into a battering ram of death. The elephant looked like a spiky hedgehog or porcupine. The red mist finished by coalescing on its tusks and trunk. The tusks became huge, curved sabers of death, and the trunk grew to resemble a morningstar head.

He looked over to see the Enbarr's red glow begin to fade as Gyr pulled an ax from its chest. Azrael checked his Ether pool to find it at seventy-eight percent. That fight and the talking had lasted just around five minutes, based on his Ether recovery rate. He felt a desire to give up, but clenched his jaw in stubborn refusal as he glared at Oberan.

Ogma jumped in to replace the Enbarr, and both Oberan and Ogma blurred as bangs sounded from a half dozen places in their twenty-foot sparring circle. They separated a moment later, and Oberan crowed, "Come now, cousin. If you force me to, I will kill you!"

Ogma was cut in half a dozen places, and Oberan seemed only to have minor injuries. Azrael couldn't tell if those were from the Enbarr or Ogma. Azrael looked to Musth to see it destroying what remained of the bees. The Queen was just a twitching corpse on the end of one of its morningstar flanges.

Azrael saw Jophi firing spell after spell and Dara running around to collect arrows as the fighting continued throughout the room. Azrael desperately tried to think of something to do. His eyes flicked to the ceiling. He looked over to Bat, who was on the other side of the room, cowering in a relatively safe area. He shouted, "Get to Bat—both of you!" He didn't care about Ogma at the moment. He might need him to hold Oberan back for the time being, but what his fate became didn't matter.

Azrael charged his blade with seven Soul Strikes and thrust the sword towards an enormous crack he could see. Simultaneously, he shouted, "Release ten!" Seventeen stacks launched from his blade, and Azrael felt his feet slide backward along the stone floor. He didn't watch to see what would happen and began following Dara and Jophi toward Bat. Arms grabbed him around the waist and easily lifted him.

Azrael had a moment to register that Ogma had caught him, and was now aiding his retreat as the grinding of his skill started up. The cracks above Musth grew until suddenly the falling dust became chunks of rock. They pelted Musth, and Azrael attempted to locate Oberan and his two guards. They had retreated in the other direction which, unfortunately, was their path out of this place. Based on their quick actions, Azrael could only hope that Musth would die.

His group watched as the ceiling caved in, and dust filled the air. Jophi coughed, "Do you think that killed it?"

Bat squeaked, "Did it have any more recovery abilities?"

Ogma sneezed before responding, "Many, but I doubt it can recover from being under a pile of stone."

They had won—but didn't have time to enjoy the victory as a massive sucking wind evacuated the dust from the chamber to reveal Oberan, Gyr, and Yonel standing at the peninsula of the collapse.

Azrael thought they would begin attacking them but saw that they were, in fact, looking up at something. Azrael followed their gaze to see a massive, transparent glass tank. The tank was sloshing liquid he couldn't identify until Ogma cried, "Oberan, you were keeping the vat of Essence down here?"

Oberan looked at Ogma and then at the massive glass pool of… Essence. He blinked and shouted, "That whole thing is Essence! You're kidding, your mother wouldn't have trusted me with the location. The amount of power right there, for the taking. What are the other two colors around the dungeon core?"

Azrael felt his confusion grow. He couldn't even see all the edges of the container holding the Essence. What he could see was easily the volume of a small lake. Because of Oberan's question, he looked to the space above the vessel and found a rainbow of colors. In the center was a glowing blue orb that could be nothing other than the Pit's dungeon core. Around it, there was a pink string that pulsed in time with Oberan's pommel. Wrapped around the pink strand was a red string, and then tying the entire contraption together was a thick orange band. All the colors pulsed and ebbed, creating a kaleidoscope of color.

Oberan answered his own question, "Danu must have placed two additional Heartstrings around the core! No wonder I could never discover the location of the Essence. That also explains why the Pit has been sluggish to my commands. She had control the entire time…"

Azrael noticed something glowing green from near his hand. He looked down to see Apep's core surfacing beside him. He touched it, and Apep whispered into his mind, "If you can get me into that reservoir, I will have the power to get us out of here."

Azrael whispered, "That is easier said than done! Why haven't you gotten yourself in?"

"I am not powerful enough to break the capping device," was Apep's short response.

Azrael lifted the orb from the ground and said, "Then I won't be strong enough either, but I will try…"

Should I really rely on someone else? Maybe the agreement with the dungeon core will be enough?

Oberan heard him speaking and sneered at them all. "Plotting some more, are you?" He looked at Gyr and Yonel, who looked at the reservoir greedily. In a single swing, he decapitated Yonel, who didn't even have a chance to react. Gyr began to turn with a crinkle on his nose as he made an angry disgusted face. His head followed Yonel's to the floor on Oberan's backswing.

Ogma shouted, "What are you doing! They were your loyal supporters! Wait, you plan to try to take this—?" He was cut off as Oberan flew over the ground and stabbed him through the chest. Jophi howled and attempted to run to Ogma. His eyes widened, and he coughed blood. Oberan shoved Jophi away and even the casual shove was enough to knock her unconscious when she hit the wall. Azrael swallowed something that formed in his throat. Was that fear?

"Ogma!" A piercing shriek echoed through the depths of the hypogeum.

Oberan's eyes widened, and his face morphed to an unreadable expression. "By Morrigan's black feathers, Danu is here! I must hurry then," he muttered to himself, his voice filled with what Azrael would describe as fear.

Azrael huffed a breath out in a sad chuckle at the comical turn of events. If Danu was here, they were all going to die—including Oberan. All because of this stupid man's greed. It was ironic because Azrael was going to die either way. So, Oberan had caused his own death.

So much for choosing how I die.

Oberan sneered at him and came over to lift him by the collar of his ragged black shirt. "Perhaps I should cut out your tongue and blame you for the deed—she always did hate the Sovereign Empire." He looked up at the sound of something crashing. Dust began to fall all around Azrael and Oberan.

Azrael tried to fight back, his hands scrabbling over the hood and powerful enchanted fabrics Oberan wore. Azrael felt like a puppy scrabbling at the jaws of a bear. Maybe if he had used a skill he would have annoyed the arena master, but his intention wasn't to beat Oberan. Only to escape...

With a casual flick, Azrael careened into the wall, and Oberan jumped up into the crevasse the roof collapse had caused. Azrael felt his back crash into the wall. His neck whipped and strained, softening the blow slightly to his head as it struck the wall with a crack. A stunned debuff floated up into his interface. The armor had saved him from unconsciousness, but he wouldn't have moved even if he could have, slumped against the wall as he was.

When the stun wore off, he looked up to find Oberan climbing the rough crack from the inside. Distantly he wondered what would happen if someone entered that reddish pool of power. A massive boom echoed from the doorway nearby, and the colossal stone slab flew to collide with the pile of rubble at the center of the chamber.

A fiery-haired woman with pale skin entered the room. She held a spear in one hand, and her plaited red hair hung down past her knee. She surveyed the room with bright blue eyes that took in everything at a glance. Azrael shivered as her penetrating gaze passed over him, but she continued looking up at the vessel and Oberan's climbing form.

She shouted, "Oberan, you know that is for Ogma! Get down here—you can't use it while already being on a planet, anyway!"

Oberan cackled back, "How can Ogma use it if you don't save his life, Danu?"

Danu's head snapped back to Ogma's form, which she had passed over earlier. Azrael blinked, and she was kneeling beside her son, her hands glowing bright gold. Azrael wasn't sure she could save him—hadn't it been too long?

Danu sent one spell into his body with a touch, and then breathed through the other hand to create a golden mist. The mist hung around Ogma, but nothing happened. A tear fell from Danu's cheek. She cried, "Breathe, you ungrateful boy!"

She hit him with another pulse of golden light from her hand. Ogma took a stuttering breath that drew all of the golden mist into his body. His face immediately became less pale, and Danu smiled. She then turned and, with natural grace, threw her spear at Oberan's climbing form. It seemed like she would hit him until he blurred and was standing on the rounded edge of the vessel.

The glowing spear course-corrected, and Oberan deflected it with ease – causing it to crash into the glass. The glass cracked, and Oberan shouted, "Thanks for the assist, *Mother!*"

Oberan struck the crack with his sword and widened it. Then stepped into the hole he'd created in the container, with a flash of green accompanying him from inside his hood. Azrael grinned.

Despite the improbability, he had gotten Apep into the container.

CHAPTER FORTY-THREE

Danu shrieked in rage and lifted Ogma over a shoulder—then blurred, carrying him out of the chamber faster than Azrael's eyes could follow.

Azrael collected Jophi and passed her off to Dara after she helped Bat to his feet. The Essence vat flashed ominously red and began to slosh. Azrael called to Dara and Bat, "Follow the crashing—Danu is probably headed to the shipyard, to escape!"

He took lead of the group because he had the Ether-Tech armor. He still hoped they wouldn't run into any creatures in the hypogeum or that Danu cleared them on her mad dash for her ship.

Bat was able to follow the trail she took thanks to something obvious only to the blind batman. He redirected them several times as the floor bucked under the fleeing group. Unfortunately, a moment later he shouted, "There is a Wendigo headed right for us. I think it heard the noise of Danu's flight as well."

The hypogeum floor seemed to jump under the group's feet. Everyone but Azrael fell. That seemed to wake up Jophi, at least. The destabilization of the dungeon was getting worse at an alarming rate. Azrael wondered if the quakes were localized to the dungeon even. Last time, placing a person in a vat of Essence had resulted in the creation of a planet, according to Ogma. What would happen if a Planetary God ascended while on another planet?

He took quick stock of his arsenal. He didn't have any stored attacks in his Soul Storage, and a quick check of his Ether pool showed it had recovered to near the thirty percent mark. He only had the armor and his sword which, admittedly, were huge advantages.

"Just one?" Azrael asked Bat. At the batman's nod, Azrael nodded too. In his Ether-Tech armor, he had a single advantage he hadn't had during the challenge competition. He could probably take a hit and avoid the disease debuff for a time. But there was also no healer here to save him. He still needed to be very careful.

Azrael glanced at the recovering group. Dara was out of arrows and was currently helping a dizzy and disoriented Jophi to her feet; they wouldn't be of any use. Bat may be of help, though.

"Assist me in any way you can, Bat," Azrael commanded as he pushed the suit of armor to its full capacity. He sprinted towards the direction Bat indicated the Wendigo approached from, wanting to create a buffer zone between him and the group. Considering this creature's undead nature, he worried it may attempt to ignore an opponent surrounded by mechanical metal.

The floor began to vibrate below him and he adjusted his plan on the fly. There was no chance to play the long game now. This dungeon, and possibly the entire planet, would soon be a death trap. He turned a corner and saw the smile first.

His body shivered as the inhuman expression met him. He shook it off and charged two Soul Strikes into his sword. He activated Soul Cloak as well, and just in the nick of time as four claws of the creature shot towards him like ninja stars.

He couldn't afford to waste the Soul Strike Ether on knocking any of the projectiles out of the air. He could only maneuver his body to help his Cloak in making them miss. He heard the sound of metal screeching as two of the ninja star-like claws sunk into the Ether-Tech armor. Azrael sighed in relief. They hadn't punctured the armor; his debuff bar was clear.

The Wendigo slashed its arms at him and he swung his sword. He severed a single appendage at the wrist but the other collided with his shoulder. More whining metal screeched from his shoulder. The Wendigo latched on, attempting to pry into the tin can he wore.

Azrael tried to attack the creature but it pressed itself in close to him, making it impossible to connect his sword to undead flesh.

Bat shouted, "It's immune to my sonic attacks! I don't think it feels pain."

Well, so much for that option. Azrael took a deep breath. There was a single option left. He stored his sword in his Ring of Holding and bear hugged the Wendigo. Once he was sure he had the creature locked down, he initiated the self-destruct sequence of the armor and commanded it to release him.

He stepped out of the back of the suit and immediately ran towards Bat. Without him inside, the armor wouldn't hold the Wendigo for long, but that was why he had set the fuse for such a short time. He tackled the batman and pulled him around the corner just as an explosion rocked the hallway they had just been down. Dust billowed around the corner and coated them.

"Ouch," Bat said as he tried to disentangle Azrael from him.

Azrael stood up and asked, "Did that kill it?"

Bat nodded and motioned to the approaching Dara and Jophi. "We need to hurry, this whole place is about to fall on top of us."

Azrael could feel the constant shake of the tunnel and went to go help Dara with Jophi. Together they fled down the tunnel until Bat called, "We need to go up. Danu ascended here!"

They were forced to climb the walls, as none of them had the strength of Danu, who had likely jumped up the levels. Once Azrael reached the top, he found some chains and managed to hoist Jophi through the hole. Dara and Bat climbed up.

The group continued to follow Bat's instructions.

"There is a large group of guards up ahead attempting to hold the combatants back. I think both groups are trying to get to the shipyard," Bat exclaimed.

A large section of stone a hundred meters behind them collapsed with a loud cracking sound. "Straight through," Azrael shouted as he grabbed Jophi and slung her over a shoulder.

"Stop that, I can do…" Jophi started to say but Azrael took off running and the rest of her words cut off in a shriek.

They turned a corner to see a massive Battle Royale taking place. On all sides, people were releasing skills, killing and maiming each other. Azrael hoped his Soul Cloak could help protect him and dove into the ranks. Jophi and Bat were right behind him.

Maybe it was because they didn't attack anyone or maybe it was chance, but Azrael made it past the skirmish and into a hallway on the other side. Bat came after him, but at a glance he couldn't see Dara. Azrael cursed but made the cold decision. "Leave her, let's keep going."

Jophi's abdomen tensed and she grabbed his shoulder hard. "You have to go back—"

Azrael began running again. Now was not the time for emotional responses. Now was the time to escape. Dara was one of his trainers and she would understand his decision. The floor continued to quake violently as they hurried through a set of doors into a shipyard. A massive Destroyer pulled away from the dock and ambled out of the port. Azrael pointed to a tiny dropship, the only other ship present, and shouted, "That's our best chance!"

Dara's voice carried through the doorway and he glanced back. She was running down the hallway towards them, Torin and Papi hot on her heels. Jophi slapped his back. "Put me down, so I can cover her escape." Bat nodded beside him and Azrael complied.

He took up a stance at the door. If his two *friends* failed he would close the gate to the shipyard, effectively locking out all three of the fighters. Jophi shot ice lances at Papi and Torin. They didn't appear to do much damage, but they did freeze their legs to the ground. Torin shouted, "I am going ta kill ya. Dan't you leave us here!"

Bat used some of his sonic attacks to add small stuns and slow the two guards further.

Azrael smiled as Dara crossed the threshold into the room and he closed the door. It would take them some time to break through the enchanted stone.

Dara took a deep breath and took over the escape from there. They rushed towards the dropship, and Azrael noted its black paint and skull and crossbones decal. This was a mercenary pirate vessel, likely here dropping off slaves. The four of them rushed to seats and strapped themselves in as the shaking continued.

Dara sat in the pilot chair and pointed to the co-pilot chair, motioning at it and Azrael with a gesture. He took the seat. She knew his teaching and skill, but trusted her experience more in this situation.

She clicked the ignition and with a practiced hand began toggling switches. He heard the clamps release the ship and the shaking he felt stabilized into the hum of the engines. Dara managed to pilot the ship out of the dock before it jerked and began to shake—alarms began sounding in the cockpit.

She looked at the warning lights and swore. "The normal thrust is not getting us away from the dungeon. Maybe it is some kind of forcefield or something? Azrael, push the throttle to forty percent. We're going to have to try to break through it."

He did so and the ship inched forward, but the shaking intensified. "That won't be enough! Go to fifty percent." The ship slipped sideways in the air, but barely budged forward. Jophi and Bat made distressed noises as everyone in the ship was tossed around like popping corn. Good thing they were strapped in.

Dara shouted, "Go full throttle! Hold together, you piece of junk—hold!"

The engines revved and for a heartbeat the ship didn't move. Azrael felt his hope start to die, but then the ship shot forward like an arrow from a bow. He felt his head slam into the seat's headrest, his body pressed firmly into it.

They shot out of the field and Azrael struggled to reach the throttle to dial it back. Dara shouted, "No, don't! We are still fighting something. Look at the gauges."

Azrael did so and saw what she meant. The drag meter and the speedometer were both in strange positions for a ship of this category. It was almost like they were flying a battleship and not a dropship. The weight the meters seemed to indicate were too high. He didn't reach for the throttle again.

When they exited the atmosphere, Azrael looked through a side window back at the planet. Massive lightning flashes jogged through the skies. Some of the clouds began to turn green, others pink, and they began to fight for dominance. The green clouds seemed to obliterate the pink, crushing them down until only a small circle held. Just as Azrael thought it was over, the pink cloud got absorbed by the green, and everything turned black. The lightning redoubled—then calmed.

Finally able to speak, Azrael called, "What is happening?"

Dara pointed to the calibration tools, which finally seemed to be stabilizing, somewhat. She adjusted some switches and motioned to throttle back. She turned the ship slightly onto a new heading as she said, "I don't know, but the gravity is still nearly doubled. It's time to get out of here!"

They sped away as the ship shook violently.

EPILOGUE

A quest line has been abandoned.
Dungeon Quest
      Initiate Combatant
            Survival Challenges
The Arena Pit Dungeon no longer exists. This quest was removed from your log because it can no longer be completed.

Azrael had a brief moment of regret for the Etherience he would have gained from continual questing in the dungeon, but assuaged the feeling with a promise to adventure on other planets.

Jophi, Dara, Azrael, and Bat sat in the small mercenary pirate dropship and surveyed what Azrael would describe as a hole in space. It had taken the majority of the power to escape the insane gravity of the anomaly, and they were currently waiting for the Ether Converters to replenish it.

Bat squeaked, "Can anyone explain to me what has all of you so fixated? What just happened, did we escape the gravity anomaly?"

Azrael blinked. Bat's 'vision' must have been confined to the dropship since they got onboard. He tried to think of a good way to explain the events that led to this moment. Jophi beat him to it, "We have escaped, but Tech Duinn got sucked through a literal hole in space."

Jophi looked to Azrael, lost for what else to say. He just shrugged at her, as he couldn't think of a better explanation. He doubted anyone truly knew what this massive hole in space was.

<I'm ascending, Azrael,> something whispered. It sounded strangely like Apep but was layered with other voices. Oberan clearly among them. Azrael couldn't place the others.

Bat's ears flicked like he heard the same thing.

Azrael looked at the others, who hadn't reacted at all. Was he hearing things?

Bat pointed to Azrael, "You have some strand of dark black Ether connecting you to something off the ship. Do you know what it is?"

Azrael shivered. Maybe he really was hearing Apep's voice. If humanoids became Planetary Gods and Dragons became Star Gods—what in the Sovereign Halls did dungeons become when they ascended?

He shook his head, dismissing the question from his mind for now. "Are you sure, Bat? I don't feel any different..." he said instead.

Bat shrugged and stopped questioning. The others gave him a strange look and he shrugged as well. They had somehow survived the destruction of Tech Duinn. That was enough for now.

Whatever was happening now was beyond the ken of everyone aboard. Dara voiced a more immediate concern, "We have no food on this ship and likely can only make it to a nearby planetary star port. According to the navigation system, we are nearest to a planet called Athas Four. Anyone heard of it?"

Jophi came to look down at the information and clicked a few buttons to navigate around. She pointed to Gaia, which was listed at less than a light year away. Then she scrolled back to Athas Four and pointed out Athas One through Three. Then she nodded, "If I am not mistaken, these are the planets that surround the Star God Skard. The Dark Elves control these planets, but they are all colonies of either Gaia or Mars. The surfaces are too extreme to be habitable. So, they have massive cities deep underground and a spaceport that always remains on the dark side of the planet."

Azrael chimed in, recalling a few lessons himself, "Are these the planets that were too close to the Star God? Or the Star God that grew too large? The surfaces range from 372 degrees during the day to absolute zero at night?"

Dara snapped her fingers, recalling what she knew as well. "Yes," she said and looked to Jophi. "Can you get the group passage onto a ship bound for the Sovereign Empire?"

Jophi clicked a few more buttons and pointed to the results. Dara blinked. Azrael felt his breath catch and he stood up for a closer look at the screen.

This can't be right.

Bat asked, "What is it?"

The list of planets owned by the Sovereign Empire contained a single entry. Each world Azrael knew implicitly, due to long hours of rote lessons, was labeled as captured. Only a few of the planets were listed as Tuathan owned. Some were now the property of Martian Guilds and others were Gaian Guilds. It would seem that one of the Etherverse Superpowers, the Sovereign Empire, had been reduced to a single planet in the time they were on Tech Duinn.

Dara looked to Azrael before she spoke, "I am going to try to get back there. What's your plan?"

Azrael thought about it. Did he owe anything to his father? Maybe—but it would seem that the addition of Guilds had entirely upset the balance in the Etherverse. He looked to Jophi, who was going to head to Gaia and her Cathodiem Guild. Then to Dara, who intended to rejoin the Empire.

Gaia was the most powerful Planetary God in existence. Surely that meant it had the greatest opportunity to advance! Why would he join the losing side? He and Dara wouldn't be able to turn the tide of the conflict. Not if the Empire was down to a single planet. But he might be able to gain strength and take some revenge…

Azrael shook his head and responded, "I think I will try to go with Jophi." Then to soften the blow, he added, "Perhaps on Gaia, I can petition the Atlantean Council to halt the fighting."

Dara turned to Bat and he squeaked, "I'm going with Azrael."

Jophi shrugged. "If we can get to the spaceport of Athas Two, I have contacts. If we can find a fast transport, we can make it to Gaia in under a year, Dara. With the war, I doubt it will be easy to find a way onto Sovereign Prime."

Dara nodded and smiled softly, "I have to try. Verimy's family lives on Sovereign Prime. Perhaps I can help them survive whatever comes next."

Azrael surveyed the people on the ship. What was this strange warmth he felt when he looked at them all?

Probably just euphoria from surviving Tech Duinn— yeah, that must be it!

Afterword

We hope you enjoyed Tech Duinn! Since reviews are the lifeblood of indie publishing, we'd love it if you could leave a positive review on Amazon! Please use this link to go to the Ether Flows: Tech Duinn Amazon product page to leave your review: geni.us/TechDuinn.

As always, thank you for your support! You are the reason we're able to bring these stories to life.

About Ryan DeBruyn

Ryan has always been a dream chaser. His first career was as a professional athlete, which taught him the dedication and perseverance needed to chase fantastic goals. A devastating injury removed Ryan from this world before his prime, and taught him the value of an education.

His first book began as a hobby project while he attended Georgian College. Using his hard fought lessons, in motivation, discipline and hard work Ryan published his first book in February 2019.

He is a recent graduate in the field of Electrical Engineering and a full-time author.

Here's hoping you enjoy the worlds he creates as much as he does!

Connect with Ryan:
Facebook.com/RyanDeBruyn
Instagram.com/RyRyDubs
Patreon.com/RyanDeBruyn

About Mountaindale Press

Dakota and Danielle Krout, a husband and wife team, strive to create as well as publish excellent fantasy and science fiction novels. Self-publishing *The Divine Dungeon: Dungeon Born* in 2016 transformed their careers from Dakota's military and programming background and Danielle's Ph.D. in pharmacology to President and CEO, respectively, of a small press. Their goal is to share their success with other authors and provide captivating fiction to readers with the purpose of solidifying Mountaindale Press as the place 'Where Fantasy Transforms Reality.'

Connect with Mountaindale Press:
MountaindalePress.com
Facebook.com/MountaindalePress
Twitter.com/_Mountaindale
Krout@MountaindalePress.com

Mountaindale Press Titles

GameLit and LitRPG

The Completionist Chronicles Series
The Divine Dungeon Series
By: Dakota Krout

King's League Series
By: Jason Anspach and J.N. Chaney

A Touch of Power: Series
By: Jay Boyce

Red Mage Series
By: Xander Boyce

Space Seasons Series
By: Dawn Chapman

Ether Collapse Series
Ether Flows Series
By: Ryan DeBruyn

Bloodgames Series
By: Christian J. Gilliland

Wolfman Warlock Series
By: James Hunter and Dakota Krout

Axe Druid Series
Mephisto's Magic Online Series
By: Christopher Johns

Skeleton in Space Series
By: ANDRIES LOUWS

Chronicles of Ethan Series
By: JOHN L. MONK

Pixel Dust Series
By: DAVID PETRIE

Artorian's Archives Series
By: DENNIS VANDERKERKEN AND DAKOTA KROUT

APPENDIX

Apep – An arena dungeon that is stumbled upon by Azrael. A map to the dungeon is purchased by Dara and Verimy during their brief trip into Mur.

Analyze – A skill that is common for almost all the individuals of the Etherverse. When scrutinizing an object or a person, the system will reveal some information based on your level in the skill. Skill can be countered or obfuscated.

Arbuckle – A very rare metal that can be inscribed with powerful runes, and has the ability to convert hold a large Ether Pool to power them. This metal is required to create a shop, and seed shops. It is somewhat alive and grows more of itself.

Atlantean Academy – A school on Gaia. This school was attached to Atlantis and held a neutral faction for the guilds. All attendees were either nobility or very skilled.

Azrael Sovereign – The main character of the novel. Son of the Sovereign King who is considered quite powerful. His mother is unknown and dropped him off at the Sovereign Halls after he was born.

Bat – Bat is saved by Azrael and quickly becomes his friend. As he gains in levels, he slowly becomes more and more powerful. Azrael who hasn't ever had a friend before thinks of him as a tool through most of the book.

Cathodiem Guild – Guild that was situated on Gaia over a billion years ago. Guild was very powerful and had great influence with a seat on the Atlantean Council.

Chain Quest – A type of quest that contains multiple parts.

Citizen Accessible Shop – An addon for a shop. This allows an assistant to scan through the merchant's wares that reside in a shop and purchase items on the behest of individuals. This limits interactions and messages that can be transmitted through spies. Still, it doesn't stop them…

Class Template – Another relatively new addition to the Etherverse. First utilized by the Martians, a template creates a known path through the fog of war that creates a 'powerful' class. These classes are only added to the list once the individual ranks up. However, this has created a bit of a problem.

Crystals – Crystallized Ether. Crystals is the short form. A type of currency.

Dagda Tract – Brother of Ogma and son of Danu. He is used in an experiment by Danu to create a Planetary God that the Tuatha De Danaan controls.

Danu Tract – Mother of both Dagda and Ogma. She has a stepson Lin as well. She is a high-ranking member of the Tuatha De Danaan and a powerful woman.

Dara and Verimy – Two guards turned hunting trainers from the Sovereign Halls. They manage to escape and save Azrael during the attack and following enslavement of the planet.

Debuff – An effect that makes a character weaker: a negative status effect.

Delving Dungeon – A type of dungeon that digs down into the ground creating descending levels with increasing difficulty.

Diamond Chip – A type of currency. This is the lowest form of currency. 10 Diamond Chips = 1 Ruby Mark.

Dincarn Abylos – A werewolf who attempts to escape during one of the tasks assigned to the slaves.

Dwarf – A slang name for the race of Karacy.

Elf – A slang name for the race of Aretrean.

Enchanting – A crafting skill that is of immense value. Enchanting uses Glyphs or Runes to circulate Ether and create powerful effects.

Essence – Essence is the primary resource of a Planetary God. It is filtered from Ether through living beings but can also be recovered from dead organisms. Gaia wakes to find almost all of her vast stores pillaged (oil).

Ether – Cosmic energy of the universe. It is the primary unfiltered raw power that allows life and Planetary Gods to form.

Ether Pool – A pool of power that skills draw upon to initiate. Synonymous with Mana pool from games.

Ether Tech – A very powerful type of armor. Combines the mechanical advantages of robotic gear with enchantments of Bio Enhanced gear.

Etherience – A measurement of the amount of power the individual has gained through completing tasks or slaying enemies. Gaming equivalent of Experience.

Guild – A new addition the Etherverse. The creation of guilds was voted into existence by the Atlantean Council. Now that guilds are created powerful individuals and family's group together to garner more power. This creates a major change to the powers of the Etherverse.

Gyr Hoff – A troll guard of Oberan's. One of the sparring partners with a tanking class. Doesn't speak but is very dangerous.

Jopiel Turendal – Daughter of Raphael Turendal a high-ranking member of the Cathodiem guild from Gaia.

Louis Darft – A cook who takes on quests to bring food to the cell block of Azrael's group. At first Louis is scared of the group but slowly becomes an acquaintance. He is likely swallowed by the black hole...

Mark – A greasy dwarf merchant. He helps Verimy and Dara sneak Azrael into cities and stay hidden during those trips.

Melee Weapon – A weapon that is used in close quarters.

NPCs – Non-Power Classes

Oberan Faedon – An assistant of Danu's who is promoted to a Territorial Leader when he discovers a better way to farm Essence. He quickly begins rising in power and conquering other Territories on Tech Duinn.

Ogma Tract – A son of Danu Tract one of the powerful council members of the Tuatha De Danaan guild.

Papi Vears – A crony of Torin's. He is a bear beastkin and is also a guard for the Pit Arena.

Perception Skill – A skill that highlights things that you might not notice otherwise.

Quests – Can be issued by Gaia directly (Red) or can be issued by Atlantean Net which is the system put in place by ancient Gaians to improve leveling and compatibility with Gaia and Ether.

Questing – Accepting quests and completing them for Etherience. This is a common way to quickly increase levels within the Etherverse.

Ring of Holding – A ring that has been enchanted to contain a massive Ethereal space inside. Our hero has a ring of holding.

Silver Spires –The home town of the Cathodiem Guild and a very beautiful place.

Soul Blade – A weapon that is spiritually bound to the user. Gains power and is able to level up. Seems to change as it levels.

Stealth Skill – A skill that Rockland learns in Book 1. He purchases it as a scroll in the Aretrean Bazaar.

Tech Duinn – The name of the planet that Dagda is the Planetary God of. Named by Ogma during creation.

Territory – A Territory is a piece of land that will level along with the leader who owns it. The Territory conveys many bonuses to the inhabitants and stabilizes Ether flow, making the immediate area more structured for monster growth.

Torin Tarzac – A particularly vicious orc guard. Azrael and Torin quickly become enemies after the orc bullies Azrael. He is left on the planet as it becomes a black hole. More to come in future books … ;)

UI – User Interface

Yonel Getz – A red skinned orc. A personal guard of Oberan. Yonel is a sword master who works closely with Gyr.

Void God – Opposite of a Sun God. The equivalent to a blackhole that is constantly trying to suck in more Sun Gods and Planetary Gods.

Made in the USA
Middletown, DE
06 April 2021